I0766355

WALKING THE TIGHTROPE

HER FREAKS BOOK 3

ERIN O'KANE AND K.A. KNIGHT

To all those who have ever felt oppressed, to all those that have ever felt alone, to all those who are threatened for simply existing...

This one is for you.

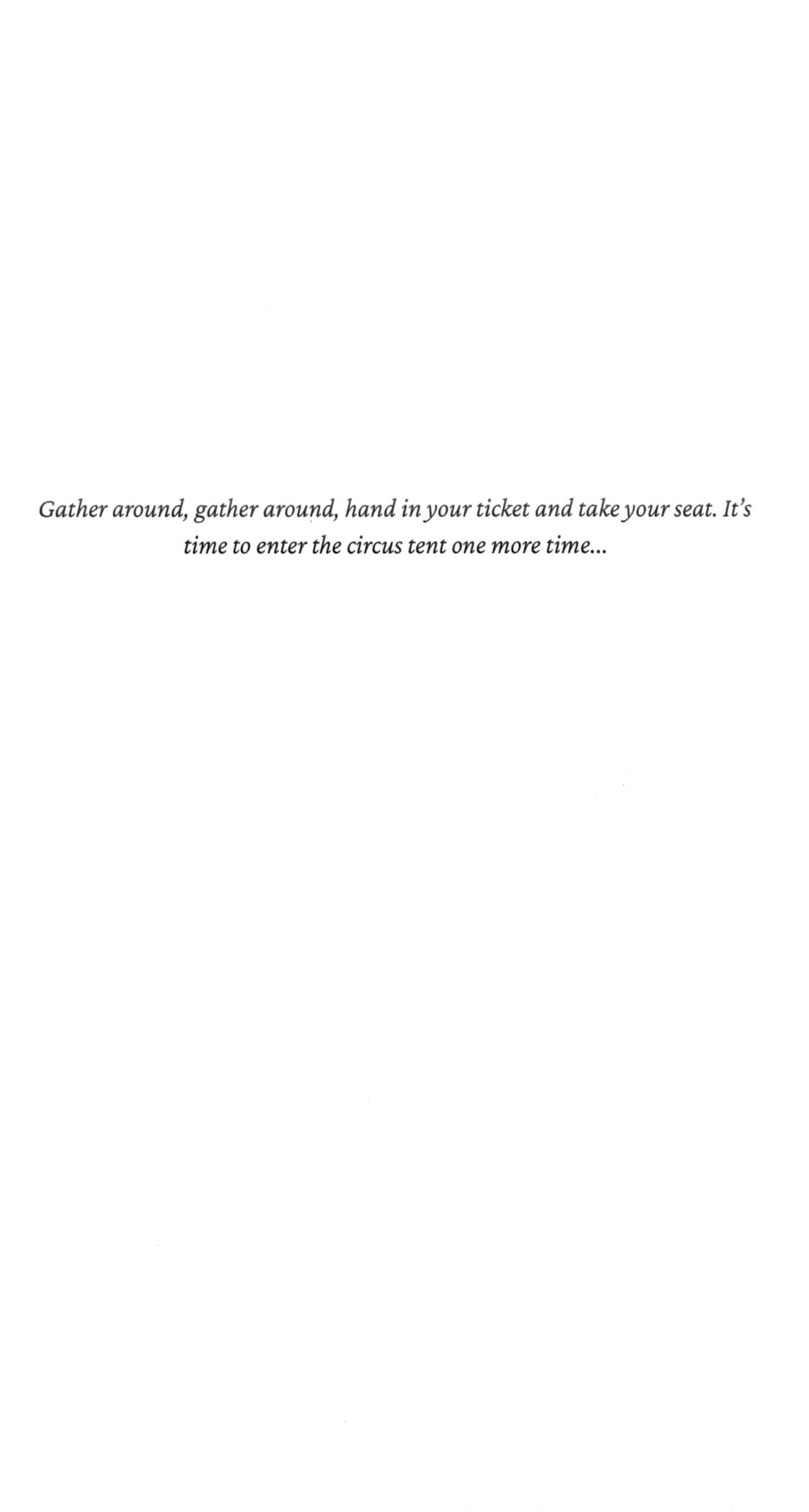

Gather around, gather around, hand in your ticket and take your seat. It's time to enter the circus tent one more time...

Chapter One

We died for you, now live for us.

The boy's words echo in my head as I hold him close, blood dripping down his chin. My world stops for a moment as I sit on the dirty, cold ground, holding him in my arms.

"Firecracker," Jesse pleads, cupping my face. His frantic tone forces me to drag my gaze away from the child, whose eyes are empty. This child sacrificed everything, including his life. He warned me and tried to save me, and in the end... he did just that. "We have to go."

An explosion rocks through the city. Jesse hunches over me as the others turn outwards to watch our backs. Their faces are hard and soaked in sweat, dirt, and blood, but they refuse to bow down or give up. I cover the child's body, my own pain and grief filling me, but he's right, we have to go. I can't let his sacrifice be in vain. Once the ground stops shaking, I lift my head. The sound of running footsteps and screams are far away, at the arena.

"I know he said Gregor," I rasp out of a raw, grief-filled throat.

"Let's go then," Xavier barks. He holds his sword out, his eyes alert in case we're attacked.

"Let me carry him, Wildcat," Rex offers sadly. I shake my head, refusing to dash my tears away. Someone should cry. A strong, innocent soul was taken from this world. It should matter, people should care.

"*Cariño*," Alcide begs softly.

"No," I snap, tightening my hold on the boy as I use the wall behind me to help me get to my feet. The weight makes my arms drop slightly, so with a grunt, I lift him higher, cradling him in my arms like a baby. I face the others, feeling determined. Nixon nods at me, and Jesse gets to his feet, squeezing my shoulder. Blain frowns but doesn't protest, seeing I won't bend on this.

"Let's go," I demand before I stride through their masses without waiting for them. Holding the dead child in my arms; I keep my eyes on the road ahead, each step heavy with the weight of the loss. I can't think about the future right now, I can only focus only on the next moment. The city is at war with the rebels. We need to get to safety, but I refuse to leave the boy behind. I refuse to leave his body like trash in the streets. He deserves more.

He deserved more than this world.

Xavier steps up to my side, protecting me and the child. None of them question it again or try to take the weight in my arms. It is my burden, my duty, to carry the weight of this child's death. Jesse slips past me, silently leading the way. We move as fast as we dare while making sure we aren't being followed or walking into a trap. The boy's weight gets heavier with each step, my exhausted body failing. My arms quiver, but I gnash my teeth and force one foot in front of the other, even when it hurts, even when I almost stumble.

We find Gregor's shop easily enough, the black, three-story building unchanged. The gold calligraphy I saw when we first came here fills the frosted windows, proudly declaring Gregoria's Tailoring. We quickly move inside and shut the door just as several guards troop past. I turn to find the shop empty and frown, shifting the boy's weight in my arms. Why did he send us here?

Just then, the curtain is pulled aside and Gregor comes running out. He rushes to the window, muttering to himself before turning to us. Unlike the last time I saw him, he seems almost frazzled. The golden decorations in his hair have changed to a set of red jewels, and the top of his locks are fluffy and curly but wild, untamed, like he hasn't had time to do anything with it. Instead of a suit, he's wearing a flowing red dress with a slit up the side and jewels around it, but his feet are bare. "Quickly, before they search here. Yes, yes, they will search, come." He blinks and then focuses on the child in my arms.

He sighs, his expression drooping with sadness.

"Such a good boy. I should have warned him. He knew though, he knew." He nods and then rushes through the curtain. I frown after him but move to follow, knowing he's right. I can hear guards streaming into the streets; so it won't be long before the chaos is under control and they will look for us.

We follow him to the back room again, and this time there's no joy of discovery, just a bone-deep exhaustion and sadness. The mirrors and podium are in the same place, but it feels like everything should have changed... maybe it's just me.

I watch as Gregor heads to one, seemingly the same as the others, and presses his hand against it. A white print forms around it, and a moment later, the mirror folds up and away, revealing an old stone staircase that leads down. "Go, go, you must go."

Xavier looks at me, and I nod.

"You can trust him, he helped us," I assure him.

"Fuck it," he mutters and troops down first. Nixon trails after him, while the others wait to follow behind me. Gregor bounces on his toes next to the entrance, looking back at the curtain as I step through.

"Thank you," I tell him softly.

"No thanks needed. Go quickly," he urges, and I step to the side, letting the others in before I meet his eyes again. He reaches out and touches my arm, and his eyes go distant for a moment before he frowns at me sadly. "Follow your heart, Rhea the Immortal. Your life will never be easy, but you're the change. Yes you are. It will never lead you wrong. Stay true." With that, he steps back, and the mirror shuts.

All the light disappears.

I turn to look down at the steps. My vision easily adjusts, getting better and better as I slowly walk down the steps, being extra careful with the precious boy in my arms. Nixon waits at the bottom, and I search for Xavier.

"Nix?" I question. Just then, Xavier pops out from the left with a stunned expression.

"Follow me. You are going to want to see this."

We share a look before following him. The stone under my feet is old and dirty. It reminds me of the ancient buildings on the outskirts of Cinders, the ones from before the bombs. The ceiling is high and made of stone, with old lights buzzing above us flicking off and on. As we walk, we pass a metal sign on the left pointing in the direction we're heading.

"Hartford Station."

The sign is dusty and old, but still readable. Xavier keeps going, and I hurry after him, our breathing and footsteps loud as we twist through some tunnels, which continue to become wider. Dust rains from above as the world shakes, and I almost fall into the wall before righting myself. I briefly wonder what's happening above, but all those thoughts disappear when I see what he meant.

There's a huge metal door before us, the orange and grey twisted metal rusted and thick. It looks like a bomb shelter door. It's propped open, and through it, I see people and hear their voices. I just stand there for a moment, in the semi dark of the tunnel, and stare. Above the door is the same black mark inked on the boy and me.

Rebels.

Freaks.

I step through the door, trusting my gut and heart like Gregor told me to, and once again, shock fills me. I wondered where all those rebels had come from, and now I don't have to wonder any longer. We're in a huge tunnel with round walls and ceilings that are so high, even Nixon doesn't have to duck. The area is so wide, our wagons could probably fit through it. The floor is a dusty off-white tile, and the walls are an old dark red brick with signs upon it. There is a bench to the left with a man in rags sleeping on it, his hand thrown over his dirt-covered face.

I scan the people, their voices increasing. There are so many voices, so many faces, all haggard and dirty. Their clothes are rags, and their bones stick through their skin, yet their voices, their determination, is loud.

I step farther into the room, and someone's head turns to me, then a whistle goes out. I see a mother hide a child behind her skirt, and someone screams. I try to show them we mean peace, but my voice fails.

"They have the mark!"

"Rebels!"

"The Immortals!"

I hear yelling, and the congregation opens, creating a path between them. Swallowing, I slowly walk forward, feeling every eye turn to me. Their voices quiet, and the silence becomes so prominent I can hear my heart race. I hold my head higher under their watchful, fearful eyes. Some look angry, others hopeful.

I don't bother to hide the tear tracks on my face. I'm covered in dirt and blood just like them... we blend in. My men are behind me, and I still hold the boy in my arms when I stop about halfway down the tunnel. At the end are more lights, and it opens up into an old subway station. I've seen one before in pre-war magazines. There's even a subway train next to it with yet more people on the platform. There are so many people, so many rebels, and so much pain hiding down here in the dark.

They are hiding from the masters, like us.

I see some eyes drop to the child and a call goes up. "I'm sorry," I whisper, the words catching in my throat. I hear running feet, more voices, and then a man and woman break through the crowd before me. Her eyes are the same as the child's, her gaunt face sorrowful as she cries out when she sees the boy. A ragged brown shawl falls from her thin shoulders, exposing her scarred, dusty skin as she drops to her knees with a scream. The man with her watches me, his eyes tight and filled with tears. He places his hand on the woman's shoulder. He's wearing nothing but low-slung tattered pants, and he's covered in tattoos. His dark hair is short and jagged, and his face is gaunt, but in his eyes I see intelligence, strength, and pain, so much pain.

The symbol on the child's arm, on my arm, is tattooed on his belly.

"I'm sorry," I whisper again.

The woman's screams turn into sobs as she presses her face into the ground. Her body shakes from the force of it. I look at the man as he kneels next to her, holding her.

"My son!" she screams. "My boy!"

My own tears start again from the very raw pain I hear in her tone, her agony vibrating the ragged octaves. Those around us lower their eyes. I feel their loss, their pain, too, knowing what she is going through.

I step closer and fall to my knees before her, still holding the boy. "I'm sorry," I say louder, big tears rolling down my face. "He saved us. I couldn't leave him there, I couldn't—"

"Thank you," the man rasps, and then crawls to me and extracts his son from my arms, cradling him softly against his chest like a baby as he looks down at him. His grief is so palpable I can taste it. "We've got you, you're home, your fight is over."

"Your fight is over, may you rest," everyone around us repeats, their fists going to their chests in respect. I repeat the movement as the man cradles his child and moves to his wife. I stumble to my feet, but my men catch me, holding me up, as I watch the crowd and the couple. I feel like I'm intruding on their pain and grief as they cry and hold him. Those who watch are angry on their behalf.

"I'm so sorry," I repeat, stepping back.

"We should leave," Blain murmurs. "We need to get to the

wagons and out of the city. We need to get our animals from their hiding spot up top."

I watch the people, and I know we can't leave them. I turn to face my men, my own anger written across my face. I feel rage for what has happened and the lives that have been lost—no, *taken.*

"We can't."

"Rhea?" Xavier asks, confused.

"We can't leave them. Look at them, they need us. He was right." I look back to the boy then. "They can't do this without us. We're staying."

Someone overhears and steps forward, touching my shoulder. "You are one of us." His eyes lock on the tattoo before focusing back on us. "Thank you for bringing one of our own back, we will not forget that."

Others move forward, offering their gratitude and greeting us as I search their dirty, starved faces. They live like rats down in the dark, hungry and scared, yet there's such hope in their eyes for a better world, a better city.

Better lives.

"Looks like we joined the rebels!" Jesse whoops.

It does indeed.

Just then, the ground shakes again, and dust rains down from above where a war is being fought for our future, the freaks' futures.

For the city's future.

Now, we are a part of it, helping those who helped us.

Chapter Two

It's chaos in the tunnels. No one seems to know what's going on, and many of the rebels come and go, bringing more and more injured back down with them. The cries of the wounded and grieving all seem to meld together in a symphony of pain. I've seen some atrocities in my life, like my time in Cinders or every time I've been beaten and degraded, but I've never seen anything like this.

The pure, raw pain and disregard for life.

It shatters my heart all the more, and I know if it weren't for the men standing behind me, I'd have fallen apart by now. The taste of my salty tears still coats my lips as they surround me with their steady, unquestioning love, which is the only thing holding me together.

So many more than just the boy will die today. They fight to live freely, just as those above live, so they no longer have to hide underground because of who they are.

Anger boils in my blood, pushing past the grief. It calls to those powers flowing through my veins, ones that want to avenge the losses, change the world, and make those who use others like discardable rubbish pay.

Everywhere I look, there is someone who's suffering, and it only increases with every minute. When we arrived, my guys and I listened to the first group we came across as they were planning. We offered suggestions and told them what we saw before we were brought here. They were trying to come up with a counterattack, but it was obvious from their grim looks that they knew they were losing. The might of the army above us is too strong for a group of misfits with little to no training.

The ground rocks again, and I swear I can hear screams from above, although we're so far below ground that can't be possible. The masters are destroying the city they worked so hard to build. How many of their citizens are they going to kill in the quest to get us back and regain their control?

All I want to do is curl up in a ball and be surrounded by my guys without bars separating us. We've been divided for so long, forced to fight in the masters' amphitheatre as entertainment, I want to revel in the fact we're all still alive and spend every moment appreciating them. I want to run my hands over their bodies and relearn the feel of them—not in a sexual way, but to know that this is real, that we made it out, and that we're alive. Except there are many who lost their lives today—loved ones, children, friends, husbands, and wives. It would be selfish of me to retreat now when there are so many who weren't lucky like I was.

In the chaos, I allow myself a minute and turn to face them—a minute where I can memorise their faces before we're needed elsewhere. After all, you never know what's around the corner, and this could be the last time I see them all together. What would my last words be to these men who love me, the other parts of my soul?

No. I can't think like that. It won't help me, and it certainly won't help anyone else.

They guard my back, standing in a semi-circle formation, their eyes all dropping to me as I turn. Their hardened, wary expressions soften a bit as they see my face and my love for them shining through.

I try to speak, but my voice cracks, my throat tight. Taking a deep breath, I try again. "Whatever happens today, know that I love you." I meet each of their gazes before I finally come to Xavier who's standing at my side, his face tight. He feels like he's always been here, always been a part of us. The cells had a way of warping time, and if I'm the last person he sees today, I need him to know. "All of you."

Something on his face changes then, and a light enters his eyes. We've not said 'I love you' to each other yet, but I needed him to know my feelings just in case.

"Rhea," Blain barks, stepping forward. Rex puts a hand on his shoulder, calling his name, but Blain shakes it off. "No, she's talking like she's giving up!" he growls. Anyone who doesn't know him might think he's angry, but I can see the fear in his eyes.

I reach up and capture his face between my hands, forcing him to look at me. "I'm not, I swear it," I promise, holding on until I know he believes me. Releasing him, I glance at the others. "But look at what happened today. Look at what we just escaped. Any one of us could have died at any moment, and I didn't want my last words to you to be something trivial." Even just the thought of losing them makes my voice break again, but I push through. I lost Jesse once, and I had so many regrets. I never want to feel like that ever again. "I just needed you to know how I feel."

Alcide hums his agreement, and I glance over at my usually pristine ringmaster. "She's right, Blain. There is so much out of our control here," Alcide admits, and I know how hard this must be for him. Despite addressing Blain, his eyes remain locked on me while he speaks, and I know the events and what he had to do in the last couple of weeks is playing on his mind.

"We love you too, Firecracker." Jesse bustles forward and wraps his arms around me. He presses a kiss to the top of my head, effectively breaking the tension.

I'm passed between them, sharing kisses and whispered I love yous, but soon enough, the wails of pain break through our moment, and I can't ignore them any longer. Sighing, I take a step back, not able to think clearly with them all touching me. "Okay, let's see where they need us."

Gathering all of my strength and courage, I turn back to the rebels. There's still a group of them discussing plans, their faces grim. They look up as I step forward, and the earlier hope I saw is dimming, but several of them meet my gaze with a determination that shows these people are fighters, survivors, just like us.

"We're here to help. Where do you need us?"

I WAS ASKED to assist with the wounded, and after what feels like hours, or days even, I step back and wipe the sweat from my face before moving to the next patient. None of my gifts can help them, but I can fetch water from the water barrels and help dress some of the wounds. Mostly, I sit with them, brushing their dirty hair back from their bruised and battered faces, wishing I could do more. They've been set up on the floor in the main tunnel. Everyone bustles around, knowing their jobs as the wounded cry out and scream in pain.

Nixon has been carrying the wounded, his strength an asset in times like these. Blain, Alcide, and Xavier volunteered to help rescue any rebels stuck above ground. I hadn't wanted them to go, but they promised to stick together and return to me. Jesse and Rex have been directing people where to go when they arrive. The tunnels are far more vast than I'd imagined, seemingly going on forever. The section of the platform I'm on has been dedicated to helping the injured— the least injured on the far right, and those whose injuries are critical to the left.

I move from patient to patient, fetching items that those helping the unwell rebels need. I stay busy, because if I stay still, that's when the thoughts and doubts hit me. What if Alcide, Blain, and Xavier never come back? What if they are the next patients I tend to? Every time I hear someone enter the tunnel, my head jerks up. Sometimes it's my men carrying a rebel between them, but they always leave again, returning to the combat above. I wonder what happened to the others from the circus who I've not seen in weeks. I don't even know if they survived when we were first taken or if they escaped. I certainly didn't see any of them in the pits.

I gently squeeze the hand of the woman I've been sitting with, brushing her hair back from her flushed face before grabbing her empty water cup. I've been holding the cup to her lips as she sipped the room temperature liquid. Standing, I cross to the water barrels, pick up the communal bucket we've been using, and queue behind the others collecting water. Rex passes me, his eyes tight with worry, and I know he's thinking about the animals. Reaching out, I stop him and pull him closer, breathing in his scent as he holds me.

"Have you heard anything?" I murmur into his chest.

He sighs, and I glance up in time to see him nod once. "Alcide told me that they retrieved the animals from their hiding place. One of the rebels showed him to another set of tunnels."

I almost sink to the ground with my relief. I release my pent-up breath, feeling some of the tightness around my chest loosen as a small smile crosses my lips. "So they are safe."

He shifts his weight, his face still tight. "Yeah, but they are alone. What if…"

He's feeling guilty. While we love the animals like family, they've always been more than that to Rex. His abilities bring him closer to them, allowing him to feel their emotions on a much deeper level. I feel sick with worry, but I know I need to be strong for him. I silence him with a soft press of my lips. It's so light and gentle that it almost can't be called a kiss, but when I pull back, he seems calmer.

"When things settle down, we'll get them and bring them here," I promise, my hand resting on the side of his face, making sure he's listening to me. "But until then, we should just be grateful that they are safe."

Rex blows out a breath and nods, pulling me in for another kiss. "You're right. Thank you, Wildcat. I needed that."

Returning his kiss, I want to fall into his embrace, but the line moves and it's my turn to get water. We say our goodbyes, my heart slightly lighter than it was just a moment before. The animals are just as much a part of this family as the guys are—we'll get them back, of that I'm sure.

After filling my bucket, I amble back to where the patients are lying, the weight of the water making it slow going. Reaching the platform, I let out a noise of relief and set it down. I grab the glass from before and go to scoop some water into it for the woman.

A panicked yell fills the air. "Can I have some help here please?"

My head jerks up, and I see a woman about my age with her hands on the chest of a man as blood seeps through her fingers. Without giving it any thought, I jump up and hurry over. Dropping to the floor beside her, I ignore the tingling as my skin hardens to protect me from the impact. The fact it was able to react that quickly gives me pause, but I don't have time to think on it. Taking in the patient, my expression turns grim. There's no way someone could survive a wound like that. A wicked slash stretches from his neck to his navel. It looks like someone was trying to cut him in half, and it's a miracle he made it this far and is still alive. The unconscious man's skin is pale, the rich red of the blood pouring out of him bright against his dying body.

"I need you to place your hands where mine are and press down *hard*," the woman instructs clearly. She's calm despite the chaos, her face determined. "I can't heal him because every time I move my hands, he starts to bleed out."

Nodding, I line my hands up over the top of hers, following her instructions. It's only then that I take in what she just said—she is going to *heal* him. Glancing up in wonder, I watch the woman with wide eyes, ignoring the feel of the hot blood pumping through my fingers.

"Okay, one, two, go!" she counts, snapping me out of my thoughts, and I quickly press down, grimacing at the blood that oozes through my fingers. "Good." She nods and places a hand on the man's forehead.

A strange rippling sensation moves over me, and I realise that I can feel her using her power. I can't see anything happening, but I know she's doing something. Silence falls over us as she works, and my mind starts to wander, remembering the atrocities we've seen today, the bodies of citizens lying dead and forgotten on the ground, regardless of whether or not they are actually the freaks the masters hate so much, and the screams of the injured. Taking a deep, shuddering breath, I push those thoughts away and watch the woman.

"I'm Rhea," I tell her, needing a distraction.

Until now, she'd been very still, her gaze on the man below, but now her eyes flick up to mine, a solemn look on her face. "I know who you are, Rhea the Immortal. I don't think there is a single person down here who doesn't."

I don't know why, but that makes me uncomfortable. I spent most of my life trying not to be noticed, then when I joined the circus, I was taught that with them, I could be my true self and should share it with the world. Except, most of the audience thought it was smoke and mirrors, a trick. Knowing that there's been a whole underground group of people who know who I am, know what I can do... it's disconcerting.

I duck my head slightly, and sensing my discomfort, the healer's face softens a little before she glances back down at her patient. "I'm Maria."

Looking at the healer in front of me, I realise her face is familiar. I'm sure I've never met her before, but the shape of her face, the blond hair and blue eyes... There are some thin silver scars across her left cheek, almost making it appear like shattered glass. It's beautiful. She must feel my assessing gaze, but she doesn't look up from her hand, which is pressed against the man's pallid skin.

"You've probably met my father." Her comment is quiet, but I hear the mix of emotions in the statement—sadness, regret, and a whole bunch of anger.

That's when I realise who she is. Her name, her power of healing —why didn't I see it before? "You're Chester's daughter," I blurt out, shock coursing through me as I stare at her. "But he said you were dead."

I don't know why I'm so surprised. The rebels saved Jesse when I thought he died, so it makes sense they'd do it for others. Not to mention she was the daughter of one of the masters of the city, one of the people who rule this place and orders the death of people like me, like her, for entertainment. Having someone like her on the side of the rebels...

"That's how I'd like to keep it," she says sharply, and her eyes flash up to meet mine. "The rebels saved me, and I've been with them ever since. I hoped my 'death' would make him realise what he's doing is wrong, would change him, but instead he lost all hope and gave up, gave in to the others' demands. He let them make him into one of their sadistic 'masters.'" Her face twists with anger and disgust, but her eyes sparkle with pain. I can't even imagine that feeling of betrayal, or how she's survived knowing that her father continues to condemn us.

I don't know what to say or how to make this better, so I stay silent and just absorb what she told me. My attention turns to our patient, and I see his colour looks better and his blood no longer seeps through my fingers. Whatever she's doing, it's working. Her power is miraculous, and I've never seen anything like it.

"He told you about me?" Maria asks quietly, startling me. The question is tentative, and as I watch her, I can tell she's been debating whether or not to ask, as if she might not really want to know the answer.

"He helped me when I was in there, in his own way," I reply truthfully. "He made sure that no one 'bought' me in the evenings. He also taught me to play chess. It was during one of those evenings that he told me about you, said I reminded him of you."

Maria is silent as I speak, her face pale. "Maybe he's not completely soulless then," she whispers, and I get the impression she's not really talking to me, but voicing something she'd secretly hoped for a very long time. Letting out a deep breath through her mouth, she rolls her shoulders but keeps her hands on her patient. "He taught me how to play chess too. We used to play together."

I don't say anything, simply nodding as she takes in all the information I just dumped at her feet. She's obviously angry, having seen him as one way for a long time and then to help someone else when he didn't, couldn't, help her. Hearing that he might not be who she thought he was has to be hard.

"You can remove your hand now, I've stemmed the bleeding."

Nodding, I remove my bloodstained hands, marvelling at the mostly closed wound, the edges knitting together before my eyes. Her gift is amazing. How could anyone want her dead because she possesses this power? This incredible, life-saving gift?

Shaking my head, I push to my feet. I feel grimy and dirty, and I'll need to clean up before I can help anyone else, but there's still plenty of work to do and people who need aid. Besides, I can't stop until all of my guys are safely back here. Taking a deep breath, I look for a place where I can wash my hands.

"Thank you, Rhea." Maria's voice stops me in my tracks. Turning back to face her, I see she's watching me closely, and as I meet her gaze once more, I know she's not thanking me for helping with the patient, but for giving her new hope.

Smiling slightly, I dip my head in acknowledgement and turn away. After finding somewhere to wash my hands, I return to the injured and help someone else to keep my mind busy from the fight that still rages above us.

THE BATTLE UP top seemed to have stopped a few hours ago, or at least moved to a different part of the city, as it's gotten quieter. My men came back stating they couldn't find any more rebels, and I overheard someone say they were probably hiding, waiting out the night.

Night... It's hard to tell down here, but my body is exhausted. I helped as many as I could, alongside Marie, until the injured were finally settled or healed. She helped as many as she could before she had to rest, her powers taking their toll. She almost burnt herself out while trying to save everyone. We helped those with the worst injuries first, and those who could survive a few more days were lined up next, ready to be healed when she was feeling stronger.

The tunnels are quiet now, almost peaceful, and the injured are resting on the edge of the platform. Someone came around a few hours ago and turned out the lights, and fires were lit inside of metal barrels that were spread throughout the tunnel system. Rebels huddle around them, their stark, hungry, and dirty faces drawn. Their whispers fill the air as they share each other's sorrow and hopes. It makes me feel like an outsider, as if I'm just watching their pain and conflict. They have suffered and lost so much. Haven't we all though?

Others are sleeping—some sit up, some are propped up against walls, and some are lying down wherever they can, sometimes pressed against the next person. No one complains, though, as they are clearly used to the cold, hard floor and lack of space. We moved away to give them privacy, sitting against the platform wall way down at the bottom of the tunnel. I sit in Nixon's lap with Jesse's head in mine as I stroke his hair and reassure myself he's really here. Xavier and Blain glare at anyone who gets too close, even when I ask them to stop. They are wary, protective, and unsure, which I can understand, but I know no one down here will hurt us. They are like us.

Freaks. Hated. Cast-offs.

We're all fighting for the same cause, and we need to help where we can. I don't know if it's the guilt or sense of responsibility I feel, but I need to do something, anything, more than helping the injured. I need to... well, fight. They came to save me. These people died and were hurt to set us free. I know it wasn't only just for us, but deep down, that's what it feels like. As if it's my fault so many have been lost or scarred. It's the masters' doing, I know that, but it doesn't stop my eyes from tracing each hungry, sad face, memorising each one, and adding to my guilt until I'm almost choking on it. I need to make their sacrifice *mean* something.

I'm debating moving Jesse without waking Rex and Nixon when a man stops in front of us. He looks around before crouching, his hands dangling before him. They are scarred and covered in dirt, but he has a wide grin on his face that instantly sets me at ease. Alcide leans forward, but the man ignores him and focuses on me, the lights from the nearby fire catching on his bright green eyes and red hair. It's lighter than mine and messy, sticking up from his head at all angles. His entire left ear is covered in piercings, and his right has iridescent flame tattoos climbing across it. His chest is bare, showing off more flame tattoos and a really bad burn on his stomach, leading to his low-slung leather trousers. He wears a thick brown fur coat on his shoulders and arms.

"You Rhea the Undead?" he teases, making me smile.

"I'm Rhea, but I don't know about the undead part."

He chuckles and stretches out his hand, which I shake, ignoring the others' glares.

"I'm Smoke. Someone wants to meet you." He stands and waits for me to get up. "All of you," he adds when he notices the others just glaring at him. He raises his hands, and I see his nails are a deep black at the bottom, fading to red at the tips.

"Jesse," I coo, and he wakes up, groaning as he rolls over. "Come on."

He gets to his feet sleepily, blinking like he's not really awake, which makes my heart flutter. Not long ago, I thought I'd never see him like this again, or even see him at all.

Alcide climbs to his feet and helps me up as the others stand. Smoke rocks on the balls of his feet while he waits. He doesn't seem afraid of the guys who surround me in the slightest. He even meets Xavier's stare head-on. "You're the phoenix, right? How cool!" He sticks out his hand. Xavier just stares at it, and he drops it with a laugh. "Fire here too." He winks at me and claps his hands softly. "Well then, time to meet the big guy." With his hands in his pockets, he turns and starts to weave through the mass of people without once disturbing or tripping over anyone, displaying more of his tattooed chest and side as the movement pushes back his fur coat.

I share a look with Alcide before I follow after Smoke, and the others quickly catch up, not willing to let me go alone. I keep quiet, not wanting to disturb anyone—they deserve their rest.

We move deeper into the platform and stop at the train car I spotted earlier. I had seen light peeking through tattered curtains that covered the windows, but the door was closed, and I figured it was private, so I didn't pay it much attention until now. It's still a deep red, but it's faded and peeling in places. Smoke knocks on the door and waits. A few moments later, it opens with a barely audible groan, and Smoke bows, his hand outstretched to welcome me in.

"He's waiting," is all he says.

How dramatic, I think as I take a deep breath.

Stepping up onto the hard floor of the small, one-person entrance, I glance around. Before me is a toilet door. The green and red locked symbol is gone, but it still seems functional. The wall opposite me has a covered window, a door, and a chair with a small lantern on top of it. To the left is a door that would traditionally lead to the next car, which obviously isn't there, so it's been boarded up, and a curtain now hangs there. To the right is a partial glass door, which opens, so I step inside, my men following behind me. They crowd me, not willing to let me go into the unknown alone. My powers rise, but I tamp them down, knowing whoever we're meeting is a rebel. They are the good guys, but it doesn't stop my nervousness. When you become so used to being betrayed, hurt, and attacked, you can become a little jaded.

I stop just inside the doorway, blinking in surprise at what I see. I expected to find a man sitting on a spare seat, but that's not what greets me. The whole car has been ripped apart, as has the other one beyond it, to create one long living space. It almost looks like a... home.

At the very back, I spot a bed peeking out from behind a separation curtain, as well as a sink and a basin on a box. More lanterns are dotted throughout, some hanging from the ceiling and some on the floor. The metal shelves close to the ceiling haven't been removed, and I spot clothes and bags stored up there. The chairs I expected to see have been ripped out except four to my very left, and there's a table separating them. To the right of the door is an old wooden coat rack holding a leather coat and a long brown duster. The floor is covered in a red and gold runner, which has seen better days, and it leads right up to a wooden plank held up by four boxes, creating a large table where a man leans with his fists pressed to the top as he scans a paper.

He's a big man. When he stands, his head nearly touches the train car's roof. I watch as his icy, calculating eyes flick up to me. He has a square, scary-looking face, and he has a scar slashing through his pink lips. His head is shaved, and there's a red bandana around his forehead. His huge arms are encased in a white shirt, and I can see that his black cargo pants are tucked into ankle high black laced boots from here. He leans back and crosses his massive arms, displaying many more scars and some intricate black ink. In the middle is the rebel symbol, the same symbol we all have courtesy of the masters, but his is different. It's surrounded by flames, making it look like the symbol is on fire. So much fire.

"You must be Rhea," he comments, but he doesn't seem impressed as he scans me angrily. His lips turn down as if I didn't pass some kind of test.

"I am." I step forward, unwilling to be cowed by him. "And these are my men, my family." He nods and waves his hand, gesturing me over. I stop beside him on the left side of the table, my men around me. He leans back into it, scanning a map of Last Stop. He turns his head, meeting my eyes again.

"I need to know if you're staying," is all he says. There's no introduction, just business.

"And if I am?" I ask, unwilling to give more than he is. I don't like his hostility or his scrutiny, like he is testing me again. I've had enough with games and word play.

"Then I would agree. It's a good move for the rebellion." He stands again and extends his meaty hand. "I'm Regnor, leader of the rebels."

I shake it, making sure to add some strength, and his lips finally tip up a bit.

"Nice to meet you. You're happy we're staying? So that means you need or want us," I surmise, and he makes a noise of agreement.

"I like that you're blunt." He nods. "I appreciate that, so I will return the favour. Yes, we need you. I'm the leader, but the rebels need a face, someone to rally around. That is not me. I'm good with war tactics, with ordering people around and planning missions, but inspiring hope and love? Not so much," he grumbles. "I'm told to keep the flames of anarchy and hope burning, but I need help... your help, to be exact. All of you. You stood up to the masters. You defied them and showed them who you truly are. You sent up a flag of declaration that freaks are not weak. You showed them exactly why we fight, and it brought a lot of numbers to our side."

Even though he says he's not good at inspiring hope, I find myself standing taller. His words make me feel important, like I had a strategic game plan and not just a desperate need to save my family and myself.

"What do you need from us?" I inquire.

"I need you to help turn more to our side and strengthen our numbers. I also need you to incite hope in flagging soldiers, those tired and battle weary." He points at locations on the map that are marked with a flame. "These are our locations. I need help keeping them secure, keeping them fighting for the cause even though we are struggling. The masters are strong, really strong, and they will prey on any weakness. You know that. Love, hope, family, friends... anything they can get their hands on. We need to show them that's not a bad thing. With your help."

"And what do we get from this?" Alcide demands, standing by

my side. "We could leave if we wanted to, correct?" I hear his power in his charming voice, and the man narrows his eyes in anger.

"Do not try your powers on me, silver tongue, they will not work. I have the ability to detect powers, amplify them, and grow them. It gives me a lot of protection against their effects." He turns to me then, answering the question and clearly not liking Alcide's attempts to win him over. What he doesn't realise, however, is that it's a habit for my ringmaster. "Yes, you're free. You could leave. We could even give you supplies and safe passage. But I'm really hoping you choose to stay. We need you. They need you. You started something up there in the fights, and now it's time to finish it."

"I agree." I sigh. "We need to stay." I look to the others who simply nod. We had already discussed staying, but I have to check. This is their life too, and I can't sign them up for a war, to be a rebel, without their agreement. I should have known better, though, they would never leave anyone in need. "We will help in any way we can."

A noise has my head jerking up to the door.

"Okay, I know I said I would rest, but I healed a few more—" Marie stops in the door and blinks at us before smiling softly, but she looks tired. There are lines around her eyes and lips, and her shoulders are slumped as she walks forward. "Hello again, Rhea."

"I told you to rest," Regnor mutters angrily, crossing his arms as he straightens. His expression is grumpy and tight. She just laughs and waves it away as she wanders closer, leans on her toes, and kisses him softly. He melts. It's the only way I can describe it. His arms uncross, his eyes soften, and a smile even tilts up his lips. "You will hurt yourself again, my love."

"I'm fine," she murmurs as she leans into his side and turns to us. "What's going on? Planning?"

I expect him to dismiss her or order her to rest, but he turns with her and leans into the map, explaining what we had been discussing. She listens raptly, nodding in certain places, and I realise he is getting her opinion and approval. They are a real team. "I agree, others would trust them, especially Rhea. A lot of people are more hopeful after seeing her. She gave them a reason to fight by showing them that being a freak is both beautiful and resilient. She stood up to the masters, and they respect that, so it would be a good advantage to press." She smiles at me to let me know she understands I'm a person with a choice, but she is assessing the situation and offering her input, which I respect. She is clearly very intelligent and experienced in helping with the rebels' plans as well as healing. If Chester could see her now...

As if her thoughts align with mine, she whispers, "I know we need to bring them down, but my father..."

He kisses her head and holds her tighter. "We can talk about that later, my love, don't worry."

Just then we hear more footsteps. Do people just let themselves in and out of his quarters? It seems so. The footsteps are slow, almost dragging, and there's a deep cough before an old, raspy voice sounds from beyond the first door.

"Oh stop it, you asshole, or I'll put you back in the fire I saved you from," they grumble, and then an old man steps through the door and smiles at us as Smoke towers behind him with a roll of his eyes. "Oh, just wanted to make sure you haven't killed yourself again by helping others, Marie," he greets, and then his eyes land on Jesse and he whoops.

"J-dog!" he calls. Jesse laughs and rushes over to embrace the man.

"Tobin," Jesse responds, smacking the old man on the back harder than I would have expected. I almost wince from it as he turns, his arm across the man's shoulders, and pulls him over to us.

"Firecracker, this is Tobin. He's the one who brought me back from the dead." He grins widely.

Tobin snorts and elbows him. "I told you chicks dig scars, didn't I?" He reaches out and shakes my hand as he winks, making my eyes widen. "Nice to finally meet you. Jesse here wouldn't shut up about you when I healed him." Jesse blushes but keeps grinning and watching me.

"You healed him?" I exclaim, and then I rush closer and hug him. "Thank you, thank you, thank you. I owe you everything."

"Well, if you're offering," he jokes as I step back. He acts like someone our age, flirting and laughing, but his hair is grey and short, his face is wrinkled, and his back is hunched. He looks about seventy years old.

"Tobin," Jesse snaps and smacks the back of his head. "Ignore him, Firecracker, he's a pig."

"Tobin, everything okay?" Regnor sighs like he is used to this.

"Fine, fine. Was just checking on Marie." He sits and watches us. Regnor blinks but turns back to us.

"If you are really with us, it's time. Inspire the people to fight. We're going to start missions again, this isn't over. We'll let them think we are defeated and low in numbers while they fortify and lick their wounds. We have spies inside, so for now, we lay low, get information, and gather our forces before we take back the city," he says strongly. Each word is filled with conviction for the cause, for the rebellion.

I meet Marie's worried eyes, but she smiles at me in reassurance.

I guess I just became the face of the rebellion.

Staring into my bowl of porridge, I try to force my drooping eyelids to stay open, the gentle hustle and bustle of everyone around us doing nothing to keep me awake.

After our meeting with Regnor last night, we left the train carriage and tried to get some rest. The others managed to get a few hours in, but sleep evaded me. Every time I closed my eyes, I could only see flashes from the explosions and the look on the boy's face as he died in my arms. The screams and pleas of those dying down here pierced the fog of my dreams as they called out to any god who might be listening. So I stayed awake and thought over everything Regnor told us.

I'm to be the face of the rebellion.

In the circus, I'm used to performing, to putting on an act and giving people what they want, but this... this is different. It means so much more. It's not a show, it's the difference between life and death. We could save lives and change things for the better for the persecuted freaks like us. We could implement real change. If that means I get the limelight in this rebellion, then so be it. I know the guys are worried that this will put me, put *us* at risk, but they understand what's at stake here.

"Rhea? Firecracker?" Jesse's gentle voice pulls me from my daydreams. Blinking sleepily, I drag my gaze from my tarnished spoon, glance around, and see all the guys watching me with varying degrees of worry etched into their faces.

"Sorry, did you say something?" I try to erase their concerns with a smile as I stir my breakfast. Leaning back against Nixon, I hum happily as his warmth surrounds me.

Blain snorts, his brows pulled low in a frown. "You were falling asleep in your porridge."

"Did you get any sleep at all?" Passing me a glass of water, Rex reaches out and brushes a finger along the purple bruises under my eyes as he speaks.

Shrugging, I take the cloudy glass gratefully and drain it in a couple of gulps, not realising how thirsty I was. "I had a lot on my mind," I reply, not wanting to worry them, but I should have known it wouldn't work.

"Rhea, if you don't want to do this, we can leave," Alcide offers, but in his eyes, I can see that he knows we're needed here. My love for him flares in my chest but I shake my head. No, we won't be leaving. Not until we've finished what we started.

We finish our simple breakfast in companionable silence. It's obvious the others are just as exhausted as I am, but there's a fire in their eyes that motivates me and gives me strength. Movement catches my eye, and I glance up to see Smoke making his way over to us.

"Morning, oh chosen one." He drops to the ground across from me and crosses his legs, a huge smile on his face. The others stiffen at his proximity to me, but they don't say anything. Blain and Xavier openly glare, but I set my bowl down and place a hand on their shoulders to calm them.

Smoke rolls his eyes at the guys' alpha male behaviour and winks at me.

He may be odd, and I'm sure half of the things he does is just to annoy my two most protective guys, but he makes me smile. "Morning, Smoke." My smile slowly drops as I see his hands tapping on his knees, his actions full of nervous energy. "Have they got a mission for us?"

Excitement, fear, and a little bit of dread run through me, but my overriding emotion is one of relief. I need to be doing something, helping people, and being useful, not just sitting here overthinking and listening to the pained cries of those grieving the lost.

He nods, ignoring the others completely as he locks his eyes on mine. "You ready?"

I know he's asking more than if we're ready to learn the plan. He's asking if we're ready for everything that being the face of a rebellion entails. I'd spoken to the guys last night, needing to check that they were okay with all of this. I might be the figurehead that the rebels will look up to, but without the guys behind me, I'm nothing.

With one last look at my men to ensure they are with me, I nod, and we climb to our feet, leaving our half-eaten breakfast on the platform. As we pick our way through the small groups of resting rebels, I'm amazed and a little perturbed by their reaction to me. Some call my name, while others reach out to brush my hands as we pass them. I'd been here all afternoon helping with the wounded, so it's not like this is the first time they've seen me. But yesterday was so hectic and laden with grief, and from their whispered, "You stayed," I get the impression they didn't think we would stick around. I smile faintly at them, and the hope flashing in their eyes makes my chest tighten. I hope I can do them justice.

Following Smoke, I climb up onto the back of the train car, rolling my eyes at his dramatics as he knocks on the door before grandly gesturing for me to enter. Glancing over my shoulder, I make sure the guys are behind me and head in. I pause when I reach the second door, hearing voices from the other side.

"Rhea, stop hanging around and get in here," Regnor demands.

Entering the room, I see Tobin resting in one of the remaining chairs, and he winks at me as I pass. Regnor and Marie are standing beside the table listening to a man. I can't quite make out what he's saying, but his eyes widen when he sees me. He finishes whatever he was saying, nods at the leader of the rebels, and leaves the car, hurrying past me and the guys.

Regnor gestures for us to come closer, and as we approach the table, I see a large red circle drawn on the map. Frowning, I lean forward to inspect it further, but I don't really understand the symbols they are using. They have probably done so on purpose in case the map was ever taken by the masters. If they couldn't read the symbols, it would be difficult for them to work out where the rebels are based.

"We've discovered that the masters have learned of one of our main entrances to the tunnels," Regnor grumbles, anger flashing in his eyes. "They've set up a trap to catch us, knowing they would get lost in the tunnels without one of us to guide them here."

"What's your plan?" Xavier steps up to my side, examining the map closely. I keep forgetting he's been here a lot longer than we have. It feels so natural with him, with all of us, it's like we've always had him with us.

Maria places her hand on Regnor's arm before taking a step forward. "We're going to send a team to disarm the trap. We can't risk any rebels who try to reach us getting caught or inadvertently leading the masters to us."

"Okay." When I glance at the guys, they nod in agreement, knowing what I'm going to say. "We're ready. What do you need us to do?"

Regnor gives me a strange look. "If you think you're going anywhere near that trap, then you're wrong."

Silence fills the carriage. He can't be serious. What happened to me becoming the face of the rebellion? Was that all a lie? Has he changed his mind? Or does he think we're not strong enough to fight against the masters? I can feel my guys' confusion. Alcide pushes forward so he's standing at my other side, frowning at the leader. Anger rouses within me, and I feel my power rise with it, but this time I don't try to dampen it.

"We have to do something! I'm not just staying down here while people put their lives at risk!" My voice echoes with power, and I'm not a hundred percent sure what my body has done, how it's adapted, but the others are watching me with awe.

"Regnor..." Marie places her hand on his arm, and his face softens. "You have to let her help."

Sighing, he rubs his hands across his face. Whatever relationship they have between them, she can influence him where others can't. The love between them is practically palpable. As they gaze into each other's eyes, they seem to have a silent conversation. Growling low in his throat, he turns back to us. "Fine. We'll have someone take you through the tunnels to the other camps. You can meet the other rebels and help with the injured."

His voice is firm, his decision final, and I realise he's being serious. This is not what I agreed to when I said I wanted to help. Frowning, I step forward. "Wait—"

"No," he barks. "Rhea, you're our figurehead. If you die, how will that look? It would destroy the rebellion."

There's a shuffling sound behind me, and I know the guys are bristling at the way Regnor is speaking to me. Knowing they'll have my back no matter what, I face off with the leader of the rebellion. "Or it would give them a cause to fight for," I retort, keeping my voice steady. I place my hands on my hips. "When I agreed to help, it wasn't just so you could cart me around like a prized cow and cheer people up. These guys are risking their lives, so I should too. I'm not afraid to fight," I insist, knowing they've seen me in the arena. They wouldn't have chosen me if they didn't know about my abilities. All of the fighters who were forced to battle the guards were freaks, and he could have picked any of them, but he didn't. He chose me and the guys I love.

"Besides," I continue with a small smile, "I'm Rhea the Immortal."

"As much as I hate to agree, she's right." Alcide places his hand on my shoulder. I know how difficult this must be for him to say, considering how protective he is of me, but we're doing this together, the seven of us. "They need to see her helping the same cause and fighting the same battles they are."

Regnor is silent, shifting his narrowed eyes from me to my ringmaster. The others make sounds of agreement behind me, and my heart beats painfully at their support. I can understand his frustration, since we agreed to follow him and we're already disagreeing with his orders, but he knows that if we pull this off, it's only going to help their cause.

"I'll be with them." Smoke steps forward, shoving his hands into his pockets as he leans against the table. He's acting nonchalant, but it's obvious he agrees with what I said. "I'll make sure nothing happens."

Throwing his hands in the air in disgust, Regnor shakes his head. "If anything happens or doesn't go to plan, you leave immediately. Am I clear?"

WE HURRY through the dark tunnel with only the light of Smoke's small lamp to illuminate the way. Thankfully my eyes adjust to the minimal light, and I'm able to see better, but I can hear the guys quietly cursing behind me as they trip over the tracks and stray stones.

I'm not sure how long we run in the dark for, but it seems to be a long, winding route, which I suppose is what they want. It wouldn't do for the masters' armies to come into the tunnels and instantly find the rebel base. Finally, we start to slow down, and I see Smoke looking around for something.

He makes a small hum of achievement, and I see what he's found. "Bingo," he whispers.

There's a ladder screwed into the wall and the smallest beam of light. It's so tiny I almost can't see it. We all pause for breath as Smoke climbs up, pressing his eye against a small hole in the cover above him. Breathing in the stale air, I look around the tunnel. It's obvious that this route is hardly used, which is exactly why we're using it. When we were planning this, we were told this is one of the emergency escape routes, but the roof isn't stable, so it's not used often.

I turn to look at the rest of our group and my chest twinges with anxiety. Blain, Xavier, and Nixon are dressed in good quality cloaks that hide their dirty, ripped clothing. Of my six guys, Regnor thought these three would be the best in a fight. Well, he actually picked Jesse, but Nixon threatened to follow anyway, refusing to let me out of his sight. One thing was clear, however—the leader of the rebels wouldn't let all of us leave on the mission. He said it was because he couldn't risk losing all of us if something went wrong, but that doesn't quite ring true. I hate not having the others with us, but this was the only way we were allowed to go on the mission. Alcide was mad that he wasn't allowed to come and got into an argument with Regnor, not used to being denied, but when he eventually realised that the leader wasn't going to budge, my ringmaster conceded.

Behind my guys is another rebel—Nico. Blain hadn't wanted him with us, but after seeing his power, he quickly stopped complaining. He can become invisible, and if he's touching someone, they disappear from view too. I like Nico, but he's quiet, and I think we intimidate him a little. Although if I had a knife thrower and an immortal gladiator glaring at me, I think I'd be intimidated too.

"Okay, it's clear." Smoke climbs down the ladder and meets each of our gazes. "You remember the plan?"

We nod. As plans go, it's fairly simple. Using Nico's power, we hurry across the city to where the masters set the trap. If there are too many guards, we're to leave and return to base to form a new plan. If there aren't too many, we go in, kill the guards, destroy the entrance, and leave a message for any freaks looking for refuge. They have developed their own symbols, much like the symbols on the map. Now that the masters know of a way into the tunnels, we need to stop them from entering and stumbling across the base.

I feel sick at the prospect of killing the guards. I've killed before, but that's always been to save my life or protect my family. Here, we're attacking them, we're the killers. I can justify it to myself in a hundred different ways. They've killed so many of us and are *still* trying to, but I know their deaths will stay with me all the same.

Smoke grins as he sees our nods of agreement. "Then let's go cause chaos." He rubs his hands together like a greedy kid and winks at me, making me smile even in the face of what's to come. He seems to have a way of making people smile. His happy, unfearful personality is slightly addictive. It makes me feel braver, like when I'm with my men. Or maybe he's just insane and it's rubbing off on me.

Nico goes first, disappearing completely, and the only reason I know he's climbing the ladder is because of the quiet metallic ring as his boots hit the rungs. A crack of light appears above, making us all wince. After a few seconds, the manhole opens farther, seemingly on its own. We wait as Nico checks to see if the coast is clear. A quiet rapping sound has me looking at Smoke for confirmation, and he gestures for us to go.

Blain goes first, reaching up as he gets to the top. My heart stops as he disappears, but I know this is because Nico has expanded his power over him. Knowing this and seeing it is something different entirely though. I'm to go next, followed by Nixon, Xavier, and lastly, Smoke. I start climbing, stretching my hand up as soon as I reach the top, my heart pounding in my chest. A strange feeling runs over me as a hand clasps mine, and looking down, I see my body's gone. Pushing past the discomfort, I use the hand to climb from the tunnel. The same process is repeated with the other three, then we're all out, holding hands to keep Nico's power over us and out of sight.

Smoke covers the entrance to the tunnel with the manhole cover, and slowly, we all move forward in an invisible human chain. It's strange. I can't see much of the others, but I can feel Blain's and Nixon's hands in mine, so I know they are still here.

We carefully make our way across the city. Regnor thought it was important we used an exit that wasn't close to the one we're about to destroy. If we're followed, we can lose them in the maze of streets.

The city seems deserted, only the masters' soldiers and the bodies of the dead are visible. It's the strangest feeling, and as we pass groups of soldiers, I keep expecting them to shout and point at us, but we walk by with no problems. Finally, we reach the square where the hidden entrance is. The open area seems stark compared to all the huge, dilapidated buildings surrounding it. A broken fountain sits in the middle, and Smoke points out where the entrance is on the other side. At first glance, the square is empty, but as I pay attention, I see guards hidden in shop windows and behind buildings, all waiting for someone to trigger their trap. Quietly, Smoke and Nico point out all the exits, explaining the best way to get back to the base. I feel my body shifting, my powers working to protect me. I have no idea what form it has chosen, but I trust it'll keep me safe.

This is the tricky part of the plan. We're to split into groups and try to covertly take down the guards. Nixon and Xavier will take the south side of the square, and Blain and I will take the north. The only exceptions to this plan are Smoke and Nico. They are to walk straight to the entrance under the cover of Nico's power and destroy the entrance. Boom.

Nixon instantly pulls me into his arms, kissing the top of my head. "Stay safe," he mumbles into my hair before releasing me. Xavier takes his place, running his eyes over my body as he arches an eyebrow. Glancing down, I see that my skin is entirely covered in thick scales, my nails long and sharp.

"Harpy," Blain says quietly, seeing the same thing I've just noticed, but I keep my eyes on Xavier.

Pulling me close, Xavier presses his forehead against mine, staring into my eyes. "Don't take any risks. I don't want to have to come rescue you." Grinning up at him, I'm about to demand he does the same, but his lips come crashing down on mine in a fierce kiss that steals my breath.

I hate this. It feels like we're saying goodbye, but we're not. I won't let this be our final day together. Pulling away without another word, Xavier and Nixon start moving towards their first target. Blain squeezes my hand, and I know I've got to focus on getting through the next couple of minutes.

"How cute. You memorised the route back to the manhole?" Smoke asks, his face fully serious for once. We all nod. Reaching out, Nico touches Smoke and they both disappear.

Blain starts running, skirting around a building, and I follow closely behind. Rounding a corner, we come face to face with a guard. Acting instinctively, I whip my hand out, and my dagger sharp nails slice along his throat. The guard dies before he can even voice his surprise. My heart slams against my ribcage. *What did I just do?* Nausea rises, and I think I'm going to vomit my breakfast all over the side of the building, but Blain's gentle hand on my back helps to ground me.

"Are you okay?" he whispers, his eyes flicking from the bleeding body at our feet to my pale face.

I take a deep breath and nod. I can fall apart later, we've got a job to do now.

They might be people that I'm killing, but it's either us or them. I don't enjoy it or particularly want to kill people, but if it's what it takes to save lives, to save freaks who have been persecuted their entire lives for simply being born, then I will. I'll bear that stain on my soul.

I don't know how much time passes, but Blain and I fall into a grim pattern, moving from building to building, our bodies splattered in the blood of our victims. I've become numb to what we're doing- it's the only way I can get through this. We've made it almost halfway around the square and are just about to move over to the next building when a huge explosion rocks the ground.

I'm thrown from my feet, and I land on the ground with an *oomph* as the air rushes from my lungs, but my scales protect me. Quickly scrambling to my hands and knees, I look around to find Blain. I breathe a sigh of relief when I see him sitting up. He's wincing, and judging by how he's holding himself, I'd say he's broken a rib, but he's alive. Glancing across the square, I see the building where the entrance was is now rubble. Flames reach up high into the sky courtesy of Smoke's fire ability.

Now we just have to get back to the tunnel.

Taking my hand, Blain starts to jog, staying close to the buildings as we head back. All of the guards are running towards the fire as we go the other way. It's going well—until a shout rings out. Spinning around, I see a guard pointing, but it's not at us. I follow his finger, and dread runs through me as Nixon and Xavier race towards us. The guard looks in the direction they are running, and his face pales.

"It's the Immortals! They are still in the city!" the guard cries out, drawing attention to us. We should go after him, but our instructions were clear—if anything happens, we're to return to base.

Blain curses and flicks his arm out in a sharp movement, the flash of silver the only indication he's used his power. The blade hits home, silencing the guard, but it's too late, he's already sounded the alarm. More guards swarm the area. We have to go.

We can't go the same way as Nixon and Xavier; we have to split up and lose any guards who try to follow. Blain points towards an alleyway, and we duck into it, sprinting now.

As we wind our way through the dark streets, my stomach twists at the prospect of anyone getting hurt. We achieved our goal, but it didn't exactly go to plan, and now two of my guys are somewhere in the city, running for their lives.

I can't fucking lose anyone. We dart between alleyways and hide between buildings as we try to find our way back. I pray to any of the forgotten gods that they'll keep the others safe.

WE KEEP RUNNING, my hand clutched in Blain's. The sound of our breathing and heavy footsteps smacking against the rough cobbles of the side streets seems loud. We keep getting cut off as we try to get back. The yells and stamping feet of the guards make us turn, duck, and weave through the city until we're almost boxed in. Their shouts as they search for us get louder and louder. They'll find us any moment now. Terror fills me as I search for a way out, any way out.

"Here," I hiss to Blain and yank open the door of the dusty, abandoned shop to our left. The floor is covered in abandoned jewellery. Clearly whoever was here left in a hurry. The inside is a giant square with a door at the back, which Blain rushes to check. As I take a step towards the front bay windows that look out onto the side street, I hear footsteps. A moment later, I'm dragged down by an invisible hand. I yelp, but a warm hand covers my mouth, and I'm pinned to the floor by someone's weight, but I can't see them. My heart slams inside my chest as I'm restrained, unable to see who's behind me. I dart my gaze around the room, looking for Blain, but he's gone too.

It must be Nico and Smoke, but how? I jerk my head up when there's a bang. There's a soldier with a stern face peering into the shop, his hands cupped around his eyes as they rove around the interior of the store. I hold my breath, and as if he can hear it, his eyes land directly where I am, but he seems to see nothing. With a snarl, he turns away and rushes after the others, so I let out a slow breath into someone's warm hand.

"Shh, they aren't gone yet," comes a soft, low whisper from above me. The voice is familiar—Smoke. His body is pressed so close to mine I can hear his racing heart. We lie like that for a few more moments before he removes his hand, and then I can finally see him. He leans back, getting to his knees with a grin. I drop my head to the floor and see Nico sitting there, his hand outstretched to the right where Blain is glaring at Smoke.

They saved us.

"Thank you," I say instantly, trying to diffuse the situation as I get to my own knees and nod at Smoke. "How did you find us?"

"We saw you run in here with some guards on your tail. You're too pretty to die, so we thought we'd help." Smoke grins, winking at me.

Blain snarls and rushes towards him, but I hold him back with my arm. "Thanks, I think." I snort. "Did you see the others?" My voice holds my worry, and for once, Smoke's face turns serious.

"We saw them run, and we chased them for a little bit, but those fuckers are fast. They were heading to the south entrance of the subway, so they are fine."

I swallow my fear, sighing in relief. He might be an odd one, but I don't think Smoke would lie to us and then help us. No, we're working for the same team, and we need to trust each other. I look to Blain and tell him that with my eyes. He narrows his own as we have a silent staring contest before he snarls and turns away, conceding.

"He was touching you," he mutters, and I smile at his jealousy as I peer out of the window for any sign of the soldiers. They won't give up so easily, so we need to lay low, make our way back underground, and meet up with the others.

"Have they gone?" I ask hesitantly.

"Maybe," Nico whispers. "We should check before we go out there."

"Blain, you and Nico go see," Smoke calls.

I turn to see Blain about to demand why he can't when both our mouths drop open. Smoke is on fire. Bright orange and red flames burn in his eyes, obscuring the pupils entirely. His lips are cracked and have bright orange flames sliding through the fissures like lava. His coat is discarded on the floor, and his head is tilted down as his chest heaves. I'm surprised he's even able to talk. Flames are caught in his clenched fists, licking along his arms before being absorbed back into the skin as he grunts.

"He'll need a moment," Nico tells us. There's concern but no surprise in his voice, like he's seen this before. That settles some of my shock, but I still can't look away. "Come on." He holds his hand out to Blain.

"I'll be back, Harpy," Blain snarls and kisses me hard before glaring at a struggling, flaming Smoke. "You let anyone hurt or even touch her, and I'll wear your skin like that fucking fur coat," he warns.

"Understood." Smoke nods but doesn't seem scared. Distracted, yes. I would be too if I were on fire. I watch Blain disappear, and then the door opens and shuts softly. I search the alley for them, but I don't see anything, so I turn back to Smoke, keeping one eye outside just in case any soldiers sneak up on us.

"Are you okay?" I ask softly, not wanting to disrupt what's happening but needing to know.

"Peachy," he grumbles, shivering as he hunches forward. The flames engulf his chest. I cover my mouth to hold in my horrified gasp. His back is covered in mottled flesh, like the burned skin on his stomach, but this covers his entire back. It looks like molten gold has been woven into his flesh, it even shimmers.

"Smoke," I murmur sadly. I reach out but then retract my hand as he turns away—to protect me from the flames, no doubt. It's a few agonising moments of me splitting my gaze between him and the window before he sighs and flops back with a smile on his face.

"Damn, that shit hurts at first, but when it's over? Bliss, like a good orgasm," he comments, his eyes closed. I snort, and his eyelids crack open as his smile widens. "Go on, you can ask."

"I wasn't going to—"

"You were, it's fine." He sits up, turning to face the window, his eyes flicking back to me as he starts to talk without waiting for my questions. "I'm still learning to control it. It's getting more powerful.

Usually I have to release the build-up. I let some out to destroy the trap, but not enough. I've been cooped up too long, so letting that small bit out opened the door and caused the rest to try and flow out. I managed to hold it back and not hurt Nico or you, but some of it escaped. I apologise, I am usually better at controlling it." He winks at me. "It seems a pretty girl is too much of a distraction though, you could even say you fanned the flames."

"Charmer," I tease. We hear a noise and duck, but nothing happens, so a moment later, I peek over to see the coast is clear. "Were you born with it?" I inquire, trying to be kind. His scars are his own, but he brought it up, and my curiosity is getting the better of me.

"Yes and no." He sighs. "I didn't know about it until I was a teenager. I never got hurt by fire, but honestly, I never really noticed. If we played jump the campfire, I noticed it didn't burn me, it almost felt... good, like it was warming my skin. But it wasn't until we were attacked that I found out."

"Attacked?" I hesitate. "You don't have to tell me if you don't want to."

"Might as well kill some time." He grins, but there are ghosts in those bright eyes. "I lived in a little village on the outskirts of the city. My father was a day trader, selling the animals we raised in the city. I was asleep, but my mother was awake with my little sister who had a nightmare. That's when they came. I didn't even hear them. I only knew when our hut went up in flames. I was awakened by their screams. Every door had been blocked, so we were trapped. I tried to punch, kick, and fight my way out, but it was no use. The flames were too strong, as were the barriers they put up to stop us from getting out. They'd overhead my dad make a joke about me being special—this was when freaks were still hunted. I could hear their taunts and comments about freaks. My mother and sister were so scared—I..." He sighs. "I tried to save them. I wrapped myself around them as they screamed and burned. I did too, burn that is. Their skin burned into mine." He touches the scar on his stomach.

"This is where they were, and my legs too. My back is from the ceiling eventually caving in on me, and the golden light my mother had made burned through my skin. The flames were so hot, I couldn't see, couldn't think. It was pure agony for hours. I thought I died, that I was with them, but I never did, and eventually, I could hear our assailants' laughter as our screams died down. I could feel the ashes of my mother and sister, and I just... exploded. I sucked the flames in and let them burst out of me. I heard their screams before the pain became too much and I passed out. When I woke up, I was being pulled from the embers by my father. I remember him falling to his knees, sobbing over their ashes, and yet there I was alive, burnt but alive." He looks at me sadly, his voice muted in the small shop, and for a moment, I'm not there. I'm transported into his past with him, choking on the smoke and ash.

"He never blamed me. We knew we had to leave and fast. As he carried me away from our home, I saw the scorch marks on the earth from the men who I had clearly killed, but I said nothing. How could I describe what had happened? What I didn't know was that my father had been attacked in the city, and that's why he wasn't there. He was hurt badly by the men who killed my mother and sister to stop him from getting to us, but he still came back and found us dead. Yet he carried me to an outpost, one he had heard rumours of. They didn't want to let him in, but he begged. He explained I was like them before he collapsed. I was in and out of consciousness, the pain was too much. When I eventually came around, they told me what happened."

"What—what did happen?" I ask, tears in my eyes for what he went through. It seems everyone like me, like us, has these horrific stories simply for being alive. I can't imagine the pain this man has been through, the fear, the feel of hiding your family as they died, unable to help them at such a young age. Yet this man can still smile, and he is still fighting.

For them, no doubt.

"The rebels, it was their outpost. One took a chance on us, a young man— Regnor. He saw my powers and convinced them to let us through. My father, he was hurt too badly. He died at my bedside while I was knocked out. I almost died, in fact I did, according to Tobin. He saved me, brought me back. I was the first human he had ever done that to. He'd healed animals before, never a human, but he took a chance on me." He swallows and blinks. "He saved me from death and helped the flames on my skin settle inside me—my power. I was a freak like them. I had no home, no more family. That's why they called me Smoke. I was reborn in it. I was lost, but Regnor and the others wouldn't allow me to be alone. They saved me, gave me a purpose, a home, and a reason to fight and continue on, even when I didn't want to. Even when I blamed myself for my family's deaths. He's a brilliant man, cold, but only because he has seen so much death, so many horrors. His own family, his wife and children..." He pauses. "Don't tell him I told you that part, but you should know what you fight for." He turns fully towards me then and takes my hand. His palms are warm and scarred. "He's the type of man who risks it all to save a boy on the brink of death simply because he's like him. We aren't numbers or soldiers to him, we're people. He feels each death for our cause. He hides it, feeling as though he has to be strong, but I see the toll it takes on my friend."

"I—" I swallow. "I don't even know what to say other than I'm sorry for your loss. I hope you still don't blame yourself. You should blame the ones responsible, the men you killed, and I'm glad you killed them, glad Regnor saved you. You have turned out to be an amazing man, and I bet your family would be proud."

He blinks, searching my face. "Thank you, I—I guess I needed to hear that."

I nod and squeeze his hand again, showing him I'm not afraid of his power. "And thank you for sharing your story. I will keep it alongside my own memories and those of my family."

The door opens, and I pull my hand away as Blain becomes visible. "They are gone, there's a path, let's go." I nod, and he helps me to my feet. I hear Smoke moving, and when there's a tap on my shoulder, I turn to see him holding something in his hand. It's a black stone. It's long with a pointed tip, and it's set on a gold necklace. His eyes drop to it, and he curls his fingers around it. I gasp as I watch flames crawl along the stone and then sink into it, like it did his skin. It lights up from the inside, swirling like a live flame. "Here, in case you forget the reason why we fight. This flame will bring you the truth when you feel doubt." He hands it over. I hesitate, fearing getting burnt, but I decided to trust him and take it. Surprisingly, it's not hot, and I carefully loop it over my head.

"Thank you," I whisper.

"Of course. Now let's get back home, so you can tell the others of my heroics," he teases. I laugh as Nico takes my hand and I am once again made invisible. Even as we leave the shop, the story I learned stays with me. The pain in Smoke's eyes is the one we all carry, the one only people like us could understand—those who have lost, who have suffered so much. The way his eyes burned with grief, hope, and pain fills my soul, and even as we head back to the tunnels, it stays with me like the stone hanging above my heart.

When we get back, Nixon and Xavier are waiting at the tunnel entrance. I release Blain's hand and run to them. Xavier reaches me first and swings me up into his arms before passing me to Nixon.

"I'm so glad you're okay," I murmur.

"I am too," Nixon replies as he kisses me softly. He eventually puts me down and wraps his arm around my shoulders. "Come on, the others are waiting." With that, he leads me to the subway car where my men and Regnor are. I'm passed around before Regnor clears his throat.

"Yes, I'm glad she's okay, but please save this for later," he teases, but when I turn, I see him looking Smoke over as if to see if his friend is okay. "Report," he demands.

"The trap is destroyed. Nixon and Xavier brought in the troops,

I'm guessing. We got separated before we found Rhea and Blain, and then we made our way back down here. They are searching the city for us, so I would lay low for now," Smoke tells him.

"Good job, go get some rest. The remainder of the night is your own," Regnor says, dismissing us.

I nod, and as I turn with Jesse's hand in mine, there's a clearing of a throat. "Oh, Smoke, won't you show Rhea and her... family to their new quarters?"

"You've got it." Smoke stops before me. "Let's go, oh fancy leader lady," he jokes and turns, expecting us to follow again. I do with a grin, my men following behind me.

Instead of heading back the way we came, he moves to the other end of the car and past the bed to an old metal door. He opens it and hops down to the tracks, then he holds his arms up and helps me down before turning. I check to see that the others are following as we move down the darkened tracks. Smoke lifts his hand, and a ball of flames fills it. The fire shines off something deeper down the tunnel, and I blink as we draw closer. It's another car.

This one seems older, a lot older, with big windows on the side that are rolled down to let in fresh air. It's a deep purple and brown colour with panelled walls. The door is wooden with a curtain covering the small, built-in window. It looks ancient and adorable. There's a lantern hanging above the door, and Smoke climbs up the ladder and lights it before opening the door and gesturing for us to come up.

"You can stay here from now on. We save this for anyone who might need space. It's the nicest place," he offers and disappears inside. I hop up and follow him inside. It's smaller than Regnor's two carriages, but just as cosy. We enter into a little space with a hallway on the right lined with purple carpet. There's a small wooden wall to the left, and when I tread down the corridor, I see it's what used to be sleeping cars. It blocks off the door, but the walls between them have been taken down to make one big sleeping room. There are beds along the floor and more lanterns, which Smoke lights as he goes. We move farther down to the end of the corridor to see a small table and mismatched chairs, a little sink, and a bathroom cubicle with a golden chain hanging from the ceiling to flush the toilet. "If you need anything, let us know. We'll send some food down," Smoke informs us as he lights the rest of the lanterns and turns to us as we stand near the beds.

"Thank you," I tell him, "for everything."

He grins and moves past us. "Get some sleep, I'll see you tomorrow." With those parting words, I hear the door shut, and then we are alone.

At the end of the car is another door leading to the back end of the train and a darkened tunnel, which makes me shiver. "I guess this is home for now."

"I guess so," Alcide murmurs. "Let's get comfortable."

"I call dibs for spooning Rhea!" Jesse calls, lightening the mood and making us all laugh—me included.

We settle down, pushing the beds and blankets together. There's a knock at the door, and Rex answers it, bringing back a whole load of food and drink. We sit around the table and beds and eat and talk. I stay quiet, and I know they notice, so I try to involve myself so they won't worry, but when a yawn splits my lips, Alcide decides it's time to rest. Everyone quickly gets ready as I lie down on the left side, with Jesse on one side and Rex on the other. Some of the lanterns are extinguished as I lie on my back, my eyes on the wooden ceiling.

"Goodnight," I call softly to everyone.

"Goodnight, *cariño*," Alcide replies.

"Night, Firecracker," Jesse murmurs.

"If that is your cock, I'm going to kill you," Blain snaps to someone, and there's a moment of silence before we all burst into laughter. When we settle down, I close my eyes and try to sleep. I attempt to empty my mind as I hear the others start to snore.

I lie here for what feels like hours, with their warmth on either side of me, unable to get any rest. I hear a noise, but I can't see much in the dark without changing my eyes. I hear a door open and jerk, but there is nothing else, so I settle down, wondering if it was one of the guys needing the bathroom.

I'm exhausted from not sleeping last night, not to mention the long day it's been filled with worry, fear, and guilt for the lives I took. It's giving me whiplash and making me emotionally tired, but the day's events still weigh heavily on me. Even with the car filled with the snores of my loves, I can't succumb to the waiting darkness. I killed men today who could have had families, children. Eventually I give up and sit upright. I spot Xavier sitting outside and blink. I can see his back through the door at the bottom of the car. Standing, I creep over my other men, open the door, and slip out. He's sitting on the end of the train, leaning into the bars with his legs dangling down to the tracks. I sit next to him, wrapping my arms around myself. He stares out into the dark tunnel before us as I search his face.

"Are you okay?" I ask.

He turns to see me, and he's not surprised, so he must have heard me coming out. "Are you?" he asks instead. "Today was difficult, and you didn't sleep last night. You should be conked out by now."

"I couldn't," I murmur, turning back to the tunnel. "I keep thinking of those men I killed today, wondering if they had children to miss them—"

"Don't," he snaps and wraps his arm around my shoulders, pulling me into his side where I settle with a sigh. "Don't do that to yourself. I was the same at the beginning. The guilt of the lives I took consumed me, but it does nothing except make you suffer. It was you or them."

"Only it wasn't," I whisper. "This wasn't like in the ring. I had a choice, and I chose to kill them."

"To save others, to save us and all these children and women down here," he reasons, kissing the top of my head, determined to not let me wallow. "Don't beat yourself up. This is a war, Rhea. There will be death, but remember why you fight—for you, for people like us, who have been used and abused. They have been killing us for years, we are simply repaying the favour."

"But does a life for a life work?" I whisper.

"I guess we'll find out," he murmurs, kissing my head again.

I become quiet then, just absorbing his warmth and strength. I let him comfort me as I think through what has been happening. He's quiet most of the time, which is fine. I enjoy his silence as much as his voice. It's different though, we've crossed a line together. He's one of us now, and I don't know where that leaves us. I admitted I loved him, and I do, I fell for him the moment I saw him.

I didn't mean to, but it just happened. He stole my heart with one blood-soaked look, and again every moment after when he tried to save and protect me. Yet we've never been together, we have hardly even touched, but it just seems to make our love that much deeper. Comfortable, that's what this is. He makes me feel relaxed, and there is no judgement. Nothing I could ever do would disgust Xavier. He has seen and lived it all and understands my scars and brain. He offers his strengths and weaknesses. Hell, he became part of this war for us.

I do love him, a whole lot.

I love him as much as I love my other men. I never expected my life to turn out like this, but with his arms around me and my men sleeping behind me, I realise it's better than I could have ever imagined. I'm spoiled with love, and no matter what is to come, I can handle it all with them at my side. Fight, live, or die, we do it together. It's time I stopped holding back out of fear. Xavier is mine, and it's time I showed him that, because tomorrow isn't guaranteed, and if we are going to die, he needs to know that and I need... him. I need to know what he tastes like and to feel that conviction, that strength, that immortality painted across my skin.

I lift my head and he senses it, looking down at me. I can't speak as I run my eyes across his face before dropping my gaze to his lips.

"Rhea," he whispers, shivering under my stare, but he doesn't move away. No, he leans closer, and the gesture gives me all the permission I need. I lift my head and press my lips to his, softly at first. He stays still under my kiss as I tilt my head and press harder. He gasps, finally kissing me back. His huge hand fists my hair to tug me closer as he takes over. He kisses me hard, controlling my movements. I moan, a sound he swallows before slipping his tongue into my mouth and tangling it with mine. Each action is strong, sure, and so raw.

Just like my warrior.

He leans me back into the door of the car, following me down and pressing his body to mine. I lift my chest, pressing it against his, and he slides his hand up my leg, over my hip, and up my stomach. His fingers glide across my breast, making me shiver even over my shirt, before he circles my throat like a necklace, anchoring me as he tilts my head farther back for access. With one sure kiss, he steals what is left of my soul and heart, making me his.

He pulls back, and I chase his lips. He chuckles softly, and I swallow and open my eyes to meet his happy ones. His gaze is filled with hunger, but he's smiling so wide, something I've never seen him do before. He leans in and kisses both cheeks, both eyes, and my forehead before kissing my lips again. "Thank you," he whispers breathlessly.

"For what?" I gulp. "I should be thanking you. That was one hell of a kiss."

"For giving me a chance, for seeing past the scarred, blood-stained warrior to the man hiding beneath," he murmurs as he drags his lips across mine again. "For seeing me, for saving me and putting my broken heart back together so I could give it to you." He leans back a little then. "I didn't say it back the other day because I wanted the first time to just be us. But I love you too, my little warrior. You stole my heart in the cells and during the fights. Each day, I watched you grow, watched your strength and confidence increase, and you stole it piece by broken piece. You glued together each shard they splintered with my family's death, each round of torture, and each violation. You took it back and made it yours, and I swear it will be yours forever. Even if you don't want me anymore, I'm yours, Rhea the immortal... my love."

My eyes fill with tears and I kiss him again. "Mine is yours as well, has been since the moment I saw you." My words pale in comparison to his, so I kiss him again, letting him feel everything in that sweet kiss—my dedication, my love for this man, my awe at what he has survived and the life I know we will have together. When I lean back, he's grinning. "When this is over, we can start anew, and they will never touch you again."

"Nor you," he promises and lifts me, sitting me in his lap as he turns to stare at the dark. I snuggle close, closing my eyes as exhaustion hits me again, tangling with the ebbing desire from his kiss.

"Sleep, I'll protect you," he vows.

"I know you will." I sigh. "How can you stare into the dark like that?" I ask, trying to fight the sleep attempting to claim me.

"The dark is all I know. It was my constant down there in the fights after I lost my family. Night was the only time I was left alone. Even when I was sold. I closed my eyes, and the dark is what saved me. It gives me solace, and it promises better times, oblivion. I wasn't there, I wasn't feeling their hands on my body or the pain they liked to inflict. I wasn't being used or taken, my firsts.... First kiss, first time being touched, taken. I was floating in the warmth of that nothingness."

"I used to fear it," I admit, and my heart breaks at hearing the pain in his voice, so I move closer, trying to hold it at bay with my body. "I'm sorry for everything you went through. If I could, I would kill them all for what they did to you."

He kisses me softly. "I know, but my life shaped me into this man. They might have taken my firsts, Rhea, but you have all my lasts."

"I will cherish them," I murmur around a yawn. "Forever, my warrior."

Sleep claims me as he settles back, musing over our words.

He kisses my forehead again. "You made it all worthwhile. I was ready to end it, to finally meet my fate in those fights, and then you came. The dark doesn't scare me, Rhea, but losing you does."

"We're going back to our tent," I announce as I approach the rebel leader.

If Regnor's surprised at our sudden entrance in his carriage, then he hides it well. In fact, he doesn't even look up from his maps spread out on the table before him.

This morning, the guys and I all sat together and discussed yesterday's events. Alcide, used to being in charge, hadn't liked being left behind and wanted to know every detail. We'd only just escaped, and that spooked him, so we didn't mind going through every minute step of the mission. When he suggested that we go back to the big top, we looked at him in surprise. He explained that we could get more intel on the masters and grab some precious items that were left behind. Blain pointed out that the tent had probably been ransacked, but Alcide was insistent.

One of the worries that swirls around my head at night is the safety of the rest of our crew. They all had powers too, but nothing as obvious as ours, and they certainly hadn't been in the cells with us. Had they been killed, or were they hiding somewhere? They are a resourceful group, they have had to be thanks to their abilities, so I'm sure they survived, and I am betting they are in hiding. They might have even left us clues to lead us to their location. Once I explained my worries to the others, they all agreed. I know they have also been worried about our friends, so it didn't take much convincing.

Now all we have to do is convince Regnor.

"Out of the question," he drawls, still studying the map, jotting down notes in a small, tattered book. This is a man who's used to being obeyed, used to people following his orders, so we need to take this steadily, not plough on—

"You can't stop us." Alcide steps forward, his dark eyes narrowed on the rebel leader. I wince at the challenging tone he uses, knowing that Regnor won't respond well to this. I lay a hand on Alcide's arm to try to contain him.

Slowly, and with exaggerated care, Regnor lowers his pen to the table and turns before pinning his outraged expression on my ringmaster. His anger at Alcide's audacity is clear. "Excuse me?" he demands, resting his hands on his hips as if daring us to retort.

To his credit, Alcide doesn't baulk under the weight of Regnor's stare, and I feel the guys shuffle behind me as the atmosphere becomes tense. "You might be the leader here, but you don't rule me, us. We're going."

Needing to de-escalate the situation, I step in front of Alcide. "We need to go back to see if any of our stage crew are still there," I explain kindly, begging Regnor to understand. "We can spy on the masters at the same time. Think of it as a reconnaissance mission."

He finally pulls his gaze from Alcide and scans the others at my back before turning his scrutiny on me. He's angry but trying to keep it under control, knowing if he pushes us too far, we'll just leave. Right now, he needs us.

"Did you not hear what Smoke said last night?" He gestures behind him, and my eyes follow the movement, finding said rebel leaning against the carriage wall. A snort comes from behind us, and I see Tobin sitting in the chairs by the door. I'd been so focused on our mission that I hadn't noticed them until now.

Rookie move, Rhea.

"The whole city is on alert and looking for you. You killed their guards and have openly joined the rebels. They won't stop until they have you," Regnor reasons, frustration lining his words.

The guys move closer, as if needing to protect me from the threat the rebel leader speaks of, Nixon's chest pressing against my back. It helps ground me, and I find the touch comforting. Taking a deep breath, I meet his unwavering stare. "Regnor, we're going. This was a simple courtesy to let you know."

Hands balled into fists, he steps forward, his teeth bared. "You're going to get yourself killed."

Blain surges forward, blocking the rebel leader from coming any closer, a blade appearing in his hand. I'm sure it's just a threat to remind Regnor who we are. He wouldn't really kill him... would he?

"We survived yesterday, and that was far more dangerous," Xavier inserts as he watches the rebels carefully. He appears relaxed on the surface, but I can tell he's ready to strike if he needs to. "We'll be moving away from the middle of the city. They won't expect it."

No. None of this is going as planned. We agreed to work with them, but the guys are so protective of me that if they don't calm down soon, this will end in a fight we can't win. My mind spins, trying to think of a way to insist on going without sounding like I'm challenging his authority or asking permission.

Pushing away from the wall, Smoke walks to Regnor's side, patting him on the shoulder. "I'll go with them." Smoke meets the leader's heavy gaze as Regnor turns to him. The two of them share a look, seeming to communicate without words.

Finally, Regnor growls in the back of his throat, the tension heavy in the train carriage, but after a second, he waves us forward and jabs a finger down at the map. "This is where we are now."

Glancing down, I see a small mark on the map, one I probably wouldn't have noticed if he hadn't pointed it out. The map is covered in circles and markers, yet their base is hardly recognisable. I suppose that's been done on purpose, in case the map was ever in the masters' hands. Regnor's finger moves across, jabbing at another spot.

"This is where your tent is." Looking up from the map, he locks eyes with me, his face deadly serious. "You get in, do what you need to do, and get the hell out of there."

The guys had discussed the plan over and over with Regnor, talking through every possibility and scenario. Smoke chipped in with useful bits of information about the best tunnels to use and ways to avoid getting caught. Regnor wanted some of my guys to stay behind, but that was loudly dismissed. I go with all my guys, end of discussion. I suspect he wanted them here as an insurance policy, knowing I'd never leave without them. I thought we proved ourselves to him yesterday, but he still seems uncertain.

Eventually, after what felt like hours of talking and arguing, Smoke leads us through the tunnels to our exit point. How he can navigate them so well is a mystery to me, especially when we reach parts where it's not safe to use a light and have to walk in the dark.

We've been walking for a long time now, far away from the rebel camp, but I have no idea how much time has passed. We're currently in a section where we have to walk in total darkness. Smoke's in the lead with us behind him in a human chain, holding hands so we don't get lost. Something starts to change. The stale air seems to move, a soft breeze caressing my cheek, and I realise that the darkness is starting to give way to light.

Thank God. I know the tunnels are our refuge, but my chest always tightens with anxiety as we descend beneath the city.

As we get closer, I realise that the streams of weak light that I can see are shining through wooden slats. Smoke turns to me, and in the light, I see him press his finger to his lips before gesturing for me to stay where I am. As he breaks away from our small group, pushes the slats up, and climbs out of the tunnel, my stomach flips with nerves. I'm surprised that I'm feeling this anxious about his safety. Sure, I like the cheeky rebel, but when did I start to worry for him like a friend? Memories of what he told me yesterday flash in my mind as I wait for him to return.

The shadow of a figure blocks the light filtering down on us, and I have to bite back my cry of surprise. The guys crowd around me, and I see weapons glinting in the light. We won't go down without a fight. The slats are pulled back abruptly, and I see Smoke grinning down at us.

"You miss me?" His voice is barely above a whisper, but he can't seem to help teasing us. Offering me his hand, he helps me climb out of the tunnel. "We shouldn't have a problem on the streets."

"What do you mean?" Rex asks quietly, but my attention is diverted by the room we're standing in.

It must have been a house at one point, but now it's just a dilapidated ruin. Stained, pink floral wallpaper covers what remains of the walls, and I see part of a fireplace in the corner. Thanks to the collapsed roof, large wooden beams cut off most of the room, and I wonder if all of us will even fit in this small space.

"See for yourself." Smoke chuckles, stepping back to give the guys space to leave the tunnel. "Follow me." He starts to make his way through the debris, ducking low to avoid a beam, and I realise now why he took so long to scout the area. Glancing over my shoulder, I see the wooden slats are back in place, making the entrance appear like a pile of wood and rubble. It's well hidden, and I know we wouldn't have found it by ourselves. I can see why the rebels have stayed safe in the tunnels for so long.

Shouts and the sound of running feet have me frowning, but Smoke just waves me forward, unworried about the noise. When I reach his side, I see why. The streets are packed. The young, old, rich, and poor have streamed into the street with banners and signs as they move towards the middle of the capitol.

"They are protesting," Alcide whispers in shock, peering over my shoulder.

"We have to go, we don't have much time, but this will work in our favour." Smoke does a head count before nodding. "Remember the plan, and make sure to follow me." Uncharacteristically serious, he meets each of our eyes to make sure we understand. His gaze slides to me, and his lips quirk up in a smile. "Here, wrap this over your hair, you're too recognisable." He winks, handing me a small bundle of fabric before pulling up his hood, hiding his own flame-like hair. It's just a strip of pale fabric, about the size of a scarf, but it's obviously been torn from something else.

Squeezing through a hole just big enough to fit a person, Smoke disappears onto the streets. Taking a deep breath, I meet the eyes of my guys before I quickly wrap the makeshift scarf around my head and follow the rebel. I'm instantly hit with the sounds of the crowd, their shouts bouncing off the buildings around us. There are screams, but they are deeper in the city, probably where the masters have sent their guards to protect them. People mill about, and I'm thrown off by being surrounded by so many people, but I'm soon enveloped by the guys.

Smoke appears at my side, his face strained as he looks back at the crowd. I don't know how he managed to disappear and get back to us so quickly, blending in with the masses like he's been doing this for years. Although, I guess he has, considering most of the rebels have been blending in and hiding in plain sight.

Taking a deep breath, he gestures for us to follow. "There's no way through the crowd unless you're willing to split up—" He's cut off by a chorus of noes. Grinning over his shoulder, he weaves through the edges of the crowd with us staying close so we can hear him. "I thought not. Okay, change of plan. We can't get close enough to see what the masters are up to, but they look pretty preoccupied at the moment." Gesturing towards the thickening group of people, he shakes his head. "We go straight to the tent, then come back here."

Nodding in agreement, we break away from the crowd, using the people in the street to blend in as we weave in and out of side streets to avoid notice. Thankfully, the tunnel we used isn't far from where the big top was set up, so it's not long before I see the peak of the red and white striped tent. Our home. We only came across two guards, but they'd been running in the opposite direction, towards the protest. I held my breath the whole time they were in view, my body screaming at me to hide, but the guards paid us no attention.

Rounding the final building, we come to the clearing where we'd set up camp. I'm filled with a myriad of emotions as I see our beautiful tent and what they've done to it. Large slashes are cleaved through the walls, the material flapping in the breeze. Even from here, I can see the carriages and carts we travel in have been raided and trashed. Grief grips me tightly. I know it's just a tent and I should be pleased that we're all alive, but this place was the first home I've ever had.

"They've destroyed it," Alcide whispers at my side, grief making his voice crack. Taking his hand, I squeeze it tightly as we look at the ruins of our life. "That was our home."

"No." I pull him towards me, his expression showing his devastation. Reaching up, I place my hand on his cheek and wait until he meets my eyes. "The tent is an important part of us, but it doesn't define us. A house doesn't make a home." The latter part of my statement is a quote from an old woman I'd once overheard talking back in Cinders. I hadn't understood it at the time, since surely a house and a home were the same thing, but I get it now. "You guys, *you* are my home. As long as we are together, we will be okay. We can rebuild and make it bigger and better than before."

The others surround us, each reaching out to lay a hand on me or Alcide, comforting us and agreeing with my statement. I become aware of a set of eyes on me, and as I look up, I see Smoke watching us with a strange expression.

Realising that I've caught him watching, he grins. "While this is very touching, we shouldn't just be standing out here in the open."

For one more second, we indulge in each other's touch before breaking apart. After checking the area for guards, we jog over to the tent and hurry inside. Once in the huge structure, I realise that the damage to the tent looked worse on the outside. Most of the structure and seats are still intact.

Smoke has been looking around with wide eyes like he's never seen anything like this before. As I glance over, he sees me and coughs as if hiding his embarrassment at me seeing this side of him. "Okay, split up, but stay in sight of each other."

The others call out their agreement and jog across the space. We all head through the curtained section at the back of the tent, away from where we would perform and into where we would get ready and prepare for the show. My chest is tight as we hurry through, the tent feeling strange without the animals and crew here. It feels much bigger, lonely. Heading straight to the practice area, I start to cross the flat, sand-covered training ring.

On the other side are the wooden crates where we used to store some of our belongings, but just as I'm about to cross over the boundary of the training ring, I trip over something. With a noise of surprise, I fall to the ground, my body instantly shifting to protect me from the fall. I sit up, my body returning to normal as I glance at the sand, trying to find what caused me to trip. I can't see anything —wait, there. A strange, slightly circular object is sticking up out of the sand. I might not have noticed if it wasn't for the fact it glistens in the light. Crawling forward, I try to get a better look, aware of the others in the tent moving around me.

"Look! I found a letter! One of the stagehands left it for us!" Jesse calls with excitement on the other side of the tent, but I'm only partially paying attention, the shiny object distracting me. Something about it gives me a really bad feeling. Digging in the sand with my bare hands, I finally reach the object, and dread fills me.

"Alcide!"

He must hear the urgency in my voice as he runs over, Nixon close behind. "Rhea, is everything... What's that?"

Turning, I move out of the way so he can kneel beside me. I hear his sharp intake of breath as he realises what it is, putting together the circumstances of our capture. The others jog over to see what the commotion is about, calling out in confusion.

"It's a camera," I whisper, glancing up at the guys gathered behind me, their eyes wide at the implications. "The masters were watching us all along."

After finding one camera, it wasn't hard to spot the others, and we decided it was best to get out of there as soon as possible. Who knows if the masters are still watching? We don't want to get caught, but luckily the protest is still in full swing, so we use it as cover to get back to the ruined house and into the tunnels. We follow Smoke and head back to the rebels, holding hands again. Smoke's is clasped in mine, and he squeezes and lets go as we get into a more lit area.

"So that's the circus, huh?" he whispers.

I look over at him and he grins.

"Never been myself. You know, rebel plans to make, leaders to overthrow."

"It is—was an amazing place." I sigh, correcting myself. I drop my gaze to the wet tunnel floor to hide my sad eyes.

"I'm sure it will be again," he soothes, and then we fall silent as we merge into the main tunnel—right into Regnor. He's waiting there with his arms crossed and face stern, and there are men behind him. I recoil, my own men converging on my back until we're facing off. Smoke stands between us, stepping closer to the rebel leader and his friend with a frown.

"What's going on?" he questions. "Is everyone okay?"

"Everyone is just fine," Regnor replies, and then his eyes flit to mine. "Just wanted to ensure our face of the rebellion didn't get hurt. I was so worried, in fact, that I had a good idea—guards to ensure her safety at all times." He jerks his head at the equally stern-faced men behind him, each one cold and calculating.

Guards?

He wants to put protection on me?

"Guards?" I snap, a bad feeling churning in my stomach. "To protect me or to restrain me?" I demand, his sudden anger taking me by surprise. My powers rise in response to being ambushed, to not being trusted, and I try to keep them in check.

"Can't they do both?" Regnor admits openly, and if I had Smoke's powers, I swear the glare I throw at the cocky leader would have set him on fire.

"So not only do you want these guards to follow me everywhere, but you probably want them to report my actions to you. You're spying on us just like the masters," I snap.

"Is that what you want? To spy on us?" Xavier snarls. "Because

I've been controlled by the masters far too long to bow to another man who wants the same thing."

I step in front of him before he does something, like attack Regnor, but with the way this is going, I don't blame him.

This is to stop what he believes is our defiance. It's because we pushed him earlier and gave him no choice but to let us go. He's worked a way around it to try and control us, but I've been controlled my whole life, and I'm tired of it. I had a taste of freedom and I want it back. I'm not Rhea the slave girl anymore. No, I'm Rhea, face of the rebellion, and it's time I acted and was treated like it. I won't be controlled, I won't be told what to do, where to go, and what to say.

This is my fight too, and it's time Regnor realised that.

When I'm sure Xavier and the others won't attack the rebel leader, I stride past Smoke and get right in Regnor's face. A crowd gathers, and I raise my voice to let them hear what I have to say.

"You seek to control me like the masters? To use me like your little puppet? Something to look at and keep silent and submissive?" I turn to address the crowd. "Are we not equals here? We are all freaks, and we are all fighting the same fight to free this city and our people from tyrannical control... and this is how you want to start it? By persecuting one of your biggest supporters because she wanted to go up top to find her friends, her people, and protect them?"

Murmurs begin in the throng as people question what happened, if what I'm saying is true. I see anger, disgust, and confusion at my statement.

I lower my voice, ensuring only Regnor and Smoke can hear me. "If you do this, if you try to control me like every other man has since I was born, I will disappear so fast you will never even see it happening. You need me for this rebellion, and I hold no malice towards you, I just want to help. You would be ruining a friendship, a working relationship with some of the strongest freaks in this city. Do you really want that? The enemy of my enemy is my friend, so let us work together. Let us stop this fight and free our people, and then we can go our separate ways. But until then, Regnor," I snarl, "do not ever seek to control me again. I am no weak-willed female. I am Rhea the Immortal, and it would be the biggest mistake of your life, just like capturing me was theirs. Do we understand each other, or should I continue to make a scene? To split your people who look to you for leadership, who have seen me and my men fight for them, die for them, and continue to do so?"

Regnor looks at the whispering crowd, obviously seeing the tension and separation. He doesn't have as many supporters who would blindly follow him as he thought. These people need a united leadership, not one that requires choosing sides. "No, we understand each other," he mutters and steps back. "We will work together, Rhea, for our people."

"Good." I begin to walk past him before stopping at his side. "Lose the guards. If they try to follow me, they will be following me up into the city as I leave."

I storm away, my men following. Before I turn the corner, I look back to see the crowd dispersing as Smoke and Regnor argue heatedly. When I face forward to head to our car, I run straight into Marie, who is undoubtedly moving towards the commotion.

"Sorry, are you okay?" she asks, stepping back with a friendly smile. It's evident she doesn't know what Regnor did, and when she sees my face, she frowns and steps closer with a worried look. "Rhea, what's going on?"

"I—" I shake my head. I shouldn't involve her, since she clearly cares for Regnor, but she touches my arm and pleads with me with her eyes. "I'm tired of being told how I should act and what I should do. I'm tired of being controlled by men as if I'm lesser for being a woman. First because I'm a freak, now because of the gender I was born into. I'm so fucking tired. And angry."

She glances over my head, irritation entering her eyes. "He means well, but sometimes his dedication to the cause blinds him to the hurt he creates." She looks at me and must see my shock. "I love him, Rhea, but not blindly. I know his faults. He's always under so much pressure, wanting to save this world. It means he sometimes makes the wrong decision, and I'm not defending that. Your anger, your emotions are justified." She squeezes my arm. "And I'm sorry, so sorry for everything you've been through."

"Thank you," I offer softly, and she smiles and steps back, looking at my men behind me. "Come on, let me show you somewhere private. There are no prying eyes there, and I feel like you could use it about now."

She turns, and I follow after her gratefully. I saw the honesty in her gaze. She doesn't agree with Regnor, even though she loves him. What a complicated relationship they must have, but it does endear me to her more. She's a thoughtful, smart, and caring woman.

She leads me to the empty end of the platform before hopping down onto the tracks and continuing on. I hesitate but leap down after her, landing with a stumble before righting myself. I peer into the dark and spot her a little way down. She's standing on some steps with a lantern hanging above her, illuminating her frame. I hurry towards her and up the steps, and she opens an old blue metal door. It squeaks but gives and bangs against the wall. Reaching in, she hits the lights, and they actually work, flicking on with a buzz.

"Here, take as long as you need. I'll have Smoke come and watch the door, I know you trust him." With that, she departs, and I watch her go. I trust Smoke?

Do I?

I guess I do, but that's a problem for a different time. I move into the room, my eyes widening at what I find.

It's a bathroom, a huge one at that, probably built down here for workers. It's old for sure, definitely pre-bombs, but it's in good condition and the cleanest bathroom I've ever seen. The walls are tiled from floor to ceiling, and old white tile covers every inch except for the five blue toilet cubicles to the right, which have open swinging doors, showing the toilets inside. To the left are six white freestanding sinks with small rectangular mirrors above them. On the back wall are three showers with no separators, other than some obviously hung white curtains. The lips of the shower lower to smaller white tiles, and the three silver showerheads are sparkling.

Obviously this space is maintained and cleaned.

"Anyone thinking of the showers in the cells?" Xavier grins as he walks towards them, flicks one on, and sticks his hand underneath. With a groan, he looks at me. "They are warm."

That's all it takes. He rips off his clothes. My eyes widen, and I let out a little noise as he ducks under the spray. I take in every scarred inch of his magnificent body before I quickly avert my gaze, but it doesn't help, because everyone else is stripping too. Rex smiles at me and leans in.

"Come on, Wildcat. Let's get cleaned up." His soft, assuring smile helps settle my nerves, and I strip, passing my clothes over. After all, everyone here has already seen me naked, but as I step towards the showers, six pairs of male eyes lock on me—dark, hungry, and unblinking. I swallow and channel some of my newfound confidence as I head towards them, stepping under the spray as they make room for me. Slicking back my hair, I sigh in contentment as the hot water beats against my skin, washing away blood, sweat, and the tightness in my muscles.

I hear someone groan and open my eyes as I turn, meeting Jesse's cocky smirk. "Firecracker, are you trying to give us all a heart attack?"

"More like a hard-on," Xavier mutters as Alcide grins. Blain rolls his eyes but spanks me as he passes to duck under the water. Nixon just smiles, but his eyes roam down to my body too. Propping my hand on my hip, I wag my other finger at Jesse.

"Down, boy," I tease.

His brow arches in answer, and then he suddenly knocks me to the floor and rolls, splaying me on top of him as he grins up at me. I yelp when he squeezes my ass. With a smile, he runs his hands up my body, making my breath catch and my pussy clench. I tilt my head down, ready to meet his lips when his touch changes.

Instead of being sensual, he tickles me.

I laugh, my body jerking above him as I try to get him to stop, but I can't. I hear the others laughing as my face turns red, and he still doesn't relent, even as I pant and writhe.

"Jesse!" I whine through my laughter.

"What was that, Firecracker? Moaning my name already?"

"I didn't hear that," Rex teases. "Maybe try harder."

Suddenly more hands join in, tickling my feet and arms until I can barely breathe because I'm laughing so hard.

"Oh God, stop, please!" I cry as they surround me, working as a team to torture me with laughter.

"You heard her," Alcide jokes. "Stop, gods."

Jesse laughs, stroking my sides as I suck in desperate breaths and slump. He cups my cheek and lifts his head, beads of water caught in his long black lashes. His plump lips part as he moves to kiss me, and my heart skips a beat. Thoughts of us together fill my head... How I thought he was dead and haven't been alone with him since. I can barely breathe with my need to kiss him.

There's a deep rap of knuckles on the metal door, and it reverberates around the room. I freeze on top of Jesse, looking up as the knock comes again, more insistent this time. Jesse groans in frustration.

"Let's go!" Smoke hollers.

"Busy!" I call back with a giggle, but he pounds on the door again, and I frown, wondering what is going on. All thoughts of Jesse's lips and the making up we have to do disappear at his next words.

"Hurry up, cutie! Get your dick on later. Something's happened!"

We dry and throw on our clothes in silence. The sense of urgency in the air twists my gut with dread. I know Smoke wouldn't bother us unless it was an emergency, so whatever's happened obviously can't wait.

Glancing around, I meet Rex's gaze as he watches me pull on my shirt. It's not in a sexual way, no, all of that disappeared with Smoke's words, but he seems to be checking that I'm okay. In fact, as I look at the others, I catch them all throwing glances at me. At first, annoyance bubbles within me. They are not giving each other those looks, so why just me? Is it because I'm a woman?

No, that's not fair. They love me, so of course they want to check if I'm okay. The guys love each other as brothers, whereas I mean something different to them. Having this many partners isn't always easy, and the pressures of a normal relationship are six times greater. I guess Regnor's actions are still annoying me, but it's not fair of me to push those feelings on the guys. They have done nothing but support and protect me, whereas Regnor sought to control me. It's completely different, and I won't let my run-in with the rebel leader taint my relationships.

Instead, I push back my annoyance and smile at Rex as I walk over and place my hand on his shoulder, reassuring him with a touch. The tightness around his eyes seems to ease, and he leans down, pressing a gentle kiss against my lips. Suddenly remembering we're not alone, I pull back and see the other guys watching us with heat-filled eyes. We were all interrupted at the worst time, and their expressions of frustration show exactly that. Raising my eyebrow, I open my mouth to comment that we'll make up for lost time later when a shout sounds outside.

Blain growls low in his throat, practically ripping the door open, and faces off with Smoke. "This better be important."

"Something's happened," Smoke repeats, and as I join Blain by the door, I see the rebel's face is uncharacteristically solemn. "Regnor's about to give a speech. I didn't think you'd want to miss it."

Nodding, I throw a look over my shoulder at the guys, all of whom are now fully dressed. Blain jumps down first before placing his hands on my waist and lifting me down, pressing a kiss to my forehead in a rare show of public affection. Smiling up at him, I gently squeeze his arm and step out of the way so the others can climb down. Before I do though, I notice a look of sorrow on Smoke's face as he watches us. It's only there for a second, and as soon as our eyes meet, he winks at me, shifting back to his usual light-hearted self, but I'm beginning to see through it. It's a mask, his way of coping in this crazy world.

Once we're all together, Smoke takes the lead, guiding us back to the main station. The tunnels seem to be alive with action. Voices and shouts echo towards us, the sounds distorting, and I see several people running ahead.

Jogging up to Smoke's side, I place a hand on his arm. "What's going on? Are we being attacked?"

He glances down at where I'm touching him, appearing surprised for a second before looking ahead, a frown marring his face. "No, but you'll find out soon enough."

Peering back at the guys, I notice their disturbed expressions. We continue the rest of the short journey in silence, all lost in our own thoughts. What could be happening? Smoke said Regnor had called a meeting, and although the two of us came to an agreement, I briefly wonder if this is a way of him pulling rank over me again? No, I don't think he'd do that. Whatever his opinions of me are, he cares too much about this rebellion to risk me causing a scene and splitting it apart.

Reaching the station, I see everyone gathered around in small groups, all looking up at Regnor with weathered, worried expressions. They have all been through so much.

As soon as I appear, the whispers start, and the whole atmosphere begins to change, hope blooming on their faces. Regnor sees me and gestures for us to join him, his expression carefully blank. Some of the gathered rebels reach out to touch me as we pass, as if even just my presence gives them hope that they can get through this.

The guys move in closer behind me, their grumbles and stiff bodies telling me they don't like everyone touching me, but they do nothing to stop it. They know as well as I do how much the rebels need something to believe in.

Climbing up onto the platform, the guys and I walk over to Regnor. Smoke's already on his other side, speaking to the rebel leader in a low voice. I see Marie standing behind Regnor, her arms crossed over her chest and expression tense. Catching our movement, she glances over and smiles in greeting, but it's tight, like the world is resting on her shoulders and this is all she can manage. After a few seconds, she becomes distracted, and she scans the crowd once more.

While we're waiting for him to begin, I take a moment to look over Regnor. He's practically vibrating with energy, and as he turns, he notices me, and I see anger burning in his eyes. I don't think it's aimed at me, but it's due to whatever's the cause of this meeting. Nodding his head at me in greeting, he turns back to the gathered rebels.

"Rebels, thank you for coming on such short notice." His voice rings out across the station, and everyone falls silent as they listen to their leader. "You might have heard that the streets above are in chaos. The people were protesting and surging towards the capitol where the masters were hiding like the cowards they are."

Low murmurs fill the space, and I notice several of the rebels spitting on the ground at the mention of the masters.

"Around the same time, three of our scouts went missing." The muttering stops as all attention returns to Regnor. "They were looking for food, and in the chaos, they were captured. They were immediately dragged to the front of the crowd and hung in front of everyone."

Horror fills me, and from the looks on the guys' faces, they feel the same way. The guards could have taken them in for questioning and given them a trial, but no, they were killed, their dignity taken from them and their deaths turned into a spectacle. I shouldn't be surprised by any of this. The masters turned killing freaks into a sport, and we all have the scars to prove it. Yet the suddenness of it... It feels like a child having a tantrum, lashing out and hurting anyone who's close by.

"Some of the crowd was also killed in the same way. I don't know if they were mistaken for rebels or if the masters were just sending out a message," Regnor continues, confirming my thoughts. The masters didn't care who got hurt as long as they showed us their might.

"Either way, it had the desired effect, and most of the crowd dispersed." Regnor's words are strong and unwavering, purely factual, but I see his hands balled into fists at his sides.

Turning my attention to the gathered rebels, I'm taken aback by what I see. Their grief is palpable, the air thick with their sorrow. They don't shout or look surprised, and I realise this is nothing new to them, yet that doesn't take away from the pain of this loss. Tears stream down their faces, both men and women alike. Regnor pauses, allowing his words to sink in, and I suspect he's attempting to contain his own anger and anguish. When Marie steps forward and squeezes his shoulder, he turns and shares a look with her. I can't see his expression, but I don't miss her whispered encouragement to him.

Taking a deep breath, he turns back to his rebels. "They have treated us like scum for too long." He steps forward, his hand going to the knife strapped to his hip.

The crowd murmurs their agreement, the mood of the tunnel changing from grief and sadness to anger and the need for retribution.

"We will not stand for this!" His shout is echoed by the cries of the rebels. The air vibrates with tension, and I realise exactly what this is.

A call to arms.

"The timeline is being moved up. Your group leader will be in touch about your role soon, so be ready." Regnor's voice rings above the din, and they quickly hush so they can hear what he's saying. "Tonight, we rest and mourn. Tomorrow, we plan."

The rebel leader suddenly turns to me, and I feel everyone's eyes follow. I straighten my back at the attention, holding my head high.

He seems to be waiting for something, and I realise he's expecting my agreement, a sign that I will support him on this. I'm taken aback and hate being put on the spot, but ultimately, I agree with what he's saying. We can't let this continue. I nod my head once, and he grins, his eyes bright.

"And then we'll take back this city once and for all!" He thrusts his arm into the air, and the rebels eat it up, bellowing their agreement. Jumping down into the crowd, Regnor joins his people, and a chant begins.

The guys surround me as soon as Regnor's gone, their expressions a mixture of sorrow, anger, and acceptance. I notice Smoke is still standing on the platform, frowning as he watches the others. I feel the urge to go to him, but right now my guys need me, and I need them. We need to be surrounded by love as we remember those who lost their lives and prepare for what's to come.

We're going to war, and I just have to pray it doesn't cost us everything.

THE NIGHT CLOSES IN FAST. There's chaos everywhere, but it's organised chaos as everyone prepares for tomorrow, for what is to come. They work together like a well-oiled machine as weapons are found and cleaned, and clothes are fixed. Groups of people gather to learn their orders and positions. We withdraw, making sure to show our faces and help where we can, but we stay together, unsure of our place and our orders. I hope Regnor doesn't make us stay back, I won't tolerate it. Not when the streets run red with the blood of my people. But for now, we wait and watch, offering hope when the rebels turn their downcast, scared, angry eyes to us.

We are a show of force, we are their beacon in the dark.

"What do we think our orders will be?" Jesse murmurs from my side, which he's seldom left since coming back from the dead.

"I don't know," I murmur.

"Whatever it is, we stick together," Alcide promises, noticing my hesitation and uncertainty and becoming the leader he is.

As if Nixon has picked up on my worry, he lays his hand on my shoulder. "We will," he states.

Xavier nudges my shoulder, much like when he did when we faced enemies in the fights. "Whatever happens, we are together," he murmurs.

"Let's give them some space, I feel like a spare part," Blain mutters as he pushes from the wall and starts to move through the crowd.

"I agree." Rex takes my hand and tugs me after them. "I hope we can see our animals soon too."

"I do as well." I lean into him as we walk. "I miss them. I hope they are okay."

"They are strong, Wildcat, just like you. We will win this, free our people, and get back to them." He sounds so sure, so strong that I can't help but straighten and trust in his words, in their confidence.

I have to be strong, not just for them, but for all the freaks—the fighters, the feeders, the healers, and those who are spread across this city, hiding and scared. They are the ones who need us now, and doubts or not, I have to be there. I have to stand tall alongside this rebellion, because if you aren't part of the solution, you are part of the problem. I refuse to be the problem, so it's time I stayed. It's time I stood up to those reigning over our world and our people with tyranny.

It's time for a change, starting right here, with these rebels, with us freaks.

We head back to our train car to prepare for tomorrow. Blain sharpens his blades—the ones he still has, not the ones he produces. Rex and, surprisingly, Xavier fix the patches in the clothing some rebels have dropped off. Xavier said he learned from his mum and that it came in handy in the cells, which I can understand. Jesse works on making our space our own and comfortable under Nixon's watchful calm eyes. Nixon is mostly silent until he points out a weakness in Jesse's new setup.

Alcide sighs, wrapping his arms around me and placing his head on my shoulder. "I miss the tents, I miss the road," he admits softly, so softly my other men wouldn't hear. For our ringmaster to admit a weakness to me? It makes me shudder. He's so strong, so sure and in charge, and for him to let me see his vulnerable side shows me just how much he loves me.

"Me too." I turn in his arms and peer up at him as his hands stroke up and down my back, assuring himself I'm here and okay. It makes me wonder how much he struggled during our imprisonment. He was in the snake's nest, trying to charm them and play the game to keep us safe. Did he miss me as much as I missed him? I think so. "But it's what gets me through. It's my hope and my determination. How could we live there, happy and together, and safe on the road when others are dying and struggling? We couldn't, not when we can help. But when it's over, when the city is free, it will be our reward. We will have our lives back, and be safe and happy once again."

"What if it's never over? What if this is just the beginning?" he whispers, voicing his concerns.

"What do you mean?" I ask, reaching up to cup his cheek. He leans into my touch, closing his eyes for a moment, his pink lips parting.

"What if this is just the beginning, the start of a change that will spread across the world? This isn't the only city where our people are hunted and killed. What if this is the turning point and we are right in the middle? We might never get our lives back, always fighting to free our people. Maybe we will even be killed doing so."

"Then we do it knowing we are doing the right thing. This world has been allowed to remain in a man's control for too long. Women are used and abused, killed. Freaks are used as entertainment and then tortured and murdered. Maybe change is just what this world needs? And, my love, if we are in the heart of it, then that makes me proud and hopeful for what we could create, and how we could change the world. Alcide... think of everything we could do. It might not be the future we planned, but it's a good one, albeit unsafe, although our whole existence is unsafe. We will never be truly secure and safe until this world is free."

"When did you get so smart?" he murmurs, searching my eyes with awe. "Cariño, you are the reason I fight. My family, my heart... you. I fight for a better life and to be the man I see when I look into your eyes."

"You are already him," I promise. "You gave freaks a home, a job, and safety. Let's finish what you started, my ringmaster."

I lean up and kiss him softly at first, but his hand slides up my back, along the nape of my neck, and cups the back of my head. He tangles his fingers in my hair, pulling me closer until not an inch separates us as he deepens the kiss. He steals my breath and swallows my moan as I shiver against him. All that desire explodes through me again. I need him. The fact that we could die tomorrow, that we are going to war only enhances it. Each second we have left is precious, and we need to make the most of it.

As if his thoughts are the same as mine, he pulls away and stares into my eyes, his own dark with desire. "Walk with me?" he asks hoarsely.

I blink, confused, but nod mutely. He clasps my hand and pulls me from the car, setting a brisk pace. I don't know where we are going, but I would follow my ringmaster anywhere. My lips ache from his kiss, and the warmth of his hands still burns across my skin.

I follow him blindly as he leads us down the tunnel, but he doesn't stop. He keeps going into the dark. I grip his hand tighter, my eyes adjusting until I can see. "Where are we going?" I ask slowly, the fires and rebels' voices far away as we follow the tunnel. He lifts me over some fallen debris and broken tracks, remaining silent until we come upon a lantern perched on a wooden box. There's a fur on the ground next to it with pillows, blankets, a water canteen, and some food. Before it is a metal gate that looks to lead farther into the tunnels.

"Smoke showed me this. It's an abandoned watch point. They don't use this exit anymore, since it leads to the middle of the city. They bolted the gate and left this lantern burning in case they ever needed it again," he explains as he turns to me and grins. "It's the perfect place to worship you."

"Alcide," I hedge as he pulls me closer, tilting his head down and stroking my cheek.

"Where were we?" he teases, and without waiting for a reply, he leans down and captures my lips again. I gasp, and he sweeps his tongue in, tangling it with mine, but I'm not the same hesitant girl I was when I ran away with the freaks. I grip his shirt and drag him closer, kissing him right back. He will always be my ringmaster, but I'm his *cariño*.

I'm his girl, and what he gives, I take.

He groans into my mouth and backs me up to the fur, grabbing my hips and slowly lowering me. He follows me down, never breaking the kiss. When my back hits the softness, I gasp and pull away, turning my head to suck in air. I look down the tunnel, my abilities altering my vision so that even in the soft light, I can see even the smallest detail right down to the corner.

That's where I see Smoke.

He's watching us... watching me.

His mouth is parted, and his eyes are wide, like he didn't expect to come upon us but can't look away. I should say something, I should stop Alcide as he starts to kiss my face and down my neck to my thumping pulse. Smoke's eyes meet mine. I know it's impossible, but I swear he knows I see him, and he blows me a kiss before disappearing into the darkness.

Turning with a moan, I grab Alcide's face and drag his lips back to mine, kissing him hard as I wrap my legs around his waist and he blankets my body with his. I feel his hardness through his thin trousers as he presses against my hot core, grinding into me as he swallows my noises of passion. I claw at his hair and then his shirt, trying to strip him. I want to feel his skin against mine, to get closer.

Chuckling breathlessly, he pulls away, brushing my hair across the fur before leaning down and kissing my forehead. "We have time, *cariño*."

"That's the one thing we don't have," I remind him as I caress his face, catching his lip with my thumb before running it down his chest to the bottom of his shirt. With a grin, I grab the hem and pull it up, working it off his well-built, tanned chest. He sits back and reaches behind him, pulling it off completely before tossing it away. He's bare from the waist up. My pussy clenches at the sight of my ringmaster, especially when he crawls up my body and stops above my heaving chest, placing a kiss above my heart.

"Alcide," I whimper, and hearing his name on my lips spurs him on. He captures the edge of my shirt with his teeth and drags it down, exposing my breasts and stomach. Grabbing it, he wiggles it over my hips before taking off my shoes, kissing each foot, and then trailing his fingers up my legs to my waistband. He hooks his fingers in it and pulls down my trousers, laying them next to us in a pile with the rest of our clothes. I shiver under his gaze, not the least bit embarrassed as he looks me over. His deep inhale makes me grin as his eyes roam over every inch like he's seeing me for the first time. His teeth catch his bottom lip, and he closes his eyes for a second.

"How can you be so beautiful, *cariño*? You steal my breath every single time," he whispers before he meets my eyes. "The only time I ever feel weak is around you, did you know that?"

I shake my head, and he leans down, murmuring against the sensitive skin below my belly button. "You're my biggest weakness and my greatest strength rolled into one. You are strong" —kiss— "sexy" —kiss— "confident" —kiss— "and amazing." He kisses me again. "You're the whole package."

"Alcide," I whisper, unsure what else to say.

He brushes his lips across my belly and up the valley of my breasts before kissing the crest of each one. I tunnel my hands into his hair, holding on, when his lips finally wrap around one of my nipples. He sucks it, licks it, and teases it into a hard point, making me whimper before he releases it and does the same to the other one. Bolts of pleasure head straight from my nipples to my throbbing clit.

Popping it free of his talented mouth, he licks around it before nipping at the skin under my breast and kissing back down my stomach, heading right for where I need him—my aching, empty pussy. I hike my leg up and wrap it around him as he buries his head between my thighs. He kisses along each before brushing his lips across my pelvis and hips, teasing me as those laughing, hungry eyes meet mine again.

He halts above my pussy, his warm breath sinking into my intimate flesh. I groan and part my legs wider, but he continues to stare, licking his lips like he doesn't even know where to begin. Just when I'm about to demand for him to touch me, he leans down and places a teasing kiss right on my clit. I lift my hips, but he presses them down with his hands, holding me still as he kisses and licks me, teasingly, tauntingly. I roll my hips in his grip, so turned on I can't help but move. My pussy aches, needing to be filled, touched. The need for release is so strong it steals my voice.

He licks a long line down my folds, circling my hole before pushing inside. It's enough to make me moan before he pulls back and focuses on my clit—circling it, flicking it, each touch teasing. It makes me wild, but it's not enough to make me come.

My ringmaster is reminding me whom I belong to, who is in control, and that's him.

"Please," I beg.

"Please what, *cariño*?" he murmurs between my thighs, pressing his fingers to my pussy.

"I need to come," I whimper pathetically, grinding into his touch, needing more.

"Be a good girl and I'll let you," he promises as he slowly pushes two fingers inside of me, stretching me around them. My eyes close in bliss as he sucks on my clit at the same time. The pleasure is so sudden and too much, yet just enough. Pulling his digits out slowly, he pushes them back in, setting a slow, punishing rhythm as he attacks my clit like a starving man.

His fingers keep up that pace inside me, curling and stroking along my walls. Each thrust, each touch of his mouth and tongue drive me higher and higher until I can't take it anymore. My release explodes through me, making me cry out as I come on his fingers, my pussy clamping around them as I shake and shiver. I arch my chest, my eyes closed as the orgasm keeps rolling through me. He licks me through it until I finally slump. With another kiss on my throbbing clit, he sits back on his heels, my release glistening across his face as he takes off his trousers, his hard cock glistening at the tip. He crawls up my body and kisses me. I taste myself on his tongue. My legs are still weak from my release, so he grabs my thigh and helps me wrap it around his waist.

"I love the way you scream for me, the way you come for me. I want to feel that around me while my cock is deep inside of you and you look into my eyes. I want you to be mine."

"I am," I tell him roughly and kiss him back. "Always."

Groaning, he presses the tip of his huge cock to my hole. Stealing my breath with a heart stopping kiss, he pushes inside of me in one smooth thrust before pulling out and pushing in, burying an inch at a time. We work together until he finally bottoms out, and then I rip my mouth away, panting.

"I love the way you feel wrapped around me, so fucking hot and tight, gripping me." His dirty talk causes me to clench around him as I bring my other leg up and lock my ankles behind him, urging him on. He holds himself above me, motionless, as he kisses me again. "Utter perfection, just like you. Nothing in this world compares to you, Rhea."

With that heart stealing line, he starts to fuck me. He moves slowly at first, before speeding up at my urging. He hits that spot inside of me that has another release building as we come together with lips, teeth, hands, and tongue. We lose ourselves in each other in the firelight.

He slides his fingers softly up my arms before twining our hands together as he lifts them over my head. He presses them down to the fur as he continues to make love to me with strong, sure thrusts. We are so close, it's like we are one person.

He grinds into my oversensitive clit with each thrust, the pain and pleasure from that making me clench his hand so hard it has to hurt. I clamp around him, trying to hold back my release, wanting this to go on forever. I want to see those flames lovingly light up my ringmaster's face above me, and feel his heart racing in time with mine as we move together.

My name is on his lips, and his is on mine.

I lift my hips to meet his thrusts, each one driving us towards that release we are both chasing, and when he groans into my mouth, I know he's close. So am I. All it takes is one touch of my clit to set me off again. I come screaming his name, milking his cock as he slams into me before stilling with a yell as he finds his own release. He fills me with it before he slumps, finding my lips and swallowing my moans as I shiver with the aftershocks. My pussy still pulses, trapping him within me.

He leisurely kisses me and strokes my body through it before pulling free and wrapping me in his arms. The flames flicker across our naked bodies. We should get back to the others, they will be worried, but for now I steal one more moment alone with my ringmaster.

It's the quiet before the storm.

Or the silence before the war, I should say.

WITH A SLEEPY SMILE on my face and warm bodies surrounding me, I stretch out. The glorious pull on my aching muscles makes me sigh with pleasure. The steady breathing of the others lets me know they are all still asleep, and I use the rare moment of quiet to take stock of my feelings.

Last night was exactly what I needed. Not the sex, although that had been needed, but the closeness and intimacy. Ever since we were the masters' playthings and he was separated from us, whispering in their ears, there was distance between us. I don't know how I ever doubted him, but seeing him up in the masters' box at the amphitheatre when we were fighting and bleeding in the sands... it had broken a part of me. We've spoken about it, but last night was a chance to heal each other in a way that words couldn't.

I still have a happy glow from my evening with Alcide, but as I think about what's ahead, what's happening today, that glow fades. Today we plan. The rebels are not going to sit back any longer, hiding out in the tunnels. No, they are going to make a final stand, and we're going to be part of it. My stomach twists, not necessarily with nerves, but at the thought of losing anyone. People die in war, that much is certain, but will any of us come out of it unscathed? I'm not sure what I would do if any of the guys died... When I thought I'd lost Jesse, my heart was fractured and it felt like it would never be whole again. Not without my sweet, funny acrobat.

Even just thinking about it makes my chest ache, and I have to sit up and search the sleeping bodies until his face comes into view. Taking several deep, calming breaths, I realise I was wrong—I'm not the only one awake. Leaning against the carriage wall, watching me with hooded eyes, is Xavier. Slowly, so as not to wake anyone, I stand and step over the guys until I reach Xavier's side. He smiles slightly, shifting over to make space for me beside him. I sit and lean over so my side is pressed against him, resting my head on his shoulder. I don't say anything or press him to tell me what's wrong, knowing he'll talk when he wants to. I don't have to wait long.

"Everything's about to change," he murmurs, his voice low.

I don't lift my head, stroking my hand up and down his arm in a gesture of comfort. "Yes, but if we win, it will be for the better."

"I know, I just..." He trails off with a noise of frustration, and I pull back to see his expression. "Most of my adult life, I fought for the masters. I became a mindless beast. Then you found me and brought me back from an edge I thought I'd crossed a long time ago."

My heart breaks for him as he speaks. I remember how hard it was to break through to him at first, but I always knew that beneath the tough exterior there was a good man. He saved me on many occasions in the arena and the cells. I want to comfort him, to tell him that he's not that person anymore, and I would always be there, but he's not done yet.

Shaking his head, he pulls his gaze from the guys to look at me. "Helping the rebels, attacking the masters... It's one thing to defend ourselves against their attacks, but to formulate our own plan and attack them?" He huffs with frustration. "I know why we're doing this, it's to create a better world, but at some point, they must have felt the same. You spent time with Chester, you know he had a vision. Are we really any better than them if we attack?" His eyes are full of confusion, and I realise he's been fighting with this for a while.

He has a valid point, one that's been churning in my mind. I've always fought to protect myself and my family, but this is one step further than that. I just have to make sure I keep the reason why we're doing it in the forefront of my mind.

I'm quiet for a moment, nodding as I think about how to respond thoughtfully. "I think for some of the masters, they did have a vision to keep everyone safe, but greed twisted them." I take his hand in mine. "It changed them and their plans until they couldn't even remember why they first began. They kill, torture, and force us to fight for their pleasure and to earn them money. We are fighting for freedom from their tyranny." I hope my earnest words get through to him. "We are nothing like them." As I say this, I squeeze his hand, emphasising my statement.

He nods slowly, but I can still see the angst in his eyes, the shadows of his past not letting him go. "I just worry that when we get out there that I'll turn back into the mindless killing machine that I was before." He looks away with his admission, his shame obvious.

My heart breaks for him a little more. "That will never happen, Xavier. Look at me," I insist, reaching out and cupping his face when he turns back to me. His expression is wary. Kneeling so we're eye to eye, I bring my face close to his. "I won't allow that to happen. You've found your place with us, you're one of us now, and we protect each other, even from ourselves."

He makes a small noise, and before I know it, I'm pulled against his chest as he presses his lips to mine. It's a slow, passionate kiss and completely unhurried as he shows me what my words mean to him. I return the kiss, loving the feel of being in his arms. When we break away, we're both smiling.

The room is quiet, and even the heavy breathing has stopped, so I know the others are awake, but they are pretending not to be to give us privacy. From the look on Xavier's face, I know he's aware of this too, and he releases me from his arms. Still kneeling, I lean forward to kiss him again, not caring that the others are listening in.

"Thank you," he whispers against my lips, and I know he's not talking about the kiss.

Jesse yawns loudly, far louder than necessary, but it's a warning that he's about to get up. The others follow suit and start moving around as they get ready for the day.

As we fall into our morning routine, I pick up on the nervous energy in the room. Everyone knows that today is an important day and that we will soon be attacking the masters. As we move around the carriage, the guys keep finding ways to touch me. It's just little touches here and there, but it helps ground us.

A knock on the door startles me. Making a sound of surprise, Alcide goes to the door and opens it. Leaning out, he seems to look around before crouching down to pick something up. Frowning, he shuts the door and turns to face us.

"Who was it?" Rex queries.

Raising what appears to be a small, folded piece of paper, Alcide frowns. "There was no one there, only this note."

A note. Why wouldn't someone stick around and speak to us, preferring to leave a note instead? And how had Alcide not seen who left it there? Unless they hid directly under the train, there's no way they could have gotten out of sight that quickly.

Nixon makes a noise of displeasure, moving closer as if to protect me. "What does it say?"

Alcide unfolds the paper and scans the words, his expression turning dark. "There's a meeting happening right now, they are planning without us."

"The fuckers! Why do they keep doing this to us?" Blain exclaims, his hands hovering over the knives strapped to his belt.

Sighing, I scrub my hands over my face. Fighting the masters is going to be hard enough without this constant infighting with Regnor. "Let's go." I don't bother to say anything else or express my disappointment, because they already know. I can see the anger and frustration on their faces as we pull on our boots.

As we jump from the carriage and onto the tracks, and make our way to Regnor's little base, I can't help but wonder who left the note. Someone who wanted to warn us, apparently. I would say Smoke, but I can't imagine the meeting going ahead without him there, besides, he would have warned us face to face. Whoever this was, they didn't want to be seen. Nico's face flashes in my mind, and I remember that his ability is invisibility. He would be the perfect messenger.

My movements are sharp, powered by anger, but I don't miss all the sleeping bodies as we walk through the tunnels. It must still be early, and I realise that they did this on purpose. By organising the meeting so early, they were hoping I would miss it, blissfully sleeping through their plans.

I don't have time to theorise any further as we reach Regnor's carriage. Climbing up, I push past the guard and storm in, walking through until I reach them, the guys at my back. The guard behind me calls out weakly, but he doesn't bother to try to stop me. I swing open the door to find a meeting in full swing. Regnor, Smoke, Marie, and several other rebels I've seen around over the last couple of days are present.

Keeping my gaze on the rebel leader, I come to a stop by the bottom of the map and cross my arms. "I thought we were past this, Regnor."

I see the muscles in his shoulders tense, and slowly, he looks up at me. He keeps his expression calm, but his frustration is clear in the creases around his eyes. "Rhea, you were not invited to this meeting."

I laugh, but it contains no humour, as I gesture around. "I can see that, and I want to know why." Standing up to his full height, Regnor crosses his arms over his chest and stares down at me, remaining silent. The guys shuffle behind me, their anger at this noiseless threat obvious. Raising my eyebrows, I don't let his silence faze me. "If I'm to be the face of this rebellion, I need to know the plans."

I can't believe we're having to have this conversation *again*. He just wants a quiet, pretty figurehead he can order around, but that's not who I am, not anymore.

"No, you just need to know your orders."

I'm taken aback by his comment, and I'm sure my surprise shows on my face. "Orders? Are you serious?" If he thinks we are just more soldiers for him to order around, then he's got another thing coming.

Smoke steps forward from the carriage wall, looking uncomfortable by the whole situation. "Regnor, she should be involved."

Smoke has been honest with us the entire time we've been with the rebels, and he has helped us with our own missions, standing up for us against his leader. This must be difficult for him, but I appreciate the support, and as our eyes meet over the table, he dips his chin in acknowledgement.

Regnor, however, doesn't look pleased at this development. Turning to face his friend, he opens his mouth to speak, but he is cut off as someone else steps forward.

"He's right." My eyes widen as Marie challenges the leader.

Regnor must be just as surprised, but he hides it well. "I thought you had my back. Don't go against me now." Anger rumbles in his voice, and I see his eyes darken. This was the last thing he expected to happen, that much is clear.

"I do have your back, but I know a stupid idea when I see one," she retorts, placing a hand on his arm to soften the blow. I know they are close, so this must be difficult for her, but I'm so glad she's on our side. Chester always said his daughter was soft, that she couldn't survive in this world, but he couldn't be more wrong.

Xavier moves to my side, frowning down at the map on the table that's currently covered in markers. "That's the town hall. Is that your plan? You're going to use the hall?" Shaking his head, he leans over to examine it closer. "You'll never capture them there. There are too many places where they could ambush you."

Looking down at the map, I see he's right. The town hall and the stretch of land before it is covered in markers. That spot of land, however, is where our tent is. Is that part of the plan? To lure them out by sending us back in?

"Not to mention your information is out of date," Xavier mutters, standing up to his full height. Pointing to the back of the town hall, which has been circled, he shakes his head. "If you take that entrance, you'll be caught immediately. The masters placed a trap there weeks ago, I overheard them talking about it."

Raising my eyebrows, I glance up at him in surprise. We'd only been in our tent the other day, and he hadn't once mentioned a trap, yet we hadn't gone anywhere near the hall, so I suppose it wasn't necessary. I'm still going to grill him about it later though.

Regnor looks just as surprised. Frustration practically oozes from him, but he keeps his calm in front of his fellow rebels. Glancing around, he takes in the concerned expressions of the others, realising he needs us.

"Fine," he grumbles, scrubbing his hands over his face. "You can stay, but only to share information." He holds up a hand to stop me from arguing, knowing before I've even said anything that I was going to protest. "No. You're going to be on the front lines, so I can't allow you to know all of the plan. It would be stupid. What if you were captured?"

Begrudgingly, I have to admit that what he says makes sense. Turning, I look at each of my guys, meeting their gazes and waiting for their confirmation. I don't like it, but I won't be left behind while everyone else fights, so I guess this is a compromise.

"Fine," I agree, bringing my gaze back to him. I hold his stare, unwavering as I face him down. "Let's plan."

Regnor only let us update him with the information we knew, and then he gave us our orders and made us leave. He stated it was for security, that every unit only knows their orders, so if we're captured, they cannot blow the whole plan. It makes sense, and we were testing his patience by pushing him, so we agreed. We graciously left, but I could see some of the rebels didn't agree with keeping us in the dark.

Especially Smoke, he seemed troubled as he watched us go. Marie too.

I understand Regnor's position. He has the whole rebellion depending on him, but he seems to dislike us, and rather than using us and letting us help, he's trying to play god and prove he's stronger, more important. He's attempting to diminish our loss and our need to complete this mission, but I won't let it happen, regardless of the in-house squabbling.

This is more important than him and me.

This is about them and their freedom. It's so much bigger than us, and I refuse to let him jade me or sway me from my plans. It, of course, infuriated my men. Alcide was so angry he had a full-blown argument with Jesse about it. I can sense my teasing man's sadness. These people saved his life, but we are his family. It's not a choice though, he can care for both. Blain ducks away to throw knives—I suspect to get his anger out—and Rex follows him to ensure he's okay. Nixon stays with Alcide, calming him like always, and Jesse remains with Xavier and me.

We prepare for tomorrow, practicing our roles and gathering anything we need to take with us just in case... in case we don't make it back. We all know what is at stake, but we know just how much we could lose as well. It means we share longing looks full of concern and panic.

There's a knock at the door a few hours later, after we are all back in our car, and a huge package is placed inside by Smoke, who winks at me. "Gotta look good for the big day," is all he says before he disappears again. Frowning, I take in the brown parcelled square with the perfectly tied golden ribbon before crouching and opening it. I gasp when I touch the silky materials inside, from glitter to hard, durable fabric.

Battle clothes for tomorrow. I start to pull out outfits and realise there is one for each of us, perfect for fighting a war but also for the distraction we are to cause tomorrow morning. Mine is a tight ribbon top with black feathers stretching downwards to lovingly cup my stomach and breasts. The pants are tight, not flared like normal, with more feathers, but they fade to orange, so it makes it look like the outfit quite literally is on fire.

"Beautiful," I breathe, and when I test the fabric, it stretches but doesn't tear, seemingly very thick and strong. I find a note at the bottom with perfectly penned calligraphy scrawled on white paper with golden ink.

I knew you would need these. They will keep you safe but also allow you to do what you do best—stun people. I will always believe in you, Rhea. You are finally on the path intended for you since your birth. Stay safe.

—Gregor

I re-read the note a few times. "Who sent it?" Jesse asks, the others huddled around, testing their outfits. I hand the note over wordlessly and meet their eyes.

"What do you think he means?" I whisper.

They all analyse it, but it's Nixon who speaks. "It means you have been foretold, Rhea, and right now you are exactly where you are meant to be."

When Nixon talks, I listen, and that settles me even as I ponder Gregor's words. How long ago did he see we would need this? They must have taken a while to make. To have all that knowledge, all those visions in his head... it must be exhausting.

We carefully hang them, ready for tomorrow, before we gather around to have a meal together. The mood is subdued at first before Jesse starts to make jokes and regales us with tales. Rex soon joins in, then Blain adds his snarky comments. Nixon's booming, simple laugh sounds around us, while Xavier asks questions, laughing as well. Alcide smiles the entire time, his hand in mine as we gather around the beds. He meets my eyes and leans in.

"This is why we fight, Rhea, for our family. You were right. I have hope. Nothing this perfect, this pure and filled with love, could ever be wrong." He kisses me, and there are some catcalls. I blush, even as I pull away with a grin.

"Alright, alright, perverts," I tease, leaning into Rex's shoulder where he's sitting on my left. "A toast," I declare in the silence, grabbing my drink, "to us, to what we are fighting for. To all freaks and to everything that is to come."

"To the freaks!" they call and toss their drinks back. After swallowing, Xavier meets my eyes and smiles.

"To Rhea, our heart," he says, and the others join in as tears fill my eyes.

I run my gaze over the men surrounding me, wondering how I could have ever gotten so lucky. Not just to fall in love with such incredible, caring, fearless men... but to have them as my best friends, my biggest supporters, and my forever.

No matter what happens tomorrow or the next day, I have no doubt that as long as we are together, we can achieve anything.

The night goes on, the drinks flow, and tongues get looser. My face flushes as I giggle at a story Alcide's telling when there's another knock and Smoke sticks his head in. "I heard a party and wondered if I could join."

I go to answer but hiccup and look to the others. I want him to, but it's not just up to me. "Come in, you are welcome here anytime," Alcide offers and purposely looks at me, making me smile.

Smoke shuts the door and takes off his coat. "Thank you." He grins as Xavier hands him a drink, and then he sits down heavily, leaning back on his elbow with his leg raised as he relaxes. "I'm sorry about earlier. I told him you should be there." He frowns, his eyes going to the flames. "But it wasn't my call." He sighs deeply, and Xavier lays a hand on his arm.

"It's okay, you tried."

"Still, it's wrong. Everyone can see how hard you fight for this, for us, and we should trust you with everything, but the truth is he doesn't even trust Marie or me with it all. Sometimes I doubt he even fully trusts himself. It's just who Regnor is, he feels every loss keenly, and this is how he thinks he wins—alone."

"That's very lonely," I comment, and he nods, meeting my eyes.

"It is. I prefer your method." He grins and toasts me. "Drinking, company, and laughter."

"Well, we have plenty of that. Now who remembers that time when Blain accidentally stabbed Rex?" Jesse starts, and Alcide howls with laughter, clearly remembering. I just grin, listening to him explain how it happened. Poor Blain looks so put out, but I see a smile twisting his lips as Rex exaggerates how big the wound was and Blain calls him a liar.

"Or the time Nixon dared Jesse to fit into a barrel and he couldn't get out," Alcide adds, making Nixon grin as I gasp at him.

"Nix!" I scold, and he shrugs.

"It was funny."

I laugh harder, and as I catch my breath, my eyes lock on Smoke's. He's smiling a full genuine smile as he looks around at my men, but in his eyes, I see sadness. Longing. Does he not have a family here like this? One to share stories and embarrassing memories?

Is he alone like I was?

I think so, and when he meets my eyes, I see the truth in those orange depths. He's lonely here among the rebels. He's aching for a home, maybe searching for the one he lost. When this fight is over, what will he do? Will the rebels disband, leaving him alone again? Regnor, despite being a good leader, prioritises himself and Marie. I think Smoke would be a secondary concern.

Where will he go?

Why am I so worried for him? His smile dips, but his eyes lighten as he watches me. "I'm okay," he mouths. "Thanks to you."

I blink at that, and then he averts his gaze and leans forward. "Okay, okay, so who here has worn the tightest outfit?" he asks, blending right in with our family like he was never supposed to be anywhere else. I guess only time will tell how he would fit in, and only if he would want to be part of our family after everything is over.

One thing is for sure, I have another mission before I leave this city—to ensure Smoke finds a home, finds happiness, because he deserves it.

After we finish our drinks, we all bed down for the night. Our hearts are light, despite the anticipation for tomorrow. When Smoke gets up to leave, I sit up. "Hey, it's okay, you can stay," I offer, knowing it's late.

"Oh, I wouldn't want to intrude."

"Since when?" Blain snorts.

"Just lie down, she won't stop until you do," Rex murmurs with a chuckle.

With a wide grin, Smoke lies on the very end and turns to me, winking before closing his eyes. I fall asleep easily, my heart full and body humming.

But my dreams are dark, filled with all the possibilities of tomorrow. I watch my men fall, watch them die over and over with no way to stop it, and eventually, I jerk awake as a warm hand touches mine. In the dark, Smoke crouches above me.

"It's just a bad dream, you're okay."

I nod, and he stands. "I have to go get into my position." He glances at my men who are still sleeping and snoring. "Take care of them." He looks back at me. "And yourself. I better see you when we take down the masters."

"You will," I promise, and I think he will just leave. He turns to do so before he mutters something, turns back, leans down, and kisses me. I recoil in shock, my eyes wide and lips burning from his heat as he chuckles softly.

"I had to take my shot. I could die today, after all." He winks.

It's a joke, but with my dreams still lingering and the way he said it, I can't handle it. I grab his cheeks, and then I do something reckless, something I've wanted to do since I saw him, but I felt too greedy, awkward, and unsure. I kiss him. Hard. He groans gently and I pull away, looking into his eyes.

"Don't you dare die."

"How could I when I've got that to live for?" he murmurs, and then with one last look, he leaves. I stare after him, wondering if I just crossed a line. Smoke isn't mine. I have six incredible men who love me, and I shouldn't need another, but it's not about need. It's about what my heart wants. It's about seeing something in someone that calls to a part of you no other can understand. My heart isn't a solid, dividable object. It stretches and grows to encompass all that is mine. Is it starting to think of Smoke as mine as well?

I don't know, but we have bigger things to worry about. As I lay my head down, though, I see Jesse watching me. I freeze as guilt fills me, but he reaches out and pulls me into his arms, kissing my head.

"It's okay. Try to sleep, Firecracker. You'll need it." His reassurance, and his lack of disgust or blame, allows me to relax enough to nod, but I don't really sleep, and when it's time to get up, I'm tired but determined.

There is no laughter this morning. We wash, eat, and then help each other get dressed solemnly. Each and every one of our faces is set in concentration and purpose.

Today is the day we go to war, the day we carry out our part of the plan.

We are to do what we do best—put on a show.

THE SLASHED sides of the big top flap in the breeze, the bright colours making the rest of the town square look drab and dreary. A handful of citizens pass by, but the space seems empty of military presence. However, we know otherwise. We know that the masters are holed up in the town hall with several troupes of guards. Thanks to our information, Regnor and his rebels know where the guards are stationed and where the traps are set, so they should be able to enter without springing the traps. We don't know when, where, or how many of them there are, thanks to being kept from the plans. Hell, I don't even know if they plan to enter the town hall, but they seemed pretty keen on the information we had.

The sky is just starting to lighten as the sun rises, but the thick layer of cloud makes everything still look dark. A flyer blows through the open space, and I realise that it's advertising our circus. It must have been from our first show here, before we were captured.

How things have changed.

A bird chirps, and for anyone walking by, it wouldn't sound out of place, but for us, it's something more—our signal. Glancing back at my guys, I meet their gazes, each one of them determined as they nod to indicate they are ready.

Making sure my dark cloak is in place and hiding the outfit beneath, I climb from the tunnel and into the dilapidated building, using the same tunnel we did the other day. A silent rebel led us here this morning, then he disappeared into the darkness before I could even open my mouth to say thank you.

This is the part of the plan that makes me the most nervous. So much could go wrong here, and we don't know what's going to happen, but I've got to trust that Regnor's plan will work. Moving to the front of the destroyed building, I peer out onto the streets. Dozens of people have appeared seemingly from nowhere, all wearing similar dark cloaks or jackets—rebels. We've got to get to the big top without attracting attention. We were told to focus only on getting there, and that a distraction would be provided.

I climb from the house, and the guys quickly join me. We start walking across the town square, keeping to the shadows while trying not to look like we're deliberately hiding. I can't help but worry that flooding the streets with rebels won't be enough of a distraction. It's just going to bring attention to us, right? Just as I think that, an explosion rocks the streets. With a gasp, I fall to my knees, and I feel the tingle of my powers quickly thicken my skin before I even make contact with the hard earth. Spinning, I see my guys covering their heads with their arms, but they all look okay. My ears are ringing, but after a few seconds, my body readjusts, and I can hear screams and panicked voices as more people flood the streets. The black cloaks blend in with the bright colours of the citizens. It's chaos as everyone runs and tries to work out what just happened.

So this was the distraction Regnor promised us. Making the most of it, we jump to our feet and run across the square. With so many people in the streets, it would make it impossible for the masters to notice and recognise the seven of us, never mind getting to us through the screaming crowds. We make it into the tent without incident, our chests heaving from the sudden exertion and shock of the explosion.

The guys hurry through the big top, getting everything ready as fast as they can, the time ticking away, but I linger by the entrance, hiding behind one of the thick tent poles as I watch what's happening in the square. Guards flood out of the town hall and hurry over to the now collapsed building. Guilt churns in my stomach. I really hope no one was hurt in the explosion. I know there will be casualties, but I pray we can avoid innocent citizens dying in our mission. I know if the situation were reversed, they wouldn't stop to help us or worry about freaks getting hurt, but that doesn't mean we should stoop to their level.

We're better than that, even though we are outcasts.

Those tasked with protecting this city have hurt it more than the rebels trying to overthrow it. Years of rot and murder taint the streets they walk through.

"Rhea, come," Alcide calls, jogging towards me. "We need to get ready while everyone is distracted..." He trails off, noticing what I'm looking at, and his hand lands on my shoulder. "Regnor would have made sure the building was empty before collapsing it." His words are gentle, somehow knowing exactly where my mind is at without me having to voice my concerns.

Turning to face him, I smile at my ringmaster, trying to push my worries aside and focus on the mission ahead of us. I let him guide me across the tent and into the ring of sand in the middle. Shedding my cloak, I notice the others have already done the same. I jog over to the guys who are waiting by the far end of the ring, opposite where the audience would sit. Everyone other than Alcide is warming up, stretching, and bouncing on the balls of their feet. As I join in, I watch Alcide. He's walking the perimeter of the ring, glancing out at the empty stalls. We all have a role to play here, and his is as our ringmaster, as always. It's a role he's used to, but today is different.

This performance is more than entertainment, it's a stand. It's our one chance to save our people and this city. Alcide's outfit had been the only one that was different from the others. While the underlayers are the same as ours, his includes his smart, black tailored jacket and ringmaster's hat, which has a red ribbon tied around the base. Seeing him dressed like that again stirs something within me, a nostalgia that makes my heart squeeze tightly in my chest even as desire fills me. His beauty, his muscles, and his confidence stir that lust low in my belly, even when I should be focused on what comes next.

"Stop fidgeting," Blain mutters, causing me to turn around to see what's happening.

I can't hide my smile as I see who he's talking to. Poor Xavier is tugging at his skin-tight outfit, not used to wearing something so figure hugging.

"These costumes are so snug," Xavier grumbles, pulling at the legs of the costume. The bodysuits are all made of lycra, and are a mix of reds, oranges, and golds that twist around our forms in feather patterns. They glisten in the light, and I know under the stage lights, they'll look amazing, like flames come to life. "I don't know how you wore them every day."

My eyes are drawn to the movement, and I can't help but notice how the clothing hugs certain parts of his body, leaving nothing to the imagination. His bulge makes me swallow before I quickly jerk my eyes away, my face heating. Of course he notices me watching, and a wicked grin stretches across his face as my cheeks flush hotter.

"Maybe they are not so bad after all," he teases, his dark eyes filling with hunger and a cocky gleam that has me shifting on my feet as he prowls towards me. The others snort their laughter.

"Okay, everyone, get into your positions. It's time." Alcide strides over, interrupting the moment and saving me from Xavier's consuming nature. His expression is confident, but I can tell from the tightness around his eyes that this is a mask. "Just remember, don't step outside the ring. Stay on the sand, and you'll be safe," he instructs, his voice firm, but not knowing the full plan is making him worry.

Getting into position, the guys surround me in a tight circle, their bodies hiding me from view as Alcide strides towards the front of the ring.

Put on a show, stay inside the ring, and draw attention. Regnor would deal with the rest. Those were our instructions. Trust him, he said. I have no idea how we're going to attract a crowd or get the masters' attention when we have no lights, no music. Just as I'm thinking this, bright spotlights beam down on us, lighting up the ring. Only the light isn't coming from the broken ones in the tent, instead shining *through* the fabric of the tent.

"They must have installed spotlights on the top of the buildings around the square," Jesse mutters, coming to the same conclusion as me. Standing in the biggest spotlight is our ringmaster, his head tipped back. His lips slowly curve up in his usual smile, and for the briefest moment, under those dazzling lights, he takes my breath away.

"Welcome, ladies and gentlemen, to Alcide's Circus!" Alcide's voice cuts off anything else we might have said. His voice has always had a way of reaching all areas of the tent, but somehow, it seems to project even farther today, and I wouldn't be surprised if the whole city couldn't hear his booming welcome. He's putting on a show and falling back into his role with an ease I envy. As if he has no worries, his body is loose yet controlled.

"We have a treat for you tonight. A special, one night only show! We will be showing you feats you never thought possible, and how strong we truly are. Freaks and citizens, gather close if you dare..."

I know this last line is aimed at the masters. While it might sound like he's talking about physical strength, he's actually taunting the masters. He's showing them that we're still alive and fighting, and that we snuck past them without their notice. That despite the fact they trashed our home, we're still here and stronger than ever.

"So come join us. You don't want to miss this." His voice turns whiskey smooth. "And run away with the circus one last time."

I can hear the wicked grin in his voice as he dials up his persuasion, calling them to us. Like the Pied Piper, he will lead them to the tent—they will have no other option. Even I can feel his power washing over me, making me sway towards him before I remember it's our job to give them something to see.

The lights dim, throwing the tent into shadows, allowing Alcide to join us. Our low, heavy breathing fills the darkness, our hands tingling from almost touching with how close we are standing. My heart slams and starts to race as the excitement of performing fills me, like always, even though I know this isn't a normal show. I turn my head, sharing a look with our ringmaster. His dark eyes are filled with heat and love as he nods at me. Taking a deep breath, I step forward, and they follow me. The lights rise as we walk forward as a unit, and loud music fills the town square. There's no way the masters can ignore us now.

And so we perform.

We lose ourselves in the music, our bodies moving automatically.

We start with an intricate dance, the guys passing me between them. The music somehow perfectly fits with the melancholy feeling of the dance. I'm held over heads, flipped, and turned, remembering to keep my hands and toes pointed and my eyes closed to focus on the beat rather than who is marching towards us. Each slide of my feet almost seems to vibrate with the stomping boots of the guards and the masters as they head our way. My heart races faster with each step, awaiting the moment they find us. It's strange to perform without our stagehands and animals, but we make do. As the song nears its end, Jesse pulls me away from the others, spinning me as they back away. Together, we perform acrobatics.

Jesse's abilities allow him to execute incredible tricks, and as I focus on my body, it adapts, stretching and bending in ways that shouldn't be possible. Once the song is through, there is a moment of complete silence, our panting loud in the tent. My heart slams so hard they must hear it as we bow and slip back into the darkness. Another song starts, and Blain does a knife throwing act, starting with showing his powers. His expression is angry as he slams a knife into a post, clearly imagining the masters as I am strapped to his target. He turns me, and we share a wordless look before our part of the show begins. He throws knives at a target strapped to my waist while I perform cartwheels around the ring. He hits the bullseye every time. The others perform as we wait. Time ticks away, and the more minutes that pass, the tenser we get, even as we try to remain calm and carry on. Just as Nixon throws a huge boulder, smashing it into a hundred pieces, we finally hear them.

They are drawing closer.

A movement outside the tent tells me it's time. Glancing at Alcide, I see he's noticed the same thing. He strides to the middle of the ring, and we back away to give him space.

"And now, for our final act, please welcome our very own Immortals! You saw them fight for their lives, now see them fight for their freedom!" Our ringmaster's voice echoes around us.

A call to war.

A promise of what is to come.

Nerves flutter in my stomach as Xavier and I step forward, our hands clasped together tightly. We practiced this routine last night, but Xavier is new to this and accidents happen. There's no time to dwell, though, since it's our moment to shine. Taking deep breaths, we start to dance. Just like in the fights, we move and work together, protecting each other, relying on our strengths and fighting with everything we have in us. I can feel many sets of eyes on us now as they troop into the tent, but I don't allow that to put me off, focusing instead on the moves. Their voices rise, but they are drowned out by the music that grows louder.

This isn't just any dance, but our story. The dance tells of how we were taken from our home, our family broken and scattered, and how we were forced to fight. Xavier spins me out before yanking me back to him, capturing me against his chest. As we move back and forth, my movements fluid and sure, I put all my hatred into the dance. When we reach the end, I become aware of movement outside the ring. Dozens of guards flood into the space, pouring in from the city. Just like Regnor thought, they are coming to protect their leaders, and there, in the middle of the stalls, are the masters. They watch with satisfied, if not evil, smiles, but they seem content to let us finish our act. I spin, my hair blocking them from view for a moment before I meet their gazes once more, and it's my turn to smile—a huge, cocky one.

Time for the big finale.

Locking eyes with Xavier, I subtly nod my head. Enacting the final battle scene, he drops me, and I crumple to the ground, raising a hand above my head as if to protect myself. Stretching up to his full height, he catches a knife that Blain produced before flinging it across the ring. With the blade in his hands, he raises it above me before dropping to his knees and slamming it into my shoulder without hesitation—a warrior to the very end. My cry of pain isn't feigned, and as Xavier bends over me, I see the guilt in his eyes as he scans my face anxiously to make sure I'm okay. Shielded from the masters, I rip the blade out, my teeth clenched to hold back my cry of agony, but as quickly as the sharp pain came, it disappears, my body healing the wound.

I nod mutely at Xavier when it's done, and he lets out a slight breath before he grabs my body. I go limp as he cradles me to his chest. Lifting me into the air with a roar of agony, he begins to spin, faster and faster, until the world is a blur. With another earth-shattering roar, he flings me up into the air right as Jesse uses his own gift. Fire envelops me, and I hear the watching guards gasp. My skin instantly adapts to the fire, trying to protect me from the heat, but I focus on changing my skin and allowing the flames to run along it. As I start to fall back to the ground, the air whistling past me, I flip and land on my feet, my arms outstretched to keep my balance.

A sparkle catches my eye, and as I glance down, I see my outfit is glowing. The feathers that make up the bodice look like radiant embers, and I realise why Gregor chose this.

I look like a flame, a beacon.

I look like the freak I am.

I look like the embers to the fire that will end this and bring victory to the rebellion.

Returning my gaze to the audience, I meet the masters' eyes with a proud smile on my face as my body ripples with flames. They may have reduced our home and lives to rubble, but from the ashes, a phoenix will rise.

I watch their faces as comprehension dawns, their expressions changing. Slowly, one of the masters begins to move forward, but with the light shining down on us, I can't see who it is. I can, however, hear his condescending clapping. He walks right up to the edge of the ring, and I can finally make out his face—Chester. A sense of betrayal rocks me, but I shouldn't be surprised. He was never on our side. Sure, he helped me in the cells, but only because I reminded him of his daughter. There was more he could have done, only he chose the coward's way out and went along with all their plans.

"Well done." His smirk makes hatred rise within me, and the fire covering my body burns brighter with my anger. "One final show together before we take you all down," he says wistfully before glancing around like he's looking for someone. "Where are your rebel friends now? You should have stayed in hiding."

As the last word trails off, a hissing noise fills the tent, and I realise what's happening as clouds of gas fill the space. It's not a show, not dramatics, just a perfectly laid out plan. It's like the night we were taken, and for a few seconds, I think the rebels have forsaken us, poisoning us as well as the masters, but then I notice that as the gas floats closer, it seems to stop at the edge of the ring, as if hitting an invisible barrier. Glancing up, I see an invisible dome around us, protecting us from it. I can only make out the shape because of the gas surrounding us, but as the guards and masters begin to fall, some yells and screams fill the tent. They are trapped. Some try to escape, I see them running through the gas, but they slow and suddenly collapse to the floor. Hacking coughs, gasping breaths, and cries take the place of screams until they fade as well. The masters and guards are succumbing to their own weapon. It's only then that I realise we're safe. *Stay in the ring.* That one instruction had been repeated over and over again, and now I realise why.

Chester falls, gasping as he tries to crawl away, as if that's going to save him. He makes a gurgling noise, stretching his hand up into the air as if calling for help. A sense of satisfaction fills me, and I step towards him, the guys at my back. Stopping at the edge of the ring, my hand almost pressed to the barrier, I wait until Chester looks up at me through the misty gas. His wide, bloodshot, panicked eyes beg me to save him, to give him mercy they never offered us.

"Please!" He claws at his throat as he chokes on the fumes. I see bodies surrounding him, some face down, some on their sides and backs. All still.

Kneeling, with the invisible dome separating us, I lean forward with a smirk on my face. "You see, Chester, you think we're weak, but look at you now." I ignore his reaching hand and get to my feet, letting the flames on my skin flare once more. "Only the strong adapt to survive, and you? You are weak."

We stand inside of the invisible dome, watching as the slightly green gas dissipates, leaving nothing but the prone, still bodies of the guards and masters. Here, unprotected and vulnerable, they look so easy to kill. Too easy. Maybe that's why I hesitate. We've spent so long under their rule or trying to defeat them—not as long as the rebels, but still. Did we really do it?

Did we trick them at their own game? It doesn't seem real.

Was their confidence their downfall? I guess what they say about rich men is true—they underestimate everyone else, believing they are untouchable. We are their greatest mistake. The dome suddenly falls, and I step back, but no gas rushes in. Regnor and Smoke, covered in sweat, dirt, and blood, step into the tent, looking around with a grin.

"Good job," Regnor praises. "We never could have distracted them or got them all in one place without you." He nods and more rebels come in, tying up the knocked out guards and hauling them out. Stepping from the ring, I double-check to see if Smoke is okay and find him doing the same to me. We share a small smile.

"Good job, Rhea. What a show!" He winks. "Though I do wish

you were there to see me kicking ass. I was a badass, if I do say so myself."

"I bet." I grin wider before Regnor coughs and interrupts us.

"Enough, we have more important things to do than flirt."

I blush and drop my gaze as Smoke chuckles.

"You're just mad I'm not flirting with you, boss," he teases.

"Shut up, Smoke." Regnor sighs, and I get the feeling he says that a lot. "Have Marie and Tobin check them over, and then lock them up under their precious fighting pit. Put them in the same cells in which they tortured and killed our people."

"And then?" I ask, stepping forward. "What do you plan to do to them then?"

"Kill them of course." He frowns at me as Smoke moves away to sort out the guards.

"The city is yours, you've won," I start. Something is not sitting right with me at the casual way he admitted to planning to commit mass murder.

"But we will never be truly free while they still breathe. They will never give up. If we let them live, they will come back, like mould infecting the city. No, Rhea, you will not sway me on this. This isn't your decision, this isn't a game. This is life and death, and here, I am the judge, jury, and executioner. You are nothing but a tool I used to win the war. Remember your place."

"A tool you couldn't have won without," I snap, refusing to back down. Smoke returns, catching that, and frowns hard. "Do not dismiss me, do not overlook me and mistake my soft-spoken nature or womanhood for weakness." I jerk my head at the masters, who are being carried out. "They did, and look where they are now." I step closer again, going toe-to-toe with the rebel leader. "If you kill them all, if you do this, then you are no better than they are. At least think about it and talk to your people."

"And if I don't?" he challenges, glaring down at me with his arms crossed. I feel my men beside me, and Smoke hesitates next to us.

"Regnor—" Smoke begins, but Regnor holds his hand up, silencing him.

"If I don't?" he repeats, gritting out each word. I refuse to bow, to be scared, or to lower my voice because it's not what he wants to hear.

"Then I will be forced to stop you. Murder on this scale isn't something you can just snap your fingers and decide—"

"They did," he snarls.

"And we are supposed to be better than them!" I yell in his face, breathing heavily. "Do not become the monsters they want us to be. Do not make them martyrs for their cause. Think, talk, take a fucking vote!" I demand. "Do not let them win this way when we are so close to victory. I cannot stand idly by while you murder innocents. I admit the masters are evil monsters and deserve their fate, but we are not God. We do not get to decide this alone and on a whim. We did this to free the city and our people, so let them decide. This is bigger than you or me. This is bigger than our anger and need for vengeance. This is about creating a future we are proud of. Can you really do that if it's built on so much bloodshed?"

"Regnor, she's right. This wasn't the plan, this must be discussed. You don't get to just decide that," Smoke reasons and steps up next to me. I hear Regnor's inhale at Smoke's gesture, at him leaving his best friend and saviour's side.

"They killed your family," he says sadly, looking at his friend as if he can't understand why he's taking our side of the argument.

"They did." Smoke nods. "And I, more than anyone, have cause to want to kill them, but it's not up to me. She's right. Don't let the power go to your head. We follow you and fight for you because of your integrity and dedication to our people and city. Do not ruin that now just to get revenge." Smoke steps forward, clasping Regnor's hand. "Brother, take a moment and think. Let our people decide. Let us do this together, like always."

Regnor searches his gaze, looking pained before he wipes his face blank. "Before her, you would have followed me blindly."

"Maybe, but that would be wrong. No one should have that much sway and go unchecked. I do this to save you, my friend, like you did me. Don't damn your soul over them. Please, Regnor, listen to your people like you always do. Be the leader we need, the man I know you are. You don't want to do this. I know the pressure you feel to protect us, but it's not all your responsibility. We have won, now let's dole out punishments and fresh starts as one. As rebels."

"Fine. Keep them locked up down there tonight. I want guards on them the entire time. Give them the same treatment we got," Regnor bites out.

"Of course," Smoke replies and claps his shoulder. "You're doing the right thing, brother."

"I hope so," Regnor says, his face twisted as he looks at me.

Smoke rushes away to give the orders, and Regnor and I stare at each other.

"Do not hurt him," he warns me quietly.

"What?" I ask in confusion, even as my eyes go to Smoke.

"He is the most loyal man you'll ever meet. Once you have earned that, he will follow you to the gates of hell itself. He is fearless, funny, kind, and strong. He deserves someone who knows that, who knows everything he has survived."

"I—" I stop, unsure what to say, my face heating. I want to deny everything, but even now there's a pull between Smoke and me. My eyes automatically seek him, and he glances back as if he feels the same thing. "It's not like that," I lie.

"Sure it isn't. I said that too. Take my advice, don't blind yourself out of duty or love." He takes a deep breath. "And keep him safe for me. It might not seem like it, but he's all the family I have left now."

He turns and storms from the tent, and I watch him go, my head hurting from the subject change. Smoke stares after his friend, frowning hard. I feel guilty for causing issues with their friendship, but at least Regnor listened to reason. I don't even know why I'm fighting for the masters' lives. They have taken so many themselves, but it doesn't sit well with me. My stomach is in knots at the thought. Some of the guards were only doing their job—not all, but some. Where does it stop?

We have to be better than them.

We just have to.

Otherwise, what are we fighting for?

WE DON'T GO BACK to the tunnels. I feel like doing so would only anger Regnor further. He needs time to cool off and talk to his people without feeling like I have swayed their vote. Instead, we help in the city by clearing up rubble from the many explosions caused by the rebels' battle and burying the bodies of those lost in the fight over the past few days—both rebels and guards alike. The loss of life saddens me, and as I look at the tear-stained, dirty faces of the people around me, I can't help but wonder if this could have been stopped before now.

But it's done, and all we can do is pick up the pieces.

Rebels, guards, and even the citizens of the city surprise me by pitching in, helping rebuild their city. The doors to shops are open, providing refuge and goods. Bakers give out free food and water is passed around from rebel hands, to ex-guards, to the higher class of the city. Here in the rubble, with dirty faces and tired, sad hearts, we are all the same—freaks and normals alike.

This is what it should always be like—shoulder to shoulder. Love, not hate. We are all the same, and this world is ours. It's the only one we have left, and we need to do better than those before us, learn from their mistakes, and make this once dead world thrive again so it is peaceful and happy.

There will still be problems, I know that, caused by those who don't want progress. It might be an idealistic view, maybe even naïve, but I have hope as I look around today. Hope for this world and the people in it.

Hours later, when the sun is setting, we finally sit down and eat something. My mind won't stray from the thoughts plaguing me. Is what we're doing right? We locked them in the very cells they built to trap us, but what if...what if it was a trap? What if it's what they want? What if Regnor changes his mind?

What if they vote to kill them all?

I have too many questions and no one to ask. I keep my head down and my eyes locked on my filthy feet as I try to sort out the madness in my head.

A hand lands on my shoulder. "I can sense your hesitation." Smoke sighs, crouching next to me. "Would it help to see them?"

"See them?"

"The masters," he clarifies, his voice low. "Would it help to look into their eyes?"

His gaze is open, unguarded, and offers nothing but kindness. He sensed my worry, my own second guesses, and wanted to help.

"I think so." I nod.

He squeezes my shoulder. "Stay here." With that, he disappears into the crowd. I watch him go before turning to my men. Xavier bumps my shoulder and offers me some water.

"You should know by now you only have to ask for something and any single one of us would move mountains to make it happen," he murmurs. "Now drink, you haven't had one in a while. You have to take care of yourself first."

"Yeah, Firecracker," Jesse teases, making me grin at him as they surround me, passing around and sharing our supplies. I join in the low conversation but jerk when Smoke suddenly appears before me and holds out his hand. "Come with me."

He waits patiently as I scan his relaxed face before placing my hand in his. "Where to?"

"Where you want to go, of course. I'll go with her. I can probably get one more of you in there as well," he offers nervously.

"Xavier," Alcide decides, and I blink at him. His eyes soften, and he kisses my other hand. "He needs that too," he murmurs as Xavier stands.

I follow his gaze and nod, and with one last look at my exhausted men, I turn and follow Smoke through the crowd. We head through the filled streets, taking shortcuts until we're before the arena. I suck in a breath as I'm led down a familiar set of stairs just as the sun sets. The last time I took this route, I was in chains, but this time, I'm free. Still, each step is heavy and unsure, and when we reach the bottom, I spot the cells filled with guards, and at the very back, cramped in separate cells with no water or beds, are the masters. They are in the very cells we stayed in. They watch us, their faces twisted in hate, but they remain silent as we approach. I search their gazes, seeing defeat. They know they have lost and what is in store for them. They look weak like this, covered in dirt and left in the dark. Without that seat of power, they are nothing but plain, weak little men. We gave them that, the power, and now we have taken it away. All that is left is the lingering taint of their rot throughout the city, but that will soon be gone.

Regnor is right, isn't he?

How could we ever move on with them still alive? But is death the only way?

Turning away, I look at Smoke for a moment. "I need to speak to Chester," I mutter, knowing I have things left unsaid, and he's the only one who will speak.

He nods and whistles. "Go down there, there's a room—"

"I know the way," I interject, and he flinches, remembering why I know the way, so I smile. "It's okay, it wasn't all bad down here..." I glance at Xavier who is standing rigidly beside me, looking around at the place he grew up in. "Some of it was very good," I finish, and then drag my gaze back to Smoke to see understanding dawning in his eyes.

"I'll stay with him," he offers and moves to Xavier's side, being there for him as he says goodbye to that part of his life.

Walking to the room Chester and I used to meet in is surreal. So many memories hound each step—the heartache I had down here, the pain, the loss—and yet all I can think about is how I would have never found Xavier without this place. I never would have discovered my own strength or changed anything in this world.

Maybe everything happens for a reason.

As I sit in the very seat Chester used to sit in and set up the board out of habit, I wonder if that reason is why I was born.

A moment later, he is dragged into the room and forced into a chair, the snarling guard almost spitting on him. "If he so much as looks at you wrong, let me know." He kicks the chair as he passes before slamming the door. Chester looks worse for wear as I meet those familiar eyes.

I nod at the board. "Play," I demand.

He hesitates before making a move, and so we play in silence as I debate why I came here. Was it to say goodbye like Xavier? To ensure Regnor had not gone back on his word? Or to get some closure on this myself?

"Why are you here?" he asks finally as I deliberate my next move.

"I was just wondering that too," I admit, moving my knight. "I guess a part of me needed this, to feel the end in these walls." I look around. "Can't you feel it? The change in the air? We have been fighting for so long, not just here, but in Cinders. I have been fighting my entire life to be free, and now I have it."

"And you don't know what to do with it," he offers with an arched eyebrow, making a move. I analyse the game and move as well.

"Oh no, I do, unlike you. You see, for people like me, like those men out there, like my family, we have spent so long dreaming of our freedom that when it's finally here, we don't squander it. No, we make the most of every last second because we know what it's like to wonder if there will be any more. Another sunrise, another moment, another day, week, year. We live it to the fullest with no regrets. That's the problem with men like you. You think you have all the time in the world, that your money can stop the inevitable. You live in your big, fancy house, looking out at the world, too scared to make a move without thinking of every possible option.

You see nothing but things to corrupt, whereas we see beauty and places to explore, live, and see. You are blind to the world around you, and in that, you are poor. You have lost everything, and what do you have left? Nothing and no one. No, I know what to do with my freedom. The question is, Chester, what will you do with your final days?"

"So that's it? That's to be my future? You'll kill me?"

"I don't know," I reply, moving another piece and meeting his eyes. "It's out of my hands now and in theirs—the people you hurt, enslaved, and used. I wouldn't expect them to be as forgiving as me."

Sitting back, he debates his next move, his mouth drawn tight and his eyes downcast.

"Your daughter is alive." I don't know why I tell him other than I want to see his face. He doesn't disappoint. He recoils, his expression showing his shock as he gapes at me.

"What did you say?" he whispers.

"Your daughter," I say, slowly moving my piece. I stroke the carved wood, remembering him teaching me as he gave me a reprieve from the desolation down here. "Marie, she's alive. I met her. She's in love with the very man who brought you to your knees. She's a healer now. She's incredible and so strong. She has this inner steel, unwilling to break even when she bends. Everything you did, everything you became... she saw. You gave up on her and yourself, and in doing so, you really did lose your daughter. She still loves you, a part of you, but I wouldn't expect her to visit. She detests the monster you've become."

He flinches, and tears well in his eyes.

I nod at the board. "Your move."

"Any move I make will make me lose," he admits.

"You set that path in motion a long time ago. Plus, those who always worry about the end, about winning, always lose," I reply. "Is there anything you wish for me to tell her?"

"I'm sorry," he says, moving without looking. "Tell her I'm sorry."

"For not fighting? For giving up? Or for being a horrible human being?" I snap.

"All of them." He shakes his head. "Alive. She's alive. At least that brings me some comfort."

Pursing my lips, I take in his slumped posture. "It shouldn't. You could have been happy, could have been with her, but instead you stood idly by. You made the wrong move, and now you are out of them. You should know that every single decision has an effect, and if you had fought, she might not be with the rebels. There might not have been a need for them. Instead, you did nothing. I've learned that if you aren't part of the solution, you're part of the problem. And Chester? You're part of the problem, and you have lost everything." Grabbing his queen with one finger, I knock it over. "Checkmate."

I stand, leaving him staring at the board, and head out. Once outside I press my back to the wall, and I let out a long breath, ignoring the guards' confused looks. It's done. I feel better now that I've seen him. Now that I got that off my chest, I can finally walk away without looking back, knowing that unlike these monstrous men, I've done everything I could.

It takes everything in me to walk the tightrope of life without falling like they have.

Now, their future and that of the city they built is to be decided, and I can't help but wonder what the future will bring.

DESPITE OUR VICTORY, I don't sleep well. Leaning against the open doorway of the train car, I look out into the dark tunnel, my thoughts plaguing me. I sigh softly, glancing at my men who are peacefully sleeping behind me.

When we were finally forced back to the tunnels due to exhaustion, we returned to our carriage, removed our clothes, and curled up together on the mattresses. None of us said anything, but we didn't need to voice our thoughts—they all know what I'm feeling. Needing the comfort of each other's bodies, we created a puppy pile. My back was pressed up against Nixon's broad chest, and the others all lay around us, touching me in some way. Eventually, they fell asleep.

I spent most of the night awake, going over every decision, every move, and every action. I worry that we've removed one set of masters from power and just replaced them with another. I'd seen how quickly Regnor was to demand the masters' execution, the rush of the victory going straight to his head. He'd been so quick to dismiss us now that we'd helped him win the battle, like we were something he could use and discard. I'm still horrified that he was going to act on his thoughts without speaking with the other rebels, and that the only way he thinks he can get true justice is to murder the ones who caused him pain.

But no, he's better than the masters, I know that. He agreed to speak to the rebels and to get their vote before doing anything. He's a good leader, they wouldn't have gotten this far if he wasn't, but he's impulsive, and I saw the gleam of power that entered his eyes when he realised he'd won. Shaking my head, I squeeze my eyes shut. No, Regnor wouldn't become like the masters, not with Marie behind him. She's his calming influence, and thankfully, she can get through to him in a way the rest of us can't.

Shuffling sounds behind me, and I can't help but smile as I look at the pile of men. I should get up and join them and try to get a few more hours of rest. The sun must only just be rising, so we should have more time before we'll be needed. Yet as soon as I close my eyes, I just see the look on Chester's face when he found out that Marie was still alive. No, I don't think I'll be sleeping for a while yet, even as exhaustion hangs heavily on my weary body.

I can hear the sounds of people stirring in the tunnels, getting ready for the day ahead. I'd been surprised by how many of them returned down here after the fight, but I suppose this is all they've known for a long time, and there's some comfort in the tunnels. Of course, there had been plenty of them who refused to return here and were making homes for themselves in the abandoned buildings. I overheard one rebel stating that returning to the tunnels would be letting the masters win. Is that what we're doing? Of course not, but our every move seems to be watched and analysed.

Shaking my head to rid it of those thoughts, I prepare to get up when I hear footsteps quietly making their way towards our carriage. Leaning slightly out of the door, I see a familiar face, and a small smile spreads across my lips.

"Rhea," Smoke greets, his own smile wide. "I never thought I'd be happy to come back down here." Winking, he walks up to me, running his eyes over my body as I do the same to him. He looks tired, like he's not slept. I want to say something, but then I guess I look just as bad, if not worse.

A sombre mood settles over us, and his smile drops as a frown pulls at his brow. "You guys might want to get ready. They are about to make a decision about the masters."

"Shit. They started without us?"

Growling under my breath and cursing silently, I jump to my feet. This is something Regnor would do. I know he thinks I meddle, and I guess I do, but it's in the best interest of everyone, not just the few.

"They have been talking all night. I would have come to get you sooner, but most of it was boring and you needed to sleep. But they have called for a vote amongst the other rebel leaders, and I thought you'd want to be there."

Rubbing a hand across my face, I nod wearily. "Thank you. Give us ten minutes, and we'll be there."

Stepping up into the carriage, he holds something out to me. "You might want this. Although I won't complain if you want to run around in that little leotard again."

I look up and see that quirky smile is back in place, and there's a glint in his eyes.

"I don't know what's in it, but Gregor gave it to me, said that you would need it."

I can hear the others moving behind me and know we woke them. Nixon wanders over in a pair of boxers and takes the bag from me, pulling outfits out and laying them on the end of the bed. A smart, form-fitting black dress catches my eye, and I run my fingers along the fabric.

"I'm guessing that one's yours," Alcide says with a wink, which is quickly followed by a yawn.

"I don't know, I think I could pull it off." Jesse holds the dress up against his chest, making me snort in amusement. The others chuckle as he prances around.

Everyone is reaching for the clothes, pulling them on and marvelling at how their attire fits them perfectly. Casual shirts and trousers are pulled on first, but what really makes them stand out is the fitted black jackets. Embroidered on the breast is a golden circus tent. Standing together, they look like a unit—a family or an army. My jacket is draped next to the dress, and I realise something with a frown.

"Smoke, there's another outfit in here." I turn to face him, our eyes lock, and there's a beat of silence. "I guess Gregor saw you coming with us."

He reaches out and brushes the fabric with his fingers, indecision crossing his features. "If I enter the meeting with you guys wearing this... it will be crossing a line."

He's right. It will show that he's with us, that he agrees with our feelings on the masters' future. It will show Regnor that Smoke no longer follows him. A sense of rightness settles over me. He should be with us, but this isn't an easy choice and shouldn't be rushed into, no matter how much I want it. "I know this is a huge decision, and I don't envy you for having to make it. You need to do what's best for you, but know that there's a place here with us if you need it."

"She's right, you should come with us. It's a new start," Xavier speaks up, startling me. Then again, if anyone knows anything about what's been going on here and starting over, it's Xavier.

"The more the fucking merrier," Blain complains from the other side of the carriage, but I see the upturn of his lips and know he's joking.

A strange look crosses Smoke's face, and I know he's struggling with this new knowledge. If Gregor knew to make an extra jacket, then he saw Smoke with us. I don't know how the tailor's ability works—if what he sees *always* comes to be or if there's an element of change.

"Thank you, that means more than you could imagine," Smoke replies, pulling his gaze from the jacket. "I agree that we should give the vote to the rebels and give the masters a chance to speak before their fate is sealed. But I'm not sure I'm ready to walk away from Regnor yet, because that's exactly what this would mean. He would feel like I've betrayed him and wouldn't trust me again."

My heart twists in my chest, and guilt rises at coming between their friendship, but he has to know his options. Placing a hand on his shoulder, I squeeze gently. "I understand, there's no pressure."

Holding my gaze, he seems to search my face for something. He must find it, because he nods and steps back, my hand falling between us. "I'll just be outside while you get changed."

My thoughts are turbulent, but I don't have time to sort through them. We need to get to that meeting before they make a decision. Closing the door, I turn and see the guys are mostly dressed. I shed the oversized shirt I was wearing and ignore the heated gazes of the guys as they watch me, my skin burning from their hungry eyes as desire settles low in my belly.

Slipping into the dress, I marvel at the soft fabric. The fit is perfect. It's a crossover dress that cinches in at the waist with two ties, the cut showing off the curves of my waist and hips. The deep V of the neckline accentuates my bust without being indecent. Small, capped sleeves finish off the top half, with the skirt ending just below my knees. As I move, I see golden flashes. Frowning, I examine the hem of the dress, looking to see if the lining is the cause of the bursts of colour, but no, it's all black. I turn to see if the guys can see anything, and the gold flashes again. Eyes wide, the guys watch me silently as I spin to test a theory. Golden sparks fill the room and I know I'm right. Every time I move, sparks emit from the dress. A smile crosses my lips. We're about to make one hell of an entrance.

The guys look smart in their jackets. The golden embroidery glimmers, showing everyone just who we are. I slip my own jacket on, along with my boots.

We're ready.

With a nod, Blain walks over to the door, slides it open, and jumps down to join Smoke where he waits for us. The other guys start to file out, and when I look back to check that we've got everything, I see that Smoke's jacket is no longer on the bed.

WE FOLLOW Smoke to the town hall. I don't know why I'm surprised, of course Regnor would set himself up here, but it makes my stomach twist. I get the feeling this meeting isn't going to be easy. We've all been quiet on the journey over, even Smoke, which is unusual. Four rebels stand outside the main doors to the town hall, and as we make our way closer, they watch us with narrowed eyes, but the presence of Smoke seems to settle them. He doesn't stop to talk to the guards, just merely nods before passing straight through. Leading us through the maze of corridors, he takes us to the back of the building. A large set of wooden double doors stands closed before us, but I can hear Regnor's voice behind them, and I know this is our destination. The last time we were here, there were metal detectors and the place was crawling with city guards. How different it is now, the doorway empty and unguarded.

Smoke knocks once before opening the doors, not waiting for a reply. Stepping into the room, I take in the scene in front me. A large, crescent-shaped table takes up most of the space, with maps and papers spread over the top. Regnor stands in the middle, his face set into a frown as he watches us walk in. On his left sits Tobin, the old healer, and on his right is Marie. It looks like we interrupted something, because her face is flushed and her arms are raised as if in mid gesture, but as she turns to look at us, hope blooms in her eyes. The other five seats are taken up by males I've not seen before. No, scratch that, I recognise the one at the far end of the table. I don't know his name, but I've seen him at some of the meetings before. He's maybe about Alcide's age. He nods at us in greeting but doesn't look particularly happy at our presence.

The others look at us with outright hostility. I don't know where these guys have been hiding, but I knew that some of the rebels had been on reconnaissance missions. They all appear to be middle-aged but don't have any particular features that make them stand out, which is good for a spy.

"Rhea, oh good, you made it." Sarcasm drips from Regnor's voice, and I focus on him.

Raising a single brow, I nod at the papers on the table and gesture at the others. "It appears you started without us," I drawl and take in the room. Bags, supplies, and mattresses are piled up in one of the corners, telling me that he has no intention of living in the tunnels. "It also looks like you've made yourself pretty comfortable up here."

The guys gather closely behind me. I feel Alcide's hand on my shoulder, and I know they'll follow my lead here. Smoke is standing just to the left, leaning against the wall as if none of this bothers him, but I've noticed how he's still with us and hasn't gone to stand with the other rebels. Regnor notices it at the same time I do, his eyes narrowing on his friend. When he drags his gaze back to me, I see the anger he's trying to keep in check.

"We're not pests hiding in the sewers anymore, we're victors! Victors don't hide like rats."

I know that's a dig at us, but I don't care. He may see himself as a victor, but I see us as survivors, and survivors do what they have to in order to stay alive, including living in tunnels until they know it's safe to do otherwise. "Many of your own people are still living down in the tunnels," I counter, trying to keep my own frustrations locked down. "They are scared, and the tunnels offer them security. They don't know how the citizens of the city will react to freaks being in control. They need you to reassure them."

"That's why we're here. They will never feel safe until the masters are dealt with," a nasally voice insists.

Slowly, I turn to look at the man who spoke. "And what do you mean by 'dealt with?'"

"We were just about to vote before you barged in," another of the rebels says. "I say they should be killed. They've killed thousands of us, and we will never be truly free until they are dead!"

Grumbles fill the room, and the guys shift their weight behind me, clearly unhappy at the easy way they are speaking of the masters' deaths.

"I have another option," Regnor inserts, and the room falls silent as all eyes turn to him. "We make them fight. They made us fight and die in the pits, so they should be subjected to the same punishment."

Horror fills me. There's execution, and then there's this. The masters are purely human with not a lick of power at their disposal, not to mention they have never had to fight. They won't last two minutes in the pits. It doesn't matter that they did the exact same thing to us freaks. If we do the same as they did, and let history repeat itself, then we're no better than them. It is cruel and unnecessary. I may not get on with Regnor, but we've come to a truce before and worked through our issues. This, though... I thought better of him, and from the look on Marie's face, she did too. Anger rises within me and I stride forward, aware of my dress sparking with the movement. The rebels eye me nervously, my fury radiating from my body.

"So an eye for an eye, right? That's how you're going to rule?" I address this last question to Regnor. "When is it going to stop? You make the masters fight, then what about their soldiers? What about their supporters? Will they all be forced to fight?" I throw my arms up in frustration. How can they not see how wrong this is? "If you go down that route, you are no better than them. If someone annoys you, will they be forced to fight for their lives? For your entertainment? Does any of this sound familiar to you?"

Regnor appears calm as he watches me, but I can feel his anger that I'm once again stepping in and causing trouble. "Don't you want to get justice for everything they did? Out of everyone, I thought you'd understand this, having been forced to fight."

He really doesn't get it.

Striding up to the table, I slam my hands down on it, losing my temper. "And it's because of that that I'm saying this!" I'm inches from Regnor now. "We got justice! We won, we have the city under rebel control, and no freak will ever be forced to fight again. Can't that be enough of a victory for you?"

There's a tense silence, and I see his hands ball on the table as if he's trying to stop himself from acting on his anger.

"Regnor, she's right," Marie speaks up, placing her palm over one of his fists.

He seems to jerk at the contact, pulling his gaze from mine as he looks down at the woman he loves. Marie's father is one of the captive men, one of the men Regnor is trying to make fight to the death, and he knows he has to tread carefully here.

Jaw stiff, he lets out a sharp breath through clenched teeth. "Let's hold a vote." Looking around the room, he meets the eyes of his fellow rebels, pointedly ignoring me and the guys gathered behind me. "You know where I stand. Execution by fighting in the ring or imprisonment."

I look at him with disgust. "When I said you needed to speak to the rebels before you made these decisions, I didn't mean your friends. All of your people deserve a vote, otherwise, how are you any better than the masters?"

"I agree with her, Regnor. We shouldn't be making these kinds of decisions without speaking with our people," Tobin says, speaking up for the first time, and I see some of the others nodding. Obviously his opinion has an impact on these men.

Regnor sees the same thing and deflates a little, knowing he isn't going to win. "All in favour of extending the vote to the rest of the rebels, say aye."

Marie, Tobin, Smoke, and the guys behind me all say "Aye" immediately, and after a couple of tense seconds, the others around the table do so as well. Regnor doesn't look surprised, but his eyes glisten with an emotion I can't quite describe.

"It's been decided then. We'll keep the masters locked up until we can get everyone together and let them vote."

I hear the disappointment in his voice, and he won't meet my eyes as he dismisses us with a wave of his hand. Smoke grins at me as he leads us from the room, the guys chatting behind me, but something's bothering me, and I can't help but replay the moment over in my head. That's when I realise what it is—Regnor never voted.

I EXPECT A PUBLIC VOTE. We hang around, waiting for the declaration, but none comes, and we eventually head underground to eat and rest. At dawn, word arrives, only it says nothing about voting or justice, just to meet at the arena for the masters' punishment. Spurred on by panic that Regnor has gone behind all of our backs and decided to hold the fights anyway, I jump up, and my men and I search for clothes.

That's when I find the dress Gregor made me. We packed it and brought it back from the tent, and here it sits, unworn. I don't have his gifts or powers, but as I hold the material in my hands, I know that today I have to wear this—not should, but *have* to—as if it was meant for this all along, and maybe it was. After all, he seems to have foretold everything and been prepared. The dress is just as beautiful as I remember and hasn't wrinkled at all, hanging to my thighs in swathes of black fabric. The feathers from the sweetheart bodice still look ethereal and fluid. Wordlessly, Xavier helps me dress, adding the leather braces and scabbard Gregor made. Jesse fixes the ends as Blain does my hair. The mood is sombre, troubled. I even see it in

Nixon's, Rex's, and Alcide's eyes. They are worried about what will happen, not just to the masters... but to us.

It won't stop me from fighting for what is right, for what is just, however. We cannot become the monsters they were. We have to do better, and if it takes my voice, my life, then so be it. That's what my men can feel, my determination, and I know they worry what Regnor will do if I stand in his way. He's a good man, I can see that, and I think that maybe in a different time, he could have been a great man, but the power and revenge is going to his head. If he's not careful, he's going to lose everything—his position, his love, and his people.

I watch as they dress in the same outfits as yesterday, their lips turned down before Alcide turns to me, cupping my face. He searches my gaze. "I won't stop you."

I go to speak, but he silences me by pressing a finger to my lips.

"What is going to happen is what you must do. It's the right thing for everyone. I know that, and I'm so proud of you, Rhea, for fighting, for never giving up, and for doing the right thing even when it isn't easy and everyone seems to be against you. But remember we're here until the very end. We're at your side, you are never alone. We do this together." He leans in, moving his finger. "And we love you, our brave, brave girl." He seals it with a kiss as tears fill my eyes, the droplets catching on my lashes as I try to blink them away.

He moves back, and Blain takes his place, searching my face before he grabs my cheeks, yanks me to him, and kisses me soundly. "Whatever happens, Harpy," he murmurs before nipping my full bottom lip. "I'll kill them all for you if I have to." With that declaration, he moves to the side and Jesse moves forward with a sad grin.

"You astound me, Firecracker. You know that's why I call you that, right? Because I saw it in you, even in that first moment. Your fire, your refusal to go out or deflate, and now, standing before me is the woman I saw hiding in those eyes in Cinders. We're not hiding anymore. Be who you are, my love. I am with you." He gives me a long, lingering kiss before Nixon moves him.

Silently, Nixon meets my eyes before kissing my head ever so gently, and in the gesture I sense a million words. It chokes me up, and then Rex is there, surrounding me in his warmth and protection. "We'll survive this like we do everything else. It's just another show, and then we can be free again. Happy and on the road." I kiss him this time, and he grins as he pulls away.

Xavier stands to the side, hesitating. He watches my men before he storms over with a muttered curse. He closes the distance and lifts me into his arms. "One last round in the arena, that's all it is. We fight now like we did then. Together." He slams his lips onto mine, and it's so fast that when he pulls away, I'm gasping for breath.

Swallowing, I try to control my racing heart as I look at them all. "Together," I repeat. Knowing they are with me means the world to me. It also makes me more confident that what I'm doing is the right thing. Even if it costs us everything, I cannot sit idly by. Not anymore. "I love you all. No matter what happens today, I wouldn't change anything. Not meeting you in Cinders. Not the hurt, the loss, or the pain. I would not alter a second because it's all worth it for you. For us. I was just a slave girl with no family, no purpose, and no future. You gave me all that. You showed me what love was, what right and wrong was. You gave me the tools I needed to fight, to stand tall and never to be cowed again by the order of men. So I don't know what awaits us inside the arena, but I need you to know... Thank you for loving me, for saving me, and for being my everything. I've lived more in this short amount of time than I have my whole life, and I have you to thank." I step back with a watery smile on my face.

It's the last weakness I will allow myself.

WHEN I ARRIVE at the arena, I can hear the rebels and citizens inside. Their confusion, excitement, and hope are palpable. Waiting outside is Regnor, Marie, Tobin, Smoke, and some of the men I wasn't introduced to. Regnor nods at me then turns away with a clenched jaw. Marie smiles as Smoke moves closer.

"We voted to wait for you," he murmurs as he takes my hand, kissing it before looking me over. His jaw literally drops. "Holy fuck on a dick. Jesus, Rhea, are you trying to kill me?"

"What?" I ask, looking down at the dress.

"You look—" He stumbles over his words. It's the first time I've ever seen that happen. "You look beautiful, but that doesn't even do it justice. You look regal, like a queen, but powerful too, like a freak." He shakes his head, grinning. "You look like you belong here more than Regnor." He kisses my hand again and turns as Regnor claps.

Without a word, they start moving forward, walking into the arena. I refuse to trail behind, to be forgotten. I, more than him, know what this place means, what it stands for, and how much blood can never be purged from the sand. Him? He might be the rebel leader, but this is our arena, and every step I take towards it only makes my shoulders go back and chin rise higher until I'm striding through their masses and catching up to Regnor as he enters. He gives me an annoyed look but nods at the stands as we pass through them.

There are cheers and whistles. I hear my name called and chanted. Not his. It makes me smile as I stride across the sand. There is no pomp or show, no, Regnor heads straight to the masters' box, and we follow. Even though being here makes me feel sick, makes memories crowd my head, I force a smile onto my face as I take in the throng. They are all waiting for what is to come, for the masters' punishment, for Regnor's justice.

As am I.

Nerves churn in my stomach at what Regnor might do.

When he steps forward, he raises his hands to silence the crowd. The audience slowly lowers their voices until only soft whispers and shuffling feet remain. "Bring them," he calls loudly, and the gate, the fighters' gate, starts to rise. I almost gasp and physically recoil as the masters are marched out onto the sand. Their hands and feet are in chains, and they are attached to each other. They are dragged behind some rebel guards, thrown forward, and shoved until they are forced to kneel before us.

A sense of dread fills me and bile rises in my throat as I look down at their faces, pale and scared. I gaze into their human, terror-filled eyes as they wait for judgement, wondering if this is what they saw every time they were in this box. Did they feel the same? Maybe at first, but by the end they didn't care. I'm not them, though, so I cannot look down on them and feel nothing. This is wrong. I hate that this is what we've become and what has transpired. I wish we could go back and change the outcome, but we can't. All we can do is change the future, and as they watch us, waiting for their sentence, I know they may not deserve forgiveness for their crimes against humanity, but it doesn't mean we get to choose their fates either. If we are the executioners, the torturers, then we are no better than them.

I have one last fight to do in this arena.

One I may not win, but I still have to try.

Regnor steps to the edge of the balcony, shooting an enraged look at the masters before his expression becomes blank and he looks out at the crowd, at all the rebel and non-rebel faces. They are waiting to see if we will be better than those before us, and when his words come, I realise we aren't. Part of me hoped he wouldn't... but I was wrong.

"Today, we get our revenge. Today, we get our justice for our people and our city!" he roars. "These men—I refuse to call them masters—that's all they are: men. They are weak, stupid men who we let rule us for too long. They will finally pay the price for their crimes. I will not hand them their deaths, no, they will fight to survive like so many of us were forced to." Cheers go up as I look around in disgust. "They will fight, and they will die. We shall finally see how strong they truly are," he sneers, looking down at them. The cheers and chants grow louder, but I notice how uncomfortable many people look, and not only the rebels, but some of the guards too. This is blood sport. This is about Regnor's sick need to see them suffer. I know they did him and Marie wrong, but they hurt many people.

This is murder.

As the cheering continues to grow, so does my anger, disgust, and need to do something. I cannot remain silent and let this happen. I refuse to be like them—killers. I refuse to be like Chester, who is staring at his daughter, accepting of his fate.

I refuse to be weak.

Never again.

No, today I speak my mind. Today I stop the city from falling into yet another reign of terror and death.

I look back at my men and see I'm not the only angry one as they look around in horror. I meet Xavier's eyes last. He more than anyone has suffered under the masters' cruel hands, but even he doesn't agree with this. He wants his revenge too, wants justice for what he went through, but this isn't the way. He must see what I want to do in my eyes because he nods, a smile forming on his lips. I've faced worse odds, I've faced worse people, and I've looked death in the eye. As I turn forward, my powers surge so strongly I almost can't breathe, but I know now that this is where I am supposed to be.

This is where I was always destined to end up, to make a change and to make this world better.

With my family at my side.

I step forward, and the crowd starts to quiet down as they see me. I tilt my head back, my eyes going to Regnor as I pass him and stand before the masters and the audience. The crowd becomes silent without me needing to force them to, and then I begin to speak. I am unaware of what I'm going to say until it flows from my tongue as if coming from a force deeper than me.

From everything that runs through this world.

From the balance of right and wrong.

Good and evil.

Nature and death.

"You speak of revenge, and I think that's very telling," I tell Regnor before addressing the crowd. "That's all this is, revenge. This isn't justice, this isn't the fresh start so many of you seek. This is an eye for an eye, this is blood for blood! The fighters, those who survived these pits, sit silent in the stands, haunted by their experiences, yet you don't see them crying out for blood because they know! They know it won't change what happened to them. Spilling the masters' blood on this sand won't change the horrors they endured. I know that, I was one of them. I *am* one of them. I fought, died, and lost my love on these sands. I grieved, I hated, I lost hope. But doing this doesn't change what happened to me. To us. It won't make the memories, the nightmares, easier. It won't make the scars any less real, and it won't bring our people back. All it will do is add more souls to those we carry on our conscience, those of the dead." While some boo, baying for blood, I hear some cheers, and that fortifies me.

"If that's how we start this new life, the new city, then where does it stop? If we make them fight now, then who's next? Anyone that wrongs you? One man doesn't get to decide the fate of the future of so many. That is wrong, and that makes you no better than them, the masters, who lorded their power and made decisions without listening. Listen to your people. They don't want death and combat, they want peace!" I look down at the masters. "I don't pardon you for your crimes, I don't forgive you, but I refuse to watch you suffer and be slaughtered the way I watched friends, strangers, and fellow fighters die. I will not. Even if I have to stand alone before the whip that will force you to fight, I will." I swallow and look around. "Who else will stand with me? Who else will start this city with hope and not death? Who else will fight, not for them, but for our souls? Who will stand with me?"

"I will," comes a strong voice. I look back to see Xavier stepping up next to me. Alcide and the others are soon to follow.

"I will," Smoke calls, moving to my left. I hear other voices and look to see the crowd standing now. More voices fill the air, blending into one until nearly all of the audience is standing. My heart hammers with hope, pride, and relief.

"I will," comes a soft feminine voice, and I turn in shock to see Marie stepping up next to Regnor. He looks stricken, betrayed. She meets his eyes, tears welling in her own before she looks at me with a nod. "It's the right thing to do. I refuse to build on my father's crimes. I refuse to be like him. I will be more. I will be better." Taking a deep breath, she looks back at Regnor. "I will save instead of damn, unlike you. I will even save you from yourself, from the hatred blinding you. I have lost everyone, and I won't lose you as well. Even if you hate me for this, my love."

Regnor's tears fall freely as more voices join until the whole arena is on its feet, and I look to Regnor.

"You have their vote, their choice," I tell him.

"No, they must pay! They stole my child, my wife! They stole my love, my future," he roars as Marie flinches in pain. Her gaze drops to the floor as she slumps and moves away from him, but he's so enraged he doesn't notice he's losing her too.

His tone is so heartbroken that it cracks my own heart, and his motives, his reasons for this hatred make sense now. I see the unwillingness to give up in his eyes. My powers jump through me, and before I can even wonder what is happening, I start to rise from the masters' box and into the air. I hear gasps and wonderment as I float eye to eye with Regnor, above the masters. The dress flares like a flame burning up from my feet and engulfing everything, yet I am unburnt. My hair floats behind me on its own breeze, and the ground explodes upwards in vines and rock, forming a cage around the masters. Water dribbles down my arm.

"They will not. We have spoken." My voice echoes around the arena, deep and not my own, as if it hails from my very soul, from the energy connecting me to the earth. "If you do this, you are not a rebellion, you are murderers. Will you ignore the voices of the people you fight for? Will you ignore that of your own love? Of your friends, family, and followers? Will you become nothing but an angry, revenge-seeking man just like them?"

He glares at me. If he could kill me from the force of that look, he would. The crowd is silent now, waiting. He looks to Marie and she nods, reaching out to grab his hand, letting him know she is there for him even though he hurt her. His lips twist, and he glowers back at me with a dark, hateful look. I know it is her who sways him, not me or his friends. He may think he lost everything, but in Marie he found a second chance. He found love, and I hope he doesn't throw it away or lose it.

"Then it is done. I will listen to my people. The masters will not fight today. Take them back down."

He turns and storms away, leaving me with an arena full of staring rebels and citizens. My heart is lighter than it has been for a long time, even if Regnor hates me.

I know I did the right thing.

THE REBEL LEADERS leave pretty quickly after that. Marie shoots me a grateful look and mouths her thanks before hurrying after Regnor. We saved Regnor from himself today, but from the look of loathing he shot me, it might only be a matter of time before we're faced with something like this again. You can't force people to save themselves, just help them find the right path. His need for revenge for his dead wife and child has obviously been his key motive this whole time. I know that he cares for the rebels, for the freaks, but that's become lost in his hatred for the masters. What he can't see is that in that hatred, he's becoming exactly like the people he detests so much.

"We should go, *cariño*," Alcide murmurs at my side.

The arena is emptying since the masters were dragged back to the underground cells. However, as I gaze down into the arena, I see many are staring up at us, watching and waiting. For what, I don't know, but a shiver runs down my spine. Regnor had a lot of support, but most of the people agreed with me, and judging by some of the looks of those still waiting in the arena, I think they are losing faith in their leader. That's not what I want, I never wanted to turn anyone against Regnor, but what he was about to do was wrong.

Releasing a shaky breath, I step back and into the comfort of my guys. Looking around, I realise with a pang that Smoke isn't here with us. I know he probably went to smooth any ruffled feathers with Regnor, but my heart aches at him not being here. He supported me, so I know he's not going to turn his back on me now; but Regnor is his best friend and leader. We've put him in an awkward position, so I hold back on the panic that's threatening to overwhelm me.

Smoke will be back, I'm sure of it. A pulse of comfort spreads through me from my powers and beyond, from the connection I now understand is to the Earth.

Nodding at Alcide's suggestion, I turn and give the guys a shaky smile, but I can tell I'm not fooling any of them. Xavier squeezes my arm gently as he passes me, his expression understanding as he takes point and leads us back towards the tunnels. We're quiet and on alert for the short journey, but other than a few stares, no one tries to interact with us.

Back in the darkness of the tunnels, we reach our carriage. The guys climb up into it, but I hold back.

"Everything okay, Firecracker?" Jesse asks, hanging out of the train door with a questioning smile. I can see his concern, but he's trying to keep it off his face.

Returning his smile, I nod, but I know I'm not convincing when his brow pulls into a frown.

"Yeah, I think I'm just going to take a walk." I gesture behind me towards the darkened tunnels, hoping he doesn't try to stop me.

There's a pause as his eyes flit over my face. He wants to say no, or at least offer to come with me, but he just smiles. It doesn't hide the tension around his eyes, but I appreciate it all the same. "Okay, don't go too far though."

I nod, trusting he can see the appreciation on my face.

With a wink, he climbs back into the carriage. I immediately hear the guys' rumbling voices as they complain, wanting to follow me, but Jesse's voice cuts through it all. "She needs a break, give her some time."

I'm sure that doesn't go down well, especially with Nixon who's particularly protective, but I'm grateful when no one appears behind me. I've got so much on my mind, and although Regnor agreed not to make the masters fight today, I get the feeling I've fractured our relationship beyond repair. Who knows what will happen now? Just because I saved the masters from that fate doesn't mean they won't be facing something just as bad tomorrow. I need to try and speak to him, to get him to listen. He only backed down today because he couldn't go against the vote of those in the arena.

As I wander through the dark tunnels, my mind is twisted and my thoughts are so heavy that I almost miss them until the sharp voices cut through my haze.

I hear their voices before I see them and freeze, expecting to see their familiar forms—Regnor and Smoke. Just ahead, another tunnel breaks off from the one I'm walking along, and echoes of their words reach me. They must be down there as I can't see them ahead of me. I should turn around, they wouldn't want me overhearing this, yet I can't seem to stop myself from slowly creeping forward. Pausing by the opening, I press my back against the wall and listen.

Regnor's angry voice whips out. "I can't believe you went against me. You sided with her. I thought you supported me!" The words seem to reverberate around me, making me wince.

"I do support you! Can't you see what you're becoming?" Smoke retorts. "I did this to save you. You're becoming more and more like them and pushing everyone away in the process. I know losing Tash and Molly broke you, and you want your revenge, but you're about to lose everything." Frustration lines Smoke's tone, but I can hear the pain hiding there too.

There's a pause as Regnor takes in what his friend said. "What do you mean?"

"Marie!" Smoke sounds exasperated, like he can't believe he's having to explain this to him. "Can't you see how much all of this is hurting her?"

"I'm doing this to protect her, to protect all of you so we never have to go through anything like this again!" Frustration and anger return to the rebel leader's voice.

"That might have been true once, but right now when I look at you, all I see is another master."

My eyes well with tears at the pain in Smoke's voice. Marie isn't the only one Regnor's actions are hurting. I can't even imagine how difficult it is to watch your friend change like this before your eyes.

A tense pause fills the air. "I can't believe you said that."

"We're trying to help you, Regnor!" Smoke retorts, and I hear footsteps as if one of them is pacing.

I shouldn't be listening to this, I've already heard too much. Pushing away from the wall, I start to quietly move away.

"We? You mean Rhea and her merry band of followers. Is that what you're going to become? Another male for her to collect?"

I freeze in place. Anger stirs to life inside me. He doesn't understand us, many don't, and that's why he scorns us. He's allowing his dislike of me to cloud his judgement. Spinning on my heel, I step from the shadows and into view. Neither of them seem to notice me, both caught up in their argument.

"Don't speak about her like that," Smoke sneers, taking a step forward until he's chest to chest with Regnor. "She's shown me something I didn't think was possible for someone like me—acceptance, maybe even love."

Something crosses Regnor's face. It looks like shock, like he never truly expected Smoke to side with me. "So that's it then."

Smoke shakes his head, refusing to back down despite how much this must be hurting him. "It doesn't have to be. You're the one who's drawing a line in the sand."

Regnor opens his mouth to speak when he suddenly realises they are not alone. His head snaps around and his eyes land on me, his expression turning into a sneer.

"Why doesn't it surprise me that you're here?" he bites out. With one last look at Smoke, he turns and stalks away.

"Regnor!" Smoke calls after him, but the rebel leader doesn't so much as flinch as he disappears into the darkness.

I watch Smoke, and my heart constricts tightly in my chest, knowing I'm the reason behind all this. "I'm sorry."

Pulling his gaze from the dark tunnel, he runs his eyes over me as if checking for injury. He smiles as he walks closer, but it's missing the usual spark that I'm used to seeing on his face.

"No, it's not your fault." He lightly brushes his fingers along my cheek before dropping his hand and nodding towards the way I'd come. "Come on, let's get you back to the others."

My skin still tingles from where he touched it, but I nod and follow him back to the guys, noticing he looks back for Regnor, but all that's left is the dust of their relationship. Climbing up into the car, I find the guys looking tense, but their faces relax when they see me. Nixon grumbles something incomprehensible and stomps over to my side before pulling me against him. Sighing with pleasure, I wrap my arms around him as the others surround us in a group hug.

"I guess I'll leave you to it."

Smoke's words are light, and as I peek over, I find him grinning, but I see right through it. He doesn't want to leave. After what just happened with Regnor, he probably doesn't feel like he has anywhere to go. Untangling myself from the guys' limbs, I offer my hand to him.

"Stay with us." It's a statement, not a question, and as Smoke eyes the guys behind me, I know they echo my sentiment. He's one of us now.

He's chosen.

We spend the next couple of hours chatting and playing games. Smoke found a pack of cards, and they have been trying to teach me how to play. I'm useless at it and keep losing, despite Nixon and Rex cheating to try to help me win. It's fun and helps lift the tension that's been around us since we first captured the masters. The apprehensions are still there in the back of my mind, like I'm sure they are for the others, but for those few hours, we can all be together as a family.

A loud bang on the side of the carriage has my heart jumping into my throat, and as I look at the others, I see they are surprised too. We sit in frozen silence as we wait to see what happens next.

"Rhea! Come out."

Regnor.

Smoke is instantly on his feet, his face twisted with mixed emotions as he hurries to the carriage door. Before he can say anything, the rebel leader speaks again.

"I want to speak to Rhea. She can't keep hiding behind her *pets*."

Nixon growls as he lumbers to his feet. Xavier and Blain immediately stand in front of me, creating a protective wall of muscle. Rex and Jesse have my back as Alcide strides forward. I've never seen him look so mad before, my usually calm, controlled ringmaster is close to losing control. I need to do something before things escalate.

Pushing to my feet, I place my hands on Blain's and Xavier's shoulders and wait for them to let me pass. It's obvious they don't want to, their faces etched with disapproval, but they don't argue with me. Releasing a long breath, I stand straight and raise my head. I won't let Regnor see that my pulse is jumping around like a startled bird trying to take flight. We knew a confrontation was coming, I just didn't think it would be so soon. Glancing at each of my men, I meet their eyes and nod my head. It's time to put on another performance.

I make my way to the carriage door. Smoke appears concerned, but at my look, he steps aside. Alcide is practically vibrating with rage, so instead of getting him to move, I grip his hand with mine and lead him through the carriage door. My touch seems to calm him a little, but my attention is fixed on Regnor. He's come alone, but his stance is that of someone ready to fight. I open my mouth to say something, to question him about why he's come here, but he beats me to it.

"We're about to vote. Come."

That's all he says before he spins around and marches down the tracks. Frowning, I look at the others who have gathered behind me.

"They must be voting on the fate of the masters," Xavier suggests.

"Why did he look so angry though? He looked like he wanted to hit me." I lose my fight against a shudder, and it makes all the hair on my arms stand on end. Nixon grumbles unhappily, stepping closer until my back is pressed against his front and his arms are around me.

"You've foiled his plans, again. Plus, his partner and best friend sided with you," Blain points out, flipping a knife I hadn't noticed in his hand just a moment ago.

"I suppose we should go," I say, trying to sound confident, but from their looks of concern, I don't pull it off. However, they nod in agreement, and we start walking towards the meeting that could change everything. I find myself spinning the silver bracelet on my arm. It's always been a comfort knowing I have it, and it's become a bit of a crutch for me. I just pray that I don't have to use it today.

As we get closer to the carriage that the rebels use to plan, my anxiety increases, but I can't let that stop me. Arriving at the old train car, I climb through the door, the guys following me, and find the rebel leaders gathered around the large table. Marie and Tobin, the old healer, smile at me, but I notice several scowls sent our way.

"Rhea, thank you for joining us," Marie says kindly, but there's tension behind her eyes that tells me this meeting has been going on for a while.

Nodding my head in thanks, I glance around, noticing the leader watching us with his arms crossed over his chest, his expression dark. "Regnor said there would be a vote?"

"There's already been a vote," Tobin calls out. "But we're tied and need a deciding vote."

So that's why we're here. They tried to go ahead without us. This explains why Regnor was so angry. He hadn't wanted us involved, but now he needs me for this vote. Alcide mutters something in Spanish under his breath, but as I squeeze his hand, he settles down. He may be the ringmaster, but here, he lets me take the lead, and that makes me love him all the more.

Glancing around the space, I meet each of the leaders' gazes, taking note of who holds my stare and who looks away. "What are you voting on?"

"The masters' fates," Marie answers. "Some of us want them to face a fair trial, and the others want to forgo the trial and just execute them."

"They don't deserve a trial. They are guilty," Regnor snarls, losing his composure.

Although I'd been expecting something of the sort, I am still taken aback to hear it said out loud. Raising my eyebrows, I meet his frustrated gaze. "If they are guilty, then they'll face death anyway. I don't understand why you're so adamant that we shouldn't have a trial. The other rebels deserve a say."

"Because you'll talk them out of it!" Slamming his hands down on the table, Regnor turns his attention to the others. "If she has her way, the masters will go free."

There's mumbling around the table, but I cut it off as I step forward. "You can't be serious." My tone is incredulous as I pin him with a look, waiting for him to back down, but as time stretches on with no answer, the atmosphere becomes more awkward, and I realise he is. Is that what he really thinks? That I want the masters to be absolved of their crimes?

"All I was doing was stopping needless cruelty and keeping you from turning into the people you hate." I address him directly, holding his stare. The days when I'd back down from a man like this are gone. "The masters need to be brought to justice, but it should be done fairly. Hold a trial and let the people vote on the outcome. You're not God, Regnor. You shouldn't have the power to just order someone's execution."

My comment clearly shocks him as he straightens and steps back from the table. I can see my words replaying in his mind. Silence descends on us again, and some of the rebels shift their weight awkwardly, but I just wait. He needs to decide which way he's going to go—leader or dictator. That's not a decision I can make for him.

"We shall recast our votes, taking everything into consideration," he finally announces, his tone even. "You get one vote, so use it wisely." He's talking to me, but his eyes land on Smoke. He's not going to give him a vote, instead grouping him with my guys and me. His eyes flick to Xavier and then me. Uncertainty flashes across his face for a second. "You suffered first-hand under the masters, I thought you'd understand."

I understand where his hatred comes from, I do, but he would be making this decision for hundreds of people based on his desire for revenge. I know Regnor is a good man, but this has gone too far.

He must see something in my expression, because his face settles back into a mask of cool indifference. "If you think the masters should be executed, raise your hand." There's a pause, and I watch as he and several others vote. My heart hammers in my chest. More of them voted for execution than I thought they would, but I think we still have a chance.

Regnor glances around to see if there are any last-minute votes before his expression tightens. "If you think the masters should stand trial, raise your hand."

I don't need to turn to know the guys agree with me, and as someone squeezes my shoulder in support, I raise my hand. I see Marie and Tobin have their hands raised too, voting for a trial. One of the rebels beside Regnor is counting the votes, but I can tell from the leader's expression which way it's gone.

"The masters will face trial. The people will vote on their fate."

The announcement is made over the grumbles of those who lost, but I don't watch them, choosing to keep my eyes on Regnor. He walks around the table towards me. The guys stiffen and form a protective circle around me, reacting to the tension rolling off of him.

"You got what you wanted. We're thankful for everything you've done and the sacrifices you've made, but this obviously isn't the place for you." The rest of the carriage falls silent as he speaks to us. "Once the trial has been held, you should leave Last Stop for good and never come back. You're not welcome here any longer."

REGNOR DOESN'T WASTE any time, choosing to call for the trial immediately. His words still echo in my head. *You're not welcome here anymore.* They were so cruel, so intense. I shiver with fear. I know we are all worried about what that means for us, but we have no time to dwell on it as we are forced up from the tunnels and into a congregation with Regnor at the front. My men and I march behind him with the other leaders as we make our way through the streets to the town hall. We may be about to judge the masters, but it feels like we're the ones on trial. People stream from their houses, their shouts and questions filling the air as they join the loud crowd. I hold my head high, even as I clasp Rex's and Nixon's hands in mine, letting them comfort me. The echo of all the footsteps behind me is so loud it sounds like the crashing of war drums.

Can the masters hear their fate coming for them?

Despite what I want, deep down, I know the outcome of the trial. It doesn't stop me from hoping for the best, for forgiveness in people, but the need for revenge and justice is too strong. It overflows from the people following us as they chant for the masters' heads. I can taste it on my tongue, and it streams from the ground under my feet, twining through my body like an infection trying to take hold.

It almost feels like with each step we take closer to the town hall, the more the people's power rises. The freaks are on full display, and the city is alive, but this time not with the hustle of people, but with anger.

When we reach the town hall, I follow Regnor to the side, past the crowd already gathered there. When we get to the steps, they finally part far enough to allow me to see what's ahead, and it makes me gasp and recoil in disgust before I'm able to control my reaction.

There, at the top of the steps, are the masters. They kneel with their hands bound before them, their eyes wide and scared as they take in the crowd. But towering behind them, like a constant threat, are handmade, wooden gallows, with nooses waiting to be tied around their necks. A man in a black, hooded mask waits to escort them to their respective places.

They are going to hang them.

It repeats in my head, and I want to run away, to turn and leave and scream. Why can't people understand this is murder? This is wrong. Then Regnor is there with his head held high as he smiles at the crowd because he knows they will vote for their deaths. He's getting what he wants, and now it will be a public execution while also reaffirming his right as a leader in their eyes. He glances at me then and smirks before holding his hands up to silence the crowd. Eventually, they quiet down enough for him to speak.

"Since we spared the masters from the fights yesterday, today we are here to decide on the justice we deserve. I take your opinions seriously. Rhea is right. If we are to start this city off correctly, we need to do it as one. That's why I will hold a vote. I will listen, as is your right, to the people, those who have been hurt, used, and abused or affected by the masters' cruel rule. So without show or spectacles like they are known for, the vote is this—to kill the masters here today and be done with it, or to keep them locked up forever inside these walls to rot and eventually die. Know, however, that at any point, their twisted machinations could get them free. If you choose life, know I cannot predict what will happen in the future, if you choose death, to end their reign of terror, we can finally move on from this tragic, blood-filled part of the city's soon to be history."

The way he speaks, trying to convince them it's the right thing to do, has my shoulders tightening. He sounds exactly like *them*. I want to scream, to tell them no, but I can't, because he's right, my voice isn't needed. This isn't about me or him or even the masters. This is about the people of the city getting their say, getting their justice and the future they want. I fought against him so they could vote, so they could choose, and to go back on my word now, to manipulate them like him or the masters, would invalidate and lessen everything I fought for. Instead, I grip my men's hands harder, my eyes downcast as sadness and concern churn inside me. My heart is heavy as I wait for the decision, like the noose is around my own neck and squeezing tighter with each passing second.

Then it snaps, leaving me reeling as the crowd steps forward one by one, their voices loud as they shout their decisions. Each word is like a rock hitting my flesh until, eventually, I hit the floor and crumble, my heart cracking, my body aching, and tears filling my eyes.

I thought we were better than them, but I was wrong.

"Kill them!"

"Hang them all."

"They deserve it!"

"They killed our people, kill them too!"

Someone close to me raises their voice. "They killed my son, do it!"

"They killed my daughter."

"My wife!"

"My father!"

The cries fill the air along with other terrible accusations. "They raped my wife, my kid!"

"They sold my son to a man!"

On and on it goes, and their pain becomes mine, but it doesn't stop the overwhelming hopelessness I feel knowing they are all screaming for their deaths and voting with Regnor.

"Kill them, kill them! Make them pay!"

"We can't be safe until they are dead."

"We will never be safe knowing they could escape. Even if we banish them, they could come back. No, this has to happen!" someone yells, and there are cheers and mutters of agreement. It seems people didn't want to watch them suffer and fight to the death like their children and friends had to, but they are okay with them being executed.

Regnor listens, scanning the crowd, and his smile grows before he holds up his hands. "I agree, and now the decision is made—your decision." He looks at the masters. "Today you will hang for your crimes against our people and our city." He jerks his head at the executioner. "To the noose."

I watch in horror as they are led up to the gallows and the rope is tied around their necks. Tears stream down their faces. Marie turns away, her eyes glassy, and Smoke moves closer, his expression sad.

"Any last words before your last traitor's breath is stolen?" Regnor asks them.

Chester nods. "Marie, I beg for your forgiveness." She flinches but doesn't look at him. "In this life or the next, one day, I hope you forgive me and remember that despite all the horrible things I have done, that I loved you deeply. Remember me from before, not now, and, my daughter, don't look. Don't watch. I don't want that stain on your soul."

Regnor flinches, and I wonder if she will ever forgive the man who gave the order to hang her father despite her hatred of him.

"Then, for your crimes against Last Stop, I, Regnor, sentence you to death by hanging." For once, he doesn't sound happy. He almost sounds resigned.

I wrap my arms around myself, feeling sad. I understand why the people chose this. They want to feel safe, to feel some peace or solace for those they have lost and the scars they have endured, but I don't condone killing. I can understand it, but it still weighs heavily on my heart. Who am I to take away their right to avenge their families, to let out their pain and anger? This isn't my world, I'm just living in it. From the blood of the masters comes a fresh start for these people, I just wanted to be part of it. I could stop this, but it is not my duty to. Everyone deserves to feel safe, so if this is the only way for Last Stop to recover, then so be it.

The platforms drop, and their bodies do as well. Like dolls, their legs kick as their eyes bulge. One dies instantly. Chester's neck, however, doesn't snap, and he starts to choke to death instead. I turn away, unable to watch anymore. I move through my men and the surging, cheering crowd. Each step is faster than the last until I am almost running to escape his final death gasps. It's time for us to leave. We continue to walk the tightrope between good and bad. It's never just black and white, but my soul feels so very dark at the moment. With each step away from the crowd, from the gallows, it lightens just a little.

I won't say goodbye. I won't listen to the celebration.

Today, my family and I leave for good.

It's over.

We return to our carriage to pack, but really, I just need to get away from the death cries and shouts of celebration. Their need for blood and revenge makes me feel sick.

With a heavy heart, I look around the space that has been our home since we were freed from the arena. I have mixed feelings about these tunnels. On one hand, they represent where the rebels had to hide themselves away, like vermin concealed beneath the city, never able to walk freely in the sun. Yet they have also become a place of comfort for me, the first place I've actually felt safe in this city. Sure, a lot of bad things have happened here, but I've also felt excitement, love, and hope here. We were able to recover and rediscover who we were after our time in the arena and cells, where Xavier became part of our family. Where Smoke sided with us and became... I'm still not sure exactly what Smoke is to me, but I can't deny my feelings any longer.

My eyes flick over to the doorway where I last saw Smoke. His belongings are stored somewhere else, so he left a couple of minutes ago to pack. As we left the arena, he chased me down, grabbed my arm, and told me he was coming with us. I'd been too numb to do anything but nod. The guys hadn't looked surprised, and neither had Regnor when I met his narrowed eyes.

My chest tightens. I don't like being separated. A line has been drawn in the sand and it's time for us to leave.

We don't have many possessions, mostly just the clothes Gregor made for us, so it doesn't take long to gather everything together. We weren't the type to carry trinkets with us before, and anything we might have had was taken from us when we were captured. A glint catches my eyes, and I glance at the silver bracelet on my wrist. This is one of the only pieces of jewellery I have, and I'm glad I was able to keep hold of it through all of this. Gregor promised that it would help boost my powers when I needed it, and that I would know when to use it. Unease travels through me. Gregor has foresight, he knows something is coming. If I haven't needed to use it after everything we went through, just what's going to force me into using it? The sense of foreboding makes me shiver in fear.

A gentle knock sounds against the open doorway, and as I glance over, I see Smoke entering. I release a relieved breath as I scan him to make sure he's okay, and I see he's wearing a backpack and his cheeky smile. When I look closer, though, I realise he seems tense.

"There's someone here to see you."

His words freeze me in place for a few seconds. Nixon's calming presence immediately surrounds me, and I gratefully lean back against him, accepting the comfort he brings me. The others share looks as they pull on their backpacks, and I don't miss the glint of something metallic appearing in Blain's hand. We hadn't expected to fight our way out of here, and I don't think Regnor will order an attack on us, but given how our last interaction went, it's better to be safe.

When I look at Smoke again, he nods. If we were about to be attacked, he wouldn't have walked in here like this, he would have warned us. Hell, he wouldn't have let anyone get close enough to even try. So whoever is waiting for us outside doesn't mean us harm.

Releasing a sigh, I reach up and rub my temples to ease the tension headache that's developing there. The others look just as anxious, each of my guys showing it in their own way. Jesse is bouncing on the spot, full of nervous energy, while Blain and Xavier look like they are ready to murder someone. Alcide has the determined expression he always wears when he's deep in thought, and Rex is muttering to himself under his breath. Nixon, as always, has gone into protection mode, his arms around my waist as he holds me close to his body.

Knowing we can't stay in here forever, I untangle myself from Nixon's embrace and walk to the doorway. I smile at Smoke as I pass him, holding my head high and back straight. Climbing from the carriage, I find Marie waiting for us. I glance around to see if anyone else came with her, but she's alone. I feel the guys gathering closer around me, not trusting anyone now that we've had our marching orders. But this is Marie, I trust her. I slowly walk over, noticing her red eyes.

"Are you okay?" I ask by way of greeting. It's a stupid question, of course she isn't okay. She just watched her father be killed by her partner's order, yet I feel for her. I've always liked Marie, and even though I've not had the chance to get to know her well, I feel like we could have been friends under different circumstances.

"I've had better days," she replies, attempting to joke, but it falls flat. I watch as she nervously licks her lips. "I've come to say goodbye."

Does Regnor know she's here? Probably not, and I can't imagine he'd be pleased if he found out. He's made his opinion of us clear. I just worry what might happen to Marie now. Regnor made no attempt to shield her from the execution of her own father, and he's obviously going down a dangerous path. Last Stop should feel safe now that the tyrannical leaders have been killed, now that freaks can roam the streets freely, yet that's not the reality of it. Perhaps once things have settled it will be better, but the guys and I won't be here to see it.

"You could come with us." I already know she's going to say no, but she needs to know that she has a place with us if she needs it.

She shakes her head, her smile sad. "My place is here. Regnor might not admit it, but he needs me."

She's right. I dread to think how Regnor would be without Marie at his side as a calming influence—not to mention as a healer, she'll be needed in the city.

"I have a parting gift for you," she says, shaking me from my morbid thoughts.

Surprised, I hold my hands up. "You don't have to—"

"No, it's important you have this." Cutting me off, she steps closer and stretches out her hand. She waits for me to extend mine before opening her fingers. Something drops into my palm, and as I look down, I see it's a chess piece. A queen. "My father made this for me, it's the only thing I have left of him."

I open my mouth to protest. This feels wrong, I shouldn't be taking the only reminder of her father, but she cuts me off again.

"You should have it as a reminder of what you've done here." Her voice cracks as if she's overwhelmed, but she simply pushes on. "You saved us, and no matter the outcome, you should be proud of that. I know you don't approve of what was done to the masters, but you did what they didn't. You gave them a choice and a chance for a better life." She means every word she says, and it warms something inside me. "Times are changing and the world is adapting, don't get lost in that. Go and save others like you did us."

"Rhea," a familiar voice calls from behind Marie. She steps to the side with a surprised expression, revealing Gregor. It seems she's just as bewildered to see the maker here as we are. "I have a gift for you."

I'm shocked, but knowing what Gregor can do, I'd be a fool to turn down a gift from him. Glancing at the others behind me, I receive a mixture of nods and shrugs. I return my attention to Gregor and smile slightly. Walking closer, he holds out a wrapped package and sets it in my palms. I turn over the thin, slightly bendy package and reach for the tape to unwrap it, but a hand touches my arm, stopping me.

"Don't open this yet. You'll know when the time is right." His eyes seem to glaze over as he speaks, and I know he's seeing something that we can't.

His words echo what he said about the bracelet, and I get a twinge of unease. I'd been thinking about this earlier, and here he is giving me another unknown gift for later. Just what is waiting for us outside of the city gates that requires these mysterious gifts? Pushing that aside, I smile gratefully at him.

"Thank you, both of you."

"Rhea, we should leave," Alcide mutters from my side, and I turn to look up at him. He's frowning, and I know he's already forming a plan for when we leave the city.

"Your ringmaster is right," Marie agrees. "It would be best for you to depart while everyone celebrates. Your tent and remaining equipment have been packed up and left with your animals. Your carts have been stocked with supplies that should last you at least a week. I'm afraid your tent was quite badly damaged by the masters, and there wasn't much we could do to fix it."

I raise my eyebrows. They want us to leave that badly? I'm excited to see our animals again, since it's been so long since I've seen them properly, but it's overshadowed with worry. I hate that we're leaving here in secret, scurrying away while no one's looking, but we have to do what's best for all of us, and staying in Last Stop isn't that.

"Regnor thought it would be best for you to leave sooner rather than later," Marie explains. Her shoulders are tense as she speaks, confirming my suspicions that he wants us gone ASAP.

Alcide steps forward so he's standing at my side. "Thank you for seeing to our belongings. We will make our repairs ourselves. We've managed before, and we'll manage now."

Nodding, Marie turns her attention to Smoke, taking in his backpack and his place with me and the other guys.

"You're leaving?" she asks, but there's no accusation in her voice, only acceptance. She already knows the answer.

"Yeah, I don't think I'm welcome here anymore. You know, with voting against him and everything."

Marie doesn't bother to deny his comment, she simply walks towards him and embraces him. He stiffens in surprise, but quickly recovers and hugs her back. Releasing her from his embrace, he turns to Gregor and shakes hands with him, saying his goodbyes. My heart clenches in my chest as I watch him say farewell to his friends, wishing there was another way.

Marie and Gregor leave quickly after that. We're all silent for a moment until Smoke turns around and claps his hands together.

"Is everyone ready?" he asks, glancing at us and taking in our packs. "I'll take you to where the animals are being kept." Smoke starts to turn, but I stop him with a hand on his arm. He looks down at me with a question on his face, but that quickly turns to concern as he takes in my expression.

I have to inquire before he can ask what's wrong and I lose my nerve. "Are you sure this is what you want?" I feel sick even asking this, but the thought that he might only be coming with us because he doesn't feel like he has a choice makes me feel worse. I need to know that he's not going to regret coming with us. "Regnor will take you back if you—"

"Stop. I've made my choice." Closing the distance between us, he stops just a hairsbreadth from me, so close that I can feel his heat against my skin. My heart is pounding so hard it feels like it's going to jump right out of my body. "I choose a life where I feel like I can actually make a difference, and that's not here anymore. I choose a life outside of these walls. I choose you, Rhea." He cups my cheek, whispering his last words. Before I can open my mouth and say anything, he leans down and presses his lips to mine in a gentle kiss.

Heat roars through my body as I eagerly kiss him back, wrapping my arms around his neck to hold him closer. Relief and gratitude are quickly replaced by lust and the realisation of what I could have lost. Our kiss intensifies as if he can feel my need.

A pointed cough splits us apart, my cheeks flushing as I remember where we are. Smoke, however, just grins, not taking his eyes from my face.

"Can you make out later? We don't have time for this," Blain barks, and I know from glancing over that he's a little jealous.

It's only natural that someone's going to feel left out or jealous of the attention the others are getting when you have seven boyfriends, so I have to be careful. However, we'll soon get used to living together. At least I hope so.

"Jealous, Blainy? Want a kiss?" Jesse makes kissy noises and throws himself at Blain, wrapping his arms around him and puckering his lips.

Laughing, I watch as Blain curses and tries to untangle himself from our human pretzel. However, despite the expletives, he can't hide his smile. The others laugh and the mood lightens, and I know that Jesse did this on purpose.

With one last look at the now empty train carriage, I feel strangely sad. I know we need to move on, that our home is not a place but made up of the people around us, but there was a feeling of stability here. When we're back on the road, we will have all of the issues that travelling brings with it—places to stay, towns to entertain, the risk of being attacked between settlements. Not to mention I have no idea if any of our crew will be coming with us or are even still alive. I've seen flashes of them, but I know some died in the arena. Not fighting, not like us.

No, they were slaves.

Cleaners.

Turning back around, I find the guys waiting for me with expectant expressions. Releasing a shaky breath, I nod at no one in particular. "Okay, let's go."

We're silent as we walk through the tunnels. Smoke is in the lead with Rex close behind him. Rex is the only one of us who has spent much time with the animals since we've been down here. He's always been the closest to them, thanks to his gift, and honestly, I don't think he'd survive being separated from them completely. Watching them being forced to fight in the arena had almost killed him.

After the rebels rescued us, they freed the animals and moved them to one of the other tunnels. They said it wasn't safe for them to be around everyone else, and they were probably right. It was a tight fit with everyone sleeping at that particular platform. I can't wait to see them though, my heart flutters in my chest at the excitement.

Ahead, I think I see light beginning to break through the darkness and surprise fills me. I thought we were going to the tunnels where the animals were kept, not the surface. I'm about to ask Smoke where we're going when I start to hear them. A hiss from Bubbles and Rumple echoes through the tunnel, and then there's the heavy steps of Tiny moving around and the low rumbling growl of Fluffy. Rex starts to jog, knowing exactly where he's going. A crescendo of noise greets us as we round the corner and see all the animals. They rush over to greet us. Fluffy knocks me over and rubs his face against mine, purring so loudly he's vibrating. I hear a curse, and when I glance over, I see Blain being sat on by Tiny, but he still reaches up to pat the creature before trying to escape. Bubbles and Rumple slither towards me, wrapping its body around my legs. I fall to the ground with a laugh as they rest their large heads on my stomach, waiting for attention, while Fluffy rolls on the ground next to me.

I take my time greeting them all, cooing and whispering praises and apologising for being gone for so long. The others do the same. For a brief moment, I find myself surprised that the animals are greeting Smoke just as warmly as they are us. Catching my look, he grins and shrugs, telling me that this isn't the first time he's visited them. When I get a spare moment to myself, I realise why I saw light. At the end of the station that's been turned into the animals' home, there is an exit to the city. It's crumbled and looks like it's falling apart, but as I wander over, I can see sunlight streaming through the cracks.

"There's an exit just down there," Smoke says from my side, startling me. I press my hand to my chest to stop my heart from jumping out of my ribcage and raise an eyebrow at him. Grinning unapologetically, he points towards an alcove I hadn't seen before, but in the dim space, I can make out more cracks of light. "We had to put them someplace where we could get them in and out quickly, in case of an attack. We're much higher here than where we were based, and right at the edge of the city. I imagine your carts will be waiting just outside."

Nodding, I turn with the intention of looking for Alcide, but he's already walking over to me. He inclines his head at my questioning look, and I turn back to Smoke. "Will you show us how to get outside?"

Without saying anything, he holds out his hand in question. I place mine in his without hesitation, and his eyes seem to heat. Tugging gently, he leads us to the exit, moving pallets aside until we're standing outside. I breathe in the fresh air, air that's not tinged with the scent of blood and death. Our carts await us, and I can see the folded tent on the back of one of them. Nostalgia swells within me. Some of the best moments of my life happened with this circus. The last time we rode in these carts, we were entering the city with no idea what awaited us.

My eyes well with tears as I recognise some of the crew milling around the carts. Alcide immediately goes into ringmaster mode and strides forward to greet them with a big smile. We're still missing a lot of them, but it's good to see some of them survived.

Everything speeds up then as the animals are led outside and everyone helps pack up the boxes of supplies that have been left out for us. Before I know it, I'm sitting on one of the carts with Smoke and Xavier, my hand in theirs as we leave Last Stop. With a final glance over my shoulder, I take in the city. A cloud moves in front of the sun as I do, making the broken buildings look sinister. There were times I didn't think I'd ever leave this place, but now I am, with two new loves.

Releasing a pent-up breath, I turn forward and watch as the large city gates are pulled open, revealing the rest of the world. No, I won't look back anymore, but forward to our future together.

Watch out, world. Alcide's Circus is back on the road.

Chapter Three

We travel all day and most of the night to get away from Last Stop and its inky, dirty feeling. Even though the masters are dead, it's clear we all want to be as far away from it as possible, not just to escape what happened to us, but so we can relax without looking over our shoulders. I don't think Regnor would come after us, he just didn't want us in his city anymore, but after the events that led us to being imprisoned, we can never be too careful. That much is obvious, and now, every inch of the journey, each stop, is tainted by worry and eyes searching the horizon. The circus used to be a safe place, but now it's like every other ruined territory in this world—dangerous.

It saddens me to think that, but it's true. We used to feel free in our tent, and that's not the case now. We have to protect our family, including the two new men who have joined us on the way. I look at the cart they are riding in with Jesse, wondering if they want to hit him yet. I laugh at the thought, and that makes Rex look at me with a small smile.

"What?" I ask, my legs draped across his lap where he sits opposite me. Blain snores on my shoulder, cramped in the wooden walls of our cart.

"It's just nice to see you smile. For a while there, we lost it," he murmurs softly, massaging my calves. I close my eyes in bliss as my smile grows.

I meet his gaze. "I guess we did. I'm hoping we can all find our way back to the way we were," I reply.

"We can't. The past is the past for a reason, Wildcat, but it doesn't mean we can't make a new, better future," he states. I know he's right. I can never go back to the same Rhea before Last Stop. I carry more scars, both emotionally and physically. I'm different, stronger, but also more jaded. I don't know if that's a good thing or not, but he's right, I can't change that. This is who I am now, and we are all going to have to rediscover who we are after the masters' rot changed us.

"Shut the fuck up and sleep, Harpy, before I fill that mouth," Blain warns, his voice rough even as he brings me closer, cuddling me like a teddy bear. I can't help but laugh even as I force my eyes closed. As usual, he's right, but I won't tell him that, because within moments, I fall deeply asleep.

The soft lull of the carriages and the echoing, playful noises of our animals make me feel safe.

I feel right at home, and for the first time in a really long time, we are back.

We are somewhere I never thought we would be again.

We are free.

I WISH we could take some time off to rest, but we need to earn money to survive, so we stop at a town a few hundred miles away from Last Stop. For the first two days, Alcide works with the crew to patch the tent, letting us relax. We all pretty much sleep the days away, clearly needing the rest. We're a bit antsy to get back to work, to doing what we love, but I worry what has happened will colour our performance. Will we search the crowd? Will our last rebel performance have changed us as entertainers? I guess there's only one way to find out. We need to take the leap and have our first show.

Alcide clearly knows that and has it planned for tonight.

It's what we know, it's how we survive. We are the circus. It beats in our hearts in tones of red and cream like our big top. The cheer of crowds and the spotlights are all we have now, but as I get ready, my fingers linger on my outfit, wondering if I am just putting on another show for survival.

How is this different from what we were doing in Last Stop?

The answer is easy. This is our choice, but it doesn't quiet those whispering voices in the back of my head making me question everything.

My tent flap moves, and Alcide steps through in his ringmaster attire. This time, however, his hat is black, and on the back is the mark of the rebels. It's a nod to our past, to who we are and what we stand for now. I guess a lot has changed. He smiles at me as he approaches, wrapping his arms around me from behind as I stare at him in the mirror. We've done this so many times before, only now when I look at my reflection, my eyes are harder, older.

"You look beautiful." I drop my gaze and he turns me, cupping my cheeks. "No, *cariño*, I should have said you look strong."

"I don't feel it," I admit. "I have doubts. How is this different, Alcide? We perform because it's for survival, because it's what we know, so how are we different from the freaks in Last Stop?"

"Because we are free." He frowns.

"Are we really? Or are we chained to this circus the way they were chained to those tunnels? Knowing no better?" I ask, and his face drops as he thinks through my question, unable to offer an answer. I turn away and tug down my outfit. "Let's do this."

I see Alcide's worry as I perform. His eyes track me and my movements. Is what I asked resounding in him, or does he think I've finally been overwhelmed? Either is possible. My mind isn't on the performance, it doesn't need to be, I could do it in my sleep. The moves are familiar and sure, even the fake smile pursing my lips, but as I land, my arms spread wide and grin wider in the spotlight, I realise I don't enjoy this anymore.

Did the masters take that too?

Will I get it back? The exhilaration of performing? I hope so.

Either way, I force my smile to widen as everyone else comes out and we bow as the crowd surges to their feet, clapping and screaming. Flowers are thrown into the ring as we continue to bow and wave. I do my part, but I see the worried looks tossed my way. As Alcide gives his goodbye speech and we all stride from the ring, my eyes catch on four men standing to the side. I notice them because they aren't clapping or cheering. No, their faces are stern, and when I get closer, my heart hammering, they raise their arms so I can see the mark of the rebels.

I freeze, but they nod and then melt back into the crowd like they were never there, and Blain drags me backstage. "Harpy?" he demands, his hands cradling my face even as my eyes return to the closed curtain where Smoke pulls security. "What's wrong?"

"Nothing," I tell him and meet his gaze, smiling slightly. "Nothing. Come on, let's start getting packed up."

He nods, but his eyes are narrowed suspiciously, and he makes sure to stay close as I head back to my tent and get undressed. Alcide wants us back on the road tonight. It seems I'm not the only one feeling the pressure. We agreed never to stay in one place for too long.

By the time we are packed, the stars are shining brightly above us and most of the crew and my guys are snoring in the carts.

I stare out the window into the dark landscape, which stretches as far as the eye can see. Why did they do that? Why were the rebels there? Is it happening? Are they finally stepping out of the shadows across the world? If so, what does that mean for us? It will mean war, battles, and many, many deaths.

If so, do we fight?

Personally, I've had enough fighting to last a lifetime, but maybe that's not my choice anymore. My fingers catch on the bracelet on my wrist, and I twist it. Gregor predicted I will need help. Was it for this? To help some kind of freak uprising around the world? I'm no leader, and I'm not the great change. I'm just a freak slave girl from Cinders who happened to fall in love with some incredible men and tends to find herself in situations she has no choice but to step up in. I never wanted to lead anyone. The burden is too strong. Look what it did to Regnor. But will I even have a choice?

When we stop for the night and set up camp, I find myself staring at the horizon again, my arms wrapped around myself. I feel something in the air... change. I feel it, can almost taste it, and it makes my muscles clench.

With change comes sacrifice.

What will we lose this time?

Can we pay the price?

The cities and villages we passed come to mind, and I think back on what I saw. The differences were slight, but now as I analyse them, they become clear. Women fought back and said no, standing up for themselves. Freaks were not hiding any longer, and there was an upsurge in crimes and punishments. Is this really the end of the rebels' fight... or just the beginning?

My guys leave me to my thoughts, as if knowing I need the space to think, but Jesse brings me some food and sits with me silently until he heads to bed. Still, I sit and stare outside, questions running through my mind until I hear a grunt and a clang of something metal. I blink, the sounds bringing me out of my trance. I turn and search the area, but beyond our carts and diminishing campfire, there's no one. Standing with a frown, I stroll around the carts, and that's when I see Xavier. He's shirtless and without shoes, wearing only low-rise leather trousers. His face is locked in concentration, and his muscles clench as he practices with his sword. He glides through one slick move after another as he almost dances across the ground, fighting an imaginary foe. Spinning, he brings the sword down again and again until his chest is heaving and coated in sweat.

I can't help but stare, my breath catching in my throat like the first time I saw him. I follow the stark lines of his physique with my eyes, admiring the huge, bulging muscles in his arms and the deep ridges of his eight pack. The more I stare, the more heat builds within me, one I can't ignore—desire. It fills every fibre of my being, making me shiver in the warm air. He turns, freezing when he sees me.

"Rhea?" he asks, his eyebrows furrowing in worry. "Are you okay?"

"I couldn't sleep," I murmur, even as my gaze drops to his chest again, and then I jerk it up to see him smiling as he steps closer.

"Me either. I thought practicing might help." He looks down at his sword that hangs loosely at his side. "It's what I'm used to, I guess."

"Don't stop on my account," I tease, stepping closer. "I'm quite enjoying the show."

"Oh really?" He grins, flashing his white teeth at me. He prowls around me, dragging his sword through the dirt with a hiss. He's so close I can feel the heat pouring off him—from his powers or his body, I'm not sure. His breath stirs my hair as he stops behind me, grabbing my locks softly and moving it to one side as his mouth descends to my ear. Warm air caresses my ear as I feel his lips move against the sensitive lobe as he talks. "You know what I'd enjoy, baby? Having your body against mine as we spar." He darts his tongue out, licking the tip of my ear, and I can't help but gasp and lean back into him as he laughs and steps away. "It was the highlight of my day."

I turn, smirking, and step closer. "Even while you were supposed to be training me to keep us alive?"

"Even then it was the most fun I'd had ever... and it didn't hurt that you had all those curves pressed against me." He traces his teeth with his tongue as he runs his eyes over my body. He's acting brazen, as if with his freedom from the ring he's finally released all the pent-up desire I saw in his eyes and tasted on his lips. I almost choke on it, struggling to breathe over my own which rises with each look. I ache for him, for his touch and lips. "So what do you say, Rhea?" he asks, swinging his sword up in a sexy as hell movement, spinning the blade until it rests on his broad shoulder.

"Huh?"

"Want to relive the good times, but make them better? I promise not to keep my hands to myself." He grins.

"Good, so do I," I retort and then leap at him. As he ducks and spins to avoid me, he drops his sword so he doesn't hurt me, and I can't help but laugh. How did he know this is what I needed to feel in control again, to let out all my stress?

He swings his fist, not holding back. No, his punch is fast and full force, and if I didn't throw myself back into a roll, it would have connected with my face. As I spin and turn, my frown fades to a smile. My body loosens, and my heart pumps with both lust and excitement until I'm laughing as I whirl under his arm, spanking him as I move. He turns, shocked and frozen, and I smirk as I crouch.

"That's all you've got?" I purr. "You promised roaming hands, didn't you? I guess you'll have to catch me first."

"Oh, now you're getting it," he calls as he stands up and storms towards me.

"Promises, promises." I tilt my head and spin as he goes to grab me. I feint left, but he expects it after being the one to teach me the move in the first place. He wraps his arms around me and lifts me into the air, his teeth catching my ear lobe. I know I should be trying to escape, but I don't want to. He wouldn't let me get away with half-ass attempts, so I kick and buck until I can turn, and then I distract him. I lean in as if to kiss him, and he freezes, inhaling, and at the last minute, I swerve and bite his arm until he yelps and releases me. I drop to my feet and stumble back.

"You bit me." He laughs. "Oh, little Rhea, you have no idea what you've unleashed now."

It's my turn to yelp when I see the dark, predatory look in his eyes. I should fight, but I turn and start to run. Honestly, I don't want to fight, I want to be caught. In two strides, he captures me. He pulls me down to the ground, pressing my face into the dirt as he pins me there, blanketing me with his body.

"I've got you," he mumbles.

"And what do you plan to do to me?" I taunt, turning my head as if to give him better access, already feeling his hard, stiff cock pressing to my ass through our clothes. It seems he is as wound up as I am from our sparring and teasing, from all the time we have kept away from each other. Ever since the first moment I saw him covered in blood, I craved him, craved the chaos that fills his soul, and right now, I know he's going to show me exactly that and make me his.

He's going to claim me out here in the dirt, with my other men sleeping not a foot away. Sweat coats our bodies, and the stars shine above us.

"Everything," he replies, his voice rough as his hands hit the ground next to me, digging into the soil like he can't control himself. He's still holding back.

I lift my ass and push into him. It does the trick. He snarls like an animal, lifts me, turns, and slams me back to the earth. Before I can catch my breath, he yanks off my trousers and shirt, tossing them away.

I shiver as the air blows over my naked body, tightening my nipples as he groans. His eyes scan every inch of bare skin, from the tips of my heaving breasts to the hair between my clenched thighs as he straddles me, blocking out the stars. "You are fucking perfect," he murmurs, his tone soft with worship. "How the hell did this scarred, ruined warrior get so lucky? I don't even want to touch you or stain your perfect skin with these bloodstained hands."

He means it, I can see it, so I grab the closest hand and press it to my slamming heart. I hold it there as I stare into his dark eyes. "I want you to touch me. I couldn't think of a warrior more worthy to let into my body or my heart. You did what you had to in order to survive, but now it's time to live. Let me show you how." I wrap my legs around his waist and roll us again so I'm above him. I never would have done something so bold before, but now I know what I want, and I plan to take it.

His eyes widen, and his hands automatically go to my bare hips, gripping hard. I grind down on his hardness, rolling my hips as the pleasure takes over. I need to be touched and fucked. I need him inside of me more than I need my next breath. I'm done talking and it seems he is also, unsure what to say as I lean down and kiss him. I taste his desperation, his awe, and his hope.

I move against his cock, my clit throbbing as I imagine him inside me, imagine riding him right here under the stars. Gasping, I sit up and scoot back until I can reach for the tie of his trousers.

"I-I'm nervous," he admits, his cheeks turning red as he drops his head back to avoid my confused gaze.

I freeze and tilt my head. "Why?"

He blows out a breath, not looking at me. "I was taken as a boy, Rhea. I've never been with anyone I chose... only who they made me." My heart skips a beat, and he finally looks at me. "I've never wanted someone so badly in all my life. I knew it when I first saw you. Something started in me, desire, and the completely foreign feeling threw me off my game. I craved each touch, each gaze you threw my way like a dog looking for scraps. I-I want this to be good for you. You have so many other men—"

I lean down, kissing him, silencing him. "It will be good for me," I soothe. "How could it be anything but? And forget everything that came before, okay? You are here with me. Look into my eyes, feel my heart, and remember it's me. No one else. I'm your first, okay? And no matter what, I am honoured."

He groans, chasing my lips with his as he kisses me, and I unbuckle his pants. He helps me drag them off, and as I circle his huge, hard cock with my hand, he shivers. A moan escapes his lips and precum beads at the tip of his huge cock that's so big, I can't even close my fingers around him. He's also so long I don't know if he will even fit, but I want to try. God, do I want to try. I want to feel all that power inside of me, to see the weakness in his eyes he only shows me. I want to replace any other memories he has with me and show him how good it can be when it's consensual between people who care for one another. This is how it should have always been for him. I can't change what they did, but maybe I can show him true pleasure and love every day for the rest of his life.

I want to give him my body the way he deserves, my heart too, because there's no doubt this scarred warrior trembling beneath me has earned it.

Leaning down, I lick the tip of his leaking cock. He gasps and lifts his hips as he slams his eyes closed. I trace the veins down his length and back up until I can suck the tip again.

"Rhea," he begs.

"That's me," I purr. "Eyes on me, warrior."

He opens them instantly, watching me, and I grab his hand, ignoring his hesitation to touch me, and place it gently on my head. He holds my hair as I widen my lips and take more of his cock into my mouth. His eyes widen, and his mouth parts on a groan that makes me shiver with desire, my pussy clenching. He looks so amazed, so unsure that it makes me feel powerful. So even though I don't know if I can, I try to swallow all of him, dropping my mouth farther until it meets my hand at his base. I gag and quickly pull back.

"Oh God, don't stop," he pleads, desperate from just a touch of my mouth. His reaction is raw and honest and so wild, I can't help how wet I am. I can feel it dripping from my hot core, knowing this powerful warrior is submitting to me, trusting me after so many have hurt him. I want it to be perfect for him, so I keep going. Hollowing my cheeks, I bob my head up and down. His hips rise, pushing his huge cock deeper as if he can't help himself. His breathing quickens, and his hands clench into fists.

"Please, baby, I'm going to—fuck, don't. Please, I want to be inside of you when I come." He tugs me back, and I instantly pull my mouth off his cock, not wanting to take anything he isn't offering. He drops his head back and pants for a moment.

"Jesus, you're enough to kill a warrior with just one touch." He groans as his eyes meet mine. He strokes his fingers across my lips, pushing his thumb into my mouth as I suck on that, too, until his eyes narrow. Popping it free, he tucks my hair behind my ear, his wide, calloused hand dragging down the front of my throat, across my chest, and over my quivering belly to my hip. In one smooth move, he grabs my other hip and lifts me, dragging me up his body. I gasp as he positions me above his mouth until I feel his warm breath blowing across my pussy.

"I want to taste you. I have imagined it so many times even when I knew you weren't mine. I have to know," he begs, and then his lips close on me. He's clumsy at first, but so fucking good I can't stop him. My head falls back and my eyes close in bliss, my bare body poised above him as I start to move. I ride his mouth gently, back and forth, needing the friction, needing to come so badly.

His tongue darts out, lashing my clit, and when I moan in encouragement, he does it again until I cry out. His fingers dig in, holding me above him as I let him take over and control me with just his mouth, my knees spread on either side of his head. He drags his tongue down my pussy, circling my hole confidently, and groans when he tastes me. The muffled sound almost causes me to see stars as I grind down harder.

"Please, Xavier," I beg. "I can't hold on much longer." I whimper, close to coming just from tasting him and feeling his sweet, innocent mouth on my pussy. I know the need swelling within me is going to explode through my body, leaving me a heaving, shattered mess.

He laps at my hole, circling it teasingly. I'm just about to yell in frustration when he spears it inside of me. I cry out, the wind stealing the sound, as I freeze on top of him. I breathe heavily as he licks my pussy, fucking me with his tongue over and over before dragging it back to my clit. He wraps his lips around it and sucks, and I almost arch off his mouth as he lets go of my hip and moves his hand between my pussy and his mouth. Slowly, he pushes one finger inside of me, and then another. He stretches me like he did with his tongue, and then he pulls them out and pushes back in. He sets a hard, quick pace as he alternates between sucking and licking my clit until I'm a moaning, dripping mess, and when he finally adds another finger and hits that spot?

Well, my release surges through me, taking me by surprise. I clamp on his fingers as I cry out breathlessly, the pleasure pounding through my veins over and over until I can only ride it out. When the waves of pleasure start to abate, I feel weak and my muscles ache blissfully. He pulls his fingers free, and I slump as he gently laps at my fluttering pussy before he tugs me down so he can see me. His face is coated in my cream and his lips are red, and my breath catches at the sight.

"Fuck, I would die happily if I could do that every moment of the day."

"You won't hear me complaining," I croak, my voice hoarse from crying out. Laughing, I shake my head. "How can you be this amazing?" He might have helped lessen my desire, but as I stare into his smiling, proud eyes, it comes back with a vengeance, and I need him inside of me.

I crawl back down his body, kissing him to silence his protests as I position myself above his huge cock. Reaching down, I grip his length and slowly lower myself until his tip notches at my hole.

"Rhea," he breathes against my lips, still tasting of my release, and with one last kiss, I sit back and slowly drop onto him. Inch by inch, I work his huge cock into my dripping pussy. He helps by holding my hips, lifting and dropping me until he is finally buried inside me. He gives me a minute as I gasp, shivering at the full sensation. He stretches me so wide I can barely take it, and I have to move. He watches my hips as I ride him, bouncing on his dick. His heart hammers so hard I can feel it as I place my hands on his chest for leverage.

"Oh fuck." He groans. "You feel way too good, so fucking hot and wet."

Closing my eyes, I bite my lip to stop my moans, his words

making me clench around his cock, which in turn makes him groan out my name. I won't last long at this rate, but I want to make his first time perfect, so I focus past my own desire and concentrate on his.

Slowly, unsure at first, he starts to raise his hips to meet my thrusts until we work in tandem, finding a perfect pace. We are so used to moving together that it comes naturally, like we are one body. Our pleasure rolls through one to the other, our eyes remaining connected the entire time, like we can't look away. His hand covers mine, as if to remind himself who he's with and to ground him in the moment.

"I love you," he confesses breathlessly. It only spurs me on, unable to speak as I move faster, chasing another release. The wet sound of my pussy would be embarrassing if I wasn't so lost in my desire. "I do, Rhea. I love you, I love you."

"I love you too." The words slip free, but I mean them. I love him with every fibre of my being. I wouldn't be alive without him. He brought me back from the brink, and he gave me the tools to protect myself and my family. He trusted in me, fought by my side, and died for us. I love him. "I love you so much." I gasp as I rock and wind on his cock.

Grunting, he grabs my hips and takes over, slamming me down onto his huge cock. It almost feels like it grows inside of me. "I'm so close, I can't stop myself, you're just too—fuck, too much. Rhea, I need—"

"Come, baby," I order. "Come for me, I want to feel it."

He throws his head back, hitting the ground hard, his mouth clenched, his eyes narrowed and tight, and his jaw locked as he tries to hold back. I wind my hips faster and harder, chasing my own orgasm. It's close, even after he already made me come, but watching him fight his desire? Watching him beneath me? It's enough to send me over the edge, and as he bottoms out inside me, hitting that spot that makes my eyes cross, I finally let go. I tumble into another release with a cry, my pussy clenching on his cock, milking him.

He roars beneath me, arching his back as he comes, and I fall forward, holding on as he wraps his arms around me. He embraces me tight as he shivers, both of us panting through our releases and aftershocks. When I can finally open my eyes, I roll my head back to meet his gaze, and I see his flutter open with a hazy, astonished expression before they meet mine.

"I love you," he murmurs and kisses me, swallowing my own promise.

We lie under the stars wrapped in each other's arms until our hearts finally slow and the sweat on our bodies cools, and then he laughs and looks at me.

"We're doing that again."

I can't help but squeal as he flips us, pinning me to the ground, and his mouth descends on mine.

Oh hell yes.

Chapter Four

I'd forgotten how brown the world is. While trapped in Last Stop, we hadn't been able to see anything beyond the huge stone walls that were designed to protect us from the dangers beyond. Little did we know that when we arrived, the real evil was waiting for us inside, like a spider pulling us into his trap, and once there, there was no escape.

Only we did escape. I have to keep telling myself that.

Sitting at the front of the cart with a silent Nixon at my side, I watch the landscape. The barren, dying land we travel through looks just the same as it did in the previous town. It's just another example of how humans fucked up this world. I wasn't alive before everything went to shit, but I've heard tales of how the land used to be green and alive, full of life, with so many creatures that don't exist anymore. It's a shame. I would have loved to see it like that, but there's no point in wasting time on wishing for something that can never be. Honestly, I can't even imagine a world that's green and lush, with fresh water flowing through the land. Here, the water that lies in the ponds is more likely to kill you than quench your thirst.

We've been travelling for a couple of days now, and we're on our way to the next cluster of towns, but Alcide tells me it's a long way, and we'll have to stop at the nearest town to restock supplies and let the animals stretch their legs. Since our first show, all of the others have gone off without a hitch. The towns all look the same, with old buildings from before and unsteady-looking wooden houses. Other than a few disgusted looks, which we're used to, there have been no problems and we have been welcomed.

"Are you okay?" Nixon mumbles, rubbing my arm soothingly.

"Yeah, just lost in my thoughts." Smiling up at him, I hope to wipe the concerned look from his face, but it doesn't work. As usual, Nixon sees right through me. Sighing, I gaze out at the passing landscape. "Everything just feels different now, you know?"

I used to be happy with this life, travelling with my guys from town to town, entertaining, but now it just feels... empty.

Humming his agreement, Nixon pulls me closer, his body making me feel safe and protected. I soak up the moment. This is something I missed. Not the hours and hours of travelling, but the time I can spend with the guys without having to worry that we'll be separated again. Sure, we have to be careful of raiders, but we've not seen any since we left Last Stop. Even if we did, there are more of us, so I doubt they would try their luck against such odds.

And so we continue on our journey. Eventually I have to move inside the cart to avoid the burning light as the sun rises higher in the sky. Swaying from side to side with Jesse on one side of me and Nixon on the other, I quickly start to fall asleep.

The lurching of the cart wakes me. My head snaps up and my heart pounds as I look around to find the cause of the sudden stop. Glancing out the windows, I can't see anything that would cause us to pause, but all of the other carts have stopped too.

"Why are we stopping?" I mutter, watching Alcide jump from the carriage and stride towards us. Throwing open the door, I jump down onto the dusty ground. "Is everything okay?" I run my eyes over my ringmaster. He looks tense, but he is trying to hide it with his crowd pleasing smile.

"We're going to stop here for a bit."

Frowning at his explanation, I step closer and keep my voice low, not wanting to question him in front of the crew. "What about the town?" I examine his face for clues. "We're almost out of supplies." We're so close to the town it seems senseless to stop here in the middle of nowhere when we could just continue on. We'll only have to stop again to pick up the essentials, so what's the real reason behind this?

Sighing, he places a hand on my shoulder and walks with me to the cart I was riding in, away from the rest of the crew. My guys see and make their way over to join us. Once we're all together, Alcide glances around to make sure no one else can overhear us. "I don't want to stop in the town. I've got the strangest feeling, but you shouldn't go there, Rhea."

My skin tingles at his words, like a premonition. For some reason, I know he's right. This brings up a pressing question though. "What are we going to do about supplies?"

His face is tight with anxiety. "I'm going with some of the crew to pick up what we need. It's not far. We'll get what we need and come straight back."

Wait. If it's not safe for me, why would it be any better for them? I'm already shaking my head before he's even finished his sentence. "Is that a good idea? If you've got a bad feeling, maybe we should push on..." I trail off. We all know we won't last much farther without water. A group of us this big goes through a lot of food and water. We manage the way we do because we usually stop regularly in each town we pass. However, because we've been trying to put as much distance between us and Last Stop as possible, we've gone farther between shows than usual.

"No, he's right, Rhea," Xavier speaks up, meeting my gaze before turning to Alcide. "I'll go with you just in case."

I know why Xavier volunteered. As well as keeping Alcide safe, he wants to make himself useful and earn his place here. He already has, and I've told him that, but fighting and working for his next meal is all he knows. He's settled amongst us amazingly well, but it will take time.

"I'd appreciate that." Alcide reaches out and claps him on the shoulder. Feeling my burning gaze on his face, he turns to me. "We'll be fine, *cariño*. We'll be back before you know it."

Closing the remaining distance between us, I fist my hand in his shirt and pull him down until my lips lock with his. His surprised grunt makes me want to smile, but he returns the kiss. Reluctantly, I release him and meet his gaze.

"Hurry back," I whisper, my breath ragged.

He winks at me in answer, cupping my cheek for a lingering moment before turning and clapping his hands, calling everyone together. He quickly explains the plan, gathering a group of volunteers to head into town with him. Soon enough, they are all sitting on a cart and disappearing in the distance, leaving me to watch them grow smaller and smaller even as my worry increases with each moment they are away from me.

It feels strange not to have Xavier and Alcide with us, like I'm missing a limb. I can't help but worry about them, especially after my ringmaster's strange *feeling* about it being a dangerous place for me. It's a dangerous place for a woman anywhere on Earth.

Trying to keep myself busy, I spend some time with the animals. They always know how to cheer me up, but as time passes, even they can't ease my concerns. The guys try to keep me entertained and I appreciate the gesture, but I just can't focus. Standing with Jesse and Rex, I stare at our little makeshift camp. Some of the crew have set up chairs and are playing card games together, making the most of the time.

Glancing in the direction Alcide and Xavier went, I still see nothing. It's been hours now, and I'm starting to worry. I can tell the others are, too, by the stiffness in their postures as they attempt to look casual, leaning against the wagons.

"I'm going to go sit in the shade." Smiling distractedly at the guys, I wander over to a large rock that we've parked next to. The guys can clearly see me from here, so they don't put up a fight, giving me the space I need. Thanks to the size of the boulder, it provides enough shade for me when I sit down. It's so damn hot here, and that doesn't help with the rising tension as we wait for everyone to return.

Leaning my head back, I stretch out my legs and rest my hands on the dusty ground. My mind wanders as I stare at the dry landscape. We could be anywhere. It all looks the same thanks to the damage that ravaged our world. I remember my earlier thoughts of how the Earth must have been before, with greenery everywhere. Absentmindedly, I dig my fingers into the dirt as I close my eyes and imagine we are there now. Everything would be different if we lived in a world like that, where we didn't have to fight for clean, uncontaminated water. Where we could grow food on fertile land and let our cattle graze on the grass. People wouldn't need to watch each other with suspicious eyes.

My body tingles as my thoughts drift, and when my fingers brush over something smooth, I force my eyes open. A gasp escapes me as I stare down at my hand. No, not my hand, but the stalks of grass that are growing between my fingers as I watch. Lifting my gaze, I see a semi-circle of quickly growing greenery with me as its epicentre. Did I do this? I must have, there's no other reason plants would spontaneously grow where I happen to be sitting—especially considering what I was thinking about the exact moment they started to grow. My powers have been increasing, and this isn't the first time I've grown plants to help me, but that was when I needed to defend myself. This is something entirely different.

I look for the guys, wanting to show them what just happened. Only I can't see them. No, wait, I see Jesse's back. He's looking at something. The others must be with him, distracted by something. That's the only reason they would let me out of their sight. Hope blooms in me. Perhaps Alcide and Xavier have returned, and that's what they are looking at!

Pulling my feet towards me, I start to get up when I spot a dark shape moving among the carriages, heading towards the guys' unprotected backs. What is that? It moves again, and I realise it's a person. I open my mouth to warn them, but I'm stopped as something is shoved over my face. I immediately start kicking, trying to scream and dislodge the cloth from my mouth, but arms band around me, keeping me still. My nose burns from whatever's on the cloth, and my vision starts to go blurry. My body tries to react to protect me, making my skin hot and burning anyone who touches me, but it's not quick enough. They caught me by surprise. I hear them curse, but I can't hold the power any longer, and I become limp against the stranger holding me.

No, this can't be happening!

We just got free, and now someone thinks they can take that away from us again. Are they just after me, or attacking the whole circus? Did Alcide and Xavier get caught by them too? Was this the bad feeling we all had?

Who are they?

Why us?

As my body gives up completely, I have to hold onto the hope that they might be free, and if they are, they will come for me.

They will come for me.

The last thing I hear is Nixon's animalistic roar before the world goes dark.

Chapter Five

My head feels like there's a vice clamped around it, squeezing tightly. My ears are ringing, and it even feels like my body is spinning so much that bile claws at my throat. I try to force my eyes open, to move, to be sick, but I can't. My body doesn't respond, remaining unmoving on something soft.

What happened? Did I drink too much?

I search through my memories, which seem hazy. I remember sparring with Xavier. I remember stopping—

Oh fuck.

Panic and terror surge through me, burning away whatever drug they pumped through my system. My powers try to rise to help, but they seem contained under my skin. There's a crawling, almost painful feeling, one I have felt before... in the fights.

But it can't be, the masters are dead.

So who has taken me and why?

There's only one way to find out. I force my eyes open and blink through the haze, even as my anger makes me tighten my still weak fists. I am so sick of being kidnapped. This time, I won't just sit here like a good little girl.

They messed with the wrong family. My men will come for me.

I need to know as much as I can, like where I'm being kept, the layout, who is behind it, and their weaknesses. So I force myself to sit up and look around, to store every single smell, touch, taste, and sight. My survival instinct is kicking in. Before, I would have cried and hid, but the new Rhea? She's mad, and she wants to be free, no matter what it takes.

I've been captive before, never again.

I'm sitting on a silver metal shelf that is bolted to the wall on my right. Reaching out, I test the bolts until my fingers almost bleed and my nails break. I give it up with a sigh, dropping my hands to the soft but thin blanket on the metal shelf. Other than a single pillow, that's all there is. Sliding my legs over the edge, I find my feet bare, and there are no shoes in sight. That's when I realise my clothes have also been changed. A shiver goes through me at the violation, at the thought of them stripping me and dressing me while I was passed out.

Discreetly, I reach under the thin, loose, scratchy white material that hangs down to my ankles—it is almost like an old hospital gown—to make sure that's all they did, but I can't find anything else. Wanting to be extra sure, I turn to the wall and look down the top of gown. This way if anyone comes, they won't see anything. Even if they already have, I don't like the idea of giving them a free show. My underwear and bra are gone, and as I feel across my chest, my fingers catch on the edge of the collar wrapped around my throat.

With a panicked mewl, I trace the rough, cold metal that encircles all of my neck. It's the same as the one the masters used, but smoother and wider. It's a nullifier like before. Are they in league with them? Who are these people?

More determined, I drop my hand even though I want to claw at it—I know it won't do any good. It does more than keep my powers at bay, it keeps me prisoner, and nothing I can do will break it—*yet*.

Turning back to the room, I try to control my panicked breathing and slow my racing heart. Once I can breathe normally again, I put my feet down on the cold concrete floor and wiggle my toes and test my legs to see if I can stand. I still feel weak, but nowhere near as bad as when I first woke up.

Pushing up, I force myself to stand, holding onto the bed as my body tries to collapse. I drag my gaze around the room, scanning the small space I'm in. Bar the cot, there isn't much else. There's a silver toilet in the corner attached to the wall with a small shelf above it and a sink to the left. No mirror. The floor itself is grey concrete and cold, as are the walls. To my right is a huge, hulking metal door, and although I know it's useless, I slowly make my way over and twist the handle—yep, locked. Putting my back to it, I blow out a breath and try to think of a way out.

There is a buzzing, bright overhead white light, no windows, and no cracks. There is nothing but a door, so I can't escape my cell, which means I'll need to flee when they either come in or take me out. That means I need to be prepared.

I need to work on strengthening my body and fighting off this weakness so I will be prepared to take the chance when I get it. No hesitation, no worries. I refuse to sit and wallow. I could let my panic overwhelm me, I could sit and worry about my men, about what they want from me, but I can't. Not if I want to survive. So ignoring my screaming brain, I push off from the door and stretch my legs. I walk across the room. It takes a long time, and when I touch the opposite wall, my legs are shaking, but I turn back and do it again and again, speeding up each time until I can jog and then run.

Once my legs are stronger and stop shaking, I do jumps and push-ups, getting my heart pumping and brain working until I am loose and ready for when they come for me.

THEY DON'T COME for what feels like hours, but I wouldn't know, since there's no way to tell time. There's no clock, no window to see the sun or the moon, just grey walls. I don't let myself sit. I drink some water from the tap and keep my body on edge so when the door cracks open, I pounce.

The air hisses in, but I ignore it, quickly scanning the three men standing there in all black—guards. That split second is all I need. I launch myself at the first, taking him down and bringing my elbow into his face twice. The first breaks his nose, and the second knocks him out. When I jerk my head up, the second one is swearing and reaching for a needle at his hip. If he grabs that, it's game over, so like a feral animal, I latch onto him, riding him down to the floor, and grip his squat face. I smash his head into the floor until he groans and is knocked out. The third... he's too quick, and he uses my distraction.

I feel a pinprick on my shoulder and whirl to see him backing off with a needle in his hand and a smirk on his pale face.

"You bastard," I slur as whatever drug he used quickly takes hold, making me sluggish. No! I need to move! But the faster my heart pumps in panic and adrenaline, the quicker the drug pulls me under. I stumble to my feet, and instead of throwing myself at him like I wanted, I fall into him.

He easily catches me with his hands under my armpits and hoists me up. With a disgusted look at the others, he hauls me past them. "Try to escape again, I'd love to be able to punish you." He laughs, squeezing my breast before continuing to drag me. I whimper as I try to thrash, but I only manage to move my toes, my legs dragging behind me as I hang limply in his grip.

Knowing I won't get free, I relax, saving my strength and letting the drug pump through my system, hoping it won't take long to wear off. I need to be awake for wherever he is taking me. I focus on the layout, the turns we take, and the corridors. I commit doors and the black stencilled numbers on each wall to memory, even noting the moving cameras I spot in the corners of hallways. We must only walk for around fifteen minutes before we turn another corner.

This corridor feels different. To the left is a huge window, allowing me to see into the room beyond, which seems to take up the entire wing before ending in a dead end. My blood runs cold at what I see, and when he drags me to the double doors and they slide open with a hiss, I begin to fight again. He ignores me, pulling me through, and the doors shut behind him. The temperature drops as we wait in a small room between the corridor and the next room. With a ding, the other doors open, and I'm pulled inside.

Goosebumps rise on my skin, the hair on my neck stands on end, and a shiver goes through my once overheated, drug-addled body.

I struggle, and a strange whine leaves my throat. I'm unable to form words, as if the drug has frozen my vocal cords.

The room is huge, cold, and clinical. Bright lights shine above, and cupboards and fridges run all along the back wall, with a desk to the right and another closed door. It's the middle of the room, however, that makes me want to scream. Metal tables are placed in a line, with bright, standing lights above them. Lying on them, in shackles, are my men. I see the moment they spot me. They try to fight, their mouths gagged. I barely get a moment to assure myself they are okay before I'm turned and hoisted onto the last free metal bed. I try to sit up, knowing my men can't help me. No, I need to get us out. But I only manage to weakly slap the guard's hands as he roughly pushes me down. He grabs my hands and feet and yanks them until they stick out at awkward angles, and then he steps back with a sick grin.

Luckily the drug seems to be wearing off, but not fast enough. Clamps come over my ankles and hands, locking into place. With a snarl, I test them. No give. Fuck. I'm trapped in a bloody laboratory for experiments.

"Good luck. I hope you fail so I can have my fun," he hisses as he leans down and licks my face, making me twist my head away as my men cry out behind their gags.

"Enough. You can leave," a strong, cold male voice commands.

Between one heartbeat and the next, the guard straightens and his face becomes empty. He nods at whoever it is and leaves. I hear the door hissing as he departs. I try to crane my neck to see, but it's useless. I can only hear him moving around, the clatter of vials and cupboards shutting before I hear him come closer.

"Do not move. I would hate to ruin a perfectly good specimen," he orders as he suddenly towers above me. My eyes widen, and fear stops my heart. I hear the others yelling, fighting, but it's no use. We are all trapped and at the whim... of a doctor. His short grey hair is almost silver in the light, and crow's feet bracket deep brown eyes on a leathery, tanned face. His lips are thin and crooked, and his face is almost gaunt, but his tall, willowy body is encased in a pristine white coat with the label 'Doctor Sun' on it. Ironic?

I flinch when a needle presses to the crook of my arm, and he narrows his eyes. "Be still," he barks. I do, not wanting to injure myself. Instead, I'm forced to watch as he takes four vials of my blood. When he moves away, I close my eyes and slump.

But then my gown is ripped up from the side, exposing my stomach and breasts. A strangled cry escapes my lips, but he doesn't seem to even notice my exposed chest as he squirts something cold on my stomach and then presses a machine to it, looking at a screen. I can't see for a few minutes before he takes it away and covers me again. I hear him talking to himself as I shake on the table, wondering what he's going to do to me next.

Why is this happening? This isn't like the masters. Who is this doctor?

"Finally!" He claps and then rushes over, wearing the first smile I've seen on his serious face. In fact, it's more unnerving than the cold, detached look he had before. "You're fertile, and more than that, your womb is in excellent condition."

"What?" I gasp, the word garbled.

He turns slightly, and that's when I see the other door is open. In the room beyond, in tiny cages like animals, are crying women. "All of them have failed so far. We are doing further tests, but you... you are in excellent condition. The perfect specimen—strong, healthy, no diseases. It's like your freak powers have given you the perfect body for what we need. I tried to explain that to them, but did they listen? No, and all these weak, watered-down freak women have been useless. Never mind. You're here now, just like the masters said, and you are marvellous." Leaning down, he strokes my stomach.

"What are you going to do to me?" I demand, even as a sick feeling starts building in my stomach. I know what they are going to do to me, and I won't like it.

The doctor leans in with an evil sneer. "This is where we will watch you as you make the future, as you make us a freak child—or children, as many as we need. You are to be our cattle. I shall call you Specimen A."

Oh God.

I'm to be a breeding machine.

Chapter Six

After that revelation, I feel numb. Of all of the atrocities and hardships I've been through, this feels the most invasive. I've been forced to fight for my life as entertainment, been a slave and treated like I'm less than nothing, yet to be used as a broodmare... My brain seems to shut down, and as the doctor continues to examine me with glee, I'm emotionless, barely feeling whatever he injects into my arm. I can hear the guys shouting from behind their gags, but hopelessness settles over me.

The one thing that was getting me through when I was in my cell earlier was the hope that at least one of the guys was free, that they were coming for me, but no. My head falls to one side, and I see all of them looking towards me with various states of concern and fury etched into their features. Whatever they see in my expression must be bad, as there is a noticeable change to their moods. Rex is strapped to the table closest to me, his eyes begging for me to fight, to smile, to do *something,* but my fight has drained out of me, and the horror of what's to come consumes my mind.

I thought I had endured the worst of humanity, but I was wrong.

Eventually, I'm unshackled from the table and phantom arms heave me up into a standing position. My legs immediately give way, since whatever they drugged me with is still affecting me. Two guards grab me roughly under my arms, abruptly stopping my tumble to the ground, and yank me upright. I didn't even see the guards enter, and somewhere in my hazy, frightened mind, I know that's bad. The third guard is the one from before. His sneering face and dark eyes practically exude violence. He wants me to misbehave, to try and escape again so he can punish me, but he's in for disappointment.

I take a moment to run my eyes over the guys. I notice that the only one who seems calm is Xavier. His expression is dark and resigned, like he thought it was only a matter of time before his happiness was taken away. That sparks something within me, a small ember of anger deep in my soul. It's not enough to burn through the numbness that's taken over me, but it's something I won't be able to forget.

As soon as the guards start to drag me from the room, Nixon begins roaring. That breaks through my stupor, and I summon up the energy to glance over my shoulder. Tears sting my eyes as I see him straining against his bindings. His face seems to get redder and redder, his fists balling at his sides as he shouts through his gag. The doctor yells something, and I see several guards rushing forward, the glint of a needle flashing under the artificial lights. I watch as I'm dragged past the window, Nixon's eyes on me the whole time, and as I'm taken out of his sight his bellow echoes in the corridor behind me.

As I'm taken away, I have a vague sense of which corridors we're using, but my mind is elsewhere. They are going to *breed* me like an animal. I've fought off men who tried to take what I'm not willing to give before, but this... this is entirely different. They are going to use me over and over again until I produce a baby for them. And once I do, the process will begin again. When will they let me go? When I'm old and used up and unable to give them what they want?

The guards take a sharp left turn, knocking my ankle against the wall. I suck in a breath through gritted teeth, and the pain sharpens my mind enough for me to realise we're not going back to the room I woke up in. Where are they taking me? I should feel fear, but my head is pounding, probably from a mixture of stress and drugs. The third guard is walking behind us, but as we come to a stop, he walks past us, pressing his hand against something in the wall to my left. A door opens, and he steps back with a cruel grin.

"Your room awaits." He smirks, gesturing to the now open doorway.

The guards drag me inside, let go of me, and quickly back from the room, slamming the door and sliding the locks into place. The smell of bleach burns my nose, like it's recently been cleaned in here. Glancing around, I see the room is very similar to the first one I'd been in. The metal bed is a little larger, covered in a blanket, and has a single pillow waiting at the top. The concrete walls and floors look the same, and to my right I see a small room with a toilet and sink. Something feels different though, and I can't quite place it. It's almost like the lighting is different, but when I glance at the ceiling, I see it's the same artificial lighting as before. Slowly, I push to my feet, testing my balance before stumbling over to the bed. It's only as I turn to sit when I see the difference. A large rectangular window takes up most of the far wall, and I see the grinning faces of the guards.

Dread settles within me. So not only am I going to be forced to breed, but they are going to take away every scrap of my dignity by watching the whole dirty act. Turning my face away, I take deep breaths as I try to settle myself, my anger simmering within me.

Thankfully, after a few minutes, the guards leave and I'm left alone. I'm sure that won't last for long, but as I curl up on the hard metal bed, I try not to think about the horrors of what awaits me. I attempt to focus on this moment rather than what is to come. It's the only way I will survive—one minute at a time.

A question has been twisting inside my mind, one I've been trying to ignore, but it's getting louder and louder, refusing to be overlooked any longer. Who are they going to force me to have sex with? I heard stories of doctors who used to be able to make babies inside test tubes, which seems crazy, but seeing the laboratory setup they have here, it's not outside of the realm of possibilities. However, they obviously have my guys and have flaunted that in my face, so it would make sense that they plan to use them. I love them all and regularly have sex with them, but to be forced to do it at the whim of this doctor, all to create a baby, is something that twists my stomach. I feel sick. Another thought flashes through my mind. What if it's not the guys they want to breed me with? The idea that I might be forced to do it with someone else...

Nausea rolls through me, and I only just get to my feet and stumble to the toilet before I vomit up the meagre contents of my stomach. From the comment the guard made as he dragged me to the lab, it's obvious what he meant by punishments. Being raped by him or anyone else would break me, just like the caged, broken women I saw in the lab. I have no doubt that any baby I have will be taken away, and although I've never had this conversation with the guys, I couldn't let my child be taken from me. Even just the idea of it... rage boils in my gut. I don't know if any of the guys even want children, but they would agree with me no matter who the father was.

Something snaps inside me. No. Fuck them. I won't let a single one of them touch me in that way, and I'll die before I let that happen. I'm no longer someone who can be pushed around, beaten, and treated like dirt.

I had a moment of weakness, letting the fear consume me, but it's over now.

Brushing my hair from my face, I push up from where I'm curled around the toilet. Walking to the basin, I calmly wash my hands. To anyone watching, they might think I've resigned myself to my fate here, but they would be wrong. I'm plotting their demise. I might not be strong enough to escape now, but I'll find a way. I won't sit around and wait for the guys to rescue me. This time, I'll rescue them.

A commotion outside the cell catches my attention, and I turn to leave the bathroom just as someone is shoved into the room. The door is slammed shut immediately, but I'm too focused on the male before me.

"Jesse," I whisper, my heart flipping in my chest.

Stumbling towards him on shaky legs, I meet him halfway as he crashes into me, his arms wrapping tightly around my torso. Suddenly I find I can breathe a bit easier, knowing that at least one of my guys is okay.

Pulling back, he places his hands on my shoulders as he scans me from head to toe, concern radiating from him. "Rhea, are you okay? I was so worried."

"I'm fine, a little dizzy from the drugs, but fine." I wave off his concern, it's my turn to assess him. "Are you okay? Did you see where the other guys were taken?"

Jesse grimaces a little, making my heart rate speed up in anticipation. "After they took you away, they knocked Nixon out, but not before he scared the crap out of them." Laughing without any humour, he shakes his head. "I think they thought he was going to break out of the restraints."

I can only imagine how bad Nixon got when I was taken from sight, and if anyone could break solid metal, it would be Nixon. Even without his powers, he's still the strongest man I've ever met.

"Then, one by one, they took us away. We're being kept in rooms next to each other. I can sometimes hear them through the wall," Jesse continues, his usually cheerful face grim. "But instead of taking me back to my room, they brought me here." He glances up at the window, then to the bed, and then back to me. "Do you think—"

I'm pretty sure I know what he's going to ask, but he's cut off before he has the chance to fully voice his question. A high-pitched buzzing noise slashes through the room, making us both flinch.

"Specimen One and Male Four, you have been paired together to breed. Neither of you will be permitted to leave this room until coitus has been achieved."

"Fuck you," I shout at the doctor. I probably shouldn't antagonise him, but the anger inside me is burning so brightly, I feel like I'm about to combust. None of this feels real. Is this seriously happening to us right now? Who does this guy think he is?

"Rhea," Jesse calls softly, his hand on my arm pulling my attention away from the doctor behind the glass wall.

My brows shoot up as I take in his expression. Is he suggesting that we follow their orders? "You want to fuck in front of these—" I cut myself off, not having a name for the psychopaths that have caught us.

Shaking his head, he steps closer, closing the gap between us. "No, of course not. I just don't think we should antagonise them." Holding out his free hand, he turns his back to the glass wall. "Come here."

I've never been able to resist Jesse, his happiness and enthusiasm for life like a beacon to my damaged soul. My hard expression drops, and I take his hand, which he uses to pull me into his embrace. Laying my head on his shoulder, I lean against him, letting his comforting scent surround me. I can still feel the doctor's assessing gaze behind us like a laser against my skin, but I try to push him to the back of my mind.

"We'll get out of here," I promise in a low whisper.

"I know." He strokes calming circles on my back, but I can hear the tension that he's trying to hide in his voice.

He's lying.

THAT NIGHT we snuggle on the bed, sharing the pillow and looking into each other's eyes, whispering reassurances. We're not bothered by anyone, but we are aware of the constant presence of someone watching on the other side of the window. We don't make love, although I would have liked to. This is the first time I've really had a chance to be with Jesse since he died in the ring. We have been together as a group since, and with his arms around me now... I feel desire filling me, to prove he's okay, to assure myself he's truly back.

Despite him now being alive and well in front of me, I still have nightmares of the moment I watched him die.

The lights have been dimmed—the only thing that tells me the sun must have set. It's impossible to tell the time otherwise. I'm currently lying with my back pressed against his chest, his hand resting lightly on my stomach. Sleep evades me as my mind spins. I go over everything that's happened since I woke up, but my thoughts keep stopping on something the doctor said. I was too terrified about what he was going to do at the time to really take it in, but now it lights a fire within me.

"No, and all these weak, watered-down freak women have been useless. Never mind. You're here now, just like the masters said, and you are marvellous."

He knew about us. The masters told them about us, about *me*. And not only that, but it sounds like they have been sending him other freaks to try to breed. Were the masters going to just get the most out of me in the ring until I was broken and couldn't fight anymore before sending me here? I had wondered why I didn't see any female fighters in the arena, and now I know why. If they weren't already dead, I would want to tie the nooses around their necks myself. Their atrocities just seem to keep growing.

Trying to pull my thoughts from the masters and their sick games, I focus on my breathing, trying to settle myself so I don't disturb Jesse, although I'm pretty sure he's not asleep either. My mind wanders to the guys, but the pain of being separated and unable to see if they are okay rips through me so fiercely that I gasp with the agony of it. I'm determined to see them again, but I'm so tired of living this way, never knowing if we're going to live to see the next day.

We just can't seem to catch a break. Every time we're happy and think we're free, we're attacked or taken hostage. This has happened repeatedly now. They are always different faces, but the hatred and greed in their expressions is always the same.

Perhaps fate is trying to tell us something.

"Jesse, do you believe in fate?" I ask softly. His light, steady breaths tell me he's awake, and as his hand tightens around me, I wait for his response. I'm not left waiting long.

"I believe that fate brought you to us," he whispers, pressing a kiss against the back of my neck.

"Ever since I joined the circus, we've been attacked and hurt." My voice chokes off as images of the last year flash through my mind. Previously, the happy times outweighed the bad, but these things just keep happening to us. "Maybe the universe is trying to tell us that we shouldn't be together."

There's a heavy pause, and Jesse's hand stills on my stomach. My heart pounds in my chest as I wait for his answer.

"Rhea, turn around." I've never heard his voice sound so authoritative before, and I'm turning on the metal slab before I even realise I'm doing it. I can only just make out his expression in the dim lighting, but I see his frown. "Do you really believe that? That we shouldn't be together?"

"No." My answer is quick and firm. I truly believe that we're supposed to be together, these guys are my family, but I can't deny the events that keep happening to us. "But we seem to escape one form of captivity only to walk into another trap."

"We're freaks, Rhea. People don't understand us, and they seek to control us because of their own sense of fear and inadequacy." Reaching out, he rests one hand over my waist, holding me close, and the other gently grasps my chin, keeping my gaze on him. "We were attacked and persecuted long before we met you, and we will continue to be, but you have changed us all for the better." His eyes are almost glowing with his passion. "Things are changing, Rhea, for the better. We will survive this, just as we did with the masters."

I don't know how he can still be so positive after everything that's happened. Sure, we're a group of survivors, but he's wrong on one point.

"But you didn't, Jesse. You died, I watched it." My heart feels like it's breaking from just mentioning when he was stabbed through the chest. I thought I'd never see him again, but miraculously, the rebels managed to save him. My eyes sting as I try to fight back tears.

Jesse's face softens as he presses his forehead against mine. "But I came back. Nothing is going to take me away from you or the others. You're an integral part of me now, Rhea. Our souls are entwined. If we die, we go together."

The tears I've been trying to hold back finally fall, creating tracks down my cheeks. Slowly, Jesse leans forward and kisses my cheek, catching the tears against his lips. His mouth works down until our lips meet in a gentle kiss, the salty taste of my tears hitting my tongue. Our kiss becomes more passionate as I respond in turn, and I wrap one of my arms around him and hold him close. I slip my other hand under his shirt so I can feel his skin. Everything but the taste of my love disappears, and only the intense need to feel him alive and beating in my arms fills me. The muscles under my fingers ripple as he shifts even closer, our bodies pressed flush together. I can feel his growing erection against me, his arousal obvious. My own fills me, my pussy clenching and throbbing.

"I'm sorry," he whispers, breaking our kiss and resting his forehead against mine, squeezing his eyes shut. "Give me a minute."

I suddenly realise that he's trying to calm himself down, and while I know we shouldn't have sex as that will be giving the doctor exactly what he wants, I need this. The closeness of skin against skin and that intimacy you can only get when with someone you love. I need his reassurance, I need his strength... I need to know I'm not alone.

"Jesse."

His eyes open, and I don't know what he sees on my face, but I can feel how much he wants this, me. I don't have to say anything more, he knows what I'm asking for.

He glances over my shoulder towards the glass wall. "What about the doctor—"

I cut him off with a shake of my head. "Ignore him. It's just you and me."

He must be able to see how much I need this, and I know he needs this too. I've not been able to have much time with him since I discovered he was alive, and although I might look calm and put together, I'm still terrified that I'll lose him again.

His lips smash against mine, and he pulls at my clothing as I reach between us to grab his cock. He grabs for the blanket and covers us as much as he can. A frenzy settles over us, like any barrier between us is abhorrent. He squeezes my right breast, his finger brushing over my nipple, making my head fall back in bliss. Wrapping my hand around his shaft, I start to move my grip up and down. Groaning against my lips, he pulls at my clothing until I'm bare, slipping his hand between my thighs.

"Fuck," he swears as he discovers how wet I am for him. He rolls his fingers over my clit, making me moan in pleasure before sliding down my folds and pushing a finger inside me. I try to bite back my noises, not wanting to give the doctor a show. This is for us, after all, but Jesse and his talented fingers force another moan from my lips. He quickly adds a second, and then a third. My hips buck, desperate for more, and I claw at his back. His cock is rock hard in my hand, and I rub my thumb over the head, a bead of precum coating my fingers. Shifting our positions, he rolls until he's above me, and before I know it, he's lining up his cock with my entrance. His eyes quickly flick up to mine, and I know what he's asking. This has been quick, and our foreplay was much shorter than usual, so he wants to know that I'm ready. Nodding my head, I place my hands on his hips and pull him closer, encouraging him.

I need him as desperately as he needs me.

Without needing any further encouragement, he pushes forward with one quick thrust. I gasp at the sudden sense of fullness and the slight sting as my body gets used to him, but it's exactly what I need right now. He gives me a few seconds to recover, scanning my face as he leans down and kisses me softly, but he doesn't wait for me to urge him on, rolling his hips as he thrusts into me. It's frantic and fast, his movements pushing me down into the hard metal slab, but that doesn't bother us. I raise my hips to meet his thrusts, panting as that delicious heat builds deep within me. Our moans surround us, bouncing off the walls of the room, but I focus on the pleasure, on him.

As the wave crests and I free fall into my orgasm, the walls of my pussy clench around him. His thrusts become frantic, which only draws out the peak of my climax. I feel Jesse finish with a final thrust as we cling to each other and waves of bliss crash over us.

As we fall apart, we don't say anything, our breathing rapid as we shuffle on the metal slab. I rest my head on his arm, and his free hand traces lazy patterns on my arm before pulling me closer, our lips meeting in a searing kiss. It's not long before I feel him hardening against me again, and this time we don't fuck, we make love. I don't know what will happen tomorrow, but I'm going to live in the now, and right now, I'm going to enjoy this time with Jesse. They might want to make it clinical, using terms like coitus and putting us in these sterile rooms, but the love between us makes this different, and they can't take that from us.

Chapter Seven

I wake up to the clanking of the door being unlocked. Before I can even sit up, four guards pour into the room. I'm still blinking the sleep from my eyes when they grab a slumbering Jesse. Suddenly, his warmth is ripped away. I stumble from the bed, twisted in the sheets as I try to go after them, but without a word, they drag him from the room and slam the door shut once more. The loud metallic clunk of the lock sliding into place echoes in my ears.

It's all so fast that I'm left wondering what happened.

I still feel his kiss on my lips, and the warmth from his arms as he held me so tightly is suddenly just gone. I'm alone again. The stark reminder of our new reality has tears filling my eyes, but when they lift the window and I see them watching, I force them back.

Anger builds within me, generated from pain and longing, until the inferno inside of me cannot be contained.

They thought I would be weak and compliant. They were wrong. They messed with the wrong family. Turning my back on them, I start to pace. I need to come up with a plan, an escape route. My men are depending on me. I need to be strong, I need to be ready.

I splash water across my face and have a quick wash in the sink, refusing to use the shower. Even if they saw me naked last night, I feel more vulnerable today under their watchful eyes. After I put my slightly smelling gown back on, I start to work out, putting my body through familiar moves that Xavier taught me. He would normally be next to me, and it sends a pang through my heart even as I forge ahead. I am determined to stay ready. I cannot afford to be weak, not again.

Once I'm done, I have nothing else to do but scan the room. I check the walls, ceiling, and floor before finally sitting down. Time crawls by. I couldn't even tell you if it's day or night. It all muddles together until I feel like I've been here for days before a noise causes me to jerk upright.

The door doesn't open though, and my hopes for escape drop. Instead, a panel I didn't notice before slides away, leaving a small gap. A metal tray is shoved through and clanks to the floor. When it shuts, I stand and hesitantly tread closer. My nose turns up at the rations I see waiting for me there. There's water and tablets—like I would fucking take them—and bread, but when I pick it up, it's rock solid. There is also some soupy mixture next to it. They clearly don't care if I'm well beyond getting me pregnant, and as hungry as I am, I still put it back. I won't risk it. Who knows what they have pumped it with?

So although it makes my stomach clench, I turn away and begin to pace again. I focus on one step then the next until my feet ache and my eyes hurt. I can barely walk anymore, filled with exhaustion. How long has it been?

Hours? Is it the next day?

Collapsing onto the bed, I try to mentally count the minutes, but I give up after ten, closing my eyes to try and sleep.

Only I can't, because the door unlocks again. I jerk upright, ready to fight, to run, but I am surrounded. Five guards drag in a swearing, angry, red-faced Blain. He thrashes in their grip until he's thrown on the floor, and then they rush out, slamming the door as he leaps to his feet and hits the metal, yelling at them.

"Blain?" I call softly, unsure if I'm actually seeing him or if I have gone crazy.

He turns, still angry. "Harpy." He crosses the distance in two steps, sweeping me into his arms and holding me tight. I wrap my legs and arms around him as I let him carry me to the bed where he tucks me into his lap. He holds me as if he thought he might never get the chance to again.

I don't blame him, I do the same, running my hands over him to check for injuries.

"I'm okay," he promises, leaning back to look into my face. "Are you?"

I nod, and he narrows his eyes.

"Words, Harpy," he snaps, making me smile. He's still my grumpy, pissy Blain.

"I'm okay, just annoyed."

"Me too." He sighs, pulling me closer and rubbing my back. His soft and loving nature only comes out for me. Once I thought this meant he hated me, but he only snaps if he cares, and Blain loves his family more than anything. He just has a different way of showing it.

"I think they are just going to leave me in here and keep putting one of you with me to fuck me" —he flinches— "and then leave me alone again," I tell him, working through what has been happening in my head.

It's clear that's what they are doing. But they have to take me back to the lab at some point, right? I can't escape this room, so maybe I can escape that sterile space? That's where I will make my move, but for now, I let Blain hold me.

"What has been happening to you guys?" I whisper, leaning my head against his chest to hear his heart racing.

"Nothing, we are just left to fucking rot," he snarls, pulling me closer. "We have vents between the rooms though. It means we can speak, but I don't think they have realised that yet. We have been more worried for you."

"I'm fine, honestly, they didn't hurt me. They won't if they want my baby."

He stiffens, his hand drifting to my stomach. "If there ever is one, they won't get it," he promises vehemently.

"I know." I'll do whatever it takes to get out of here.

After a few minutes of just being with each other, a yawn splits my face. Blain instantly stands, rips back the messy bedding, and climbs in with me, pulling the covers over our heads until we have a cosy, warm cocoon. He strokes my face as he watches me from inches away.

"Sleep while I'm here," he begs.

"Soon," I tell him. "Our time is limited, and we need to plan."

He nods, knowing I'm right but hating it all the same.

"You can talk to the others, so you need to let them know I'm okay, and whoever they throw in here can pass messages for us. I don't have a full plan yet, but it needs to happen in the lab." He frowns but nods, following my logic. "Keep your eye on the guards, and try to figure out schedules, how many, and any ways out of here. Listen to everything you can and pass it on to me."

"Okay," he murmurs. "We'll figure this out, Rhea, just hold on."

"I will," I promise. "Make sure the others are okay for me," I beg, kissing him.

He groans and flops back. "They are a pain in the ass. Smoke keeps singing to us, Alcide is trying to plan, Nixon paces, Rex checks on everyone, and Jesse is playing with Smoke and Xavier."

I can't help but laugh as he pulls a face, and he narrows his eyes. "Don't you laugh," he warns, tickling me and making me laugh harder.

"You will have coitus," a cold voice orders through the room, making us both jerk as we're reminded we aren't alone. My laughter dries up. Blain rips the blanket back, sits up, and glares at them.

"You can't fucking make us. Only I get to see my girl like that, not you sick bastards. It's not fucking coitus, it's making love, and you bastards won't get it!" he screams. "You hear me? It's our choice and her body, not yours."

I hold onto him even as I hear the footsteps before the door opens. He turns his head and kisses me quickly, deeply. "Hold on, Harpy. I love you."

"I love you," I call as he's ripped away. I know there's no point in fighting them, it wouldn't help, instead I watch him get dragged away because he won't do as they want. But when they shock him for his disobedience, I scream at them until they finally stop.

Despite the pain he's in, we share one last determined look as the door closes.

Blain is willing to fight for us, for our future, and so am I.

Chapter Eight

I've started telling the time by the arrival and departure of my guys—one male a day, and they are usually sent in just before they lower the lights. Whether the lowering of the lights is to simulate night and make us feel like we have more privacy in a bid to encourage us to copulate, or if it's actually the end of the day, I don't know, but each 'morning' when the lights flash on and blind us, the guards swoop in and take whichever of the guys spent the night with me. I've decided that they do this on purpose when we're still groggy from sleep and trying to work out what's happening. It's harder to fight back when you don't remember why you're fighting.

Of course, reality quickly sets in, and I'm faced with another long day alone. I have a little routine now, and it's the only thing keeping me sane. Once I'm alone, I force myself to get up and wash in the small basin while still wearing the shift. I've not used the shower. There's a tiny curtain around it, offering me the façade of privacy, but I know that nothing I do in this room is truly private. They give me a fresh shift to change into every handful of days, but they never feel new, and it gives me the heebie-jeebies to think that some other poor female has worn this at some point. What happened to her? Is she still here? I try not to think about it, as that is a dark spiral of thoughts I know I'll struggle to climb out of again.

Once I've washed as best as I can, I return to my room and begin my workout. I know they watch me, but I ignore them, running through my exercises as best as I can in the small space. I must stay strong if we want any chance of escaping this hellhole. At some point during the day, well after I've collapsed from exhaustion, the hatch at the bottom of the door slides open and the usual tray of hard bread and soup is pushed through. I held out for as long as I could, but eventually, Alcide convinced me that I had to eat it. I've only seen him once, but it's clear the guys have been speaking to each other through the vents, because he scolded me as soon as he saw me. I explained why I didn't want it, that it was probably spiked, and he agreed, but he explained that if I didn't eat, there were ways they could force me to. The idea of being violated like that, force fed through a tube, horrified me, but he was right.

There is no way the doctor here would let me waste away when he is trying to breed me. Not to mention I need to stay strong, and without food, that will be impossible.

Looking down at my tray, I ignore the water and pills, as usual, and reach for the hunk of stale bread, dunking it into the soup—although calling it soup makes it sound far more appetising than it actually is. Wincing, I force myself to eat the whole meal before dropping the tray by the door, not caring that the glass of water spills. Maybe the guards will slip on it when they next come in. The thought makes me smile.

Walking back over to the bed, I sit on the edge and let out a long sigh. This is the worst part of my day. My limbs protest at the thought of more exercise, and it will be a couple of hours until one of the guys is brought in. The only thing I can do during this time is think. My mind is my own worst enemy, playing over everything that led to our capture, things I could have done better, or shouldn't have done in the first place. After a while, I get up and start pacing the room like a caged animal. This damn collar around my neck feels like it's getting tighter by the day. I know it's not, but I'm starting to feel suffocated. We have to get out of here, I don't know how much longer I can live like this.

Something else that plays on my mind is that other than that first night with Jesse, I've not had sex with any of the guys who have been brought in. The guys have been shocked for not complying, but other than that, our captors don't want to do any lasting damage to them in case it would affect their 'performance.' However, we all know that our time is limited. They won't let us keep refusing for long. When they do finally lose their patience, what will happen then?

Footsteps bring me out of my chaotic thoughts, followed by a strange noise which I soon realise is someone singing.

"And when I get that feeling, I wanna sexual healing," a familiar voice croons.

Despite the situation, a grin tugs at my lips. I don't know the song, it must be one from before the world fell to shit, but the words amuse me given our current situation. A flash of red catches my attention as one of the guys is marched past the window, but I already knew who they were bringing as soon as I heard his voice.

The singing abruptly cuts off, followed by a dull thumping sound that stokes the anger inside me. Unfortunately, I know all too well what that sound signifies. The door opens suddenly, and Smoke practically falls through it, stumbling about to keep his footing as he faces the guards. I wince as I see the swelling around his eye from where they hit him, yet that doesn't seem to stop him.

"What? Was I off key?" he asks with mock innocence before the door slams shut in his face.

Despite myself, I bark out a laugh. Smoke finally turns to face me, his lips splitting into a grin, but his eyes tighten as he looks me over. "Hey, Rhea." I hate how sad he sounds despite how hard he's trying to conceal it.

Unable to hold back any longer, I close the gap between us, flying into his arms so fast he lets out a quiet grunt of surprise. His arms wrap tightly around me, pulling me closer as he presses a kiss to the top of my head.

Pulling back, I run my eyes over him, checking for other injuries, but thankfully he looks alright. Although, unfortunately, we all know that there are ways of hurting someone without physically touching them. This is the first time I've seen him since we all woke up in the lab together, and I've missed him more than I can put into words.

"Are you okay?"

He pulls a face and shrugs his shoulders. "Well, the mattress is hard, and they need a new chef, but I've stayed in worse accommodations," he jokes, pulling a smile from me. His own smile soon drops though, replaced by a concerned frown as he reaches out and cups my chin. "How are you?"

"I'm..." I trail off as I think about my answer. I was going to say that I was fine, but that would be a lie. I'm not fine, none of us are fine. Instead, I take a deep breath and tell him the truth. "I'm scared."

I'm so much more than just that one word. I'm angry, I've had my dignity taken from me, I'm hurt, and I'm frightened we'll never make it out of here. However, he seems to get all of that from just those two words. He pulls me roughly against his chest, and I grab onto him like a lifeline, inhaling his familiar smoky scent to reassure me that I'm not in this alone.

"I know," he whispers, his voice rough as his hand strokes the length of my back. "I am too."

We stay like that for a few minutes, but I eventually pull out of his arms and take his hand, pulling him towards the bed. "How are the others? How's Nixon?"

His face tightens. Nixon is now the only one of my guys who I've not yet seen, but from what the others have told me, he's not doing so well. Smoke's expression doesn't help alleviate my fears either.

Sitting on the edge of the bed beside me, he sighs and scrubs his hands over his face. The fact that he's putting off telling me about Nixon just makes me worry all the more.

"The others are fine, but Nixon... Being separated from you and knowing what they are trying to do... He's retreated in on himself. He won't speak to any of us, but whenever the guards come near, he goes ballistic," Smoke finally admits. A sick feeling grows in my stomach with each of his words. "I've never seen anything like it," he says with a shake of his head.

My heart clenches painfully, knowing how much my gentle giant must be suffering, and I know that the longer they keep us apart, the worse it's going to get.

"We have to get out of here." I keep my voice low so we're not overheard, but that doesn't lessen the force I put behind them. They may have bound our powers, but they have found our true weakness by keeping us apart.

Smoke nods, but I can tell from his frown and the look in his eyes that he doesn't believe we can do it. "I know, but with these on, I don't see how we're going to make that happen." He pulls at the collar around his neck. "Every door has keycard access, and they keep us drugged just enough so we're not at full strength. There are always at least two guards with us when they bring us here. We can't fight them, Rhea."

His words are gentle as he places a hand on my arm, but I just look at him in shock. Where has my strong, funny, fiercely independent rebel gone? Is it just Smoke who feels this way, or are they all starting to doubt that we'll ever leave this place?

I grab his shoulders and force him to meet my eyes. "Don't you dare give up," I demand, the words sounding harsh with my desperation.

Shaking his head adamantly, he leans forward and presses his forehead against mine. "I'm not. I would never give up on you, Rhea, but I don't know how we're going to do this."

I close my eyes for a moment, enjoying the closeness between us and the intimacy of the moment as I try not to let the situation drag me down. Letting out a slow, controlled breath, I open my eyes and pull back slightly so Smoke can see the truth on my face. "I promised I'd get us out of here. I will keep that promise."

He closes his eyes, letting my promise wash through him. We stay like that for hours before lying down. I spend the night in Smoke's arms listening to the sound of his gentle breathing behind me, and instead of sleeping, I plan. They don't keep me as sedated as they do the guys, which I assume is so that it doesn't affect the possibility of me getting pregnant. The guys might not be able to get out of their cells, and we might be powerless with these collars on, but I'm valuable to our captors and that gives me an advantage.

I'm not sure how I'm going to do it yet, but I need to get back into that lab.

My family is depending on me.

Chapter Nine

A few days have passed since my promise to Smoke, and I'm acutely aware that I still haven't made a move. The more time that passes, the weaker they will get. Not only that, but their hope will diminish, which means the sooner we escape, the better.

It's not just us feeling antsy and impatient though, oh no, the doctor is too. He is annoyed I'm not having enough sex. He soon realized shocking the guys wasn't enough, and yesterday the guards beat the shit out of Jesse. I think they chose him because I slept with him before, but when we both refused, they dragged him out and beat him on the other side of the window. He was awake when he was dragged away, and that was the only thing that gave me any comfort. Now, I wait impatiently for whichever of my men they throw in with me today, so whoever it is can tell me how my funny man is.

They seem to be late today though, and I panic, wondering if they have finally had enough of our insubordination, but just as I think that, I hear them. I stand by the back wall, my heart racing as I wait for the door to open.

But when it opens, a swarm of guard's rush in. I duck, my hands coming up to defend myself, but they aren't coming for me. No, they are dragging a roaring, fighting Nixon in. Eight men try to subdue him. Rex is behind him, his eyes dark and angry, silently standing between the two guards holding him.

One on each arm.

I can't take it.

"Nix!" I yell, rushing forward. At my voice, he stills, his eyes instantly flickering to me. The guards quickly drop him to the ground and rush from the room, locking it behind them, leaving me with my two men. I share a quick sad smile with Rex before dropping to my knees before my surly giant. I cup his face. His eyes are wild, almost lost. I silently beg him to notice me, to lean into my warmth.

"Not real," he murmurs over and over, curling his hands into fists as he thrusts me away from him. I fall back onto my ass in shock, gaping at him. Rex rushes over and kneels next to me, placing his hand on my shoulder.

"We're losing him, Wildcat. It's like he's retreated and can't tell you're here."

"I'll bring him back," I promise, my voice trembling with fear. Getting on my knees again, I shuffle over to him where he's pulling at his hair. He won't hurt me, I know that, and I have to bring him back. I can't lose Nixon, I can't.

My heart freezes at the thought, and terror fills my veins as I try to think of a way to bring him back. I call out, but he only hunches. I talk to him, my voice soothing, and gently lay my hand on him, but he rolls back like the touch burns him.

It's not working.

"Nixon!" I finally yell. "I need you, come back. I love you!" I finish in a terror-filled plea.

I stare, my heart thumping hard, but when nothing happens, I slump in disappointment and close my eyes for a second as a tear escapes my eye.

There's a rough, disbelieving croak. "Rhea?"

My head jerks up and I open my eyes to see a confused Nixon

before me. He reaches for me but stops as if he doesn't dare. As if I will disappear.

"Rhea, is it really you?"

"It's me," I promise, grabbing his hand and pressing it to my racing heart. "It's me, big guy, come back to me, okay? I can't lose you, please."

"Rhea," he repeats, blinking slowly before his expression turns from ice cold to an inferno. Suddenly I'm yanked forward. I tumble against his hard chest with a grunt, and then his lips are on mine. His tongue sweeps in hard, fast, and dominant, and he slides his hands across every inch of my body to ensure I'm real. He pulls me closer, as if the inch of space between us is too much, and he groans. It's still not enough to settle those demons.

He holds me tight and stands, and I wrap my legs around his waist to stop us from falling as he turns and slams me against the closest wall. The move is hard enough to knock the breath from me, but not once does our kiss break. His huge hands drag up my legs, over my waist, and to my shoulders before cupping my cheeks as he finally pulls back, his lips raw. His expression is desperate, as if he doesn't have me, he will lose me again.

"Rhea," he whispers brokenly, "I've been going crazy without you. I-I'm sorry." He tries to put me down, but I tighten my legs, and whatever was holding him back disappears. The wild, fighting man who was ready to kill to get to me is once again before me.

He growls, his teeth bared in a snarl. I would almost be scared if I didn't know he was such a softy. But right now, my gentle giant is nowhere in sight. This is a man in love, a man who almost lost his lover—again. His family is in danger, and he knows we might die at any moment. This is a beast.

My pussy clenches at the stark hunger I see in his gaze.

"Rhea?" Rex queries, trying to make sure I'm okay.

I look over Nixon's shoulder, meeting Rex's eyes, and smile reassuringly. "I'm okay," I promise. He nods and steps back, but I see his expression tighten with his own need, his own worry. I was so focused on Nixon's feral anger, I didn't see Rex's quiet, painful one. He's missed me too, he's worried as well, and right now, he needs me.

My eyes flicker from him to Nixon as my giant scrapes his teeth down my neck, and I tilt my head to give him better access. He nips my pounding pulse, making my pussy clench as my clit throbs desperately.

They both want me, and I want both of them.

Why can't I have them? They are mine, and they love me. It wouldn't be the first time nor the last. I don't care if the doctor is watching. He wanted us to have more sex, and he is getting it—but on my terms.

I need to feel alive and get lost in the haze of pleasure I know they can both give me. It's almost a compulsion, and I can barely breathe past the thought. My nipples tighten as Nixon licks up my neck to my ear, sucking on the lobe while grinding into me, letting me feel his huge, hard length.

Tugging on his hair, I pull him closer, even as my eyes go to Rex. Decision made. "I need you both," I beg almost too quietly, but they hear it even over my thundering heart. It's only beating for them, demanding they fill me, comfort me, and promise me everything will be okay with their bodies.

Rex's eyes darken as he takes a hesitant step forward before stilling. "Rhea..." He glances at the window and then back to me. "Are you sure?"

"About wanting you both? Always." My response ends on a gasp as Nixon nips my pulse again, his hardness still pressed to my stomach. He's huge, and I have to think logically about how this will work. I want them both inside of me, but I also want their kisses and to see their faces. So no cock in my mouth, even though I also drool at the thought. No, this time they will both be inside of me, working together to bring me to release, focusing wholly on me and nothing else. Not even their fear.

They are both too out of it to take charge, so it's up to me.

Swallowing my nerves, I roughly tangle my hand in Nixon's hair and tug his head back. His teeth snap together in a bite as he fights my hold to try and get back to my skin. "Lay me down, big guy," I order. He hesitates before turning and gently dropping to the floor, covering my body. He kneels above me, blocking everything else, even most of the light with his wide shoulders.

"Rex, strip me," I demand, meeting his eyes as he drops down next to me, called to me like I am to them, the love and passion between us unable to be denied.

He reaches for me reverently, while Nixon snarls like a waiting, trapped animal. His shoulders shake with the force of obeying me, and his hands curl into the exposed skin on my thighs. I gasp from the abrupt pain, but that sudden sharpness fades to extreme pleasure as Rex leans down and, without warning, sucks my nipple through the thin gown. My back arches off the floor and my eyes close as he sucks harder and harder. The pleasure shoots down to my clit. He pulls back and does the same to the other one, and when he sits back again, he's grinning cockily. I look down to see the wet material above my nipples, which poke through the gown.

"I had to sneak a taste," he murmurs before reaching down and softly tugging the gown up. The slow exposure makes me shiver as the cool air of the sterile room wafts over my legs, my wet pussy, then my quivering belly. He hesitates, looking at me again to make sure it's okay before he takes it off. I nod confidently. I know they are watching. They can see me, I don't care. I'm not hiding anymore. Who knows what is coming next? I refuse to not take what I want— my men—due to fear. In fact, I almost feel empowered as Rex lifts the shift over my head, exposing my breasts. My damp nipples tighten further until they beg to be touched again.

Nixon growls, leaning down until his shoulders are wedged between my thighs. I have to part them almost painfully wide as he grips my inner thighs, pinning them to the floor as his hungry gaze takes in my pink pussy.

"Beautiful," he snarls, tightening his fingers on my skin until I whimper. He narrows his eyes, drops his head, and inhales, sucking in the scent of my arousal, one that even I can smell on the air. Rex watches, his eyes darkening and lips parting.

Nixon meets my gaze and waits.

"Lick me," I whisper, trying to make it sound like an order, but it's more of a plea. "Make me come. I want you inside of me, but you're so big, baby, I need to be ready." I lick my lips before they tip up in a wicked grin. "Especially if Rex is going to fill my ass at the same time."

Those bold words free me as Rex groans and closes his eyes in ecstasy and anticipation. I glance straight at the window for a moment as if to dare them to judge us, to watch us. This is my life, and these are my men. They can lock us up, abuse us, and command us to fuck, but they cannot take our love from us, or our pleasure. This is for us. But the sureness, the boldness that fills me surprises me. Without my powers, I'm usually scared and weak. Now, however, I'm still me, still the fearless warrior they all see me as.

I'm Rhea.

Just fucking Rhea, and guess what? That's enough.

They can throw their best at me, many have, and I have survived. I will survive this too, but first I want my men. I want to scream their names as a declaration against the evil breeders here. They will never get a child we make. New life might be born from our love, but it won't be here.

This isn't just us fucking, it's us reassuring ourselves we are still here. Still alive and okay.

This is a promise to the scientists. They might have locked us away, but they don't control us.

Nixon doesn't wait anymore. He drops to his front, opening his mouth over my pussy. He tastes my desire, and I cry out, tilting my hips to grind into his talented mouth. He doesn't always talk much, but he says enough with his tongue as he drags it down my folds, swirling it around my entrance before dipping it inside of me. My eyes go to Rex as I pant, reaching down to tangle my fingers into Nixon's hair as that talented tongue sweeps back up and flicks across my sensitive clit. He lashes it until I cry out again, as if he's drinking in my noises. Rex just watches with hunger etched over every line in his face as I ride Nixon's.

"Rex," I whisper, and his eyes dart up to mine. Dragging my other hand down my body, I cup my breasts, squeezing them together and offering them to him. "I need you."

"You never have to ask twice, Wildcat," he replies, leaning over me and blocking their view of my body. He brushes his lips across the sensitive, heaving flesh of my breasts, mouthing the skin. He kisses every inch, purposely avoiding my aching nipples, teasing the slight sheen of sweat covering my skin with a hum.

Nixon presses a finger to my clenching hole as his mouth wraps around my clit and sucks. I arch off the floor with a cry as that long, thick finger spears me, stretching me around him as I writhe. Rex sucks my nipple into his mouth, replacing my hand with his as it drops to the floor in ecstasy. He pushes my breasts together as he sucks, nips, and licks like they are a feast. Rex moves from one breast and nipple to the other over and over as Nixon adds another finger.

"Oh God," I cry out, my voice hoarse as he stretches them inside of me. He parts them before curling his fingers and rubbing along my walls. It's too much.

Too fucking much.

I scream as my release takes me by surprise. It explodes through me, discharging throughout my body. My pussy clenches around his fingers, greedily keeping them inside of me as my hips undulate. Rex's face is almost buried in my breasts as I arch my back.

All the while, I'm locked in the cycle of pleasure until it finally stops, fading away as I collapse. But they don't relent. Nixon adds a third finger, fighting through my fluttering channel. Rex kisses down my stomach and back up, across my neck, and to my lips, swallowing my wordless whimpers as Nixon laps at my clit. I jiggle my hips, too raw and sensitive. He gets the picture, licking and kissing down my pussy before circling my hole where his fingers are buried. Slowly, he pulls them out and pushes them back in until I relax, limp from pleasure, and only then does he speed up. He builds me up to another orgasm, then suddenly pulls them free just as I'm about to come.

I bite Rex's lip in punishment, but he just chuckles and pulls back.

"Here," Nixon snaps.

I force my eyes open to meet his and see his lower face is covered in my cream. The sight makes me shiver as he moves back.

"I won't fit in her ass, it will hurt, so take her pussy first. Make sure you are nice and wet," he instructs Rex. Even now, in his throes of desire, he ensures I'm taken care of and not hurt.

Rex replaces Nixon, who moves up my body, stroking as he goes, before he leans down and kisses me softly. Soon, his mouth speeds up, dominating and distracting me so much that when I feel Rex's hands on my thighs, lifting me into the air, I gasp and fall back. He's naked now, and his huge cock is hard, seeping at the tip as he watches me. Holding me effortlessly with one hand, he drags that leaking tip up and down my folds, coating his cock with my release until I'm impatiently thrusting my hips below him. Finally, he presses the head to my entrance, meeting my eyes as he slowly pushes in.

I cry out, but Nixon is there, swallowing my noises and kissing me as Rex slowly eases into my body. He pulls out when his hard length is halfway inside and thrusts back in until he's balls deep, filling me, spearing me. His hands go to my hips, stilling my desperate movements and letting me feel his huge length buried inside of me. He allows me to adjust until I'm fighting them both, needing to move.

Rex pulls out and plunges back in, slowly at first as I tilt my hips and quickly match his pace, urging him on as I purposely clamp around his cock. He groans and digs his nails into my skin. Usually they would be claws, but his powers aren't here—another reminder.

He doesn't notice, no, he's too busy slamming inside of me. He speeds up until he's fucking me and pushing me across the floor with the force.

My eyes close, and my head falls back, but Nixon cradles it to stop me from hurting myself as I lose myself in Rex's rhythmic movements. Both of us chase the pleasure building inside of us, drawn by the drag of his huge cock across the nerves inside of me.

"Please, please," I chant, and when I force my eyes open, I see Rex snarling and fighting his own release. It's been too long. Suddenly, he pulls out, and I whimper, empty and cold. I'm dropped to the floor and rolled. My head spins. I was in charge, but I'm not anymore.

No, they are, and they are consumed with bringing me pleasure.

With being inside of me like I wanted.

With coming together again.

Someone moves behind me, and my ass is dragged into the air. My dripping pussy almost causes me to shiver in embarrassment as my cheeks redden. Hands span my ass, and I'm lifted. My eyes widen as Nixon slides under me with his hands out to catch me as I'm lowered onto him.

He's naked, his hard cock is straining, and precum beads at the tip. Veins bulge along his inhuman length. Narrowing his eyes, he widens his hands to span my whole stomach, holding me still for a moment as I whimper. My thighs are stretched wide to accommodate his huge body. I'm almost off balance, but when he releases my right side and reaches down to take his length, I forget all about it. I watch him stroke himself in a leisurely manner before he lifts me higher due to the height difference and presses his hard cock to my empty, throbbing hole. He holds my gaze as he slowly pushes into me. I still whimper as he stretches me, even with his mouth, fingers, and Rex's cock, he's big, almost too big. The pain and pleasure as his huge length fills me makes me stiffen, and I close my eyes as it rolls through me in waves. He keeps me locked there as Rex dots reassuring kisses along my spine, begging me to relax, so I do as Nixon works in an inch at a time.

I'm tired of waiting, though, with just the tip of his massive cock inside of me. I want more.

So even though it might hurt, I open my eyes and drop my hands to his chest for leverage, then I slam down, impaling myself on his length. He roars and throws his head back, his neck straining as I cry out in both pain and pleasure. His length bottoms out inside me, filling me so deeply and stretching me so much I roll and wiggle my hips. He's stiff beneath me for a moment as I curl my nails into his wide chest, and then he slowly lowers his head. His eyes are darker than I've ever seen them, and his lips twist in a fierce snarl as he takes over. He clutches my hips, lifting me and dropping me, forcing me to bounce on his cock. The wet sound of our bodies coming together is loud, even over the sound of my panting.

Rex just waits, stroking my back and even my ass cheeks, massaging them like a promise. I shiver with anticipation, knowing what is to come. Nixon speeds up, fucking me and filling me over and over again, making me cry his name. Suddenly, he stops, and I almost collapse, closing my eyes as he heaves beneath me.

"Now," he snarls at Rex as he tries to resist moving. I need to move, to feel his length dragging along my inner walls, but I only get a whimper out as Nixon wraps his arms around me and pulls me down until my ass is in the air. The new angle makes his cock press into those nerves that have me gushing.

Rex's hands part my ass cheeks, still massaging.

"So fucking beautiful, Wildcat," he murmurs from behind me, making me cry out, so I press my lips to Nixon's chest. Rex's hands drag down my ass to my pussy, collecting my cream before sliding back up to my hole and circling it. He wets it before pushing one finger at a time past my stinging muscles. I have no choice but to relax as he starts to fuck me with them. My asshole is tight and clamps around him. The fullness of his fingers and Nixon's cock causes me to whimper, and then Rex's fingers are gone and his cock replaces them. The warm, wet heat presses against my asshole and then he starts to push in.

I can't help but bite down into Nixon's skin, digging in like a feral animal as he snarls beneath me, his involuntary thrust forcing me deeper onto Rex's cock.

"Fuck," Rex groans, holding my ass cheeks apart so he can watch as he fills me with his cock. He feeds me each inch until he has to pull out and work back in. It's slow going as he doesn't want to hurt me, and when he finally settles all the way inside of me, I'm so full it's too much. My ass and pussy are stretched to their limits. Nixon pulls my teeth from his skin as he starts to move.

Words, praises, and pleas flow from my lips. I can't even tell you what I spew, only that it urges them on. When Rex pulls out, Nixon pushes in, and each thrust heightens the pleasure already consuming me until I come again.

I scream their names, clawing at Nixon's chest, but he doesn't care. They don't stop, fighting my tight muscles until one release rolls into another. The pleasure is too much. My body's not mine anymore, but theirs, as they rock into me, working me with their cocks. My release drips down my thighs and onto Nixon below.

"Oh God, oh God, I can't... I can't anymore. I can't—"

"You can," Nixon assures me.

"You will," Rex adds. "I want to feel you come around my cock once more."

"Oh God," I whimper, my voice hoarse, and I am unable to open my eyes. My pussy and ass almost hurt, and the pleasure borders on painful, but they don't care. They drive me higher and higher, urging me on with comforting words and reassuring kisses across my body. They speed up, pummelling into me until another release explodes through me.

I almost black out as I squirt around Nixon's cock, but I fight it. Nixon's hips stutter as he fills me once, twice more, and comes with a roar. It's so loud it feels like it shakes the entire room. He holds me like he'll never let me go as his warmth splashes inside my pussy.

Rex groans and presses his head to my spine as his hips snap forward over and over until he bites my skin, muffling his cry as he finds his release. It fills my ass, dripping around his cock as he slumps into me.

We stay like that, breathing heavily. I'm basically a limp, well-used mess. I'm unable to think or see as Rex slowly sits up and pulls from me. I cry out in pain, feeling his cum drip from my ass. He helps Nixon lift me from his cock too, and when I'm finally empty, I collapse. Rex stumbles to the bathroom with me and helps clean me up before carrying me back and crumpling to the floor next to a still panting Nixon. He turns and wraps his leg over mine, opening his eyes.

"I love you," Nixon murmurs.

"I love you too," I reply, smiling widely. I'm satisfied, if a bit wet and used. Rex kisses my cheek, and I turn my head to press my lips to his. "I love you too."

"I love you forever," he says and pulls me closer. They hold me between them so tightly, I remain in a sleepy haze.

Lying in their arms, I've never felt so relaxed. Despite where we are, and knowing the doctor is smug and happy, it doesn't take away from the comfort and strength I got from my men. It's a reminder of why I'm doing this, why I'm fighting to get us free.

For them, for this.

For us.

Now if only I could get to the lab—

That's when it hits me. It's idiotically stupid, and I don't know why I didn't think of it before. Lips turning down, I consider every option before I sit up. "I know how we are getting free," I murmur.

"Come back." Rex groans, grabbing me, but I turn away.

Nixon sits as well as he watches me, his knowing mind considering the possibilities. "Whatever you are thinking... it feels right," he murmurs, and that one quiet statement fortifies my decision.

"I'm going to get to the lab." I grin at him, lowering my head for a moment as I scrub at my hair. If I'm at the lab, the guards will be too. I need to get rid of them.

Lifting my head, I meet both of their gazes. "I'm going to get us out of here and I know how. I just need your help."

"Whatever you need," Rex promises.

I smile, I can't help it. "I was hoping you would say that, because I need a distraction."

Chapter Ten

The next morning, as the guys are taken away, we share a look. Today is the day I'll get into the lab. They don't know what I've got planned, only that I've thought of a way to get there and I'll need a distraction—a distraction they are going to make for me. If they knew my plans... well, I doubt they would have agreed to help, much less be so calm about it.

Rex blows me a kiss, and Nixon gives me a lingering look. The guards appear smug as they start to lead the guys away, and I grind my teeth, trying to ignore the leering stares they throw my way.

"So that was the trick all along," one of them jokes, glancing at me as his sick gaze travels the length of my body, heating with a look of lust that makes my stomach churn. "Stick two of the freaks in there with the whore and she'll perform. Maybe we should—"

"Complete that sentence and you'll die," Nixon rumbles.

His body seems to grow with his anger, and the guard's face drains of blood quickly, leaving him white. He's seen how ferocious Nixon can get when he gets into a rage or I'm at risk. He throws me a glare like it's my fault and thrusts Nixon from the room. Rex is next. Wisely, he keeps his mouth shut and slams the door closed behind them.

I watch them through the window, hoping they can feel my love for them through the glass. If things go wrong today and I'm caught, this could be the last time I—

No. I can't think like that.

I have to keep my head clear and focused on my task. I can't let my worry about what might happen distract me. We won't escape today, but this is an important step in finding our way out. If I can access the computers in the lab, I'll have the information I need. Plus, there are all kinds of items that can be used for weapons in that room. They may not be conventional, but beggars can't be choosers. Besides, getting stabbed by a scalpel in the shin would be painful.

Once the guys are gone from sight, I have to go through my usual routine, although it's the last thing I want to do right now. If I change it now, though, the doctor might get suspicious. I don't want to give them any cause to suspect that anything is out of the ordinary. It's just a normal day of forcing women to breed. Yup, completely normal.

Pushing off from the bed, I ignore the twinge of my sore muscles from our fun last night and begin my warm-up. Going through the motions, I feel a heavy set of eyes on me. This isn't anything unusual, and on a normal day, I'd ignore it, but today my temper is frayed. Tilting my head, I look to the window where I find the doctor staring at me with a smug smile. Oh yes, he thinks we gave in last night and that we're finally performing as he wishes, and boy did we put on a show. I don't think I've ever orgasmed so much before, and honestly, I'm still a little sore from our sexcapade. Let him think we caved to his orders. Nixon, Rex, and I know the truth.

Last night was for us, not them. They just don't know it yet.

But they will soon...

As I work out, I imagine the doctor's face with each punch and kick, allowing my anger to fuel my moves, making me stronger, faster.

I have to time this perfectly, otherwise it won't work, and the guys' actions will be for nothing. When the guards bring our lunch, the guys will start counting down, giving me ten minutes to get to the lab. Once that time is up, they will cause the distraction, hopefully allowing me to be left alone. If I'm too early, then I'll be in the doctor's hands, and if I'm too late, I'll have missed my chance.

So I keep moving, doing press-ups, sit-ups, and laps around my room. At some point the doctor moves away from the window as one of the guards takes watch, but I remain focused on the plan. Footsteps sound from down the hall, and I know it's time. The hatch at the bottom of the door opens, and a tray is pushed through.

Time for action.

Ignoring the food, I walk over to the bathroom, my breathing coming in pants from my workout as well as my nerves. Adrenaline makes my heart race too. Most of the room is open, so I can be watched at all times, but there is some privacy in the shower cubicle with the flimsy curtain that pulls across, blocking the window and camera. It doesn't cover all of me, falling to my knees, but that's enough for what I need.

The only way they are going to take me to the lab is if I'm injured. They need me in prime baby making condition, after all. I'm going to need something sharp. Glancing around the room, I search for something that will do what I need it to, and my gaze stops on the round porcelain soap holder that's sitting on the edge of the sink. Smoothly, so as not to attract attention, I walk over and grab it before placing it inside the shower. Taking a deep breath, I steady myself for the next part of the plan. If they are going to believe I hurt myself accidentally, I need to make it look real.

Very real.

Pain, blood, and all that fun stuff.

My determination outweighs my self-preservation, and I've survived worse—just usually with my powers.

I grab the bottom of my shift and quickly pull it up and over my head. I shiver as I expose myself, partially from the cool air in the room, but also due to my disgust because I'm being watched. Making sure to keep my back to them, I climb into the shower and close the flimsy curtain behind me. Turning on the faucet, I suck in a gasp of air as the icy water falls down. I reach for the soap disk and quickly discard the soap. Raising the dish, I smash it against the wall of the shower, smiling as it shatters into several pieces. I let most of it fall to the floor, selecting one of the bigger, more jagged fragments. I grasp the sharp, wet shard as I take a steadying breath. Closing my eyes, I press the porcelain against the delicate skin of my inner arm as I brace myself for the pain that's to come.

I focus on the reason I'm doing this and the faces of my guys, and then I slice. Alcide and Nixon. I gasp at the sudden burn of the ragged cut, but I need to keep going. Rex and Jesse. Slice. Blain, Smoke, and Xavier. They give me the strength to do what I need to, even without being here with me. Warmth trickles down my arm, and I open my eyes to see a large, jagged cut running diagonally from just below my elbow to my wrist. Panic flashes through me when I see the blood. The skin is torn, and bright red blood runs down my arm, mixing with the water below.

Stay calm, Rhea, this is part of the plan.

Quickly turning off the shower, I push aside the curtain and grab a towel, wrapping it around myself. Covered, I stumble from the cubicle, not needing to feign the very real pain flowing through my body, and make my way towards the window. By now my powers would have healed me, but this time I'm alone, and for the first time in a long time, I feel vulnerable. However, where I would have let that stop me in the past, now I let it fuel me.

"Help me." I don't have to fake the quiver of fear or pain in my voice as my knees buckle.

The guard who had been looking away when I first emerged from the shower stares at me with wide eyes. "Shit," he curses, lifting his walkie-talkie to his mouth. He mutters something into it as he hurries around to the door. I hear several sets of footsteps running towards us, and as the door opens, the first guard rushes to my side.

He reaches out and squeezes the cut. I cry out in pain and instinctively pull away from him.

"I'm trying stop the bleeding, you stupid bitch." Jerking my arm towards him, he squeezes just below my elbow. "How the fuck did this happen?" he demands as the other guards run in.

I hear curses as they see the trail of blood that leads to my slumped form.

"I fell in the shower, cut my arm," I mumble, falling forward to make it look like I'm about to pass out. I'm in pain and I am losing blood, but I need to make it seem like I've lost a lot more than I actually have.

"Fuck. The boss will have your head if she dies," a gruff voice barks beside me, but with my eyes closed, I can't tell which guard it is.

"You think I don't know that? Shit. Let's get her to the lab," the first guard orders.

I force myself not to pull away as several sets of hands descend on me and lift me from the ground. This is what I wanted, what I needed, yet suddenly the reality of what's happening hits me. As I'm carried away, I repeat the names of my guys over and over in my mind as the guards rush through the labyrinth.

A whoosh of air startles me, but I stay slumped in the guards' arms as we step into what I assume is the lab. The air is cooler in here, more sterile, and I can smell cleaning chemicals that make me want to wrinkle my nose.

"What happened?" the doctor barks. Even with my eyes shut, I know it's him. His voice is marked in my mind.

"She was in the shower and fell, cut her arm," the guard explains quickly.

"Get her on the table. If she passed out, she probably already lost too much blood," he growls. "I'll need to give her a transfusion," he mutters to himself as I'm dumped on the bed.

Cracking my eyes open a fraction, I see the doctor rushing around as he prepares something. He raises a bag of blood, and I can't help but wonder how he got a hold of it or who it's from. The idea makes my stomach churn, and I have to swallow back bile. All the guards have moved away except for the one who found me, his hand still clamped tightly around my arm. The doctor steps forward with a tray full of medical equipment, and I close my eyes all the way, not wanting them to know I'm awake.

"If she dies, I'm holding you accountable," the doctor snarls as he reaches my side, and I assume he's talking to the guard still holding me. "Tie this below her elbow but above the cut. It needs to be tight."

"Yes, sir," the guard replies. As he lets go of my arm to apply the tourniquet, a rush of blood floods to my hand and feeling returns to my fingers- even as more blood escapes. It takes everything in me not to move or cry out at the pain coursing through my arm. The tourniquet squeezes my arm painfully, but I focus on staying still.

Something wet touches my other arm, followed by a small prick of a needle, but it's nothing compared to the overload of sensations in my injured arm.

"I don't need all of you here, she's passed out from blood loss," the doctor barks.

The guards murmur their acknowledgement, and I hear the footsteps of several people leaving the room.

"Not you," the doctor orders as he settles at my side. "This is your mess, you should stay." I'm guessing he's talking to the guard who found me, and from his heavy, unsurprised sigh, I know I'm right. Something cold wipes across my injured arm, and I try not to wince when a sharp needle pierces my skin as the doctor stitches up my arm.

I'm not quite sure how much time passes as my arm is slowly sewn together, but I start to worry that I'm going to miss the distraction. The sound of heavy booted feet running past the lab catches my attention, especially as the guard's walkie-talkie comes to life. I can't make out a lot of the words, as most of it is static, but I don't need to hear to know this is my diversion.

"What do you mean the prisoners are revolting?" my guard demands into his walkie-talkie.

More running steps and shouts fill the corridor. The door suddenly opens, the sound intensifying.

"What is the meaning of—"

A deep, unfamiliar voice cuts off the doctor. "There's an incident. We need you to trank the males."

"I have a patient—"

Nixon's roar echoes through the room, and I nearly break. The urge to jump up and run to my gentle giant, to reassure him, is screaming through my veins. But no, this is part of the distraction.

"We need all hands on deck to subdue these guys," the voice from the door calls. "She doesn't look like she's going anywhere, and she'll be locked in the lab even if she does wake up. You won't be gone long."

The doctor growls under his breath, and I hear him hurrying around and grabbing what he needs. "You, stay here," he demands before two sets of footsteps hurriedly leave the room.

"I can't believe I'm here looking after a fucking body," the first guard mutters, and I realise we're alone together. "You're not going to cause any trouble, are you?" The tone of his voice changes, and I'm suddenly afraid for a whole new reason. A hand touches my unhurt arm, and his fingers trail up to my shoulder. I know he's about to grab my breast. I try to keep still, to prepare myself. I'll do pretty much anything to get us out of here, but is this my limit?

"All guards. I repeat, *all* guards. We need you in the cell block to deal with an incident, immediately."

I've never been more glad to hear the crackly voice over the radio. The guard seems to hesitate for a moment, his hand growing hot where he's touching my shoulder. Finally, he curses and pulls away. Heavy footsteps followed by the whoosh of the lab door opening tell me he's gone.

Even so, I lie here for a minute to ensure no one's coming back. Once I'm certain, I crack my eyes open and turn my head to look around. There's a tube in my arm which is attached to a drip, as a bag of blood works its way into my body. Pulling my gaze from the blood, I focus on the room once more, and a slow smile spreads across my lips.

I'm alone in the lab.

It's time to begin.

Chapter Eleven

I waste no time. I leap off the table, stumbling from the blood loss. I don't want to pull the line in my arm out and alert them, so I grab the pole and drag it along after me, ignoring the cool tile on my feet and the shakiness in my legs. Not to mention the numbness from whatever he used to stitch me.

I search desperately for anything, something. I risked everything to get here, so there has to be something I can do. Firstly, I make my way to the now closed door where I saw the caged women when we were first brought here, but it's locked and I can't get through. I tug on it and kick it to make sure, but there's no way I can save them without a keycard.

Fuck.

Stupid, I know, because where would I even take them at the moment? But the guilt as I turn away still eats me alive. I frantically scan the room, knowing I don't have much time before they come back, and if they find me snooping? I shiver at the thought of what they could do to me. There are a lot of ways to inflict pain that wouldn't harm my ability to make a child.

My eyes land on a computer on the desk near where the doctor was stitching me up. Surely it has to hold some helpful information, right? Rushing over, I thank the stars for my luck.

It's unlocked.

He must not have had time in his haste and assumed I was not a threat. Using the mouse, I navigate the files, ignoring the data on my blood work and men, and even the pictures of us they have taken for the files. They almost look like mugshots, but I guess it could have been worse. There are no maps, but I spot a camera system and try to access it. I can only see a flashing map of where they are situated, but I can't turn them off as it asks for a password. Knowing I won't be able to get past it, I close the program, covering my tracks.

There has to be something.

Anything.

My eyes continually go back to the door in panic as more time passes. I'm acutely aware I'm running out of time, so I randomly start clicking things. Suddenly, a defence system loads and I gawk. It shows the entrance above ground, confirming we are in a bunker of some kind. There are cameras and sensors, which I again can't access because of a password, but as I scroll through, I manage to somehow access something titled 'Defences.'

Surely it can't be, can it? But when I see the information, I almost scream in glee. It is, it's their above ground defences. After all, they wouldn't want anyone just stumbling into this place. I'll need to disarm it to get free anyway, so I hover the mouse over the on/off slider for the electric fence, and with a deep hopeful breath, I slide it. A moment later, it flickers to red, off, and I have to hold back my happy dance.

Quickly, I scroll down the other defences, turning off guns, mines, trap doors, and everything else that stops anyone from getting in... and us from getting out.

It's a big step. It's not freedom, but it's a step in the process. When it's done, I close it all and rush back to the table, lying down just as I hear the doctor grumbling as he stomps back into the lab. I roll my head to the side, blinking like I've just woken up.

"Stupid males," he mutters, heading back to me. He taps my cheek as I blink innocently. "Good, you're waking up. I need to conduct some more tests, so I may as well do it while we are here."

I go cold at that. Tests?

What tests?

My tongue feels thick and numb as he moves away, and I turn to watch him. I brace myself for whatever comes next, knowing I have to survive it because my family is depending on me. We are getting free, and he's all that stands in the way. So, closing my eyes, I force my mind to drift far away from here and the cold, annoyed musings of the doctor. Instead, warmth fills me from the sun above, the smell of trees and wet earth filling my nose. My fingers twitch, as if stroking the wood of our wagons as we travel. My vision of my life keeps building. My men are there, talking and laughing. I feel myself smile as I reach for them.

Suddenly, my happy place is destroyed as two cold wet fingers shove into me.

I open my eyes as I lift my head and kick out, but he presses a button, and my legs are suddenly banded down to the table. He doesn't even look at me as his searching fingers violate me, turning inside of me. I gag, my stomach rolling as tears fill my eyes and slide down my face.

"Please," I beg, annoyed at myself as it slips out.

He ignores it and eventually pulls them out. The only saving grace is there is no hint of desire or arousal in either his touch or eyes. No, it's clinical, and although it doesn't make what happened okay, for some reason it helps me distance myself from it as I try to shut my legs to no avail. He leaves me like that, exposed to anyone who could walk in, uncaring about my dignity because I'm nothing to him.

Just a womb.

Luckily the other tests aren't as invasive. He moves around me, poking and prodding, all while making notes. He's happy, which annoys me. Anything that brings this bastard joy makes me want to rage. Eventually he covers me up and calls for the guards.

"Take her back to the cell and throw in the man I specified. They would make an interesting specimen, I think. I'd like to see the gestation and track the progress."

The fucker.

I want to swing at him as I'm pulled from the table, but I can't. Instead, the doctor comes up and removes my IV. I can't risk punishment or them hurting us so close to escape, so I force myself to breathe through my anger as I am finally led from the lab.

My stomach rolls with nerves the entire way back. So much could go wrong. They could figure out what I did. I hope not. I also hope someone trips the sensors up top, that would be a good shot at an escape, or even better, they blast their way in.

But only time will tell.

For now, we have to wait... again.

"Doc ordered us to put that powerful annoying one in."

I perk up, wondering who they are talking about.

"Smithy should be bringing him now. We'll just toss him in there with her and watch them fuck. Who knew this tiny bitch was a freaky one?" They laugh.

Ignoring the flare of anger, I let them drag me back to my cell where they march me inside, this time keeping the door open. I hesitate, staring at the possibility of freedom, but a moment later, there's more booted feet and a body is tossed inside. He rolls across the floor before the guards slam the door shut.

My eyes go back to the man and my eyes widen. "Smoke?"

SITTING CROSS-LEGGED BEFORE SMOKE, I can't help but grin. He just has a way to make me laugh. Even throughout everything that has happened, he's still cracking jokes and flirting. He left Last Stop and the only life and friends he knows for a better life—for me—and now here we are.

I was the reason he was taken prisoner, yet he still watches me with soft burning eyes, stroking the bare skin of my foot as he talks to me. "Are you sure you're okay?" he asks for the fifth time. "I've been so worried. The others have told us what was going on, but—"

"I promise I'm okay," I assure him, reaching out to lay my hand on his thigh without thinking. He grins down at it as I slowly pull it back, my cheeks reddening. He makes me feel like an innocent young girl again, all excited and embarrassed. I would say I feel butterflies, but that's not true. Smoke does excite me, but he doesn't make me nervous. No, it's the opposite—he makes me comfortable, like I've known him for years. He slots right into my life and heart like he was always there, even though it's only been a few weeks. It's like the start of a whole new relationship, if that is where this is going. I don't know if it is or how the others would react. Our love grew naturally, but at the same time, Smoke came into my life like his namesake, in a fiery oblivion that calmed to a slow burn, his smoke wrapping around me and pulling me closer each day.

When I saw him, I was relieved, but more than that, I was happy. I wanted to rush to him and kiss him. I had to actually stop myself. We've only kissed once, and I really don't know where we stand, which is a strange feeling for me, but not a bad one.

"I don't know how long we have before they come to take you," I start, but then a siren blasts through the room, cutting my sentence short. I leap to my feet, as does Smoke. He stands at my side, ready to defend me as I am him. We wait, but the siren just keeps wailing, and suddenly, the huge overhead lights turn off and we are plunged into total darkness. I curl my hands into fists and wait, straining to listen beyond the sound of the alarm.

Slowly, tiny dim lights flicker on around the room, casting it in shadows. We hear running and shouting then. I hear the words 'surface' and 'defences' mentioned, and can't help but grin and look at Smoke.

"You did this?" He laughs.

"I think so." I nod. "I took the surface defences down to buy us time. I guess it worked and someone stumbled through."

"You're a clever little thing, aren't you?" He winks. "Well then, let's make the most of it and sort out our escape." He cracks his neck.

"Let's," I repeat.

THE PLAN ISN'T COMING ALONG TOO well. We are still stuck on what to do. I want to go back to the lab, but Smoke says it's a risk, arguing they could catch on. He thinks the guys could take the guards if they work together. I don't think it's worth the gamble. But more than our scheming? We now have more time.

It seems whatever I did has sent the bunker into some kind of lockdown. Smoke isn't taken from me, not day after day. No, we are locked inside. No one comes. No one watches.

We are completely alone with nothing but time.

The days in lockdown go slowly. There are no big lights on, only low energy lights. I hear no booted feet, and trays of food only come every now and again as if they seem to suddenly remember we are here.

Whatever I did worked. It's thrown them off guard, and now they are striving to regain control. It gives me precious time to come up with our next step without being forced to fuck like a mare in heat.

On the fifth night, I lie side by side with him, closer than ever. All week we have been drifting together, trading touches, looks, and lingering chaste kisses. Each day I want more. Right now, our bodies are pressed together tightly, and he holds me like he knows me intimately, but it's not true, and the thought saddens me.

I want Smoke.

As if this week has been one long, tortuous seduction, I'm suffering the effects. My body is slick for him, my heart pounds with need, and my hands shake from the force of having to hold myself back. I'm still not sure what either of us wants, and I should be focusing on the plan, not on the way his heat warms me through or how his body fits against mine so perfectly.

"Rhea?" he murmurs, tilting my chin back until I look into those fiery eyes. "What are you thinking?"

It's now or never, who knows what will come tomorrow? I've learned that the hard way. I need to speak my mind, to take the leap, and hope he's falling with me.

"I don't know where we stand." I take a deep breath, surging ahead as his eyes widen at my blatant honesty. "You followed us into the world, sacrificing your life and friends. You kissed me like your very life depended on it, and now you hold me like you are scared I am going to slip through your fingers. You look at me like you want to consume me, but you never take it further or ask for anything else. I guess I'm wondering if you really want me, or if I'm just a passing fancy."

"Which do you want it to be?" he asks darkly, his voice rough.

"I-I don't know. I think it would hurt if you walked away, because I like you a lot, Smoke."

His eyes smoulder, burning brighter than ever like they harbour their own flames. He pulls me closer, his hands heating against my skin.

"But I would understand. I don't want you if you do not like me that way. My life is complicated." He grins at that. "And I would never be wholly yours, you would have to share me."

"Rhea," he interjects, covering my mouth. "Stop thinking so hard about this. Just focus on now, on this moment. Tomorrow isn't promised, so don't even worry about what could happen. Just enjoy the present like I am." He leans in and I inhale. "I'm focusing on the way you feel against me, the way your eyes widen when you're wondering if I will kiss you, and how sweetly you lean towards me. The honest answer is I don't know. I don't know if this is forever or just now, but this? This right here? It's enough for me for now. You have to ask yourself if it is for you. Can you commit to just living the journey with me and seeing where this goes? No plans, no assurances, just... loving one another?"

My heart stutters as he licks his lips, pulling his hand slowly away. "All I know, Rhea, is that when I'm with you, I'm happy for the first time maybe ever. My smiles are real, and I feel like I have purpose again. A family. My heart doesn't hurt." He grabs my hand and places it on his chest, where I can feel it racing in sync with mine. "I don't know if this is love, because I've never felt it. All I can tell you is that when morning comes, this is where I want to be. Right here in your arms. For a day, a month, a year, a lifetime. Whatever this world gives us."

"I want that too," I whisper, overcome by his words. He's right. I don't even know if we are going to get free, but I'm so tired of planning. With him, I want to do just what he said and see where it takes us. It will hurt if he ends up walking away, but the time we have together will be worth it, and I refuse to waste one more minute wondering.

Not when our seconds together could be limited.

Gathering my courage, and using the arousal and kindness in his eyes as an opening, I lean in and kiss him. I freeze, he does too, and then with a groan, he snaps into action. My eyes close as his big hand slides up my back, across my neck, and tunnels into my hair to pull me closer and tilt my head as his soft lips run along mine. The moan he makes against my lips steals a piece of my heart, and when he tugs on my hair, it forces a grunt from my lips. He swallows it and sweeps his tongue into my mouth, tangling it with mine, sucking on it, and licking along my teeth. He dominates my mouth, stealing every inch of me and remaking me in his fire.

I feel him heating up against me, but his powers are contained within his skin, and I don't know if that encourages him, but I feel him let go of that last shred of control as he loses himself in our kiss. I taste his desperation, his need, and the pure life that fills Smoke. He's just such a vibrant soul, I feel it in every touch, as if it's imprinted in my skin until I'll never be the same.

Needing to breathe, I pull back and press my forehead to his. I blink open my eyes to meet his inches from mine. I stare into those flames and let them burn me alive. I let them consume me until I melt. Until there is no Rhea anymore. Just us.

Together.

Our breaths and our bodies become one as he flips me. My back presses to the mattress as he blankets mine with his. He props his hand next to my head as he leans down and kisses me. Wrapping my legs around him, I lift my hips, feeling his hardness between us. Grunting into my mouth, he grinds against me, hitting a spot through the gown that has me gasping. He does it again, circling his hips, but I want more, so much more. I know we have time, there's no rush for this.

But I want him.

I want to feel that fire contained under his skin inside of me. I want to burn in his flames.

"Smoke," I murmur as I pull back. He nudges my head to the side with his own as he kisses along my cheek. His warm, wet mouth trails down my neck to that junction between my shoulder and neck, then he kisses and licks as I whimper. I wrap my arms around his neck, digging my nails into his back to pull him closer.

Smoke kisses me harder as he reaches down, grips the gown, and tugs, as if asking if it's okay. I can't pull my mouth from his to speak, so I urge him on by squeezing my legs. He takes it as permission and slowly starts to lift the gown between us, sending a shiver through my body. He has to break away, doing a rolling sit up as he tugs the shift above my breasts, exposing them to the cool air. My nipples tighten under his gaze as he stares at me hungrily, licking his lips.

Grinning, unable to help myself, I arch my back to push my chest out enticingly. "Going to take the gown off or just stare?"

"Cheeky." He winks before leaning down. "I was debating if I wanted to lick your pretty rosy nipples or your cunt first," he admits, making me fall back as I reach for him.

"Both." I grin.

"Greedy girl," he whispers as he lowers his head, still fisting the gown in one hand as he blows warm air across my nipples. I close my eyes, and then his mouth is there, so hot, so wet, sucking my nipples. A bolt of pleasure flows through me as I clench my legs around him, winding my hips desperately. Sucking harder, he digs his teeth in before pulling back and circling that hot tongue over the stinging pain. Turning his head, he does the same to my other breast, cupping it this time and squeezing as he licks and sucks. Sitting back, he tweaks them until they are throbbing and so hard the sensation borders on painful. I think I might come just from him touching them alone.

"So pretty," he coos, circling the wetness from his mouth with his fingers. "So sweet, just like you, little Rhea. I can't wait to see my marks all over this porcelain skin and feel it burn for me."

His words have fresh wetness coating my thighs, wanting just that. As if finally remembering, he tugs on the gown and pulls it over my head. I have to sit up to get it off, and just to be a tease, I lean up and stroke my hand down his chest to his hard cock and squeeze.

His hips snap forward as his eyes slowly close before he groans. He opens his eyes as he bats my hand aside and leans down, kissing between my breasts and licking down the valley to my stomach. He leaves biting hot kisses and red marks behind, not hesitating in the least as he moves down my body. He grips my hips to keep me still as he works between my thighs so they are over his shoulders, my legs parted so he can see my dripping pussy.

"Fucking hell, Rhea," he whispers. "You are going to need to relax, we are going to be here for a while." I must look at him with confusion, because he grins. "Baby, I'm setting up camp between these pretty thighs and eating this cunt all night long."

"Oh God." I roll my eyes. "Terrible jokes and—" My words fade into a moan as he drags his tongue down my pussy before circling my clit, and then he sweeps back down to dip it inside of me. He hums as he pulls away.

"You taste so sweet. What were you saying?" he asks, grinning.

"Bastard," I mutter, even as I smile.

That talented tongue drags back down my folds, shutting him up for once. I can't help but lift my hips and grind against his mouth. My clit throbs in time with my heart, begging for his touch. When he finally does, I almost come off the bed, crying out as he sucks it into his mouth.

He adds his teeth, pleasuring me until I am both pulling him closer and pushing him away. Chuckling, he moves back and lashes it with his tongue. "Rhea, you're so wet for me. So goddamn pretty and pink."

I feel his tongue thrust inside of me but it's not enough. I clamp down on it, needing more. Whispering and pulling back, he licks my clit as two fingers press to my hole. I gasp as he slowly pushes them into me.

"Fuck, you're so goddamn wet." He groans. "You feel so good, I can't wait to feel you around my cock."

His dirty words have my eyes closing as I raise my hips to meet his fingers. He begins to fuck me with them with sure, hard thrusts before adding a third, stretching me deliciously. He attacks my clit with his tongue as he curls those fingers and strokes that spot that has me screaming. Clawing at the bed, I grind into his face, reaching for the release on the horizon, and suddenly, it's there.

It bursts through me like flames, flowing through every inch of my body, drawn by the mouth still sucking on my clit as I writhe under him. As the flames ebb, he pulls back, laying a gentle kiss over my fluttering cunt.

When he moves up my body, I flip us, straddling his legs and scooting down. I need to know what he tastes like. I need to make him as wild as I feel right now without him inside of me.

He blinks and reaches for me.

"Rhea, what are you—fuck!" he exclaims as I yank down the stupid pants they gave him and grasp his huge length. He's so thick, really thick and long. Veins bulge down his steely length, and his cock is so hot it almost burns my palm, but it feels good. I lean down and swipe my tongue across the head to taste the precum beading at his tip. Fire explodes across my tongue, addictive and so fucking good.

He grabs my hair, holding on as I slide my tongue around his head and inside of the tip, searching for more of the addictive fluid. I pump him with my hand as I do, squeezing his base when I decide to swallow him whole.

With a roar, he yanks me from his cock and throws me down on the bed, covering me in an instant. He grabs my legs and presses my feet to his shoulders as he leans closer. "Keep doing that, and I'll burst before I even get inside this pretty cunt of yours, and baby? I've been dreaming of this moment, so lie back and behave."

"Never." I groan, sweeping my tongue out to catch every drop of his taste.

In punishment, he smacks my clit hard.

I cry out, my hips jerking as he does it again. "I'm not a well-behaved man, Rhea. Keep pushing, and I'll pump my cum down your pretty little throat until the flames are all you can taste and you choke on it. Then I'll take this pretty pussy, but I will not let you come again." He grins. "Now be a good girl and hold still."

Goddamn.

Why does that threat almost have me coming again? I want his cock too much to get him to follow through... this time. But there's always the next, so I do as I'm told to get what I want. I lie back, my breasts jiggling as I feel the warm head of his cock press to my fluttering hole.

The tip of his cock slides in, and he captures my lip between his teeth, biting down as he pushes inside of me. He fills me with each hard, hot delicious inch of his cock, fighting through my pussy as he releases my lip. He drags his tongue down my chin and then back up. "Next time, I want to paint you with my cum and watch you writhe in the heat."

He bottoms out and stills, letting me feel every burning inch of his cock.

"But it will be enough to see it fill you and drip out of you, to hear you scream for me," he says as he rises, placing his hands on the bed next to me as he rolls his hips. The movement makes my mouth water as he fills me.

Again and again.

He speeds up until he's slamming into me, his neck corded as if he can't resist. I don't stop him, I urge him on. I slip my legs down until I can wrap them around him and pull him deeper, and we both moan at the new angle.

"Goddamn, Rhea, you are enough to make a man believe in heaven." He pants, closing his eyes for a moment as he powers into me. "To dream of more."

Heat blasts through me with each brutal thrust. He leans down and kisses me so softly, it almost makes me cry. His thrusts slow as if he's trying to make this last as long as he can, even as I claw at the skin of his back. My fingers nearly burn as my legs tighten around him, my pussy clenching his cock.

I lean up and nip at his lips, and he continues to roll his hips, filling me time and time again with sure, slow strokes.

This isn't fucking anymore.

Smoke is making love to me.

He's showing me exactly how he feels.

"I burn for you," he whispers against my lips. "I was a slow flame before you came, and now I'm a volcano, just waiting to erupt. Controlled by you. You set me free, and you brought me to the brink of the fire and plunged in with me." He gasps. "No one but you, Rhea, could survive this, survive me. Wherever this life takes us, we have this. This moment. We have these feelings. We have each other and the fire that will never extinguish."

His words have me reaching for that peak again as he slowly makes love to me. Our bodies move in sync, fitting together perfectly. His hands caress every inch of me, his lips too. His cock is so hot I burn for him, but I've never felt so alive.

"Smoke," I whisper, wrapping my arms around him as he leans

down to kiss me again. "I knew when I saw you, knew you were meant to be mine. Down in the dark, surrounded by war, I saw the spark of forever in your eyes. Now I feel it too. This. It's perfect," I whisper raggedly, my body shaking as sweat covers me from trying to hold back.

"I love you," he murmurs against my lips, his voice rough, strained.

"I love you too," I admit freely, and it's true. In this moment, I do, and I know I always will.

The fire inside burns brighter and hotter as if those words have set it free. His hand snakes down my body, circling my clit softly as he thrusts into me, kissing me until that flame explodes.

Covering us both.

He cries out, his hips stuttering as my pussy milks him. My own silent cry escapes my lips as my body locks up from the force of my release. I feel his boiling cum fill me, and it extends my orgasm, rolling through me until I finally fall back.

I am spent, hot, and so happy I can't contain it. He kisses me again, turning us onto our sides so we are still joined. He strokes his hand down my back and cups my ass, holding me to him as he pulls away. He's the happiest I've ever seen him. "Thank you for giving me a second chance at life, Rhea, for giving me a new family and loving me. I will be at your side until the end."

Until the end, I vow sternly.

Snuggling into each other's arms, we let the heat flow between us like a circle. Our hearts are in sync, and I know we are meant to be together.

He is meant to be my forever like the others.

Lying here in a haze of comforting warm smoke, I sleep.

Chapter Twelve

As I wake up in Smoke's arms, my body warm and pleasantly sore from last night, a smile stretches across my lips. It's only as I peel my eyes open that I realise something is different. The main lights are back on, illuminating the whole room with bright sterile lights once again. Jerking into an upright position, I search the room, and my eyes land on the window and the guard watching us.

Fuck.

Does this mean all of the disabled defences have been restored? Was everything I did for nothing? Or worse yet, do they know it was me who did it? If so, we're running out of time. We need to attempt this soon, otherwise we will lose our chance and I'll never forgive myself.

Turning to the sleeping man beside me, I shake his shoulder to wake him. "Smoke."

He rolls over with a sleepy smile and leans forward to press a kiss to my lips, not hearing the panic in my voice. I hear heavy footsteps marching towards us, and then the cell door opens.

"Wha—" Smoke calls out groggily, blinking as two guards enter the room and grab his arms, dragging him from the bed. "Hey!" he shouts, trying to kick one of the guards, but they raise their batons and shock him until he becomes limp in their hold.

I know I should stay silent, since screaming won't help anything and usually only encourages them, but I can't help crying out when they hurt him, his face contorted with pain. As they drag him away, I watch through the window, meeting his eyes until he's out of sight.

This can't go on.

Anger burns inside me so brightly it's like a living thing within me, and I'm surprised it doesn't scorch me. The collar around my neck feels like it's tightening with every passing minute. A glint catches my eye, and I look down at the bracelet around my wrist—my gift from Gregor, something the guards were unable to remove from me. He told me I'd know when it was the right time to use it. Surely now would be that time? Uncertainty twists my gut. No. It doesn't feel right. I don't even know what it does, but Gregor saw a moment in the future when I would need it, and I won't ignore that unspoken warning.

Sighing, I lower my wrist and begin to pace my room. I'm about to start my exercises when I see guards approaching through the window. Realising they are coming for me, I back up, my heart pounding and my breath hitching with fear. This is different.

Two guards step into the room, eyeing me with disdain. They obviously don't think I'm a threat from the way their arms hang loosely at their sides.

"Come on, don't cause any trouble," the one closest to me orders as they march closer, reaching out to grab my biceps.

"Look at her," his companion sneers, his eyes roaming over me. There's no lust in his eyes, just frustration and disgust. "Compared with what we've been dealing with the last couple of days, taking her to the lab is piss easy."

I don't fight as they drag me away. They just gave me some very important information. Whatever damage I caused by turning off their defences has made things difficult for them. This brings me a sick sense of satisfaction. Good, the bastards deserve it. The second thing I've learned is that they are taking me back to the lab. So I stay silent, hoping they'll give away more information on our journey. My patience pays off.

"Why couldn't the Doc come and get her himself?" the gruff guard complains, his hand tightening around my arm with his frustration. "Doesn't he know how fucking busy we are with the defences down?"

My ears perk up, but I have to make sure I don't give away that I'm listening, letting my head hang forward as they haul me through the maze of corridors.

"I know," his companion agrees. "It's a nice change from running around on the surface trying to sort everything though. It's fucking hot up there, and the defences are screwed. It's going to take months to get everything re-established."

The gruff guard snorts. "Huh. Don't get used to it. We're going back up there as soon as we drop this one off."

The other guard mumbles something incoherent but doesn't reply.

The rest of the walk is in silence, but I don't care. Their defences are still down. They may have sorted some of it, but whatever damage I caused can't be fixed quickly. They also revealed another important piece of information—they are returning to the surface once I'm in the lab. It sounds like most of the guards have been sent up there too, meaning the hallways will be almost empty.

This feels too good to be true. I need to calm down and not get ahead of myself. I still don't know why the doctor ordered my presence in the lab in the first place. My gut clenches as I remember my last experience there.

Finally, we reach the lab, and I can see the doctor hunched over his computer, furiously typing away. One of the guards presses his keycard to the door and it opens with a whoosh, the cool, sterile air making me shiver.

"Good, put her on the table and leave," the doctor orders without even looking up.

The guards march me over to the examination table and strap

down my right arm. The other guard begins to reach for the next strap when the doctor spins around and pins them with a glare.

"What is taking you so long? Don't you have defences to fix?" he snarls, annoyance lacing every word.

The crabby guard who had been about to strap me in spins and glares at the doctor, his voice raising as he barks back. I'm not paying attention to what they are saying, however, since my eyes are on the metal trolley full of medical equipment. While their backs are turned, I reach over and grab a scalpel, carefully tucking it under my hip where I can easily grab it later.

I manage it just in time. The guard turns back and slams my arm down on the table, yanking the strap into place before storming from the lab while glaring at the doctor. However, I notice it's not as tight as he would usually make it.

This could be it. This could be our opportunity. Twisting my wrist, I search for the scalpel with my fingers, and hope soars through me as I feel the cold handle. The doctor turns around, and I quickly relax my hand. The guards haven't tied down my legs today, which makes me think the doctor is going to do another examination. Nausea rises within me, and I have to take a few steadying breaths.

Seeing my legs unstrapped, the doctor growls something under his breath. He reaches for my right foot, and I instinctively jerk it back, panic rising in my chest.

"Stop fighting," the doctor barks, never once looking up at my face, his whole attention on my leg.

While he's distracted, I twist my left wrist in the restraint. It's tight, but there's some give thanks to the guard's quick exit. Making my hand as small as possible, I twist and pull, trying not to alert the doctor to what I'm doing. However, I'm running out of time. As I feel the restraint tighten around my right ankle, I panic, and when he reaches for my free foot, I yank my hand with all my might, not caring about the doctor realising that the binding gives.

"What—"

I kick him with my unrestrained leg as hard as I physically can. He stumbles back, a shout of anger and surprise leaving his lips. Before I know it, he's leaning over me with his hand raised to strike me, but with my wrist finally free, I grab the hidden scalpel, sit up, and slash the blade at him. I aim for his neck, but as he raises his arms to protect himself, I cut his hands and the blade ends up jammed in his shoulder. Crying out, he rears back and trips over the trolley of instruments before falling to the ground, smacking his head in the process.

When he doesn't move, I realise he's knocked out, and I watch as blood begins to pool beneath his head.

This is it. This is my only chance. With my heart in my throat, I sit up and start tugging at my remaining restraints. I have no idea how long it will be until someone else passes. That constant pressure hangs over me, making my moves shaky.

Cursing under my breath, I force myself to focus as I undo the remaining straps.

Finally free, I jump off the table and hurry over to the doctor. Kneeling at his side, I pat his body, searching for his keycard. I'm not going to get far without it, since every door and cell are locked with these. Reaching into his right pocket, I grin when I find it, clutching onto it tightly.

This could be the key to our freedom, literally. Now I just need to figure out how to get these collars off. Once we have our powers back, nothing will stop us.

The doctor groans, and I see he's starting to come to. Grabbing the front of his jacket, I shake him until his eyes peel open, another long groan leaving his lips.

"How do I remove this collar?" I barely recognise my own voice as I bark out the demand.

Squinting, he sneers, "Why—"

I cut him off. "Don't think I won't kill you," I growl, slamming him back down onto the floor. He must see something in my eyes, as fear suddenly crosses his face.

"You need the key. It's the magnet in my pocket. It's the size of a coin," he mumbles, the words practically falling from his mouth as he hurries to save his own life.

Shaking my head in disgust, I search his pockets again, coming across something small, smooth, and round. Removing it, I frown at the object before turning my ire back to the doctor.

Does he think I'm stupid?

"Press it to the side of the collar. You'll find a seam in the metal," he insists, his eyes widening at my anger.

Slowly, while keeping my narrowed gaze on him, I do as he says. As soon as the key is near the collar, I feel it pulling my hand closer—a magnet, just like he said. Pressing it against the metal, I gasp as the collar opens and falls to the ground with a clatter. My eyes remain locked on the worn metal as my powers surge back through me. I almost cry, I'm so overwhelmed. The relief that pours through me from feeling that twirling strength racing through my veins is indescribable.

"I helped you. Now you'll let me—"

I raise my fist and slam it into his face, enjoying the sick sound of his head hitting the floor once more and silencing his whining voice. When he doesn't move, I reach down to check if he's still alive, hating every moment my fingers touch his slimy skin. Finding a pulse, I slowly stand on shaky legs, my powers already healing my bloody fist. I know I shouldn't care about whether the doctor lives or dies after what he's put us through, but killing him while he's begging for mercy... I just can't bring myself to do it.

Keycard and magnet in hand, I leave the scalpel behind. Now that I have my powers, I don't need the blade. Hurrying to the door, I raise the keycard, but before I can do anything, a noise catches my attention.

Cries for help.

The other women.

Closing my eyes, I take a deep breath. No, I can't risk my family. I need to free them.

Feeling like the worst human in existence, I press the keycard to the door and hurry into the corridor, leaving the trapped women behind.

THESE PASSAGEWAYS ARE LIKE A MAZE, but now that my powers are back, I can almost... sense my guys, like they are a beacon leading me to them, and my powers are the compass.

Thankfully I don't come across any guards until I reach the cell-block where the guys are. I skip to a stop when I see the guard. He's surprised to see me, but before he can do anything, I reach for my connection with the earth. Down here, underground, it's easier than ever, and the wall cracks as long, thick brown roots capture him. Dragging him back, they pull him into the dark soil, his cries for help muffled by one of the roots.

Slightly disturbed, I release my control of the roots. They seemed almost eager to help me, like they have been waiting. Still, I don't have time to think about that. I can hear the guys calling out, but they can't see me yet.

The first cell I come to is Jesse's. Pressing the keycard to the door, I feel tears filling my eyes as he falls out of the cell and into my arms.

"Firecracker! I knew you'd find a way to free us!" he exclaims, pressing his lips against mine in a hungry kiss.

"Save the kissing for later. Get me the fuck out of here," Blain shouts from the neighbouring cell.

Chuckling, I pass the magnet to Jesse who looks at it with a raised eyebrow, clearly confused.

"It's a key," I explain, pointing to his neck. "It removes that so you can use your powers."

His eyes widen and he quickly presses the magnet to the collar, gasping as it releases and drops to the floor with a clank.

"I'll unlock the doors if you remove their collars," I tell him.

I'm moving before Jesse has a chance to reply, trusting that he'll follow my suggestion.

One by one, Jesse and I release the guys and unlock their powers until I have only one remaining. I left Nixon until last. While that might seem cruel, I knew I needed to get everyone else released before letting him out, as I suspected he wouldn't let me go once he got his hands on me.

I was right.

As soon as his cage is opened, I'm yanked forward and pressed against his huge chest, his arms coming around me.

"Hey, big guy." The tears I've been holding back finally break through and roll down my face. Nixon takes a deep inhale and nuzzles against the top of my head as if to reassure himself that this is real.

"Nixon, let her go. We need to get moving," Alcide orders.

My gentle giant growls low in his throat, but he reluctantly places me back down. Other than me, the ringmaster is one of the only people Nixon will listen to.

Now back on two legs, I smile up at him, my heart bursting with emotion at seeing all of my guys together with their powers back. Blades gleam in Blain's hands, and I can see sparks flitting from Smoke's fingers. Jesse jogs over and presses the key to Nixon's collar.

"Let's get out of here," Xavier declares, already at the end of the hallway and looking out for guards. "I overheard the guards saying most of the defences are still down. They'll mostly be on the surface." I nod as he speaks, his words confirming what I'd worked out.

It's time to go. I did it, I freed them. No, I can't get carried away. We still need to escape the bunker first.

The others, all except Nixon, hurry towards Xavier, turning left and away from the lab—away from the women I left behind.

A vice clenches my heart and I squeeze my eyes shut as I realise I can't leave without them. I've been them, lost, abandoned, and help-less. I would be turning my back on who I am if I left them here.

That's exactly what people like Chester and the doctor would do. Well, I won't be like them.

Not today, not ever.

"Come on, Rhea, let's go!" Alcide calls, holding his hand out to me.

My heart tightens painfully in my chest. I want to leave, but I can't. What I'm about to do could risk all our lives, but I can't go until *everyone* is free.

Otherwise, what type of person am I?

Blowing out a wobbly breath, I shake my head. "You guys go ahead. I can't leave yet."

The others all turn to me in shock, disbelief marring their expressions.

"I won't go without you," Nixon mutters quietly behind me, constantly reaching out to touch me.

The others, though, don't seem quite as supportive.

"Rhea, what are you doing?" Blain storms towards me, his eyes furious.

Shoulders back and head held high, I meet his angry gaze. "No, you can't change my mind on this," I reply, feeling sick despite my calm exterior. "I'm going back to save the other women with or without you."

Chapter Thirteen

My panic makes me sloppy.

I slide into the lab without looking, expecting it to contain only the doctor whom I knocked out earlier... but I'm wrong. The guys are behind me, having followed me as I ran back into the maze of corridors.

Fuck!

There are five guards here, all staring at the unmoving body of the doctor. He's still passed out. I don't know why they came back or when, but they are here now and in my way. They spin, spot us, and gawk at our lack of collars. Their eyes narrow as they reach for their weapons. I can't help but grin sheepishly.

"Surprise?" I offer.

"Get her and kill them!" one of them orders.

Well shit, I guess it's time for us to leave. "Keep them distracted. I'm getting the women!" I yell to my men as they spread out to buy me time.

I watch Nixon crack his neck, readying himself for the fight. Smoke grins and flips his hands so fire gathers in his palms. Blain smirks and blades appear in his hands. Rex's eyes fade to yellow, Alcide's gaze narrows, and Xavier and Jesse step forward.

All of their powers rise to the surface, and I gasp at their magnificence.

"Drop your weapons," Alcide orders, persuading them with his gift, and two of the guards actually do.

Knowing they have this under control, I rush to the door which is still locked. There is no way I am leaving the women behind. We're all getting out of here. These sick bastards will never hurt or use anyone again.

A woman is more than her womb, and they are about to learn that.

I run my hands over the door, feeling for a release. I duck and jerk instinctively when I hear roars and the connecting of bodies. Something is flung my way and my eyes twitch, but I keep searching. I won't leave them behind, and the quicker I get them out, the safer my family will be. They are relying on me as much as I am relying on them.

"Argh!" I scream when I don't find a keyhole, kicking at the metal before turning and searching for the answers.

Keycard! I bet I need a different keycard.

I rush back over to the doctor's body, dropping to the floor and rolling when a shot goes over my head that was meant for my men. Sparing them a quick glance, I realise more guards have streamed into the lab, brought by the noise, but they are still holding their own.

For now. I need to be faster.

Searching his pockets, I find nothing, so I sit back and spot the computer again. Maybe... Leaping to my feet, I go to grab the mouse when I see the release button at the side of the computer. It would be inconspicuous if you weren't looking for it. Praying I'm right, I hit it and a buzz sounds. I look up and see the door opening and almost scream in happiness.

I feel the air whizz behind me. Spinning to the left, I just narrowly avoid the grabbing hands of a guard. Using the table as leverage, I kick out, my added powers giving me strength, and send him flying back into the frenzy of fighting bodies.

Time to go.

Rushing over to the women's door, I see rows upon rows of cages. Some of the women are scared, some are hopeful, and others just look... dead inside. There are even a few younger girls in here, which turns my stomach. "I'm getting you out of here, let's go." I slam my fist into the button on the left, and with a buzz, all the cage doors swing open.

Some hop out immediately, but others hesitate. "Come on! We have to go before they come back!" That gets them moving, and I lead them into the other room where my men are still fighting. "Okay, out of the door, go!" I order, moving closer to my men to help buy the women time to escape.

"Thank you," one of them calls and then turns, waving the others over to the lab door.

Holding my hands out, I quickly trip one of the guards going for Nixon's back with a vine, wrapping it around him and dragging him away. With my powers added, the tide starts to change, and we begin to win. The guards are winded and hesitating as they form a line and stare us down. We are not even breathing heavily, all of us stronger than them and willing to die for this cause.

Are they?

"We're losing! Just shoot the women and they will surrender!" one of the guards screams, and all weapons turn to the innocent, fleeing captive women.

I turn in horror as everything slows down, and I see the bullets hit their marks.

One hits a woman in the back as she tries to escape, her screams as she falls searing into my brain as I scream in horror. Another hits a little girl right between the eyes, and before she even hits the floor, her eyes are empty—dead.

"No!" I roar.

The horror, the pain, the weeks of torture, and their evil become too much. My powers grow with each bullet that finds a home. The women fight each other to get out of the door. I hear their cries for us to save them, and their fear is so palpable it invades every one of my senses.

My men are diving at me to protect me.

Me?

I turn, suddenly calm.

No more.

I tell myself no more women will die for their sick cause. No, only they will. We were just going to leave, but now? I'm going to kill them all for their crimes against us, for misusing their power, and for taking advantage of women. For playing god.

"No more!" I roar.

No. Fucking. More.

There has been too much innocent blood spilled. I can no longer remain this scared person. If they kill, so shall I. I end this here. The breeders will be wiped out. It's them or us, and I choose us. Every single time.

Even if their blood stains my soul, I know I did it for the right reasons.

Stepping into the path of the bullets, I hold up my hand, and time does actually freeze. I see my men's eyes widen, their hands outstretched mid-air but unable to move. I see the guards' wide eyes and anger, and the beads of sweat rolling down their faces. Their guns are raised, and the bullets are there too, hovering before me.

Looking up at the guards, I flick my hand.

Just like that everything speeds back up. The bullets turn in mid-air, and before anyone can move, they fire back at the men. Every single one finds a home in the ones who shot them. They scream and fall. Some die. Some writhe in agony.

Stepping towards them, I feel vines shooting through the floor, forcing the tiles up in the torture lab. Wind blows my hair back, and water evaporates from the air, crawling up my arms. My powers are stronger than ever, coming to my pain, to my defence.

To save these women and our family.

I am Rhea the freak.

I am the power.

With a blast, it rips from me with a force I can see and slams into the injured doctor and remaining guards. Their cries suddenly end, and when I stumble back, I realise what I've done.

I've killed them all.

I know they deserved it, I know they were monsters, but an eye for an eye doesn't work. Does killing them make me any better than them? Fuck, we have no time for philosophy, I realise, as Smoke grabs my hand.

"Time to go!" he yells cheerfully, dragging me away and out of the lab.

He holds my hand as we run after my guys who lead the way through the maze of corridors. My heart races as the women rush ahead. We are almost there. I know it!

Everything is chaos with so many bodies around. We are one big huddle running together. We encounter a few guards, and the guys break off to deal with them. I have to trust them, because my job is to get the women out. Turn after turn, corridor after corridor, we run.

Until we see the stairs leading up to a huge vault-looking door.

"That's the exit! Go!" I scream. I spot the control panel to the right and hurry over. I scan the many buttons and switches, but luckily, they are labelled, so I find the handle that reads 'Open' and turn it. There's a vibrating noise, the floor shakes, and then the door starts to roll to the right. Bright sunlight pierces through the dimness of the bunker. The women shield their eyes, and some fall back.

"We have no time, run, go!" I order, moving to the door and pushing them outside, making sure each one is clear. My guys have formed a barrier between it and the corridors just in case. "We are clear. Let's get out of here!" I yell.

With one last look at the corridor, they run closer, and as they do, I scan them, checking them over for injuries. Hope blooms in my chest along with love.

We did it, we're free!
But the guys... I count them again to be sure, realising...
"Wait! Xavier is missing!" I scream.
That's when I hear an unmistakable roar from my lover...

Chapter Fourteen

Xavier's agonised roar tears through me.

No, this can't be happening.

Without stopping to think about the consequences, I spin on my heel and rush back into the bunker. I hear the guys shouting my name, but they should know by now that I'm not going to leave anyone behind, especially one of our own. The sudden darkness of the underground corridors is a shock, but I feel my body tingling, adapting to the environment, and within seconds, my eyes adjust. I don't stop, I just keep running. The sound of footsteps echoes all around me, the pounding of boots on concrete matching my racing heart.

"He's immortal, he's immortal," I repeat to myself over and over, yet that doesn't stop the panic that's pulsing through my system.

"Rhea!" one of the guys shouts from behind me—Alcide, I think —but my mind is a mess right now, so I keep on running. A hand grips my shoulder, pulling me to a sudden stop. With a cry that doesn't sound human, I try to break from their grip. The sound of cursing reaches me, and before I know it, I'm wrapped in a huge pair of arms.

"I'm not leaving him behind!" I shout, thrashing against whoever's got me. After a few seconds, I realise it must be Nixon, only he has arms this big and could restrain me in a way that doesn't hurt.

We all know that I could use my powers to rip from his hold and push them all away, but something stops me, breaking through the wall of fear and fury I built around me.

There's a shuffling sound behind us before Alcide appears in front of me. Placing his hands on my shoulders, he lowers his face so we're eye to eye. I can see the panic and concern in his gaze as he scans me, which makes me wonder just how bad I look right now.

"We won't leave him behind, I promise. But stop for a minute and think," Alcide commands, his voice soothing despite the fear in his eyes. "If we race in, there's no telling what we could be walking into. Xavier is immortal, his powers will protect him. Let's come up with a plan."

Everything he'd been saying up to this point makes sense, and the logical part of me agrees. Running into danger without knowing what's happening would be like going in blindfolded, but in that moment, Xavier shouts out.

It's full of pain and rage, but it's the note of hopelessness that does it for me, like he doesn't expect to make it out alive.

No. Fuck no.

Even if I die trying to help him, I won't let him think he's alone.

"Nixon, let me go," I order, my voice sounding far calmer than I feel.

There's a pause, and then slowly, Nixon releases me. Turning, I take in my guys. They are all gathered behind Nixon and watching me with wide eyes. All except Alcide, who holds his hand out beseechingly.

"You're right," I say slowly, watching as a look of relief washes over Alcide's face. That look soon disappears, though, when I take a step back, putting some distance between us. I run my gaze over them, taking in all the things I love about them. "I won't put you guys at risk. Go back and take care of the women."

Blain pushes forward, his face twisted with his frustration. "Harpy, what the fuck are you on about? We go together," he snaps, his hands balling into fists.

"I won't leave Xavier. He's been alone for too long." I shake my head. I don't have time to argue with them anymore. They are right, this is dangerous, but there's a way I can protect them *and* get to Xavier. "I love you all."

Why does it feel like I'm saying goodbye?

They must sense it as well, because they all start moving towards me in unison. Holding my hand out, I reach for the power within me, barely even having to think as the vines and roots jump to do my bidding. The floor cracks and vines quickly start creating a wall of greenery between us. They weave together, and I watch the guys' faces disappear. I should feel exhausted from using this level of power. I've only ever caused shoots and leaves to grow before, but if anything, I feel alive, and power courses through my body.

"Rhea!" Nixon roars, pounding against the vines.

With my heart breaking, I spin and leave them behind. I know the vine wall won't hold them at bay for long, but I need to get to Xavier as soon as possible. It will take them a while to forgive me for this, but I'd rather we all escape and they be mad at me than have Xavier die because we took too long.

Pushing those thoughts aside, I run through the corridors, following the sounds of fighting. Gunshots echo around me, and I push myself to move faster. I skid to a halt as I round a corner and enter a large room, horror filling me at the scene before me.

Xavier is in the middle, fighting five separate guards. More pour into the room from a door on the other side, their guns raised as they shoot at him. His body is peppered with holes, and trickles of blood run down his skin, soaking into his clothes. His gift has stopped him from dying when many others would have already fallen, but when he sees me, his eyes widen.

"Rhea, no, run!" he roars hopelessly.

As soon as he speaks, the guards turn to see who he's talking to, and they shout when they see me. I throw up my hands, trying to block the oncoming bullets with vines. Several slip through, but my skin instantly hardens, adapting as they hit my body. A small grunt of pain leaves my lips, but I ignore it and weave through the guards, needing to reach Xavier. He doesn't look great, and his body is starting to sag, but he fights with renewed vigour as I reach his side.

"Rhea, what are you doing?" he growls, swinging his arm around as he punches one of the guards, knocking him out cold.

"Did you really think I was going to leave you?" I counter, my voice sharp as I kick the nearest guard. "Just like old times, right?" I joke even as I duck an oncoming punch.

More guards flood into the room, and I realise we might be in real trouble here. We're hopelessly outnumbered, and they look pissed. I mean, we did break out of their lab, kill some of their men, and steal the women, so I suppose they have something to prove.

Without a word, Xavier and I stand back to back, just like how we fought in the arena back in Last Stop. My heart breaks a little. I hoped we'd never be in a situation like that again, but no. Perhaps being free will never happen, not in a world where there is so much fear and hate.

The guards start to close in on us with wicked smirks on their faces, their weapons raised.

A roar echoes down the corridor I'd arrived from. I guess Nixon's free from the barrier I built. A mixture of feelings hits me. There's relief that they might be able to help us, but more than that, I feel fear. They aren't protected from bullets like Xavier and I are. I knew they wouldn't let me face this alone, but part of me hoped they would.

Jesse comes barrelling into the room first, swearing as he sees the guards, followed by the others.

That's when all hell breaks loose.

The guards turn on them, swinging weapons and firing bullets. I can't keep track of who's doing what or check if anyone is okay since I have to put all of my effort into keeping myself alive. Xavier and I fight like a team, and I get flashes of the others as they move through the room.

I'm not sure how much time passes, it moves differently when you're fighting, but when no one comes forward to take the place of the last guard I fought, I look up in surprise. Hope flashes through me. Did we do it? Did we kill them all? Are we free? That hope is instantly fractured as I see the wall of guards surrounding us. My guys and I are in the middle of the room, and as I glance around, I see the guards are everywhere. I had no idea there were so many of them in this bunker.

Heart stuttering in my chest, I realise we're not getting out of here. There's no way we can get through this many guards, even with our powers. There's just too many of them.

Something touches my hand, and I automatically jerk it away before I realise it's Xavier trying to hold my hand, resignation written across his face. He knows it too. This will be our last fight together. Looking to my left, I see Rex at my side. I offer him my hand, and he instantly links his fingers with mine, a sad smile curving his lips. A tear rolls down my cheek, and I look over my shoulder at my other guys. They have all linked hands too. It seems fitting that we're all here, even if I wish it was the other way around. If this is how we go down, at least we go down together.

Just a girl and her freaks.

Chapter Fifteen

This is it.

I know it.

I should have died many moons ago, back in Cinders as a slave, but yet here I am, surviving against all odds. I found love, and I found a family. And if this right here is how I die, surrounded by love and doing the right thing to save people, then so be it.

At least I won't die alone.

I close my eyes for a moment, and those innocent, thankful faces of the women we saved flash through my mind. At least they are gone. We have given them a chance, which is more than we have right now. Our lives seem forever doomed, moving from one tragedy to the next. Maybe it's me who is doomed, and I've led them all to the grave. They don't blame me though, no, they surround me with their arms, protecting me and standing with me as best as they can, even as they face death. We've lost so much, and all we ever wanted was to be together. We travelled the world, trying to spread hope and laughter, and in the end, it wasn't enough. The darkness of this world is so consuming, so far reaching, that it's going to blot us out.

"No, this isn't how it ends," Smoke whispers, making me open my eyes and look at him. "It isn't." He looks around, searching for a way—a way he won't find.

Sometimes even doing your best isn't enough. And that's okay. At least you tried.

"Smoke," I murmur, but he ignores me, his eyes calculating until he finally turns to me. I stare back at him as he seems to come to some sort of decision, closing his eyes as if he's in pain.

"There's a way," he murmurs as we hear the guards reloading their weapons, ready to end our lives.

I hope it's quick. Not for me, but for them.

"What—" I start to ask, but it's too late.

Smoke turns without hesitation, and fire forms in his hands. He stretches forward and blasts a hole through the guards, setting them alight. They fall back with a scream, and the others don't take their places, too scared of burning to death. "Go!" he orders. There's an opening, a chance. Nixon and the others rush through, and I grab Smoke's hand as I hurry through the opening as well. The corridor is before us, just out of reach but so close. We have a chance now!

Hope fills me.

We can still survive this.

We're going to be okay!

Smoke's hand slips from mine and I turn, my eyes widening. He stopped on the edge of the corridor. The guards slowly inch towards us. My eyes dart to them and back to Smoke. "Come on, let's go!" I yell, reaching for him again.

He takes my hand and kisses it, meeting my eyes before he steps back. I move forward, and he nods at someone behind me. "Look after her for me. Don't let her follow."

"Smoke," I whisper, trembling. I'm confused, yet a terrible feeling of foreboding builds in my stomach. "Come with us, let's go—"

"I can't, my love." He smiles sadly. "They will only follow us. You'll never be safe. You deserve to be happy and safe. I can stop them here. I can end this for good. Just promise to have a good life, Rhea. To love and laugh, and to never stop living, even when it hurts."

"Smoke, no," I beg, reaching for him again, but arms wrap

around me, keeping me from him as he steps back. Tears fill my eyes, almost blinding me. He can't mean what I think he does, can he?

"We can survive—"

"No, Rhea, there's only one way out for us. It's okay," he promises. "I'll be with my family again. Maybe that was the reason why I met you—to save you all. You have to survive, Rhea, to bring hope to this world. I am no one."

"To me you are everything!" I scream.

"Love her for me, and protect her always," he demands of the others behind me.

"We will," I hear the others echo, not arguing.

"Don't listen to him! Let's grab him and go!" I scream, pulling from their arms to see their steady, sad eyes. They won't help.

"No!" I shout. Smoke glances at the guards then back to me.

"There's no time, Rhea. Let me do this. Let me save you all. Let me make this world a bit of a better place." Rushing forward, he smashes his lips to mine. I grab him and hold him to me, trying to get him to come with us, but all too soon his lips rip away from mine despite my best attempts to hold him tight, and I'm left cold and reaching for him. "It's okay. Thank you for giving me a second chance, and for giving me a family, someone to fight for... for loving me."

"No!" I implore, but fire sprouts from the ground, stopping me from chasing him as he turns to the guards with his hands out. Fire crawls across his arms and chest, and he screams in pain. Sobbing, I try to get to him, to get through the fire, but it's too hot.

I was wrong.

There is goodness still left in this world, you just have to know where to look for it.

Smoke is that.

He is good.

He is one man standing against the evil trying to infect what is left of our broken world.

He can't stand alone, but he won't let me stand and die by his side.

He feels this is his path, his sacrifice to make. I scream and shout, kicking and fighting to get to him. I won't let him die for me, too many already have. I won't. I sob, reaching for him. I can't lose him. I can't. I just found him. We haven't had nearly enough time together, but I know one year, five, fifty... would never be enough with this man who has fire in his heart and love in his eyes.

But time and destiny stop for no man or woman. Even if you try to fight it, the world just doesn't give a shit what's right or wrong or good or evil. Death is something that happens every single day.

You can't fight it or outrun it.

Yet I still try.

"Rhea!" Jesse screams, and I look back to see the fire catching on the walls and floor, burning everything.

We are all going to die.

I have a choice to make.

My eyes flicker back to Smoke as he turns his head, those bright orange eyes alight. His lips tip up in the same teasing grin he gave me when we first met. "I love you," he mouths before turning back to the guards, his head falling back with a deafening roar as the flames engulf his entire body.

There is only the burning silhouette of a man, and then it explodes outwards. I throw my hands up instinctively. A protective bubble forms around me and my men, but I can't look away from the scene before me. My arms wobble from the strain, and agony winds through me as my powers deplete.

My eyes water, and my entire body trembles.

I scream in pain, and then I hear a crack. Looking down, I see the bracelet on my wrist brighten with its own inner light, and suddenly, more power than I've ever felt flows through me like an electric current, reinforcing the shield.

I watch as the guards shoot and yell, trying to run, but it's too late.

The flames swallow everything but us as the whole bunker burns around us.

I fall to my knees, and we huddle together, the bracelet burning my skin as it pumps more and more power into the protective bubble separating us from Smoke's wrath—from his last act as a man who loves me.

I feel the others behind me, and I know I can't give up. I can't let the agony pouring through me stop me or they will all die. Smoke is sacrificing his life to save us, and I can't let that be in vain, even if it hurts. Even if it feels like I just want to give up and go with him. Even if it's so hard I don't think I can do it.

He believes in me.

He's trusting me to save them.

So I kneel before my family, holding up the protective barrier to keep them alive. All the while, my eyes are locked on the burning man I fell so quickly and deeply in love with.

Until I can't hear anymore.

Until I can't feel anymore.

Until it's all too much.

The silhouette slowly fades into the rest of the flames as they start to go out. My body is screaming at me, but I try to hold on. I feel myself swaying before I fall to my side, holding the barrier. We are going to be entombed down here. I can't let that happen, so I send every last drop of remaining power out in a burst.

It surrounds us and blasts us to the surface.

Blackness edges my vision, and the last thing I see is his fire raging around us.

Burning it all down and killing him with it.

My eyes snap open, my chest is tight, and my entire body aches. I force myself to sit up, even though it hurts. I look around, hoping it was all a bad dream. There's sunlight piercing through the smoke surrounding us. I don't know how, but we survived. I bring my gaze back to my men to see them slowly coming to as well.

We are alive.

How?

What was once the bunker is now nothing but ashes covering us and the floor. And Smoke? He's nowhere to be seen. He's dead, I know it. There can be no Smoke without flames, and he used all of his powers to save us... to save me. My heart cracks wide open, falling to the ground in pieces like his and the bunker's remains. It hurts so much I can't breathe, can't think, and then as sudden as that sharp pain came, it goes. It floats away on ice that moves sluggishly through me, numbing me to everything. I don't know if it's my powers or just plain shock, but I'm cold.

So very cold and empty.

I spot my broken bracelet, and for some reason, that makes me shiver. Is this what Gregor saw when he gifted me with it?

I'm numb, cold, and empty.

I know it's probably shock, the pain will come later, but for now, I submerge myself in that emptiness, knowing it will hurt too much.

He's gone.

I know he's finally back with his family, but I can't help recalling Regnor's words—that I would be Smoke's downfall. He was right, I was. I led him to his death. Was it really worth it?

He left everything for me.

Friends, a purpose, a city. He survived the death of his family and a war, and it was me who finally killed him.

Now he's nothing but his namesake.

Smoke.

Chapter Sixteen

I'm not sure how long I kneel in the ashes. It could be an hour, it could be days or even minutes. Time has ceased to matter to me. It stopped registering the moment Smoke sacrificed himself for us.

My body is screaming for me to move, and my muscles are cramping from being in one position for too long, but I can't take my eyes from the last place I saw Smoke. Part of me wants to move to that spot, but I'm terrified of what I might find. If I were to find any of his remains, I would fall apart, and I'm not sure I could be put back together again. But no, I wouldn't find anything, I know that.

His flame burned too hot.

I'm vaguely aware of movement around me, low voices, and the shuffle of feet. Someone's sitting next to me. I think it's Nixon, but I'm not sure, I can't find the energy to move. They have not tried to speak to me, just attempting to comfort me with their presence, knowing nothing could help right now.

I can't believe Smoke is gone. It happened so quickly. He saved us all, but now we have to live in a world without him. He was so hopeful for his new life, and it's all over.

The sound of footsteps crunching the dirt and gravel tells me that someone is approaching, but I still don't move. A part of my brain is continuing to function enough to know that Nixon wouldn't let anyone who meant me harm close, so I dismiss anything but the numbness. Voices rumble around me, a pair of legs appear in front of me, and before I have a chance to look up, Alcide kneels before me. His face is set in a worried frown, and I can see his own grief in his eyes.

Taking me in, he sighs softly.

"Oh, *cariño*." His voice is quiet, his nickname for me a whisper across his lips. Slowly, he reaches out and starts rubbing my face with his hand. I'm slightly confused by what he's doing, but the burning hole in my heart is making it hard to focus on anything else. He pulls away, and I see his hand is covered in soot. So that's what he was doing, trying to wipe the ash from my skin. I should probably care that I'm covered in it, but if anything, it's just proof of what we went through, of the sacrifices we made to keep us alive.

Another set of feet appear at my side.

"Come on, Firecracker, we need to get moving."

Jesse. Only he calls me Firecracker.

Gentle hands land on my shoulders, and I realise they need me to stand. Numbly, as the guys help me climb to my feet, I cast my dull eyes around me.

We are in a smoking hole. Even the concrete is smoking. The walls are nothing but rubble, and the roof is gone. The bright warmth of the sun and the dark pain and loss within me are at such odds that I start laughing. It's a broken, wild laugh that tears at my throat.

"Rhea?" a soft, concerned voice calls—Rex, I think.

The laugh stops as abruptly as it started, and I turn on unsteady legs to look at him.

"Oh, Wildcat." The grief in his voice is too much for me to cope with, so I shut down, shoving my emotions away, unwilling to feel them right now.

Something catches my attention. Turning my head, I watch the black smoke from the ruined bunker spiral up into the air. I can't see anything that would have caught my attention—no, there it is. It's a butterfly, and it's flying across the ashen field like a fucking metaphor. Life will continue here, and sometimes you have to raze everything to the ground for new life to grow.

Unable to deal with the swell of emotions that are trying to overwhelm me, I push them down once again and build a wall around them until a state of numbness is all I feel once more. With the guys' hands on me, they guide me through the ruins and towards several large cars. I've never actually seen any that work before, their rusted empty husks lining the ruins of our world. These must have belonged to the scientists, which explains how they were able to capture so many women. I have no idea how they managed to keep them running or what fuel they use, but honestly, I don't care. My grief makes me walk in an indifferent daze.

The cars are filled with the women from the bunker, and I'm led to one of the vehicles in the front. This one is empty. Climbing in, I stare out at the desert before us as the guys speak in hushed voices.

Others climb into the car, and with a loud chugging noise, it starts. Everything shakes around me, and slowly, we start to move.

"It's okay, Rhea. We're going to the closest town so we can take the women somewhere safe." Xavier's voice catches my attention, but I don't look away from the window.

As we pull away, I turn and stare at the smouldering ruins, leaving the lab and Smoke behind.

I press my hand to the window in a final goodbye to the man who entered my life in an explosion of flames and left the exact same way.

THE NEXT FEW hours pass in a blur. I watch with a detached numbness as we find a town. The guys check it out and find somewhere the women can stay. Alcide assures me that the attitudes towards freaks is different here, and that the women will be safe. I don't respond, trusting their judgement.

Sitting in the dining area of the local pub, I stare down at the mug before me. It's full of a strong smelling alcohol that makes me wince every time I raise it to my lips, but a delicious warm heat settles in my belly with each sip, chasing away the cold. The guys sit around me, and I'm aware that they are discussing something, but I've not been listening. Every now and again I'll hear my name mentioned, but I continue to stare.

I'm not actually seeing the mug, but the last moments I saw Smoke alive. He was so vibrant, so *alive*. He always was. His ability to see the humour in every situation was one of the things that first brought him to my attention. I remember every time he'd saunter up to me with that cheeky smile of his, and the moment when I realised that he was more than just a friend, but someone I loved too. We didn't have enough time together, it should have been longer.

"She's catatonic!" Blain's loud exclamation shakes me from my memories. "We can't move anywhere else until she snaps out of this... state! If we get attacked on the road, we need her to be alert."

Catatonic. Is that what this is? This numbness that makes everything feel heavy and detached? I feel like I'm in a bubble that is separating and protecting me from everything happening around me.

"Staying one night won't hurt," a soft, familiar voice agrees. "We're far away enough that even if they *did* have reinforcements, they wouldn't find us tonight."

There is a deep, long sigh. "Fine, I'll speak with the owner and get us a room." The gentle accent tells me it's Alcide who's speaking. A chair screeches against the wooden floor of the pub, and I hear his heavy steps as he walks away.

The other guys continue to talk as Alcide sorts somewhere for us to stay, but I'm not focused on what they are saying. It's only when my ringmaster walks back with a key in his hand that I look up from the table.

Locking my eyes with his, I steel myself to speak the words that will change everything. "Smoke is dead."

The guys all freeze at the sound of my croaky, broken voice.

"I know, *cariño*," Alcide replies softly, scanning my weary form as if he's worried his words might cause me to break down.

Lifting the mug once more, I chug the alcohol, not stopping until I've drunk it all. Standing, I feel lightheaded and dizzy, but I doubt it's the alcohol working already, it's the toll today has taken on me. The other guys stand with me, watching me closely. As if the weight of the words I just spoke are too heavy, I stumble. Someone moves behind me, and before I know it, I'm cradled against Xavier's chest as he carries me through the room.

My eyes close of their own accord, unable to look at this dull world any longer. I must fall asleep, as the next thing I know I'm being placed in a bed, while the guys stare at me with varying expressions of concern and sympathy. My stomach knots as my pent-up emotions try to surface, but I refuse to let them. Rolling over so I face the wall, I hug my legs to my chest. I close my eyes and pray I have a dreamless sleep. I don't think I could cope if I dreamt of him tonight.

It's too fresh, too raw.

Thankfully, I feel the pull of empty darkness immediately. The events of the day and the exhaustion of depleting all of my power catch up with me, and I slip into the blissful oblivion of unconsciousness.

The heat of Smoke vanishes, just like him.

Chapter Seventeen

The walls I built around my grief and pain crumble as soon as I wake up, as if all the strength leaves my body with the clinging oblivion of sleep. The room is dark, and quiet snores fill the air as silent tears start to slide down my face. I wrap my arms around me to try and hold back the splintering pain ripping me apart so suddenly, I struggle for air.

He's gone.

I gasp out a desperate breath, blinded by my own tears. I dig my teeth into my lip in an effort to stop my wails of anguish, biting so hard I taste blood. My whole body shakes with the force of my sobs, and I hear someone stop snoring as if sensing my pain.

I can't wake them. I need to feel this alone.

They will hold me, kiss me, and try to make it better... but they can't. Nothing can make this better, and right now, I have my own storm that I need to let out.

Slipping from the bed, I stumble across the uneven, cold wooden floor, searching blindly. There has to be a bathroom. I find a door and open it, wincing at the creak before stepping out into a hallway. We must be above the pub. I remember that as the haze begins to dissipate, leaving me blinded by grief.

I tread on silent, bare feet to the next door, and I open it to find a bathroom. There's a long wire to the right as I shut the door, so I pull it, and a light blinks on above, throwing everything into a yellow hue.

I don't care.

I slide down the door, finally letting the sobs out. I pull my knees to my chest, ripping at my hair.

Gone.

Gone.

He's gone.

Fuck!

I want to roar with it. I slam my head back against the door with an audible thud. The physical pain helps chase away the emotional pain for a split second, so I do it again and again. Regnor's words repeat in my head. He knew this would happen. He knew I would be Smoke's downfall. He was right.

That hurts too.

He tried to warn his friend, and now he's lost.

At least he got to say goodbye.

I love you.

The words echo in my mind, as does the image of Smoke burning as he mouths them to me, making me cry out. I know if I become much louder, the guys will come, so I bring my arm up and bite down, muffling my sobs as the pain finally breaks free.

I don't know how long I sit here, but my tears finally dry up. My eyes are swollen and aching, my face too, and there are teeth marks in my dirty arm. My head hurts, as does my body, and I feel filthy. Filthy and so fucking tired.

Stumbling to my feet, I pass the toilet and rip back the cheap, tattered shower curtain. There's an old-style silver shower to the right, and I press a button. The deep rumbling sound is followed by that of clanking pipes before brown water shoots from the shower-head. I watch it disrupt the dust in the bottom of the old, cracked bath until it eventually turns clean.

I throw off my clothes, not wanting them to touch me for a moment more. I step under the spray, letting it wash me clean. The heat is almost unbearable, but it's better than the cold, and better than the feeling of the ash on my skin.

Ash... and probably bone.

Probably Smoke.

I know rinsing it away won't wash the day away, but I couldn't stand it touching my skin for a moment longer. My head drops, and I press my hands against the wall as the water sluices over my exhausted muscles.

Today was a nightmare.

And I don't want it to end. When the sun rises, it will finally be true. He's truly gone. I expect him to bust down the door at any moment with a cocky smile and electric eyes, but he won't. All that's left are the memories I have of him, which are far too little.

My head hangs heavily as the hot water washes over my body and face. I watch idly as dirt and ash mix with the water at my feet before being pulled into the drain. It makes me cry again, as if the final part of Smoke is leaving me.

I watch the water swirl, over and over, until it finally runs clean, and then I collapse. Sitting in the tub, I hold myself even as the spray turns cold and I shiver. Even as my heart continues to fracture in my chest.

It hurts.

It hurts too much.

I close my eyes and lose myself in memories of Smoke, his laughter, and his touch. The way he would talk. I remember everything, memorising his face as I float away on a cloud of good memories.

"Rhea?" Rex calls through the door sometime later, breaking me from my trance. "It's time to leave."

How long have I been in here?

Do I really care?

Time to leave.

Time to leave Smoke and everything we could have had behind.
But what does the future hold for us now?
Nothing but pain and heartache?
Will I lose more of my family to this world?
But the bigger question is... what do I do without him?

Chapter Eighteen

Stumbling from the shower, feeling raw and damaged, I go through the motions of drying myself. We don't have any clothes other than what we escaped in, and staring down at the dirty gown I'd been wearing, I feel my chest constrict.

I can't do it, I can't put that back on.

"Rhea," Jesse calls softly, knocking on the door. "I've got some clothes for you. They'll be too big, but they are clean."

Screwing my eyes shut, I say a silent thanks that I have these men looking out for me before opening the door and peeking out. Jesse stands there with an armful of clothing and a small, sad smile.

"How are you doing, Firecracker?"

He's asking how I'm feeling this morning after my shower, but I know his question is about more than that.

"Broken," I reply honestly. My eyes sting, but I've got no tears left to shed. Taking the bundle from his arms, I retreat back into the bathroom. "Thank you." My voice sounds as broken as my heart feels.

Closing the door quietly before he can ask me any more questions, I release a long, shaky breath.

I know Smoke had just joined our family, but that's what he was to us, and his loss is going to be felt keenly.

Slowly, I continue to dry myself, feeling exhausted from the sheer amount of energy I used to protect us yesterday and grief. It's crazy how draining it is to lose someone, like a little part of my soul has been chipped away, and without it, I'll never quite be whole again. I can hear the others moving around, since the walls are thin up here. They are discussing what happened and what they are going to do next, and while I can't make out exactly what they are saying, I hear the occasional word.

That's when it hits me—they are grieving too.

Suddenly, I feel like the worst person in the world. I might have loved Smoke in a romantic sense, but they loved him like a brother. You can't go through what we did and not form a bond. Of course they are suffering from his loss too. I need to pull myself together and be there for them. I know my grief won't just go away, but we need to stick together and help each other through this. Like a family.

Taking a deep breath, I pull on the borrowed clothes, grateful Jesse thought to bring me a belt, as the trousers are way too big around my waist. Putting on the shirt and large trousers feels like donning armour to protect my broken heart. It's as if being out of the gown and in normal clothes is peeling away everything that happened. Bit by bit, I dress myself, focusing on the task rather than the gaping hole in my chest. That makes it easier.

Finally dressed, I open the door and find Blain waiting for me. His arms are crossed as he leans back against the wall. Looking at him, you'd think he was pissed off, but as he raises his gaze to mine, I see the truth in his eyes.

He's hurting.

"You okay, Harpy?" His voice is as dark as his eyes, and his body is tense like he's expecting trouble.

Slowly, I walk towards him, stopping only when I'm inches away from him. We're not even touching, but I can feel his body heat against the parts of my skin that are still exposed. Shaking my head, I let him see the truth in my eyes. "No, I'm not okay. Are you?"

He pauses for a second, as if contemplating how he's going to answer, but finally he just sighs and shakes his head. "No. Not even in the slightest." His voice drops to a whisper as he speaks, and I can no longer hold myself back. Closing the distance between us, I wrap my arms around him and press my face against his chest. He makes a small noise in the back of his throat and holds me tightly against him, burying his face in my hair. We stand like that until he's able to speak again. "He was a cheeky shit and annoyed the fuck out of me most of the time, but I miss him."

"I know." My voice is croaky, my vocal cords tightening as the tears threaten to flow once more, but as I take a deep inhale of Blain's familiar scent, I manage to ground myself. "I hate that he did what he did, but I'll be forever grateful because he gave me another day with all of you."

Blain seems to stiffen for a moment, but then he just sighs again. "Yeah. You saved us too, you know." I feel him shake his head. I want to object, it was Smoke who saved us with his sacrifice, after all, but Blain continues before I can speak. "That shield you threw up around us... The fire would have killed us. I didn't even know you could create shields."

"Neither did I," I admit, falling quiet as I remember that moment and how fiercely the fire had been burning. The bracelet had undoubtedly saved our lives by giving me extra power. Silence descends around us again as we take comfort from each other's presence, until I can't hold back the question that's been growing in my mind. "What do we do now?" My voice sounds small, broken.

Reluctantly, he releases me from his embrace and stares down at me for a moment before replying. "The others are waiting for us downstairs. We need to decide where we'll go next."

My stomach tenses at the reminder. We're homeless. We were attacked and taken from our wagons. I have no idea what happened to our stuff or the animals, but I'm sure the carts have all been looted.

Frowning, I nod in response and let him lead the way. We're silent as we make our way downstairs into the main room of the pub, the guys sitting around a circular table at the back. They all look up as we enter, and their expressions range from concerned to sympathetic. Finally, my gaze lands on Jesse, and I see his eyes are red. He and Smoke were closer than the others. Jesse spent more time with the rebels than us, and the two had become fast friends.

And now he'll never see him again.

Stop it. Don't lose it here.

I have to repeat the order to myself over and over. Earlier, I'd thought that I'd run out of tears to cry, but it appears I was wrong. The guys stand as I approach, and one by one, they pull me into their arms. We don't say anything, we don't need to, our sadness is palpable. Once we've all reassured ourselves that we're alive, I squeeze onto the bench beside Alcide and Rex, their eyes on me.

"What do we do now?" I ask, repeating the question I asked Blain just minutes ago.

The atmosphere is heavy, and eventually, Alcide clears his throat and leans forward, resting his elbows on the table. "Nixon and Xavier went to scout out the place you were taken from to see if any of our belongings were still there."

My heart speeds up in my chest at the reminder of that day. We hadn't even seen it coming. Swallowing against the sudden lump in the back of my throat, I glance towards the two males in question.

Xavier has his arms crossed over his chest, and he has been staring at me since we sat down, but now he looks away as if knowing what he's about to say will be painful. "The wagons were smashed, but not beyond repair. However, there was nothing left on them though, they'd been picked clean. Everything's gone."

"So we're penniless and homeless. How are we going to perform if we don't have a tent and have no way to buy a new one?" Blain snaps, glaring at anyone who dares look at him.

"I've been thinking about this," Alcide starts, his voice unusually hesitant. "I think the time for the circus has passed. We're not needed anymore."

Several of the guys look shocked, and Blain snorts like this is the worst idea he's ever heard, but before anyone can say anything, I jump in.

"He's right. I don't want to keep travelling anymore, never sure what we will encounter from one town to the next." My heart pounds as I speak, not quite believing what I'm saying. I love our circus. It saved my life back in Cinders when I was nothing but a slave girl. It gave me the confidence to grow into the person I am today and meet the loves of my life.

But everything comes to an end.

"What do *you* want, Rhea?" Nixon asks, surprising us all, his deep voice soft and questioning. From someone else, it might sound like a dig, but I know he genuinely wants to know the answer.

"I want a home," I whisper. This is something I've always dreamed of but never thought possible, not for someone like me. "During our captivity, I had a lot of time to think, and I don't want to waste any more time. I want to be happy and safe with you guys." Looking around the table, I meet their gazes, my voice becoming more confident as I see several of them nodding. "I want to find someplace where we are safe and can be a proper family."

"So, no more circus?" Jesse inquires quietly. "What will we do instead?"

He's right, we have to earn money some way, but between us, I'm sure we can figure something out. It's daunting, since we're literally starting with only the clothes on our backs, but we have each other, and that's worth more than all of our previous worldly possessions.

"The world is changing," Alcide speaks up, a thoughtful expression on his handsome face. "I went for a walk in the town this morning, and there are signs for the rebellion everywhere. I even overheard two people talking openly about having powers." Leaning forward again, he meets each of our gazes, working his way around the table until he meets my eyes. "Freaks outnumber those without powers. We don't need to hide anymore."

While we always openly used our power within the circus and never denied that we had them, we managed to get away without too much aggravation because people said they were just stage tricks —a trick of the light or strings that controlled targets to make sure we always landed a bullseye. Deep down they knew the truth, but in all honesty, we hid behind that because it was safe. Since everything we went through in Last Stop before becoming the face of the rebellion, that's going to be impossible to do anymore if their reach has stretched this far.

I'll miss the circus, the acts, and our crew, but it's time to move on. This makes me pause as a thought suddenly comes to me.

"What about the animals? Did you see any sign of them?" I ask quietly, turning my attention back to Nixon and Xavier. My heart sinks as I see the former shake his head.

My expression must show my dismay, as Xavier leans forward and places his hand over mine. "There were paw prints, I think they managed to get free."

"They will find us." Rex says, speaking up for the first time, and I turn to look at him. He's got a faraway look in his eyes, but the confidence in his words makes me think that his gift is telling him something we don't know yet.

"It wouldn't hurt to look for them as we travel either," Blain suggests, his gaze still locked on my face.

The others make noises of agreement. I look at each of them, and despite the aching sadness within me, a sense of hope begins to bloom in my chest. We're really doing this. It's going to take some work, and it won't be easy, but Smoke died so we could have a future, and that's exactly what we're going to do.

"So we're in agreement?" Alcide asks, falling back into his ringmaster role as he looks around the table again, waiting for each of us to nod. "We are a circus no longer, and we'll search for somewhere to settle. We'll search for our future." I can hear how much giving up his circus means to him, but it's time.

"No, not just anywhere," I interject, a small, shaky smile pulling at my lips. "A home."

Chapter Nineteen

e set off into the horizon of the destroyed world we lived in with only one thought in mind—to find the life we promised Smoke, full of laughter and happiness.

I miss him, I do, but I refuse to let him down or ignore the legacy he provided us with. And so we travel as a family, no longer as a circus. We explore the world, searching for the perfect place that feels like home, a place to start our future together.

To settle down.

THREE MONTHS after we started our journey, we find it. I know it as soon as we see it. We stumbled across it, really, as we searched for a place to camp in the middle of the wilderness we had found ourselves in.

It's a cabin.

It stands broken and abandoned, but there is such promise in that old wood, and the world around it is breathtaking.

An oasis.

It thrives despite the bombs and wars, the scarred earth and suffering. It's peaceful and beautiful. There's a small lake just before the cabin, and the water is nearly crystal clear with some harmless birds swimming on one side. It's surrounded by blooming plants and flowers, and trees meet above to create an arch that we walked through to get here.

It's magnificent, a breath of fresh air.

A symbol of hope.

"We are home," I murmur as I stare at it.

"Then I guess we better get to work," Alcide calls, rolling up his sleeves.

And work we do, because nothing worth having in this life is easy. You have to fight every single day, and if you're lucky, you will find those willing to fight at your side.

The first night we spend under the stars near our new home, I cry. They hold me the entire time, touching and comforting me.

The next night, I let them kiss me all over to make it better.

And so the days pass, and with it, so does my sadness. I lose myself in making the cabin a home. I lose myself in them over and over, letting them take me away for just a moment. I relearn who I am, and I allow myself time to grieve and heal.

I change, just like the world.

The world is different now, we saw it on our travels. Women are taking charge, supported by men, friends, families, and lovers. The breeders are running scared, hunted by the rebels. Cities are overthrown and given a new chance at life. There are no slaves, only free men and women.

The world is adapting. It's healing.

And so are we.

Our fight is over. We have given everything we could for others, even our lives and futures, but now? It's time for our very own to begin.

As the days pass, the cabin starts to become more of a home. We will need to expand it eventually, but for now it's enough. It has one large living area with a fireplace which we sit before at night, sharing meals and stories. We found an old barn we transformed into a haven for animals. More and more show up each day like we are a mecca for them—including our own. Rex was right, they found us again.

They, too, have their freedom and future.

We renovated the back of the cabin into a large bedroom, with plans to make more for privacy. There's a kitchen, a dining room, and a bathroom with a huge copper clawfoot tub which took a lot of cleaning. There's also an outside shower which Xavier really likes, and well... I don't mind the show he puts on when he uses it.

I find myself smiling more, as if every scarred broken bit of the cabin we fix repairs something within me as well. At night, I'm surrounded by love and warmth, and even when the nightmares come, they are swiftly chased away and replaced by good dreams from my men.

Like tonight with Blain. I couldn't sleep, so I slipped from their arms and went outside, letting the cool night air soothe me. But it wasn't enough. I could still hear my own screams, mixed with the breeders' laughter, and smell burning flesh, so I walked to the edge of the lake.

I've swum in it a few times, and the water always seems to have a way of washing my worries and pain away, so I quickly strip from the sleep dress I'm wearing, leave it on the grass, and slowly walk into the water. The moonlight shines bright enough to guide me, the stars twinkling above as I submerge. The middle of the lake is deep enough to swim in, while at the edges it goes up to my waist, and that's where I stand for a moment. The cool chill of the water quickly fades to a soothing temperature as I sweep my hands through it, watching the ripples from my movements.

It reminds me of life. How one person's actions, no matter how small, can have a ripple effect, changing the world around them. That's how I feel about Smoke... and how my family feels about me.

Blain's soft voice fills the air behind me, interrupting my thoughts. "Harpy?"

Looking over my shoulder, I meet his worried eyes before turning back and diving under the water. Holding my breath, I swim and swim, letting it wash away the sweat and pain until I emerge in the middle, gasping for air. I spin to see him diving into the lake to chase me like I knew he would.

When he breaks the surface, slicking his hair back, I grin. "What the fuck, Harpy?" he snaps, pissed as always even as he reaches for me. I wrap my legs around him greedily and drape my arms around his neck, letting him hold us up as I press against his warmth. His heat chases away the rest of the nightmare. "Bloody woman."

"Let's stay like this for a moment, please?" I whisper, staring into those dark eyes. He nods, and I lie back as he holds me up. I close my eyes as I float under the night sky and forget everything for a moment.

Eventually, I realise he's breathing heavily, and I crack open an eye to see him staring hungrily at my exposed chest. My breasts sway in the water, and my nipples are tight in the cool air. His eyes meet mine for a moment before he bends down and sucks one nipple into his mouth, working it into a stiff point as I gasp. I grip his shoulders to hold on as he attacks me.

"Blain," I murmur, holding him to me.

I've been with him so much these last few months, but every time still feels like the first. The taste of his skin as I lean up and lick his face, the feel of his warm, hard body against mine. The power in his hands as he slides them down to my ass and squeezes as he continues sucking my nipple.

It sends a thrill through me as my clit throbs in time with his mouth's ministrations before he quickly switches to the other side, causing me to wiggle in his arms in no time. Yet he ignores my gasped pleas as my head falls back, my gaze going to the moon. Giving in, I let him do whatever he wants as long as he doesn't stop touching me.

As if in reward, he releases my nipple and scrapes his teeth along the valley of my breasts, squeezing and stroking my ass before he lays me back fully. The top of my body floats in the water, and my legs are wrapped around his waist, but they are stretched out now. I bring my eyes back to him, to the beauty of my tattooed lover. His are entranced by my body, as always, watching his hand as he strokes across my belly and hip to my pussy.

"Blain," I purr, knowing he loves it when I say his name.

In retaliation, he cups my cunt, squeezing it possessively as those dark eyes flash to mine. "Shh, Harpy. For once let me just make you feel better. Let me help."

I do.

I don't fight him, which we enjoy sometimes, nor do we argue or struggle for control and dominance. I relax in his hold and just let him have me in every single way he wants. His firm, possessive grip on my pussy loosens, and he strokes my wet folds so softly, I relax into the water.

His gentle touches don't speed up as he takes his time teasing me. He circles my clit before dipping his fingers inside my wet channel. I whimper and close my eyes as I reach for the release I feel on the horizon. Finally, he wrings it from my body by leaning down and closing his mouth over my pussy. He licks and sucks my clit as he thrusts his fingers inside of me.

He makes me come once...

Twice.

Three times.

I'm boneless in the water, just floating in a haze of ecstasy. A soft kiss is placed over my heart, making me open my eyes. "I will love you forever, Harpy, and I'll help heal your broken heart." Tears fill my eyes, and he kisses them away. "I promise, for as long as I live, I am yours. I will never leave you, never hurt you. I love you."

"I love you too," I whisper, pulling him closer. Sitting up, I wrap myself around him, and his hands go to my ass to support me as I feel his hard cock press against my stomach. Yet he ignores his own desire to just be there for me.

But I need him. My core is empty and almost hurting from the ache.

"Blain, please," I whisper, leaning down to nip his lips before kissing him, unleashing all my pent-up pain, worry, and hope into the kiss. I feel his huge, hard cock pressed to my entrance, and it only urges me on. I sweep my tongue inside his mouth as he lifts me slightly and drops me onto his cock.

I moan as my head falls back, ending our kiss.

His huge length stretches my pussy as he works in every hard inch. I'm wet as hell, but he's so fucking big. That tiny bit of pain soon fades to an all-consuming desire, until nothing else exists but this. Not the nightmares, not the past, nor even the future, just this moment as we come together, and when he starts to move?

I see more than the stars in the sky.

The water moves faster around us from his quick, hard thrusts. He grunts in my ear as he kisses and licks down my throat. My nails dig into his back as I hold on, using his body for leverage as much as I can to meet the wild snap of his hips.

"Love you," he snarls into my ear, fighting the clamping of my pussy as I threaten to come yet again.

I can't speak or think as he continues to hit that spot inside of me over and over, making love to me under the stars in our new home. He pulls back and cups my cheek, and I see those once angry, lonely eyes are now filled with nothing but love.

I let go, soaring away with my release as he swallows my scream of ecstasy, his own roar mixing with it.

When I finally come back to my body, he is still holding me. The sweat and water on my body cools, and I shiver. "Let's get you back to bed, Harpy." He spanks my ass. "That's an order."

My reliable, cocky Blain is back, and for some reason, that makes me smile as he wades to the embankment.

I don't bother getting dressed, instead Blain and I walk hand in hand back to our beds on the floor in the cleared room of the cabin. He tucks me between my snoring men, kissing me goodnight, and before I can reply, my eyes are closing and I'm drifting back into a dreamless slumber.

THE NEXT MORNING, I wake up to the chirping of birds. I heat some tea on the fire as the others sleep and wander outside. Sitting on the grass before the small lake, I watch the trees blow in the wind and sing with it as the ducks chase their siblings through the water. Tiny is washing in one end, making me grin, and Rumple and Bubbles laze in the morning sun. Sid bounds over and sits next to me as I stroke his back. Fluffy lounges on a branch, yawning.

It's a perfect moment.

I realise my heart is almost healed, and I'm happy.

Content.

My hand drifts to my stomach. I wondered for a while if it was true. At first I couldn't even comprehend it, but now I can.

I'm pregnant.

I feel the life growing inside of me, and my body is changing. It's only a matter of time before the others notice.

I guess the breeders got their wish, but they will never see my child. "We've made it a better world for you, little one. And when you're born, you will be so loved. You'll have a family, something most of us never did, and you will never be alone. We will never let anyone hurt you or use you. They called us freaks, my little one, but I know now that word holds power. Meaning. We are freaks, but in the very best way. And this world? It's filled with them, and whether you are born a freak or not, we will love you unconditionally."

Power is beauty. We hold a strength others could only dream of, and their jealousy became their hatred and their downfall.

I'll never shield my child from the past, instead I will let them learn from it so they can shape a better future.

So they may find their own path, just as I did.

Until then? This is paradise, and it's more than enough for a slave girl and her freaks.

Epilogue

Four Years Later

The sound of high-pitched giggling brings a smile to my face.

Peeling myself from the sofa in our sitting room, I stand and wander over to the open back door. Leaning against the door-frame, I feel my heart swell in my chest as I watch Nixon and Jesse playing in the garden with our little girl.

The dilapidated cabin we found all those years ago has been slowly turned into a home, and now I couldn't imagine living anywhere else. It wasn't all smooth sailing, especially with a newborn baby. None of us knew how to care for a child, and they are so rare in this broken world that provisions aren't exactly easy to come by. However, because babies aren't born often, the locals in the closest town absolutely doted on her. At first the guys were worried and overprotective, rightfully concerned that traffickers might try to take her from us. When you've been through what we have, it makes trusting others hard.

Only, the world is changing. In most towns, freaks and those without powers live in harmony. They finally figured out that our powers can be useful to everyday life, and there are now many places that specifically hire freaks. We still mainly keep to ourselves, though, old habits and all that.

After Smoke died, we were all adrift. We found our new home, but as soon as the guys discovered I was pregnant, everything changed. We don't know which one of the guys is her father—it's impossible to tell after everything that happened in the labs—and honestly, it doesn't matter. They are all her dad. Before the labs, I'd always assumed that I either couldn't get pregnant, like most of the population, or that my body stopped it from happening. Whatever they injected me with must have done something, however, as I've not fallen pregnant since, and there have been plenty of opportunities for it to happen.

Another high-pitched laugh brings a grin to my lips as I watch Nixon chase our daughter. My gentle giant stomps his feet and makes roaring noises, while Jesse and Hope run away.

Hope.

That's exactly what she is, my little ray of sunshine.

Our hope for a better life, for a future, together.

A barking noise pulls my attention from our daughter, and I look down at the bottom of the garden where Rex is training the new animals. He was right when he predicted our animals would find us. I still remember the day Tiny, Fluffy, Bubbles, Rumple, and Sid just appeared at our door. I was pregnant with Hope at the time, but that didn't stop me from climbing up onto Tiny's back and giving them all the greeting they deserved.

Since then, more animals have arrived. They just seem to *know* that they will be safe here, so Rex has created a haven for them. The old barn at the bottom of the garden is outfitted with everything they could need.

The sound of footsteps has me glancing over my shoulder, and I see Xavier watching the scene in the garden with a smile. I can hear Blain and Alcide talking in low voices, and if I poked my head out the door, I'm sure they'd be sitting on the porch watching Hope. None of us are ever far away. During her new-born days, she never spent one night in her crib. One of the guys always stayed up with her, whispering sweet nothings. Her favourite bedtime stories are of a circus that travelled the world, providing a safe haven for freaks where they could work and earn a living. I also make sure to tell her about her daddy Smoke who saved us all.

In the garden, Nixon pretends to fall to the ground, defeated in whatever game of chase they had been playing. Jesse cheers and Hope joins in, jumping up and down and clapping her small hands—only as she does so, sparks appear from her hands.

Created from nothing.

Startled, I push up from the doorframe, glancing at Xavier to see if he saw the same thing I did. He looks shocked, and as I turn around again, I see matching expressions on Jesse's and Nixon's faces. We'd thought that the breeders were wrong, that Hope wasn't born with powers because nothing had manifested yet. It seems we might have been the ones who were wrong.

I search for any other signs that she might be developing powers, but as quickly as it happened, it's gone, and Hope starts skipping towards me.

There was only one of us who could create fire in his palms without any accelerant.

Smoke.

"Mummy!" my daughter cries out, throwing herself towards me. Kneeling, I open my arms and catch her in a hug.

"Hey, baby girl," I murmur, kissing her red and orange hair which she inherited from me.

As she babbles at me, telling me all about the game her and Daddy Nix and Daddy Jesse had been playing, I hold her close. That familiar ache in my chest starts up as I think of Smoke, but as a tear rolls down my cheek, I find that I'm not sad. Smoke not only saved our lives, but he left a piece of himself behind with us.

He gave us Hope.

THE END

ACKNOWLEDGMENTS

Woah, what a wild ride. We can't quite believe that this series is over. Circus Save Me was our very first co-write and Erin's first ever published book. As such, it means a huge amount to us, and as Rhea developed as a character, we developed as authors. We've truly loved every minute of writing this series and hope you enjoyed reading and growing with us!

Of course, this book wouldn't be what it is without the support of our friends and family. Thank you to Jess, our wonderful editor and Norma our proofreader. Thank you to our alpha, beta and ARC readers for your constant positivity and support, without it this series wouldn't be possible! There are so many people that make up our team and help keep us on track, so a huge thanks to our PAs and author tribe who constantly keep us motivated. And of course, thank you to you. The readers. Your belief, support and constant love are the reasons we write. Without you, there is no us. From the bottom of our heart - thank you.

It's bittersweet to be ending Rhea's story, but we've loved the journey, and hope you did too.

Katie and Erin have been writing together since 2018, their friendship bloomed from the love of books and sarcasm. Nine books and three years later they are closer than ever and overjoyed to finish up the series that started their co-writing journey...

ABOUT ERIN O'KANE

Erin lives in the UK with her cat and works full time as an independent author. Now a *USA Today* bestselling author, she began writing in 2018 when she published her first book, *Hunted by Shadows*. She specialises in writing fantasy and reverse harem paranormal romance.

Previously to writing, she worked as an intensive care nurse. Despite having to now use a wheelchair, she doesn't let it stop her and loves to travel the world.

She met K.A Knight in 2018 when they became partners in crime and began writing together. In 2019, she became co-authors with Loxley Savage, writing fantasy reverse harem.

She's Disney obsessed, loves to read, craft and snack, and is always planning her next story.

Make sure to follow her on her social media pages for updates on what she's currently working on:

Facebook group: https://www.facebook.com/groups/ErinOKanesShadowRealm

Facebook author Page: https://www.-facebook.com/ErinOKaneAuthor

Newsletter: http://eepurl.com/gJhSd9

Instagram: https://www.instagram.com/erin.okane.author

ABOUT K.A. KNIGHT

K.A Knight is an USA Today bestselling indie author trying to get all of the stories and characters out of her head, writing the monsters that you love to hate. She loves reading and devours every book she can get her hands on, and she also has a worrying caffeine addiction.

She leads her double life in a sleepy English town, where she spends her days writing like a crazy person.

Read more at K.A Knight's website or join her Facebook Reader Group.
Sign up for exclusive content and my newsletter here
http://eepurl.com/drLLoj

OTHER BOOKS BY ERIN O'KANE

The Shadowborn Series:

Hunted by Shadows

Lost in Shadow

Embraced by Shadows

The Shadowborn series- the boxset

Born From Shadows Series:

Demons do it Better

The War and Deceit Series:

Fires of Hatred

Fires of Treason

Fires of Ruin

Fires of War

Fires of the Fae:

A Lady of Embers

A Spark of Promise

A Legacy of Hope and Ash

The Cursed Women Universe:: Venom and Stone

Betrayal and Curses

Fractured Wings

Bloodlines series:

Midnight Magic

Midnight Trials

Midnight Deception

Midnight Conviction

Midnight Ascension

The Complete Bloodlines Series – omnibus

The Brides of Darkness – interconnected standalones

A Kingdom of Broken Bonds

A City of Embers and Brimstone – coming soon

Standalones:

Second Chance

Love Bites

CO-WRITES

By Erin O'Kane and K.A Knight

Her Freaks Series:

Circus Save Me

Taming the Ringmaster

Walking the Tightrope

The Wild Boys:

The Wild Interview

The Wild Tour

The Wild Finale

The Wild Boys Series- The boxset

Standalones:

Hero Complex

Dark Temptations

By Erin O'Kane and Loxley Savage

Wicked Waves duet:

Twisted Tides

Tides that Bind

OTHER BOOKS BY K.A. KNIGHT

CONTEMPORARY

LEGENDS AND LOVE *CONTEMPORARY RH*

Revolt

Rebel

Riot - coming soon..

PRETTY LIARS *CONTEMPORARY RH*

Unstoppable

Unbreakable

PINE VALLEY COLLEGE *CONTEMPORARY*

Racing Hearts

DEN OF VIPERS UNIVERSE STANDALONES

Scarlett Limerence *CONTEMPORARY*

Nadia's Salvation *CONTEMPORARY*

Alena's Revenge *CONTEMPORARY*

Den of Vipers *CONTEMPORARY RH*

Gangsters and Guns (Co-Write with Loxley Savage) *CONTEMPORARY RH*

FORBIDDEN READS (STANDALONES)

Daddy's Angel *CONTEMPORARY*

Stepbrothers' Darling *CONTEMPORARY RH*

STANDALONES

The Standby *CONTEMPORARY*

Diver's Heart *CONTEMPORARY RH*

DYSTOPIAN

THEIR CHAMPION SERIES *Dystopian RH*

The Wasteland

The Summit

The Cities

The Nations

Their Champion Coloring Book

Their Champion - the omnibus

The Forgotten

The Lost

The Damned

Their Champion Companion - the omnibus

PARANORMAL

THE LOST COVEN SERIES *PNR RH*

Aurora's Coven

Aurora's Betrayal

HER MONSTERS SERIES *PNR RH*

Rage

Hate

Book 3 - *coming soon..*

COURTS AND KINGS *PNR RH*

Court of Nightmares

Court of Death

Court of Beasts

Court of Heathens - coming soon..

THE FALLEN GODS SERIES *PNR*

Pretty Painful

Pretty Bloody

Pretty Stormy

Pretty Wild

Pretty Hot

Pretty Faces

Pretty Spelled

Fallen Gods - the omnibus 1

Fallen Gods - the omnibus 2

FORGOTTEN CITY *PNR*

Monstrous Lies

Monstrous Truths

Monstrous Ends

SCIENCE FICTION

DAWNBREAKER SERIES *SCI FI RH*

Voyage to Ayama

Dreaming of Ayama

STANDALONES

Crown of Stars *SCI FI RH*

SHARED WORLD PROJECTS

Blade of Iris - Mafia Wars *CONTEMPORARY RH*

CO-WRITES

CO-AUTHOR PROJECTS - *Erin O'Kane*

HER FREAKS SERIES *PNR Dystopian RH*

Circus Save Me

Taming The Ringmaster

Walking the Tightrope

Her Freaks Series - the omnibus

STANDALONES

The Hero Complex *PNR RH*

Dark Temptations *Collection of Short Stories, ft. One Night Only & Circus Saves Christmas*

THE WILD BOYS SERIES *CONTEMPORARY RH*

The Wild Interview

The Wild Tour

The Wild Finale

The Wild Boys - the omnibus

CO-AUTHOR PROJECTS - *Ivy Fox*

Deadly Love Series *CONTEMPORARY*

Deadly Affair

Deadly Match

Deadly Encounter

CO-AUTHOR PROJECTS - *Kendra Moreno*

STANDALONES

Stolen Trophy *CONTEMPORARY RH*

Fractured Shadows *PNR RH*

Shadowed Heart

Burn Me *PNR*

Cirque Obscurum *PNR RH*

CO-AUTHOR PROJECTS - *Loxley Savage*

THE FORSAKEN SERIES *SCI FI RH*

Capturing Carmen

Stealing Shiloh

Harboring Harlow

STANDALONES

Gangsters and Guns *CONTEMPORARY*, IN DEN OF VIPERS' UNIVERSE

OTHER CO-WRITES

Shipwreck Souls *(with Kendra Moreno & Poppy Woods)*

The Horror Emporium *(with Kendra Moreno & Poppy Woods)*

AUDIOBOOKS

The Wasteland

The Summit

The Cities

The Nations - *coming soon*

Rage

Hate

Den of Vipers *(From Podium Audio)*

Gangsters and Guns *(From Podium Audio)*

Daddy's Angel *(From Podium Audio)*

Stepbrothers' Darling *(From Podium Audio)*

Blade of Iris *(From Podium Audio)*

Deadly Affair *(From Podium Audio)*

Deadly Match *(From Podium Audio)*

Deadly Encounter *(From Podium Audio)*

Stolen Trophy *(From Podium Audio)*

Crown of Stars *(From Podium Audio)*

Monstrous Lies *(From Podium Audio)*

Monstrous Truth *(From Podium Audio)*

Monstrous Ends *(From Podium Audio)*

Court of Nightmares *(From Podium Audio)*

Court of Death *(From Podium Audio)*

Unstoppable *(From Podium Audio)*

Unbreakable *(From Podium Audio)*

Fractured Shadows *(From Podium Audio)*

Shadowed Heart *(From Podium Audio)*

Revolt *(From Podium Audio)*

Rebel *(From Podium Audio) - coming soon*

FIND AN ERROR?

Please email this information to thenuttyformatter1@gmail.com:

- *the author name*
- *title of the book*
- *screenshot of the error*
- *suggested correction*

www.ingramcontent.com/pod-product-compliance
Lightning Source LLC
Chambersburg PA
CBHW051113300726
48981CB00001B/116